CHAOS NIGHTMARES

The cessation of pain is what first awoke Tyrchon. He had laid in agony for an eternity, yet in the clarity of a mind free of pain, he knew it had not been that long.

He looked around with opalescent eyes able to pierce much of the night's darkness. Around him Tyrchon saw fog-gray forms moving at incredible speed. The shaggy creatures, with thrusting muzzles and a trio of glowing eyes, were T*svortu*—Storm demons. He'd fought them before.

Their speed, now, means I'm in a slow zone. Throughout Chaos there were small areas, pockets where time ran slower or faster than elsewhere. As grievously wounded as he had been, it made sense for his companions to have left him in a slow zone while they went for help. *Because they have not returned, yet I am healed, something else is going on here.*

Sitting up, he heard a distant sound coming from behind him. The sound keened obscenely loud as the T*svortu* broke through the edge of the slow zone, her hands wrapped around the hilt of a saber raised high for an overhand slash.

Books by Michael A. Stackpole

Once a Hero
Talion: Revenant

Star Wars X-Wing Series
Rogue Squadron
Wedges Gamble
The Krytos Trap
The Bacta War

A Hero Born*
An Enemy Reborn*

*Published by HarperPrism

REALMS OF CHAOS

AN ENEMY REBORN

Michael A. Stackpole
and William F. Wu

HarperPrism
A Division of HarperCollins Publishers

HarperPrism

A Division of HarperCollins*Publishers*
10 East 53rd Street, New York, N.Y. 10022-5299

This is a work of fiction. The characters, incidents, and
dialogues are products of the author's imagination and are not to
be construed as real. Any resemblance to actual events or
persons, living or dead, is entirely coincidental.

ISBN 0-06-105681-2

HarperCollins®, 🔥®, and HarperPrism®
are trademarks of HarperCollins*Publishers,* Inc.

Cover illustration © 1998 by Paul Youll

First printing: March 1998

Printed in the United States of America

Visit HarperPrism on the World Wide Web at
http://www.harperprism.com

❖ 10 9 8 7 6 5 4 3 2 1

For Michael A. Stackpole

To the memory of
Karl Edward Wagner

For William F. Wu

Christopher N. Wu,
my brother, with love

ACKNOWLEDGMENTS

The author would like to thank, first and foremost, William F. Wu for his work on this project. (Visit him at his web site at WilliamFWu.com to learn more about his work.) I would also thank Rick Loomis for his generosity in letting me use a world I created on his time for this novel. Caitlin Blasdell deserves a big vote of thanks for her patience and gently deft method of turning the screws to get this novel out of me. Conversations with Dennis L. McKiernan about the first book inspired chunks of this second one. And above and beyond all that, Liz Danforth has my undying thanks for once again putting up with me though the ordeal of getting this monster down on paper.

AN ENEMY
REBORN

PROLOGUE

Though he had prepared for this moment, part of him had wished it would never come. Shoth Churgûn heard the whisper of tinkling tiny bells ascend from the tower room below his. He hoped it would tail away, refusing to build and refusing to call him to his station. It always had before, allowing him to avoid choices he knew he would be called upon to make.

Hard choices I don't want to make.

Feeling far older than his years, the magicker—a Warder by rank, though much more because of studies forbidden and arcane—rose from his desk and pulled a threadbare robe about himself. As he tugged the robe closed, his fingers brushed over the rank badges that proclaimed an individual's status within the Empire. On the right he had his Warder badge, a simple device of three interlinked circles surrounded by a thicker circle. It had been fixed to his robe with golden thread, indicating that magick was his chosen profession.

1

Over his heart he wore two other badges. A square design featuring two mountains, one positioned behind the other, marked him as belonging to the land in which he had been born and to which he had now returned to work. It had been attached to his robe with green thread, proclaiming his residence in and allegiance to his homeland. The Matarun—Mountain folk—though a minority in Garik province, were proud, seldom understood, and often feared by most Garikmen.

The other badge he wore had been created by an effort to bring the Mountain folk more into the mainstream of Imperial life. Lady Myat Grizar-Choth, youngest daughter of one of the most powerful Matarun lords, had been wedded to Prince Aloren of Garik seven years earlier, and had given him a son five years ago. Her emblem showed the Prince's black-and-white triskele design emblazoned on a lady's fan—a traditional design for a noblewoman connected to the Imperial house by marriage.

Shoth had sewn it to his robe with red-silk thread, and the device did not wholly cover the darker square that indicated where a previous patch had been replaced. The thread's color betokened a blood tie to the Princess. Shoth had known her all of his life, early on as an infant cousin five years his junior, and later as the reason for his existence.

The sound of the bells built, not sharply, but gradually. He trotted down the wooden stairs, ignoring their creaking protests, and passed into a windowless chamber that stood in the middle of his tower. The stairs from above or below allowed the only obvious access to the room—the lack of windows had been to keep the air as still as possible so the bells would not respond to some zephyr. The air stank of nervousness, yet made Shoth's flesh tingle as magickal energy built in the room.

His feet made no noise because the floor had been covered with carpets of all shapes and sizes, from all corners of the Empire. Herak and Garik contributed their fair share of fine rugs, but they also came from Duar and Tarris, Menal and the islands. Their distribution appeared haphazard, and many of the carpets curled against the wall as if ivy trying to scale it.

They seek to cover it with their beauty. The tower room's interior walls looked hideous. They had been coated with a patchwork of plaster made from the earth of various provinces; they had color splashed on them from pigments manufactured in yet other provinces. Mildew and mold even sprouted in places—probably from spores trapped in the carpets, Shoth thought—and he sprinkled them with water from time to time to encourage their growth.

All to protect this, the Meter.

The Meter had been of his design and built to his painstaking specifications in the center of this tower floor. The laminated hardwood ring that supported it had four legs that raised it a yard off the floor. The ring itself supported a delicate lattice of steel rods, each with tiny cuts made in them so they fit flush where they overlapped. When the grid had been laid in, Shoth had been able to pull a diaphanous sheet of silk over the surface without a single snag or hint that anything was out of place.

The wooden ring and steel lattice, as magnificent as they were, formed only the skeleton for the Meter. The most important part of it was what he had called his *scouts*. The little cruciform metal pieces had a bell linked to the bottom, and a cup on the top. The rounded arms allowed the scouts to rest on the lattice bars, with each one being so carefully balanced that a casual wave of his hand could create a breeze that would set bells ringing with a deafening peal.

Into each of the cups on the top he had placed a bit of sand, or a rock, or a little water taken from a specific location in Chaos—the vast, ever-changing wasteland beyond the Ward Walls that kept the Empire safe. Each little artifact maintained a link with the place from which it had been taken, and through his magick he had strengthened that link. While the individual footfall of a Chaos demon might land close enough to a spot from which one of his samples had come to set that bell ringing, his Meter had been devised to warn of greater forces being gathered in Chaos.

And a very great force did appear to be gathering in Chaos. The bells over in the northeast quadrant rang as the scouts to which they were attached quivered. He'd seen that sort of activity before, but it faded quickly, as if its source was passing nearby the area of Chaos his Meter covered, but not through it. The previous times a swath perhaps five or even ten ranks deep had been set to pealing, but he could watch the track and see it plunging nowhere near the center of his Meter.

This time, however, the track appeared different. It had started ten ranks of bells ringing, but on a narrow front that did arrow in toward the center of the Meter. The track broadened at the back, hinting at great power and energy, and the wild swaying of some scouts marked peaks of energy that he could not have even guessed would exist, even in Chaos.

This could be it.

He turned away from the Meter and headed back

toward the stairs, but before he could mount them, he saw her feet and heard her voice. "Is this the storm we have been waiting for?"

The sound of her voice drove his fatigue from him, and he dropped to one knee at the foot of the stairs. He bowed his head respectfully. "It may be, Highness."

He remained bent, his eyes cast to the floor, as she descended. Her footsteps came lightly and delicately, with the stairs offering no protest at her descent. She hesitated halfway down, right where she would have been able to look upon the Meter and see the wedge being driven into the scouts. He heard her gasp and wanted to look up, smiling, to see if her joy made it onto her face, but he dared not. *When she is happy, she can be most generous, but when vexed . . .*

Then he heard her complete her way down the stairs. The flowery scent she wore reminded him of high mountain meadows striped with yellow blossoms amid deep green grasses. Her left hand touched him, her fingers sliding through his blond hair—hair now tinged with premature gray—reminding him of why he was her favorite, why he needed to be her favorite, and of the fact that from the first he had felt an invisible bond linking them. Pride and shame warred within him, but pride won, as it always did in her presence, and he smiled.

"This has promise, cousin, does it not?"

Her question trailed after her as she approached the Meter. Shoth rose and moved away from her, around to the Meter's farside. He looked past the swaying scouts and at her. Like him, Myat was small for one of the Mountain people, but at least she had the coal black hair and icy blue eyes commonly associated with their kind. She was often described as petite, and it was meant in all the positive ways. Her undeniable beauty and her ability to charm those she met but did not know well made her as popular as was possible in Imperial circles for one of the Matarun. He, on the other hand, being shorter and slighter, with blond hair and gray eyes, had been seen as a misbegotten child even among his own kind. Reviled and ridiculed, he had been a loner until she—precocious and ambitious beyond her tender years—had befriended him.

He smiled at her, warming at the sight of her beauty. "It does. I will need another hour to be certain. Then we can decide if we will proceed."

She shook her head, then brushed black hair back past her shoulders, allowing him a glimpse of the cleavage displayed by her pale blue gown. "If this storm is right, we proceed. You will do what must be done."

Shoth's lower lip quivered for a moment. "There will be other storms. We have time to perfect things."

Myat gave him a sad little smile, and he blushed for having disappointed her. "Shoth, dear Shoth, have you not heard what happened at the Emperor's Bear's Eve Ball a month ago? Have you forgotten already?"

"I was not there, Highness, but I recall the stories. Fialchar, he who shattered the Seal of Reality and caused Chaos to wash over the world, he came from beyond the Ward Walls and disrupted the ball. I remember."

She nodded carefully. "And you recall that Fialchar vowed to give the Emperor a year before he would destroy the Empire; a year of which only eleven months still exist. We have eleven months to figure out a way to oppose Lord Disaster and his plans, and this Meter and the spells we have crafted will provide the Matarun all the defense we need against him."

Shoth had heard this argument before, but in different forms, all throughout the time he had known Myat. She had always been oriented to expanding the power of the Mountain lords, to allow them to go forth and guarantee their place in the Empire. Because the mountains extended through numerous provinces, and the Matarun had successfully resisted attempts to conquer them by various lowland lords and Dukes, they answered to no political power save their own Clanmasters and the Emperor, regardless of which province claimed their land. Just as the mountains formed the Empire's spine, so the Mountain folk saw themselves the strongest people of the Empire. The Matarun allegiance to their homeland and nobility superseded any other fealty, and they felt, someday, justice would be done, and their superiority would make them masters of the Empire.

Myat had been determined, even from a very young age, to see this as something she could make come to pass in her lifetime.

"Highness, I know what you are saying is true, and I know you have ever planned to protect the Matarun. You, in your wisdom, even saw a role for me in what you wanted to do, and pushed me to learn all I have." Shoth plucked at the worn Warder badge on his robe. "I learned all I could in the City of Sorcerers, and I have learned more since. Your skill as a theoretician has showed me the way to create and perform many magicks of incredible power . . ."

She smiled broadly at him and came around to his side of the Meter. She slid her right hand up along his left arm and shoulder. "You have ever been the strength I needed, Shoth; and the voice of common sense when my dreams take me too high. Now, again, you suggest caution. You're not afraid that what we will do here will be detected, are you?"

A shiver ran down his spine, but he did not let it make him twitch. "The Masters of Magicks in the City of Sorcerers are very good at what they do, but I do not believe we will be betrayed here. Within the Ward Walls, all magick is really the release of Chaos energies, and you wish us to tap into primal Chaos storm energies to work a spell, so they will not be detecting anything unusual—though the duration and power of the spell might be detectable."

"True enough, but that's why your tower is made the way it is." Myat pointed toward the mottled plaster on the walls. "As the bits of Chaos in your scouts have a link to Chaos itself, so the earth and stones used here have a link to all the spots in the Empire from which they were drawn. The magickal energy that would be detected will be diffused throughout the Empire. Even *if* it were detected, the chances of their finding this spot would be slender, even though it is in the shadow of the City of Sorcerers itself."

This should be true, and we must use the storm's power because mine is insufficient and hers is nonexistent. "And you are certain you want to go through with this?"

Myat nodded confidently and almost a bit too quickly for Shoth's peace of mind. "It is the only way. We will be fighting fire with fire."

The ringing of the bells increased sharply, causing Shoth to look away from his cousin and back at the Meter. The wedge had driven further into the circle of scouts, and the storm shook various scouts hard enough to scatter some of the sand in their cups around. Yet, even as it did that, some scouts did not move at all, allowing little pockets of stillness to erode the edges of the storm.

Myat's fingers clutched at his shoulder, her nails digging into him through his robe. "I've not seen that before. What does it mean?"

"I'm not certain. The power of the storm is right, but the distribution of energy is odd. There seem to be forming two wings to the storm."

"Will the storm split and diminish? If it splits, will you have enough power to work the spell?"

"I don't know."

"What do you mean?"

"I mean that no one has ever attempted what we will be attempting. It should work, but if the storm splits and dies, we will have to wait."

Myat frowned darkly. "Go, now. Start the spell."

Shoth shook his head. "We need the storm near the center of the Meter field. That is where your researches said our target was last seen, and that is where we are most likely to be able to bring him back. If I start now, and the storm never gets to the center, I don't know if we will be successful."

"We must be successful, and now." Her features sharpened as she applied herself to the problem. He had seen the expression countless times before and actually began to take heart in it. While Myat had little formal magickal training and had never possessed the strength to cast grand magicks, her ability to handle the intricacies of sorcerous theory had proved nothing short of stunning.

"If we fail, we will likely have no result because the storm's power was diminished, correct?"

Shoth nodded. "I believe that is true."

"And if our failure is because the storm is not over what we believe to be the point of easiest access for bringing Dashan back from his self-imposed exile, he will come back somewhere in the area, but just not where we want him, correct?"

Shoth chewed his lower lip for a moment. "I believe that is a strong possibility."

"Then we have no need for caution, cousin. We knew we would need to send people out to find him. They will just have to search harder now."

He wanted to tell her that there were many more possible problems, too many for them to be so blithely dismissed, but the cool confidence in her voice erased those doubts. In the same way, the set of her hands on her hips and the slight arch of a dark eyebrow prevented him from voicing reluctance about summoning anything into or through Chaos. "Their work will be nothing compared to ours."

She raised his hand to her mouth and kissed it. "Nor will their reward be anything compared to ours when we succeed." She pulled on his hand and led him toward the stairs going down into the tower's foundation chamber. "Come, cousin, today we save the Empire from its folly and its enemies, all for the future of the Matarun."

1

H*ere we go again!*
    Len Fong swung shut the little locker into which he had stuffed his street clothes and fastened the combination lock. He stood and turned, tugging his uniform into place, as Mr. Corbett came waddling through the shoe store's tall storage shelves. Though Corbett, as manager, wasn't required to wear the same uniform the floor staff did, he donned it as a statement of solidarity with his workers—a fact he reminded them about from time to time.

The uniform itself consisted of black slacks, a choice from a variety of approved shoe styles, and a polyester, soccer-style jersey with a collar. The shirt's design had alternating thick bands of black and emerald green, slanting down from the midline, and black sleeves. The company crest, showing a capering jester in motley, also of black and green, rode on the left breast, and Angie, one of Len's coworkers, always complained about where the little clown had his feet.

On Mr. Corbett the shirt's design just arrowed attention to his double chins and bald head. Mr. Corbett shaved his head, and, in Len's opinion, there were few things uglier in the world than a white man with his head shaved. The polyester in the shirt also stretched enough that it rippled like the skin on pudding when Mr. Corbett walked. On *him the uniform isn't a fashion statement, it's just a fashion scream.*

Corbett smiled at Len, his thick black mustache bristling broadly. "You're always a team player, Sales Associate Fong. I like that."

"Thank you . . ." *Comrade.* Len didn't know why he always mentally added that tag when speaking to his boss, but it just seemed right. The man made a show of being a fellow corporate wage-slave just like the people working for him, but he was very capable of docking someone's pay or, worse yet, exiling them to Gulag Stockroom. Corbett really despised them all, which would make things at the store miserable, but Len did his best never to let it get to him.

Corbett fished into his pocket and pulled out a thick plastic device shaped like the Dancing Joker Shoe Outlet logo character and extended it toward Len. "Because of your excellent attitude, I wanted you to be the first to get one of our new promotional tools."

Len took it, flipped it over, and felt his stomach begin to collapse in on itself. The three-inch-tall jester figure had been mated to a quarter-inch-thick disc that had a safety-pin attachment on the back. The thing had been formed out of plastic and had a little compartment for batteries, but that wasn't really enough for Len to figure out what it actually was. That didn't surprise him because the Dancing Joker promotional folks usually came up with gimmicks mysterious enough to make the Sphinx as obvious as a made-for-TV mystery.

Then again, Len knew beyond a doubt what it was, but he kept his feeling of nausea from registering on his face.

Before he could ask what it was, he noticed Mr. Corbett had fastened his own pin on the right side of his shirt, opposite the company crest. Smiling proudly, Corbett flashed his left hand up and smacked the device solidly. This sent another ripple through Corbett's flesh, which was the effect Len expected, then he got something more. A voice came from the little device.

"Welcome to Dancing Joker Shoes—the most fun shoe emporium ever!"

Corbett smiled. "They got a good one here, don't you think? I think it is brilliant. Try yours."

Len gave the device a squeeze.

"The customer is always right!"

Corbett frowned slightly, then injected a commanding tone into his voice. "No, Sales Associate Fong, put it on and try it. Bo Gester should only be used when attached to the shirt."

Len could not suppress a groan. *Bo Gester!* More than ever he was convinced the promotions folks had a diet consisting of lead-paint chips and tequila consumed from lead-glazed cups. Still, he fastened the device in place and dutifully hit it. *This is all my fault, and now I pay for my sins.*

"Our prices will leave you as happy as a clown's smile."

Corbett nodded solemnly. "There are twelve different phrases. If you haven't hit it for a while, or hit it twice, quickly, you get a greeting message. Whenever you greet a customer, you should use it. When you conclude the sale, or at a point where you want to focus the customer's attention, just hit it once. They say they can send us new phrase chips to use when we have special sales."

"That sounds great, Mr. Corbett." Len put some enthusiasm into his voice and a smile on his face, which wasn't too tough since he did it every day at work. Len marveled at how the man could stand there and instruct him in how the thing worked, when Len had suggested creating these very devices.

Well, almost these devices. Corbett had complained that keeping track of employees was difficult, and he really wanted a way to be able to talk to them wherever they were in the store, but pagers were too expensive. Len, intending on being as sarcastic as possible, had suggested Comrade Corbett might want to have the company create Star Trek–like communicator pins—the design and use of which Len considered one of the more stupid things he'd ever seen. The discussion had moved into the ridiculous at that point, to where the idea of adding merchandising slogans to a voice chip had just seemed about as logical and intelligent as possible.

I forget about it, Corbett runs it up the corporate flagpole, and merchandising guys fall all over themselves to make it happen.

"I knew I could count on you. And one other thing, there is no poking another employee in the Bo, even as a jest . . ." Corbett's chins quivered as he laughed at his own joke. "Dancing Joker Shoes does not tolerate sexual harassment of any sort."

"Got it . . ." *Comrade.*

"Good." Corbett smiled proudly. "Well, you have five minutes until your shift begins, Sales Associate

Fong. Lace up your City-trekkers and get ready to sell shoes. Since we are the first to get these prototype Bo Gesters, someone from Corporate is stopping in to see how they work. I expect a good showing from you, especially." The manager spun on his heel and returned to the front of the store, his broad hips twisting askew shoe boxes in the stack through which he walked.

Len sank back down on the changing bench and shook his head. He hated his job and knew it was a dead end, but couldn't find it in himself to walk away, no matter how much he wanted to. When he started to evaluate the job, it didn't seem that bad: no really heavy lifting, he was inside in climate-controlled comfort, the store stocked fairly young and hip styles, so few and far between were fussy old ladies who were determined to jam their size 10 dogs into size 4 stiletto heels. There were bosses out there much worse than Comrade Corbett—idea thief and crepe-soled dictator though he might be. Len had been through enough jobs to know exactly where Corbett fit in the constellation of horror-show bosses.

And his coworkers weren't bad to work with, especially Angie. One night last week, as they were closing, she'd popped her shirt off to show him where the embroidered patch was rubbing her a bit raw. She'd asked him if he knew any ancient Chinese secrets of a healing touch. He'd replied that he didn't, but he could learn, and they were going out on Saturday night after the company softball game so she could see just how much he had learned.

Yet even with Angie as incentive, he knew he could have easily walked away from Dancing Joker Shoes if not for his damned fantasy. Not a foot fetish, but kind of a Cinderella thing in reverse. It wasn't that he'd go looking for his princess with a glass shoe in hand, but that she would come looking for shoes and realize what she wanted was really him. He knew it was silly and pedestrian, and hadn't breathed a word of it to anyone, but his belief in the fantasy allowed him to differentiate himself from the others at the store.

Without it, I'd be different, but just hopelessly pathetic. Len, at twenty-three, had chosen not to pursue college past the two years he'd already done at UC Berkeley. He'd spent his first two years trying a bit of this and a bit of that, trying to find something that fit him. His grades were actually pretty good, and would have been much better if he applied himself fully to his studies, but when it came time to make that commitment to a major, he balked. His father respected his decision, but declined to offer financial support for it, so Len went to live with his grandaunt Miriam and, in return for light chores and minimal rent, endured stories of what her grandfather had told her about railroad track-laying in California.

Mr. Corbett was on a career track with the company, and the Bo Gester thing would certainly accelerate his advancement. Everyone on staff expected him to wander down to Orange County and the Costa Mesa store in a year or two. Angie and most of the others were working at DJS while going to school, so Len was the only real candidate to replace Corbett, but management just didn't seem like the career path he wanted. If not for his fantasy—and the date with Angie—Len had little more than his aunt and a voracious appetite for science-fiction and fantasy novels to call a life.

He laced up his City-trekkers and doubled the knot. He liked the low-cut hiking shoes and thought they were the best product Dancing Joker Shoes produced, though the laces they packaged with them were too long. He stood, straightened his shirt, and headed out to the front. As he passed through the curtain from the stockroom to the sales floor, he tapped his Bo.

"Welcome to Dancing Joker Shoes, the home of happy feet."

Len tossed a nod to Comrade Corbett, who had been in the perfect position to watch and see if Len used his Bo, then picked up a sizing guide and stuffed a shoehorn in his back pocket. A slender guy with a bar code of hair strands combed over his bald pate stood next to Corbett. He also wore a Bo, which told Len the guy was a corporator and there to be impressed by the way Corbett's staff utilized the Bo Gesters.

He looked around the narrow store, then caught Corbett's sharp nod as two young women stepped through the threshold. Rob Carson, a coworker who was standing closer to the women, took a step toward them, then looked up at their faces and hesitated.

He smiled unctuously at Len, feigning a gracious surrender of his commission. "Be my guest."

Len nodded and accepted the assignment. The two young women had long, straight black hair, brown eyes, and the epicanthic fold that sharpened their eyes into a tight almond shape. They could have been anything from Hawaiian to Japanese, Mongolian, or Korean; but the fact that they looked to Comrade Corbett to be of Asian extraction meant they were Chinese, and that meant Len should welcome them to the store.

By the time he got to them, one had already picked up a pair of cowboy-style boots in black with green accents. The taller of the two girls saw him and smiled before he could touch his Bo. *"You beide yanse ma?"*

Len stiffened slightly. "I'm sorry, I don't speak Mandarin, or any Chinese." He shrugged, feeling color rise to his cheeks. "I'm an American."

"Please, I'm sorry. Do you have these in another color?" Her English came with a highborn English accent." Hong Kong, Len guessed, relocated after the Beijing takeover.

"We do. Red and purple." Len waved her to a chair and seated himself on the footstool. He eased off the sandal she wore and shot Rob a quick nod toward the girl's companion. Rob licked his lips and started to wander over, but Comrade Corbett directed him to service a battle-ax with a punked-out daughter in tow. Len quickly adjusted the size indicator and width gauge, then looked up. "Six-B Dixie-trix boot. I think we have you covered. Which color?"

"Could I look at both?"

Len nodded and tapped his Bo. "It is our pleasure to serve you."

The girls giggled at that, and Len turned away to hide his blush. The giggles left him enough flustered that he took his shoe sizer with him into the back. Instead of returning to the store, he just clipped it to the top of his pants at the small of the back, using the handy-dandy belt clip that had been one of Corbett's own brainstorms. Len glanced at the stockroom shelves to determine where to find the Dixie-trix boots he needed. He cut over to the right, then shivered.

Just my luck. They're under the Death Boots.

He dragged over a wobbly fitting stool and stood on it to reach up and get the Dixie-trix, but he hesitated. The Dixie-trix boots were on top of the shelves and perched on top of them, like a pair of leather gargoyles, sat the Death Boots. Though he knew the stories about them were probably nonsense, he felt uneasy looking at the things.

Primarily because they looked back.

Way back when, well before Len had come to work for Dancing Joker Shoes, someone in promotions saw a wine label that had been designed by a famous artist and thought it would be wonderful to have some special shoes designed by an artist to display and, if anyone was mad enough to pay for them, actually buy. They wanted Salvador Dali to design the boots—and apparently had a hard time understanding why the artist's death would prevent him from doing the work. They settled for some daft Argentine artist who said he was channeling Dali and got what, to Len, had to be the ugliest pair of footwear ever imagined.

The boots were nominally cowboy boots, though no wrangler would have worn them unless he wanted to stampede cattle. Ruby red uppers with black trim, made of kangaroo skin, they had been decorated with multicolored painted-on eyeballs that were hauntingly Daliesque. The toe cap was silver and shaped like a melted watch, and the artist's signature had been stitched across the heel.

The legend of the Death Boots began—as Comrade Corbett was fond of telling during the Halloween party—when the artist who designed them tore his own eyes out and pitched himself off the Dancing Joker Shoes corporate headquarters in Muncie. While other companies might have abandoned the project right there, the run of boots had already been made, and though pretty much everyone in the company was sure even orphans in Bosnia would refuse to wear the things, even if they were a giveaway, the promotion went forward.

This store's pair had an infamous history. The boots immediately attracted the interest of a patron who bought them for herself, shelling out $1,700 for the pair, only to have her die in a traffic accident on the way home. The store, of course, took the unworn boots back. The next patron who wanted them was a tourist from New York who was determined to possess them. Mr. Greene, the manager before Comrade Corbett, waited on the customer himself, then collapsed and died of a massive coronary the second she'd agreed to take the boots.

Since then the boots had languished in the stock-room. New hires were initiated by being forced to pull the boots down, dust them off, and polish them. Most were required to do it during a hideous thunderstorm, or after hours when ghost stories and a darkened store made the ritual downright creepy. Because of it, Len had never really liked closing the store, though Angie seemed to have ideas about ways to change his mind concerning that sort of thing.

"The superstition is just stupid!" Len shook his head, then tapped his Bo for confirmation of that fact.

"Adventures begin here at Dancing Joker Shoes!" it announced in a mechanical voice Len decided he didn't like.

"The only adventure I want starts Saturday." Len frowned, then reached up for the Dixie-trix boots he wanted. Above that box, one of the Death Boots shifted. A big clump of dust leaped free and plunged toward his face. Len blew at it, disintegrating it, but when he breathed in, he got a nose full of dust. "Oh, shit!"

He sneezed, just once, but sharply and violently enough to unbalance the fitting stool. He started to pitch backward, then grabbed at the boot boxes to steady himself. He thought he had prevented a fall, but something else shifted, and a wave of nausea passed over him. As he wavered, the stool tipped out from beneath his feet, and the toppling boot boxes vaulted the Death Boots into the air. As Len fell, with Dixie-trix exploding from their boxes around him, he saw the Death Boots above it all, their eyes winking at him.

Stars exploded before his eyes as his head hit a shelf behind him. A second later he landed hard on the floor and felt the shoe sizer slam into his back. A tingling jolt of pain ran down over his rump and into the backs of his legs, then Dixie-trix by the dozen began to pummel him. He brushed them away from his face, scattering the boots and boxes, just in time to look up.

The Death Boots, in all their artsy glory, danced down on his head. He thought, for one fleeting second, that their impact couldn't be enough to knock him out, but then, with his last conscious thought, he realized he was wrong.

2

Deep in the bowels of the earth, Shoth stood naked and alone in the middle of a circle painted on the chamber's floor. From above he could still hear the Meter's bells ringing loudly, all ajangle, yet that sound barely penetrated the snapping and hissing magickal maelstrom swirling around him. Luminous threads of gold and red; blue, green, and purple danced around him. Moving always from right to left, they spiraled within the circle, part of the time serpentine and part of it lightning—always cold, but glowing with an intensity that stung his eyes.

Myat lurked toward the rear of the teardrop chamber, back where the base of the teardrop had been rounded from a natural formation. Directly away from her the room narrowed into a dark tunnel. Only the passage of light threads from his circle out, or thicker, opalescent strings coming into his circle, provided any illumination for the tunnel itself. Shoth knew well what lurked in its dim depths, but now only concerned himself with the magickal energy streaming into his spell chamber from them.

Sweat coursed down his body, droplets flicking from his hair with every turn of his head or dripping from elbows and chin. It splattered earthward onto the rusty painting beneath his feet, loosening some of the pigment and letting his feet smear it with even the most careful step. He had expected it, and thought it might cause a little trouble, but it was the least of his worries at the moment.

His right hand darted out and caught a purple thread. He grabbed a green one in his left hand and quickly knotted them together. Twisting the green one around a pulsing gold line, he brought the green back and tied the loose end back into the purple thread. With a couple more knots and threads he created a glowing net which he cast down at the painting, physically launching it at the muddy circle. The magick energy hit and lingered there for a moment, quivering like a spine-smashed snake, then melted like ice into the painting and was gone. In its wake it left a spiderweb of slender black lines, linked to other lines that radiated out through the painting.

Almost done. Sweat burned into his eyes, but he wiped it away with a forearm. Fatigue made his back ache, and his legs already trembled, but he pushed himself onward. *One more net, one more casting, and we can be certain*.

More energy pulsed in through the tunnel, taking the form of a dazzling silver tendril as thick as his wrist. Without conscious thought, Shoth grabbed it in his right hand and felt a tingle unlike any he had with previous lines. Then the silver thread bunched and wrapped itself around his arm. It began to constrict, applying pressure as it spiraled up his arm.

He heard Myat scream, but he did not let her voice panic him. With a speed even he didn't think he still possessed in his limbs, he flicked his right hand down toward the floor, hard. His sweat-slicked flesh sloughed the energy thread off with ease. The silvery line lashed down, striking the painting, then a gold gout of energy whirled its way back up the energy ribbon to Shoth's hand.

Agonies greater than any he had ever even imagined snapped his muscles taut and lifted him from the floor. He sensed himself falling, but even the pain of smashing into a table and some chairs beyond the circle, shattering them, seemed terribly distant. He felt as if he were watching the crash, not experiencing it. He felt a tug on his left thigh, and saw a slender piece of wood sticking up out of it. He even noticed blood welling up around the wound, but he felt nothing to connect it to himself.

Two things captured his attention more immediately, one of which surprised him, and the other of which did not. What had not surprised him was that his being thrown from the circle had canceled his spell. In magick, ritual defines the parameters within which great magicks can be worked. While there are countless spells that can be cast in a heartbeat, with little or no preparation—combat spells being primary among them—grand magicks require preparation and exacting attention to detail if they are going to be worked with tremendous power.

The circle in which he had been standing, for example, had been carefully painted with pigments made from dirt taken from places in Chaos. Just as the samples of earth in the scouts above gave the Meter a connection to Chaos, so the painting had allowed him to be casting spells into Chaos by proxy. He used the energy of the Chaos storm, and cast the spells within the areas being overrun by the storm, providing him with two connections to the locations where his spells took effect.

When that tendril touched the painting and me, I remained in the loop and suffered from a backlash. He shivered. That sort of thing had never happened to him before, nor to any other mage, but then he and Myat were working spells that even the Twelve at the Shattering would have hesitated to cast.

Myat crouched by his side and dabbed at the blood on his leg with the hem of her robe. "Are you . . . ?"

"I will survive, I think, Highness." Shoth could begin to feel some pain from his leg. He looked at the sliver of wood sticking up through his flesh and grabbed it at the bottom. Clenching his teeth, he whisked it free, then pressed his left hand down to close the exit wound. "My robe. At least the sash, please."

She frowned. "Why not spell it closed?"

Shoth managed a hint of a laugh. "I'm too tired. I can tie it off for the moment, and spell it afterward."

Myat crossed over to the foot of the stairs and grabbed the sash from his robe. Shoth circled his thigh with it several times, then knotted it off. He worked his way to his feet and put weight on the leg. A little pain rewarded him, but the leg seemed to work fine. "Just a flesh wound, then."

"Good." Myat smiled carefully at him. "Were you successful?"

"I don't know. Something is wrong."

"What do you mean?"

He held a hand up. "Listen."

She tilted her head down and closed her eyes for a moment. "I hear nothing."

"Exactly." Shoth limped over to the stairs, pulled his robe on over his head, and climbed to the Meter chamber. As his head broke the plane of the floor he could see a dozen or two scouts lying there. He crossed to the Meter itself and rested his hands on the wooden circle supporting the whole device.

Myat joined him a second later. "What has happened here?"

"I'm not at all certain." He studied the Meter, noting that the scouts had been knocked out of two very distinct places on the face of the Meter. One had been at the leading edge of the storm track, forming a slash two scouts wide, that cut from northeast to southwest. The other gap appeared, similarly shaped and directed, halfway across the Meter, well away from where the Chaos storm had been raging.

"The gaps appear almost to be twins of each other, don't they?"

Myat nodded slowly. "But the only way that would be possible would be if the link-medium in one set of scouts somehow contaminated the other."

"And that didn't happen here, unless the containers brought back from Chaos were mislabeled."

She frowned. "The riders who were sent out to gather these samples were from my personal guard unit, loyal Matarun, each and every one. And smart. They wouldn't make this sort of mistake."

"Unless compelled by magick to do so. It could be that one or the other of these areas has magick laid down upon it to conceal it. If it were sufficient to be undetected *and* sophisticated enough to cause individuals taking a survey to dump what they took and move elsewhere to take yet other samples, well, that's a spell the likes of which I've never seen before."

"What's there?" Myat pointed to the scar where the storm had been tracking. "Could whatever it was have caused what happened to you?"

Shoth's head came up. "What an interesting idea. Because I was projecting magick through the storm itself, whatever is there might have employed magick back against the storm. I caught a piece of it, and the magick may have even snuffed the storm."

"Is that possible?" She blinked her eyes and folded her arms around herself. "That would take incredible power, wouldn't it?"

"It would."

"Dashan had such power."

Shoth canted his head at an angle. "If you believe the legends, it's possible that he did."

"Then you succeeded in summoning him."

Shoth was about to protest that he could not claim that, but Myat reached up, pulling his mouth down to hers, silencing him. In her kiss he felt her pleasure, but also her hunger for power. He tried to ignore the latter and dwell on the former, and would have been entirely successful had she not slipped from the closing circle of his arms.

"This is good, Shoth, better than I could have hoped." Her blue eyes sparkled. "Dashan is out there and is as strong as ever. He is waiting for us to find him to help him." Her mouth opened into a horrified circle. "You don't think he was injured, do you?"

"No, but fighting the storm could have tired him out, certainly." Shoth shivered, then leaned against the Meter as his legs began to tremble again. "He's probably exhausted."

"Then you will have to go find him." Myat started the sentence as an order, but softened it toward the end. "You will rest a bit, and I will organize a squad to go with you. How long will you need?"

"With food and drink, I will need six hours, I think. Four if I must."

"No, take your six, even eight." The Princess smiled at him, then took his hand and kissed it. "You will be my ambassador to him, and you will bring him to me. I am certain, once I make my case to him, he will do all he can to help me save the Empire and set it to rights again."

Shoth studied her smile for a moment, then matched it with one of his own. "I am certain you are correct, Highness. He will be, as I am, your loyal servant. Of this I have no doubt."

3

The cessation of pain is what first awoke Tyrchon. He had lain in agony for an eternity, yet in the clarity of mind he had now, free of pain, he knew it had not been that long. He recalled crossing into Chaos with Lachlan and Roarke, determined to destroy the B*harashadi* Necroleum and break the power of the Black Shadows forever. He even remembered scouting for the group and running into a band of Black Shadows.

The fight had been bitter and fierce. His companion, Hansen, had fallen quickly, and Tyrchon had been left to slay the rest of them. And he had, though the last of the black-furred Chaos demons had driven a *vindictxvara* into his side. The magickal blade had been forged specially to kill him, and only the fact that he'd thrust his sword through the Black Shadow's chest prevented his foe from completing the job.

Not that it matters much with a vindictxvara. Tyrchon's

right hand slid across his chest and beneath his leather jerkin to probe the wound. He could feel the hole in his jerkin and smell the crusted blood there, but the flesh beneath his fingers had become smooth to his touch. *Not even a scar, which means someone used magick.*

Before he raised his head, he sniffed the air and caught a musty scent that brought him to instant alert. His ears pricked up as he rolled up into a crouch and off the stretcher on which he had lain. His mail coat had been bunched beneath his head for a pillow, while his bracers and mail gloves had been placed between his lower legs. He still wore his boots and steel greaves, and his left hand immediately went to one of the daggers riding in a boot top.

He looked around with opalescent eyes able to pierce much of the night's darkness. Around him he saw fog gray forms moving at incredible speed, which he knew was impossible. The shaggy creatures, with thrusting muzzles and a trio of glowing eyes, were *Tsvortu*— Storm demons. He'd fought them before and found them to be supple and agile, but not terribly fast.

So their speed, now, means I'm in a slow zone. It made perfect sense to him because throughout Chaos there were small areas, small pockets of reality where time ran slower or faster than elsewhere. As grievously wounded as he had been, it made sense for his companions to have left him in a slow zone while they went for help. *Because they have not returned, yet I am healed, something else is going on here. Whatever it is, though, is not my primary concern.*

He glanced back at his stretcher but saw neither his sword nor his spear. *And no time to don my armor.* Tyrchon shrugged. *Wouldn't want them to catch me with it over my head anyway.*

His lower jaw dropped open in a smile. He picked the mail coat up, shook it out, and started to gather it in his hands as if he were going to slip it on. As he ducked his head, he heard a distant sound coming from behind him. The sound keened obscenely loud as the T*svortu* broke through the edge of the slow zone, her hands wrapped around the hilt of a saber raised high for an overhand slash.

Tyrchon whirled to his right, holding fast to the hem of his mail shirt. The metal fabric came around heavily and caught the Storm demon in the ankles, smashing her legs together and tangling them up. She crashed down hard across the stretcher, but before she could even begin to turn around toward him, Tyrchon pounced on her back. He drove both his knees into her spine, transforming a snarl into a yelp of pain, then he grabbed a hank of fur and cranked her head back as far as it would go. His left hand flashed forward and stroked the knife blade across her throat, releasing a torrent of indigo blood.

He vaulted from her thrashing body and scooped up the saber she'd dropped when she fell. He let his momentum carry him from the slow zone in a roll, then he came up and slashed his blade beneath the guard of another T*svortu* warrior. She curled around his blade, mewing softly, then he wrenched it free. As she collapsed into the dust, he heard the hunting howls of two more Storm demons coming from the circle's far-side, so he darted forward and slipped between two tall rocks and crouched.

The battlefield proved to be fairly unremarkable because countless places like it existed in Chaos—or, at least, in the places he had visited in Chaos. The land itself had little or no topsoil, but somehow a variety of spiky and scrubby plants clung to life there. In the daylight most of the ground and rocks would appear blood red, but at night they remained black and concealed his enemies as well as they concealed him. Worse yet, the fine dust covering everything filled his nostrils, neutralizing one of his advantages.

An ear flicked to the right as a Tsvortu made a misstep coming around one of the boulders. Tyrchon exploded from his hiding place and slammed a shoulder into the Storm demon's flank. She twisted around to face his attack, but the blow drove her back against a low stone, which caught her heels. She tipped back and over, with the blue pads of her feet being the last thing he saw of her. Yet, even as she went down, she cried out in a sinisterly melodious voice that was part wind-howl and lightning crack.

He heard something rasp behind him and started to turn as the other Tsvortu warrior leaped from the top of a rock and slammed both feet into his left hip. He crashed into the same low, flat rock that had tripped the third Storm demon, cracking his right elbow on it. The saber flew from his hand into the darkness. The demon that had kicked him rose up at his feet and slashed down at him. Tyrchon twisted to his left, and the saber struck sparks from the rock.

He kicked backward with his right heel, raking his spur across the Tsvortu's leg. She yelped and hopped back. He started to sit up, when two big paws grabbed him by the shoulders and pulled him back down. Looking up over his head he saw a Tsvortu grin down at him, then the other one returned, with saber raised on high.

Tyrchon kicked out with both feet, hoping to drive the sword-carrying demon away. At the same time, he reached up with his hands and grabbed handfuls of

Tsvortu pelt. He yanked down and raised his head quickly, twisting so he could sink his teeth into the Storm demon's throat. He felt blood gush, all hot and bitter, and a scream rattle itself to death against his teeth. He pushed away what he had pulled toward him, letting spurting blood rain over him. The Tsvortu fell back, gurgling, then vanished.

He spat out fur and flesh, then sat up, looking for the last Storm demon. She lay at his feet, a wicked-looking blade protruding from below one breast. He recognized it from the hilt as the *vindictxvara* that had stabbed him. How it had gotten into her chest, he had no clue, but he felt quite pleased that the blade meant for him had saved him.

A rustling sound to his left built, sounding like millions upon millions of insects crawling over each other. He turned in that direction, then froze. Part of him wanted to run and another part fight, but he knew he was as good as dead if he made either choice. As much as it tore at him, he remained where he was and even managed to tug his jerkin straight.

A tall, gaunt figure pulled itself out of the shadows and nodded at him as if that gesture were worthy of celebration. The threadbare robe it wore stank of mildew, while the figure itself reeked of decay. In the creature's right hand—a hand with tattered flesh that revealed the aged ivory of bone—Tyrchon saw an onyx staff with a smoky quartz globe on the top, and knew it to be the Staff of Emeterio.

The staff we came for to destroy the Black Shadows.

Tyrchon's eyes narrowed. "You are Fialchar, the Shatterer of the Seal of Reality. Chaos is your doing."

Laughter came from the figure, though it sounded like the wet tearing sound of scavengers worrying carrion. "You do me too much credit. Chaos is its own force. I merely provided it a conduit to this place and time. I am not its creator, merely its facilitator."

"A murderer's accomplice is still evil."

Fialchar waved his free hand nonchalantly through the air. "Be that as it may, such a philosophical discussion is decidedly beside the point of our meeting."

"And that point would be?"

Fialchar's head came up, allowing his hood to slip back. A faint light began to glow within the quartz globe, glinting dully off the argent portions of the wizard's face. The patchwork flesh made him seem a silver statue from which paints had begun to flake or on which birds preferred to perch. Black pits lurked where his eyes should have been, but not seeing them did not bother Tyrchon in the least.

"That point would be legion. First, you show no gratitude at my having healed your wound. No one else could have done it, you know."

Tyrchon stood. "And I cannot imagine you doing it of your own accord. Locke made you do this, didn't he?"

The sorcerer stiffened. "It did come up in the course of our conversation, yes. I could have refused him, but I did not. Regardless, I saved you from that last Tsvortu."

"So you did." Tyrchon glanced up at the night sky and read the constellations. "But, unless the Storm demons have spread themselves thirty leagues to the east, they would not have found me here. Shall I assume their presence was your doing as well?"

A slight nod gave him his answer. "When I came to fulfill my bargain with Locke, I found you a most curious creature. Look at yourself, you're more beast than man."

Tyrchon felt a cold chill run through his insides. In

his younger days, when first becoming a Chaos Rider, he had fashioned a cowl and cloak from the skin of a huge wolf he had slain. He wore it with pride on all his adventures into Chaos, letting it become his trademark. People knew him by sight, and he hoped, someday, he would be very bit as much of an Imperial hero as Gavin Madhand or Locke's father, Cardew.

Then there came a day, well after his eyes had taken on the opalescent *Chaosfire* that marked all riders who had spent a fair amount of time in Chaos, when he could no longer remove the wolfskin. He began to hear through its ears and smell with its nose. The wolf's hackles rose when he felt threatened. Dogs feared him or respected him, and wolves considered him a brother. *And I have even torn the throats from my enemies.*

"I am a *man*, Lord Disaster, just a *different* sort of man."

"He says, awash in *Tsvortu* blood." The skeletal figure's shoulders shrugged. "Seeing you that way, I chose to test your skills. I plucked the Storm demons from their den—three to fight you, and one to bear witness to the fight. I told them only three could fight, but they ignored me."

Tyrchon walked over to the one that had been killed with the *vindictxvara* and pulled a braided-leather necklace with a small clay disc tied to it from around the Storm demon's throat. "You took them all from the same den? They are all sisters and bloodoath-bound to avenge the death of their siblings. The fourth one *had* to come after me."

"Yes, they are somewhat determined that way, aren't they?"

"Why did you test me?" Tyrchon canted his head to the side. "I'm sure that was not part of Locke's agreement with you."

"True, but circumstances have changed." Fialchar pointed off to the northwest with his staff. "When Locke destroyed the Necroleum, he unleashed an incredible amount of magickal energy. This energy helped create one of the most violent Chaos storms I have seen in a long time. This storm even had special properties, almost a sentience, as if it were alive and searching for something. It possessed wild spikes of energy and was making quite a mess of the places it touched—which were mostly old Bharashadi haunts, so of little consequence."

"All the Black Shadows are destroyed?"

Metal flesh groaned as Fialchar lifted his eyebrows in surprise. "I do not know, nor do I care terribly much. Suffice it to say, much of their realm has been *adjusted*."

Tyrchon nodded. Though he had never seen a Chaos storm up close, and had fled from several, their aftermath was simple to see and rather abundant. Theory had it that at their heart Chaos storms were actually paired cyclones, and what one touched was sent to the other and vice versa, leaving glacial patches in arid areas, or a floating bridge of prairie grasses on a lake in exchange for a narrow strip of water at the heart of a grassland. The winds shielding the cyclone itself were sufficient to move a lot of earth and rock, so even if no cyclone touched down, the damage done by a Chaos storm was considerable.

And that was just on the physical plane of things. Tyrchon had heard sorcerers theorize that a lot of magickal energy swirled around in those storms. While Chaos itself could easily work changes in creatures traveling into it—as evidenced by his new nose and ears—the changes usually took time. A Chaos storm, it was thought, could make many changes all at once. Getting used to having a pelt had been a tough enough adjustment that Tyrchon had no desire even to think about being utterly and completely warped in the blink of an eye.

"I still don't see why you needed to test me."

"The most curious thing about this storm was that it stopped, abruptly."

"Stopped?"

A little flame licked from each eyepit up to singe eyebrows. "It went away. It vanished. And before you ask the obvious, yes, this is not usual."

Tyrchon straightened up and stood. "I appreciate the report about the weather, but this is no concern of mine."

"I mean to make it a concern of yours."

Tyrchon's head came up, and his nostrils twitched. "Then tell me why this storm has made you afraid."

Fialchar took a lurching step forward, fire blazing from his eyes. "I am not afraid! I have not been afraid of anything since before shattering the Seal of Reality."

"The stink of fear is all over you."

The fire in Fialchar's eyes quelled a bit. "I believe the power in the Chaos storm was absorbed in a particular location. I do not know why or how this happened. I do find this to be of concern, but I do not *fear* it."

The warrior folded his arms across his chest. "Why don't you go there, see what happened."

"Stupid mortal, I have tried that." Silver flesh screeched as Lord Disaster's eyes tightened. "There is something in the area akin to your Ward Walls. While the feeble magicks your Warders produce are insufficient to hinder me, this phenomenon is different. It causes me pain to get too close, yet I cannot let this area go unexplored. I will have you explore it for me."

Tyrchon threw his head back and laughed. "And why would I want to do that for you?"

"Because if you do, I will grant you that which you most desire."

Both his wolf-ears snapped forward. "And what would that be?"

Fialchar's foul laughter returned. "I will give you your humanity again."

"I don't want or need it."

"You will." Fialchar shrugged. "However, to prove to you that I value your skills, I will also give you this."

The lichlord raised his left hand as if reaching out to cup a star in his palm. He teasingly drew his fingers in, tickling a twinkling green light from the sky. Tyrchon saw a star begin to move, streaking gold across the black skyvault, then it curved in toward the earth. A brilliant flash of light exploded as the wizard closed his fist, then a blast of hot air slammed into Tyrchon and knocked him flying.

He rolled twice, then sneezed dust. He looked up and saw a dull red glowing ellipse standing out from Fialchar's hand. The scarlet light slowly died, then the quartz's glow increased. The rising light revealed a double-edged longsword. The blade seemed improbably slender to Tyrchon, though the hilt was long enough for the blade to be wielded with two hands, suggesting the weapon was very strong.

Fialchar released the sword, and it floated over to Tyrchon. It hung in the air before him, slowly spinning. The pommel and cross guard had been worked with star motifs, and golden serpentine sigils snaked their way down a third of the blade's length. The pommel cap itself had a thick disc with a five-pointed star hollowed out of it. Tyrchon had never seen such a splendid weapon and longed to reach out and take it.

He did not.

Fialchar nodded carefully, and for the first time Tyrchon did not see the gesture as mocking. "You do well to fear this blade as well as covet it. This sword was fabled before the Seal was even a dream. It was shaped from metal taken from beyond this world—perhaps even from beyond this reality—which makes it very special. It is very keen and capable of slicing through anything you are strong enough to cut. One story says it was forged by gods themselves when they tired of immortality. The heroes who have used it may have been forgotten by the Empire, but I once thrilled to songs sung about them, and none of your Imperial heroes can begin to compare."

Tyrchon's eyes narrowed. "Such a blade must demand a terrible price for its use."

"It does." Fialchar's smile sent a chill down Tyrchon's spine. "Accept it—become a swordbearer—and know that there will come a challenge against which even its might will not bring you victory. That challenge will consume you. It may not kill you, but it will break you."

"And if I lay the blade down before that challenge comes to me?"

"Then you will be a greater man than all those who have wielded it before you combined."

"If I were a creature of pride, you would have me." Tyrchon shook his head, then fixed the wizard with a hard stare. "Ultimately, if I refuse you, you'll kill me, correct?"

"Stoop to murder? Me? Hardly." Fialchar pointed the staff at the dead Tsvortu at Tyrchon's feet. "She, however, is from a very large and powerful family, and you are a long way from the Empire. You'll not make it, nor will your friends."

"Friends?"

"Others Locke left behind. They're surviving, so far." The wizard grasped his staff in both hands. "The choice is yours."

Tyrchon reached out and accepted the sword. "The choice is made."

"So it is. The sword will direct you to where you want to go."

"How will I report to you?"

Fialchar smiled most coldly. "When it is time, I shall know and make arrangements. Do my bidding, do it well, and I shall be pleased. Fail me, and even death will not shield you from my wrath."

4

Len lay there, on his back, with his eyes closed. *This is embarrassing, but at least Angie isn't working today.* He wanted to kick himself. He knew better than to be standing on a fitting stool—the damned things were none too steady when he sat on them, and standing on one was just a recipe for disaster. "And I better not be injured because Comrade Corbett hates filling out workman's comp forms."

The image of his boss's sweating face and rising color brought a little smile to Len's face. On a lark he raised his left hand and slapped the Bo to see what it thought about the whole situation.

"Do that again," said the electronic voice, "and I'll bite your hand."

Len laughed aloud. "Some programmer's going to lose his job for that one."

He hit the device again, then pulled his hand away as he felt a sharp sting. *Must have broken in the fall.*

"I told you I'd bite your hand." Len heard the sound of spitting. "You should wash your hands after fondling women's feet."

Len blinked and sat up in darkness. His left hand touched gravel while his right pulled the sizing guide from beneath his back. The gravel was wrong, he knew, since his fall wouldn't have pulverized concrete, and the darkness was wrong, too, since he couldn't have lain there undiscovered past closing. He kicked at the fitting stool tangled in his legs, heard it whimper, then . . .

Whimper? Len stared through the darkness as the long, narrow bench crept away downslope, like a dog that had been kicked. The flat footrest came up, rising to the level of the padded seat and above, then lowered itself again and scraped its front through the dirt. "It's as if it's sniffing around trying to scent something."

"Nonsense, it's grazing."

"Huh?" Len looked down at his chest and the Bo Gester. The clown figure didn't seem to be in the same position he remembered. "Wait, I didn't touch you, so you can't be talking."

"Right, okay, sure. I'm not saying nothing."

Len reached up with his left hand and massaged the back of his head. He felt a bump and moaned. "Oh, man, I'm seriously messed up. I must be in a coma, dreaming this thing. But, if I was, would I be dreaming that I was dreaming?"

"Frankly, Len, if I was having a dream that was boring enough to be a dream about dreaming, I'd be doing everything I could to wake up." He heard the Bo sigh. "Since you aren't waking up, I think we can conclude you're not dreaming."

"I thought you said you weren't saying anything."

"No, I said 'I'm not saying nothing.' Double negative

there, genius, it means I *am* speaking. W*hy* I'm speaking to you, on the other hand, is anyone's guess."

"Well, just shut up, will you? I have to think."

"What a novel idea."

Len raised his left hand to his mouth and sucked at the little wound he had at the base of his middle finger. *I've got to be unconscious and dreaming. I'm back in the store, or in some hospital. I have to be. I remember falling.* He looked around, but aside from the fitting stool and his sizer and his uniform and shoehorn, there was nothing to suggest he was in the store. In fact, as nearly as he could make out in the darkness, he wasn't even in a building, but on a gently sloping hillside.

"Where the hell am I?" He gathered his feet beneath him, stood, and laughed. "I don't think we're in Kansas anymore."

"Son, Bill Gates couldn't afford the long-distance charges between this place and Kansas." The little plastic jester had folded its arms across its chest—Len didn't see it do so, but the figure appeared frozen that way when he looked at it. "Look, either you're dreaming or this is real. You've read plenty of accounts of stuff happening like this."

"Yeah, but they were all *fiction*."

"How do you know?"

"That's what it says on the spine of the book."

"Ah, so the fact that a story is labeled *nonfiction* means all these stories of alien abductions are true, then, right?"

Len frowned. "There's a difference. Fiction is stories that you know aren't true, but you're willing to believe in their own little reality, if the author has done a good job. This, wherever this is, can't be true because, in truth, I'm in a shoe store."

"If you're dreaming *me*, you're one sick puppy."

"Yeah? Maybe I'm dreaming you to let my subconscious have a voice in my dream, so there." Len squeezed his eyes shut and shook his head. "I'm seriously messed up. I'm arguing with a little plastic Bo Gester."

"And you're losing." The device gave off a tinny laugh. "And don't call me Bo Gester. I hate that name almost as much as you do."

"Oh, what would be your pleasure in a name, then?"

"Jhesti, I think. Exotic, but fitting."

"Jhesti it shall be. I'll file a memo to Corporate at my earliest convenience." *Another thing Corbett can take credit for!* Len opened his eyes and saw the fitting stool continuing to root through the gravel. "Why would I dream the stool grazing in gravel?"

"Because . . ."

"Wait, let me figure it out, it's my dream." Len crouched again and scooped up a handful of gravel. He hefted the stones, let them slip through his fingers, then raised one real close to his face. "Light's not so good, but I'm going to guess it's red, which suggests iron oxide. The stool is steel, so it's feeding on its component parts."

"Very good." Jhesti congratulated him with a hearty laugh. "Now rationalize how an inanimate object is managing to metabolize raw metal ore."

"It's a dream. C'mon, I can come up with any explanation I want, and it will work."

"Bear that in mind, pal, because your dream is keeling over into a nightmare."

The stool's front came up like the head of an animal listening for a predator, then the stool loped away from Len a few steps. The shoe clerk spun and looked off upslope just in time to see a dark form eclipse a blazing splash of stars in the sky. The creature appeared to be short and squat, with bandy little legs. It had two arms raised up past its head and, to Len's surprise, had two more arms at waist height. One upper fist clutched a spear and the other a cudgel.

Len laughed aloud. "There, proof I'm dreaming. I decided the rocks were red, like Mars is red, and here I'm seeing something that could have existed in Edgar Rice Burroughs's *Mars* novels, some of my favorites."

"That's great, sport, but you're no John Carter."

Something in those words and the soul-slashing scream the creature issued turned Len's guts into water. He turned and started to run, leaping over the cowering stool. He landed at full run, then his right foot slipped. He started to go down, then something clipped him hard in the right shoulder, pitching him forward into a somersault. That roll degenerated into an uncontrolled series of tumbles that took him to the bottom of the gully, leaving him sprawled facefirst in a dry streambed.

Len's shoulder ached, and he spat out gravel. He started to rise, then threw himself to the left. The spear *chuffed* as it sank into the sand beside him. Adrenaline sent a jolt through him, propelling him to his feet. He glanced at the spear for a second, then at the six-limbed beast galloping toward him, and made a decision.

He ran.

Len dashed off along the course of the stream, spraying sand in his wake. He leaped over small rocks and vaulted a deadfall tree. Cutting around larger obstacles, he positioned himself so that they were behind him, shielding him to prevent the creature from having a clear shot at his back. He couldn't hear it coming for him, but he knew it was, so when he reached a fourteen-foot drop, he only hesitated for a second before leaping.

Smooth rocks shifted beneath his feet as he landed, dumping him on his butt and the shoehorn in his pocket. He pulled that out with his right hand and glanced at the shoe sizer in his left hand. "They're as much a mockery of sword and shield as I am of a hero."

"Didn't hear me complaining when you ran, did you? Wouldn't have minded if you took the spear, though."

"Thanks, Jhesti." Len got to his feet again and started forward, but stopped after only a step. There, in front of him, in the streambed, he saw a circle about six feet in diameter. It glowed with a faint luminosity that he found curious and decidedly chilling. The low light illuminated a tangle of bones that appeared stacked almost as if they had been washed down the stream by some torrent. He'd read about similar things in fossil beds in a paleontology course, but noted two differences here. First, the bones weren't all jumbled up—the skeletons had pretty much held together. Second, and more importantly, the skeletons were not fossils embedded in stone, but full skeletons.

Len recoiled from the sight, back beneath the drop-off's overhang, saving his life.

The creature that had been pursuing him landed hard in the streambed, its spear driven a good six inches into the earth. It yanked the weapon clear, scattering rocks about, then snapped the spear around and pointed it at Len's chest with its upper two arms. The creature crouched to let the lower hands pick up good throwing rocks, then advanced on Len.

Len brandished his shoe sizer like a buckler, surprised that the belt clip appeared to be large enough to accommodate his left hand. He brought the shoehorn around, with his thumb resting in the curve of the top. The shoehorn seemed a bit bigger to Len than it had before, but he was fairly certain that was a trick of the light. At *best I can gouge an eye out with this thing*.

Close-up, the creature scared him less and more than it had initially. He'd thought it was much bigger, but it really only came up to his breastbone. The upper body seemed roughly proportional to that of a six-foot-tall man—one who was well muscled and had a spare pair of arms, and the bald head appeared slightly larger than it needed to be. The upper torso's being mismatched with the short bowed legs meant the creature was a bit unbalanced, and Len saw it use the lower arms to steady itself as it came forward.

The beast had a strong lower jaw, with two upthrusting tusks that almost reached its tiny, feral eyes. It had no nose to speak of, only a pair of slit nostrils. The creature appeared to be completely naked and hairless, with a patchy pattern of light and dark flesh that reminded him of Jhesti's motley outfit.

"Kin of yours?"

"Doesn't look very plastic to me."

Jhesti's comment appeared to surprise the creature because it looked at the device for a second, letting the spearpoint track to Len's right ever so slightly. *If a thrust comes now, I can parry it and then . . . die as it bashes me with a rock.*

Suddenly, with a metallic squeal that somehow communicated outrage, the fitting stool launched itself from the drop-off and crashed down onto the beast's head. The creature brought the spear up and across, battering the stool aside with the shaft. The stool flew off to the side, its metal legs striking sparks from the rocks it hit, then vanished from sight.

Without conscious thought, Len danced forward and snapped a side kick into beast's chest. He hit it solidly, putting as much power into the kick as he could. The creature began to totter backward, scrambling to stay upright, but the unstable landscape betrayed it. The creature stumbled backward, then fell. It lay still for a moment, then thrashed violently. Len cringed from its tantrum, covering his face with his hands, then peeked out as silence fell over the streambed.

"What happened?" Len glanced over at the creature and began to approach cautiously. "Must have smacked its head on a rock."

"Go find out."

Len crept forward, heartened slightly by the fitting stool coming up over a rock to join him. The stool looked as unsteady as a fawn—*and a bit larger than before*—but he found its presence reassuring. He reached out and patted it on the padded seat. "Thanks for coming to the rescue."

"Thanking a stool?"

Len frowned at Jhesti. "Hey, dream or reality or whatever, gratitude is never in poor taste."

"Point for the shoe salesman."

Len rose to his full height as he neared the beast's body. It was apparent to him that it was out cold or dead, and as his head rose high enough, he knew the latter to be the truth. The creature had not, however, hit its head on a rock to kill it.

It fell in the bone circle.

Len crouched back down near the creature's right shoulders, careful to stay away from the edge of the glowing circle. Where the creature's body had fallen into the circle, nothing was left but naked bone. "But that's not possible."

"But it happened, didn't it?"

"Yeah, but *how*?" Len grabbed the creature's spear and poked about an inch of the butt into the circle. He watched as the wood cracked, then pitted. In a matter of seconds it went from hardwood to dust. He shoved another two inches in and watched it disintegrate. He was about to do it yet again, when Jhesti's voice stopped him.

"You might want to save the spear, pal."

"Good point." Len set it down, then sat back on his haunches and clasped his hands together. "It almost seems as if something invisible in there is eating the wood, but I don't feel any gnawing or anything. Just watching it, though, looks like one of those time-lapse photography things where you see a piece of wood decaying. In fact . . ."

Len slipped his watch off, looked at the time, then swished the watch through the circle's perimeter. He looked at the time again and blanched. "Oh, wow."

"What?"

"One second in there clicked off thirty seconds on the watch. If there's a thirty-to-one time ratio going, then . . ." Len frowned. "The creature wouldn't have been in there long enough for this to happen to him."

"Really? Check the date function on the watch."

Len did and felt his throat go dry. "Well, the five-year battery here lasted for at least seven, according to the date. One second equals seven years, that's a ratio of . . ."

"Of enough speed to age this thing to death. It probably exhausted the oxygen in the blood in the brain by the time it landed, and was dead by the time the twitching started." Jhesti whistled mournfully. "Nasty little place you've dreamed up here for yourself, Len."

"This doesn't feel like something I'd dream up."

"That's been my point all along."

Len's guts just folded in on him. "I'm really not dreaming, am I?"

"I'm no supercomputer, but it doesn't seem like it to me."

"So I'm just like all these characters I've read about in stories? I'm like John Carter on Mars, or Thomas Covenant or Tarl . . ."

"Don't even say that name."

"Hey, the first few weren't bad."

"That's beside the point, Len." When he glanced down at Jhesti, he saw the figure had its hands planted firmly on its hips. "Two big differences between you and them. One, they were heroes—you, the jury's still out."

"Hey, I could be a hero."

"Len, if you were truly hero material, you'd have done more with your life than dream. You might actually have confronted Corbett about having stolen your idea. At the very least, by this time in your life, you'd have done something exciting or adventurous."

Len frowned. "Well, I asked Angie out."

"Oh, sure, that makes you a real Richard Burton." Jhesti hesitated for a moment. "And not the actor."

"I know, the explorer." He shifted his shoulders uncomfortably. "Well, maybe I'm just a late bloomer."

"Let's hope you live long enough to bloom, then."

"Right. What's the other difference between me and those heroes?"

"A simple one, but the most important one." Jhesti's

voice grew cold. "Since their continuing adventures could make money for their creators, they had an inside track on staying alive. You don't have that luxury. Right now, the only one taking care of you is *you*, and, quite frankly, that should scare you more than your little dead friend ever did."

5

Fialchar had departed abruptly, taking with him his light and any further explanations about the sword, the location of Tyrchon's friends, or the mission he had been given. Tyrchon stripped the necklaces from the other Tsvortu bodies, braided them together, and hung them around his own neck. In the slow zone he donned his armor, rebelted his sword belt over the mail shirt, then slid his new sword into the scabbard. The slender blade rattled around a bit, but he expected it would remain in place until he could return to the Empire and have a proper scabbard made. By the time he was done, because of the time differential, a bloody sun splashed a deep maroon into the dawn sky.

He gathered up the Tsvortu sabers, bound them up, and slung them onto his back. Tyrchon didn't see an immediate need for them, and he could always toss them aside if they became burdensome. While he had no doubt the new sword he had been given would last him a good long time, there never seemed to be enough weapons available in Chaos. And, at the very least, taking them with him denied them to other Storm demons, which was in no way a bad thing.

Finally he returned to the body of the Storm demon Fialchar had killed with the *vindictxvara*. Tyrchon pulled the blade free, being careful not to let the blade twist and catch on the *Tsvortu's* ribs. The dagger had a plain pommel and cross guard that had been simply decorated with a wavy-line design. He knew enough of the *Bharashadi* to know that design indicated the bloodline of the Black Shadow that had fashioned it, but he did not recognize it. *Hardly matters, they are mostly all gone now.*

The blade itself had a diamond cross section, making it quite strong. A third of the way down, on the underside of the blade, a wicked notch had been cut into the metal, forming a nasty hook. Both sides of it had been sharpened, and Tyrchon had seen such a device on a knife before. Trappers and butchers used it to help skin animals because they could hook it around tendons and slice them free with a quick tug. On a *vindictxvara*, however, the use of the hook was to tear living flesh and leave it a ruin.

Tyrchon wiped the blood off on the *Tsvortu's* fur and took a good look at the design worked into the blade. The knifesmith, when making it, had magickally worked an image of Tyrchon himself into the metal, forging a link between the man and the blade. The wound this magickal blade had created when it sank into him was beyond all proportion to the real damage it should have done. The wound had quickly festered and become putrid. It would have killed him except for Fialchar's skill in curative magicks.

And he is skilled in other things as well. The image Tyrchon now studied was not the one he'd seen stained with his own blood when he pulled the knife from his side. The foot-long blade showed his face, but it was the face he remembered from *before* he and the cowl became one. *He even lengthened my black hair to account for the growth since then.* In addition to that change—which rendered the blade inert in terms of magickal damage it could do to him—Fialchar had also repaired the bit of the hook that had broken off inside of him and splashed some gold tracery down the blade to make it more of a match for the sword.

Tyrchon shivered. He had long recognized the value of having sorcerers accompany Chaos Riders into Chaos, but magick made him uneasy. Magickers were often capable of generating spells with devastating effects, and there was simply no way to look at a magicker and gauge, given his size or species, what sort of damage he could do. As a warrior, Tyrchon was well used to sizing up foes and figuring out how to defeat them, but magickers defied simple judgments like that, *and* they had the annoying ability to cast spells at a range that never even let a warrior get close.

A sorcerer of Fialchar's rank—and Tyrchon wasn't even sure if the rank Grandmaster of Magicks would be suitable to cover what he could do—was capable of things that were legend. He didn't believe that Fialchar had actually pulled a star from the sky and fashioned it into the blade, but he didn't doubt Lord Disaster was able to do such a thing. Tyrchon had seen the emerald-towered Castel Payne, Fialchar's home, floating through the Chaos sky, and that alone dwarfed the wonders worked by the Empire's best magickers.

It was nice to know, however, that there were things

that could hurt Fialchar. *His power is not absolute.* Tyrchon found this to be somewhat reassuring, for he had no doubt that Fialchar would discard him once his mission was finished. Fialchar certainly would not want it known that he had limitations, for that would give the Empire a tool to use against him. Moreover, Tyrchon got the distinct impression that Fialchar would not like having anyone who knew of his weaknesses around, if only for the sake of pride. *I bet his metal ears burn every time some bard sings of the Lost Prince plucking whiskers from Fialchar's beard in Castel Payne.*

The mere thought of Fialchar taking umbrage at tavern songs brought a jaw-drop smile to Tyrchon's face. He tucked the *vindictxvara* through his belt at the small of his back, drew the sword he'd been given, and held it out before him. The blade's heft seemed too much for its physical size, yet it had a balance that made it easy to manipulate. Tyrchon whipped it through a couple of slashes, then thrust the blade forward, withdrew it, and brought it around in a circular parry. He wasn't certain he was any faster using this sword than he was with the one he had owned previously, but he felt more confident with it, and that counted for a lot.

"But you're supposed to point me on the way to my mission. How does that work?" He held the blade out loosely in his grip, willing it to point in the direction of the friends Fialchar said remained in Chaos. The blade just lay there. Then he held it up, resting the balance point on his right wrist so the blade had more free play, but again it didn't move.

Something else, then. Tyrchon drove the tip of the blade into the ground and crouched, letting his shadow wash over the blade. He closed one eye and peered through the star-shaped design in the pommel, but all he saw was the landscape beyond and his shadow stretching out toward it. *Nothing . . . wait.*

He looked again through the star, then stood up. With the sun at his back, his own shadow pointed unerringly at the far horizon.

The sword's shadow ran off at an angle to the right, pointing north-northeast.

The warrior smiled. "It will work during the day, anyway." He set his nose in the direction the shadow pointed, pulled the blade from the earth, and slid it home in his scabbard. "We're off, then."

Tyrchon set a decent pace and, every so often, double-checked his course, using the sword's shadow. Even as the sun rose in the sky toward noon, the sword cast a long shadow to direct him. Tyrchon did not follow the course it set exactly, but varied his route to make passage easier for him, more difficult for pursuit to follow, and to avail himself of water whenever he scented it nearby. Visits to the watering places proved doubly valuable because they often showed tracks of creatures that had visited them and, until the last one, he saw no sign of Chademons.

Just before noon, Tyrchon approached the crest of a hill, listening carefully for any sign of trouble because at the last water hole he'd seen *Hobmotli* tracks. While he'd slain a few of the Devils in Motley in the past, that had always been solitary hunters. The tracks he'd seen were enough to let him identify at least three individuals, which meant trouble. While alone he had never found them to be particularly intelligent, in groups their intelligence seemed to increase considerably.

He found himself a shadowed crack between rocks on the hilltop and peered out into the little valley beyond. Five hundred yards along the way, halfway up the valley wall on the right, he saw three *Hobmotli* sitting in the shade of a big rock. Another of their number perched on a stony overhang above the mouth of a cave. The four-armed Chademons had spears with stone tips and their knobby war clubs, as well as a pile of small throwing stones that would come easily to hand. Three of them appeared to be naked, but the fourth wore a ragged cloak festooned with feathers.

Tyrchon sniffed the air and got a snootful of *Hobmotli*. Despite the pungent tang of their unwashed bodies, he also caught a hint of two other scents. Having come all this way to find his companions, he had expected the cave to hide someone familiar to him. *That Xoayya and Nagrendra are in there is a surprise because I thought they died at First Stop Mansion the night the* Bharashadi *attacked us.* Tyrchon shrugged. *No reason truly to be surprised.* As Roarke was fond of saying, "Things like that happen in Chaos."

He crouched there, measuring distances with his eyes, looking for paths of approach so he could get to the trio and the *Hobmotli* with the cloak first, then deal with the one at the cave. Unfortunately, the valley had surprisingly little cover, and the *Hobmotli* above the cavern mouth seemed preternaturally alert. There seemed to be no way he could surprise them, so he'd just have to draw his sword, attack, and hope the sheer ferocity of his assault won the day.

Tyrchon dropped a hand to the hilt of his new sword and hesitated. *What if this is the challenge where the sword will not prevail?* His eyes narrowed. *Is there another solution to this situation, one that won't defeat me?*

He nodded and stood up. He walked to the middle of the hill, skylining himself, then slowly descended. He picked his path carefully between rocks and cacti and wished, for once, that his muzzle would allow him to pucker up his lips so he could whistle as if he had not a care in the world. It was the first time such a thought had occurred to him, and he wondered idly if dogs found whistling so intriguing because they couldn't manage it? *Fialchar has you thinking about all you have lost, but you need to remember all you have gained.*

Even at four hundred yards, he could hear the rumble of voices from inside the cave. He couldn't make out words, but there was no mistaking the tones of Nagrendra's bass voice. He suspected the Reptiad sorcerer had somehow detected his approach, but he caught nothing in what he heard to suggest panic within the cave.

Tyrchon raised both his empty hands as the *Hobmotli* hopped to their feet and brandished their weapons. "Peace. No fight. Peace."

The three naked Hobs began to jump up and down, slapping their lower hands against the ground. The cloaked *Hobmotli* took a step or two toward Tyrchon, then hesitated, adopting a three-point stance. Tyrchon immediately dropped into a crouch and waited. When the *Hobmotli* leader came back up and moved a step closer, Tyrchon resumed his approach, still holding his hands high.

The lead *Hobmotli* waved his subordinates to silence as Tyrchon closed the distance between them. Tyrchon slowed and crouched again at the foot of the small rise where the *Hobmotli* waited, then he drew the bundle of sabers from over his head and deposited them in the dust at his feet. He lowered his hands to his knees and waited.

The *Hobmotli* leader slowly descended and lowered his muzzle to the bundled blades. "Sab."

Tyrchon nodded slowly. "Sab. Tsvortu sab." He reached up and rattled the Tsvortu discs he wore around his neck. "Dead Tsvortu. Tsvortu bad. Hob not bad."

"Hob not bad." The Hobmotli sat back on his rump. One lower hand reached out and tentatively touched a saber. "Hob sab."

"Hob sab, yes." Tyrchon nodded. He pointed off toward the cave. "Hob sab, cave mine." He touched his own chest at the last.

The old Hob watched him carefully, folding all four arms over a chest that bore plenty of scars. The Hobmotli were a tribe of Chaos demons that reproduced very fast and would long since have overrun Chaos except for their love of fighting each other, and sincere efforts by other Chademon tribes to exterminate them. Like most vermin, however, a few always managed to escape and, in no time, were able to reinfest an area.

The chief advantage the other tribes and all Chaos Riders had over the Hobmotli was the Hobmotli inability to master even the most simple metalworking. Swords and armor provided their enemies with all they needed to withstand Hobmotli attacks and mercilessly slaughter the little beasts. Hobmotli battle tactics generally seemed to equate attacking with screaming, and a good attack with a really loud scream. While the mere thought of an army of Hobmotli in armor, with modern weapons, was enough to put Tyrchon in a cold sweat, he didn't think giving them four sabers would create much of a problem.

Especially when Tsvortu come looking for them.

The leader of the Hobmotli touched the blades again, this time with two hands. "Hob sab yes. Cave bad."

Tyrchon's lips peeled back to reveal some fang, and

his voice dropped into a growl. "Cave bad Hob. Good mine. Hob good. Cave good mine."

The elder Hob nodded. "*Tsvortu* dead?"

"*Tsvortu* dead yes."

The chief pointed at Tyrchon's sword. "Dead sab?"

Tyrchon snapped his teeth shut, then flashed fang again. "*Tsvortu* dead bite." He shrugged. "No sab, teeth."

The *Hobmotli*'s eyes grew wide. He turned and jabbered at the two *Hobmotli* behind him. They turned and jabbered at each other, occasionally glancing down at him, then they began to jump up and down again. The other one above the cave began to hop up and down, too, very excitedly.

Not for the first time did Tyrchon regret having the Hobs upwind of him.

The head *Hobmotli* let his hands linger on the blades. "Hob sab good. Cave good. Hob good. Good good."

Tyrchon nodded, then tapped his own chest. "Tyrchon."

"Tyrchon good." The Hob chief drummed his chest. "Fryl."

Tyrchon stood and backed away from the sabers and toward the cavern entrance. "Hob good. Fryl good."

"Tyrchon good." The *Hobmotli* lifted the bundle of swords above his head, then began to worry the cloth binding them with his teeth.

The warrior smiled and started up toward the cave, jumping aside to miss the headlong rush of the Hob from atop the cave as he engaged in a six-point gallop to get at the swords. As he climbed the hill, Tyrchon recovered the Hob's club and spear and carried them up with him.

"Hello, Nagrendra? Xoayya? Are you all right?"

"We're surviving." Nagrendra's voice sounded a bit strained, but still strong. "The Hobs, did you kill them?"

"No, just made a deal." Tyrchon smiled as he entered the cave. "You'd be surprised just how cheaply they were willing to let two magickers from beyond the Ward Walls go."

6

"Take a good look at us and you might want to renegotiate."

Tyrchon ducked his head to enter the cavern and hesitated, but not because of anything he saw. The scent of sour sweat—especially the acrid nervous sweat expected given that the Hobs had been waiting for them—didn't really surprise him. What he caught instead was the sour stink of decaying meat that he easily associated with impending death.

He cast the spear and cudgel down at the cave's entrance and slowly straightened up. "It's good to see both of you again." Tyrchon let his jaw drop in a lupine grin. "We'll get out of this, you know."

"So I have been told repeatedly by Xoayya." The large lizard-man magicker shifted uncomfortably on the ground. His eyes burned with *Chaosfire* and narrowed as he shifted his left leg around and used his thick tail to support it. Nagrendra's forked tongue slithered out of his mouth quickly and back in, then he shook his head. "We have a problem, as you can see."

An iron spike as thick as Tyrchon's thumb transfixed the lower half of Nagrendra's left leg, entering from behind his knee and poking back out at the front of his shin. The Reptiad's scales, which time in Chaos had transformed into shiny mica chips, clearly hadn't stopped the spike, which meant it had been driven through with incredible force.

"How long have you been like that?"

Nagrendra shrugged. "Two days, though it seems longer."

Xoayya stood to the Reptiad's right, her slender arms hugged around her. Tyrchon looked up at her and saw her as if for the first time. He immediately noticed that her large blue eyes had already taken on hints of *Chaosfire*, which was rather remarkable given she'd been in Chaos less than a week. Her fiery red hair had been gathered back into a ponytail and tied with a strip torn from the hem of her skirt. Dirt stained her alabaster flesh, and dark circles beneath her eyes marked a lack of rest, but she did not seem defeated by her experience.

Tyrchon realized he'd have predicted a collapse based on how she suffered on the long journey to the Ward Walls, but then he'd not spent much time with her or noticing her since coming across into Chaos. He had been preoccupied with defending the group against the *Bharashadi*, and she had been working with Nagrendra in that cause. Because she was so small— not a child but not quite yet a woman—and because she had no weapon skills, he had dismissed her. *It seems, however, Chaos agrees with her.*

Xoayya half closed her eyes. "I can use my healing magicks to stop the wound from festering too much, and to numb it a bit, but I can't block all the pain."

Nagrendra nodded. "And with the pain, my ability to concentrate enough to cast spells or even teach Xoayya spells that could help me is nonexistent." He pointed a three-fingered hand at his leg. "The spike is through the big bone. The metal has to come out if I'm going to be healed. That, or I lose the leg."

"No!" Xoayya shook her head violently. "You will not lose the leg. I've seen you walking with us." Her hands balled into fists and pounded into the tops of her thighs. "You keep the leg. That's final."

Tyrchon scratched behind his left ear. "I'd forgotten you are a clairvoyant. You're sure of this vision?"

"I'm sure of many things, Tyrchon." She dropped into a crouch beside him. "I can't get the spike out, but you can. I can heal the damage done, but you're going to have to get it out."

The wolf-warrior looked up at the lizard-man. "What do you think about me digging around in your leg?"

Nagrendra's nostrils flared slightly. "You know as well as I do that Xoayya's magick is holding infection at bay, but not wiping it out. You can smell it, too, I'm certain. Xoayya can probably dull most of the pain. I'll endure the rest."

Tyrchon reached forward and plucked a mica scale from the cave floor. Straightening up, he drew his sword and ran the scale down along the blade's edge. A slice of scale curled off easily.

Xoayya looked up at him, horrified. "You're not going to use that thing to cut the spike free, are you?"

"I don't have a hammer and chisel, and I'll be going through bone." He gave her a smile. "Trust me, though, this blade is sharp enough to go through easily. Nagrendra, I'll free the spike from bone, then we'll have to pull it out. That's going to hurt a lot."

The Reptiad sorcerer looked at Xoayya. "You didn't see me limping in this vision of yours, did you?"

She smiled shyly and patted Nagrendra on his good leg. "I did not. You will endure."

"Proceed, Tyrchon."

Tyrchon instructed Xoayya to use her belt and the Hob cudgel to create a tourniquet above Nagrendra's knee to restrict the amount of bleeding that would result during the surgery. She twisted it as tightly as she could, then Nagrendra himself took over. He smiled as he did so. "Gives me something to do."

Tyrchon dropped to his knees and wrapped his mail gloves around the sword's blade, leaving six inches exposed beyond this handhold. "I'll give you something else to do. Tell me how this thing got jammed in there and how you ended up here. Last I recall, the *Bharashadi* crushed the tower you two were in."

"They actually crushed the top of it. I should have been dead, and would have been, save for Xoayya and her prescience." The Reptiad looked away as Tyrchon lowered his blade toward the wound. "I'd raised the magickal wall I expected to hold the Black Shadows back, then I heard Xoayya scream from below. I turned to head for the stairs leading down, but I was weak from the spell. I got dizzy and tumbled down the stairs."

"And your fall was a bit faster than a controlled descent?" Tyrchon stabbed the tip of his blade into the Reptiad's flesh about two inches above the wound and traced a line down to two inches past it. He made two more crosscuts and peeled the flesh back from the wound. Because of the tourniquet, very little blood flowed. Another long cut took him through the muscles and ligaments sheathing the bone, revealing the spike itself.

"How does it look?"

Tyrchon nodded. "Not bad. The spike struck off center. A little whittling, and we should be clear. But you were telling me about your fall."

"Yes, ouch, I was." Nagrendra's tongue whiplashed from one side of his mouth to the other. "Planning on leaving your name carved in the bone there?"

"No, but I *will* ask the Carving Guild if this work qualifies me for an apprentice badge." Working carefully with the tip of the blade, Tyrchon nibbled away at the chip of bone holding the spike fast. Leaning forward, he blew the bone splinters out of the way and continued his work. "Getting there."

"Good." Nagrendra's nostrils grew as he drew in a deep breath. "My fall got me to the bottom of the tower a bit faster than the debris from the collapse. Not that much faster, though, as the spike attests. Xoayya, dear, please continue."

"Sure, Nagrendra. Just listen to my voice, concentrate on it." She laid a hand on his shoulder. "When first exploring around the tower, I had sensed tunnels and passages. I wasn't certain where they were, or even *when* they were."

"When?" Tyrchon looked up from the surgery. "I'm not sure I understand."

"I don't always know if what I see is past or future. I mean, if it concerns me, I know if it is future when I haven't lived through it yet. With other things, I don't know. It could all be potential, and that is what I sensed." She frowned. "When Nagrendra crashed down in the base of the tower, a series of paving stones on the floor gave way."

Nagrendra hissed. "They evaporated."

"They weren't there anymore and revealed a narrow trench cut in the foundation of the tower itself. Nagrendra fell into it, and I dived in after him. Above us, the timbers that had given us a moment or two of sanctuary from the falling debris finally collapsed, killing Aleix and burying us." She shivered. "We crawled forward and into a narrow tunnel. It slanted downward, and we kept going."

"Interesting." Tyrchon set his sword aside and looked up at Nagrendra. "I have the spike free of the bone. I'm going to pop it loose. This will hurt more than anything you've known . . ."

"Save the spike going in?"

"Right, maybe that." The wolf-warrior glanced over at Xoayya. "Be ready to start spelling the bone back into shape when I get this spike clear. Ready? Now!"

Holding on to the leg with his hands, Tyrchon pushed with his thumbs and worked the spike up and out of the crescent-shaped hollow in the bone. Xoayya's hands hovered above his, and a blue-white glow started from inside them. Tyrchon felt a tingle as the magickal energy pulsed down past his hands and into the wound. His jaw dropped with amazement as the tiny fragments of bone all around the wound appeared to become liquid and flow back into place.

Using his left hand to hold on to the sharp end of the spike, Tyrchon shifted around so he straddled the leg and could grasp the spike's other end with his right hand. He wiped his hand off on his pant leg, then got a good grip. He wiggled the spike, vaguely aware of Xoayya's shifting around to his left. "This comes out now."

Nagrendra's leg made a sucking sound as the spike

reluctantly slid free. When it finally cleared his leg, the Reptiad involuntarily flicked his tail, catching Tyrchon behind his right leg and dumping him on his back. Tyrchon rolled quickly to his left to get out of the tail's range, but as he came to his feet he saw Xoayya cast another spell to close the wounds, and Nagrendra's tail ceased its thrashing.

Xoayya took hold of the Hob cudgel, prying it free of Nagrendra's left hand, and slowly released the tourniquet. The Reptiad looked over at her, and vaguely in the direction of his leg, then let his head sink back. His breathing quickly became regular.

Tyrchon nodded toward Nagrendra. "You spelled him to sleep?"

"Took no effort, given all he's been through." Xoayya fastened the belt around her waist again. "He's been remarkable, really. So brave. Despite his pain, he wouldn't sleep. He wanted me to take the leg from the start, but I refused. I couldn't have done it."

"How are you holding up?"

She glanced up at him, a hint of surprise at his question on her face. "Chaos has put demands upon me that I never could have anticipated. Before coming here, before meeting Locke and you and Nagrendra and the others, I lived a life of visions and fantasy. I told Locke that visions came to me when my mind was unoccupied, and he provided me a way to occupy it, but until coming here I never realized the underlying problem I had."

Tyrchon picked up his sword, wiped it off on his pant leg, and resheathed it. "And that problem was?"

"Mortifyingly simple. The reason I had so many visions, the reason my mind was unoccupied, was because I had no real life. I had all I wanted—I was quite spoiled by my family—and had to contest with visions of my future that told me where I would be at various stages in my life. I had no responsibilities and, moreover, knew my existence would continue whether I did anything about it or not, so I had no reason for doing anything."

"But from what you told Nagrendra about seeing him walking, you still clearly believe in destiny and the futures your visions describe. Your belief in them means you still have no life of your own."

She glanced down at the ground. "There is a difference, and I am not certain I fully understand it. Locke would love this—I'm slipping closer to his position of believing in free will. The difference is the difference between being a child riding a pony being led by an adult, and someone taking the reins herself. Instead of waiting for things to happen, I am participating in them. I may not be able to affect the outcome, but I don't have to be passive, because in being passive, I become remote and dull and dead."

Xoayya pointed at Nagrendra. "These past two days with Nagrendra would have been hideous for the both of us had I been the way I have been. I would have sat here, confident that you would come because I've seen the three of us together, and that would be enough for me. I would have just waited, and not talked much with Nagrendra or been anything more than dutiful in spelling his wound. Physically I would have been here, but mentally and emotionally I would not. I can't explain it any better than that."

"You don't need to explain more, I think I understand." Tyrchon gave her a firm nod. "I do think you're wrong about destiny, though. In dealing with the Hobs, I made a choice, one that meant they didn't die, and I didn't die. I have to believe that choice will continue to have effects, for me, for you, for them. Believing in predestination means, to me, that I'm a puppet acting things out in some grand festival somewhere, and I don't like the idea."

"Not enamored of being a puppet?"

"The only kind of puppet I want to be is one who can climb his strings and bite the puppeteer's hand." Tyrchon shivered as he recalled his conversation with Fialchar. Am I *supposed to be* your *puppet, Lord Disaster?* He also realized that Fialchar's comment about the sword and the price it would demand of him was something he rejected. While the idea of frustrating Fialchar was something that caused him some personal joy, the idea that it might hurt Xoayya was something he found himself reluctant to do.

"You realize, I hope, that I mean no disrespect to you in saying that."

Xoayya shook her head. "You and Locke will just have to learn."

"Or, perhaps, you will be the one doing the learning."

"Meaning?"

Tyrchon shrugged. "Years in Chaos have taught me that everything is mutable. I see no reason to assume the future is any different."

"Interesting perspective." She gave him a careful smile. "I will think about that."

"Good." Tyrchon glanced down at Nagrendra. "From what you were saying, you crawled through a tunnel beneath First Stop Mansion? How did you end up here, then? This cave is leagues away from there."

Xoayya dropped to the cave floor and sat back against the wall. "Along the passage we came to a shimmering wall of light. It looked something like the

Ward Walls, but it was darker, more purple and red, with very little white. I didn't know what it was, but when I touched it, I felt only a little tingle. We pushed on through it and found ourselves back there, in the back of the cave. There is no curtain there—whatever it was seems to have been strictly one-way.

"Nagrendra decided, after thinking about it, that the vanishing stones in the tower and the light curtain were remnants of magick cast on First Stop Mansion before the Shattering. He said that the spells were probably cast to allow the residents to flee if ever attacked, and the use of B*harashadi* magick on the tower may have been enough to trigger them. While spells cast from before the Shattering should have long since worn off, Nagrendra thinks they remained in place because of the magick inherent in Chaos itself."

"Interesting idea, but well beyond my ken of magick." Tyrchon removed his sword belt, then sat opposite her. "You'll be happy to know the B*harashadi* Necroleum is destroyed, and their power is broken."

"And Locke and the others?"

"I don't know about all of them. Hansen is dead." The wolf-warrior tapped the rent in his armor on his left flank. "Black Shadows ambushed him and me while we were scouting. One got me with a *vindictxvara*, so the others put me in a slow zone so they could go for help. Locke apparently made a deal with Fialchar to heal me."

Xoayya's eyes grew wide. "Fialchar? He helped you?"

Tyrchon brandished his sheathed sword. "And even gave me this blade."

Her eyes narrowed. "And what does he want in return?"

"Too much, I have no doubt, but it seems like very little right now." Tyrchon shifted his shoulders uneasily. "But part of the bargain allowed me to find the two of you, so I think, so far, I'm way ahead of Lord Disaster."

7

Shoth Churgûn picked his way up the rocky outcropping with care. He avoided setting his feet on anything that looked loose and didn't grab at rocks with his hand for fear of tearing them free. Over the last two days he had endured enough reproving glares from the detachment of Myat's personal guard that accompanied him to make him wary of winning anymore. *They will never respect me for what I am, but I won't give them further grounds for despising me.*

He slid onto his belly and lay down beside Ghislaine, the Guard captain leading the group. She held a finger to her lips as she looked at him, then pointed beyond the hill to the grassy bowl below. He followed her gaze and saw a spring-fed watering place surrounded by a blanket of purple grasses, all gathered into little domelike clumps.

Grazing peacefully were a half dozen bovine creatures that were faintly reminiscent of oxen, save for the

73

third horn on the nose and the run of spiked bony plates running down the creature's neck and spine to its tail. Unlike Imperial oxen, these creatures ran to a brownish maroon in color—very much akin to the color of dried blood—and sported a shaggy coat on their flanks and undersides. A massive bull *tauroch* with a fairly long nose horn appeared to lead the group, with four cows and an immature bull completing the herd.

Ghislaine slunk back below the crest of the hill and pulled him down with her. Dark blue with only a hint of *Chaosfire*, her eyes hardened as she spoke to him. "Taking a *tauroch* will give us fresh meat. If we had horses, we could take them. On foot, it would be suicide for my people to approach."

Shoth found that hard to believe. All of the Guards—men and women alike—towered over him and, pound for pound, seemed as well muscled as the bull *tauroch*. The light leather armor they wore had been stained a dull ocher, matching it to the predominant color of Chaos. The Guards had seemed incredibly stealthy, able to move without sound, flitting from shadow to shadow effortlessly. Shoth found himself half-surprised one of her people wasn't already among the *taurochs* butchering them.

"And you are telling me this because you want me to go out there?" Shoth shook his head. "I know you and your people have no use for me . . ."

The woman grabbed a handful of his maroon tunic. "I have a use for you, magicker, and one that is more pressing than your directing us hither and yon. You are capable of casting combat magicks. I want you to kill a *tauroch*."

Shoth watched her face for any sign of deception, then shrugged almost imperceptibly. "Which one?"

"Whichever one you wish."

"Fine, consider it done." Shoth pulled his tunic free of her grasp and walked up to the hillcrest. Standing there, he could see a couple of the other Guards crouched down and assumed the remainder were scattered about in a semicircle centered on the *taurochs*. Those he could see looked at him and waved him back down and out of sight, but he ignored them. Instead, he took a step forward and started down toward the water hole.

The bull *tauroch*'s head came up. He regarded Shoth with flat black eyes. His ears flicked around, betraying some concern and irritation. Shoth had no idea what the creature's experience with human beings had been, but the sorcerer assumed nothing as big as the bull would see someone as puny as he was as a threat of any sort.

And, in that, you are not unlike all Matarun. From the outset Captain Ghislaine and her dozen Guardsmen had regarded Shoth as nothing more than a magickal signpost directing them on a long trek through Chaos. True, Shoth had not been prepared for the sort of arduous journey they had been making, but the Guards seemed barely human to him. They slept for a handful of hours each night, marched forever without complaint, and spoke to him as little as possible. They didn't help him set up his tent, nor tear it down, and required him to gather his own water and firewood.

It was not that he minded hard work, but he had been completely excluded from their society. He knew his blond hair and his gray eyes marked him as being apart from other Matarun. That was something he had lived with his entire life, but his close association with Princess Myat had brought him welcome relief from such treatment in recent years. *But the Guards, they are more Matarun than the first Mountain lords themselves.*

The bull *tauroch* snorted and took a couple of steps in Shoth's direction. The sorcerer flashed teeth at him, then slowed and stopped, staring at the beast. The *tauroch* lowered its head in a challenge. Shoth extended his right hand toward the bull. His hand glowed blue as he opened it, palm forward, then the glow intensified as Shoth balled his hand into a fist.

He heard one of the Guards gasp as he started to run at the *tauroch* and it at him. Shoth's mouth went dry and his chest tightened as he sprinted across the grasses at the galloping bull. The sorcerer kept his knees high, pulling his feet from the saw-edge grasses. *If I trip, if I go down . . .* He refused to think about it. *I cannot. I will not.*

The *tauroch* flew at him, mucus spraying from nostrils as the beast snorted angrily. Sunlight flashed from horns, especially the wickedly curved snout horn. The *tauroch* lowered his head, readying himself for an upthrust that would disembowel Shoth and fling his dead body high into the air.

At the last second Shoth cut to the left. The *tauroch* tried to move his head toward Shoth and hook him with a horn, but the sorcerer slipped past, just out of reach. Leaning back in toward the right, he drove his glowing fist into the *tauroch*'s chest, right behind the beast's left shoulder. As the bull continued past him, the tail lashed him across the face, spinning Shoth around and to his knees, stunning him just enough to leave him at the bull's mercy.

It didn't matter. The bull continued on past Shoth for a couple of steps, then collapsed. His mighty chest plowed into the grass, and a horn tore a ragged line in the earth. Hooves gouged up clumps of grass, then the great beast exhaled in a shuddering sigh and lay still. The only motion on the *tauroch* came from a trickle of blood flowing from its nose.

All around him, Guards stood and began to trot down into the grassy depression. The rest of the herd, bereft of their protector, galloped off away from the water hole. The Guards slowed as they approached the bull, first looking at it, then Shoth, and finally back at the bull again.

Shoth raised his left hand to his face and felt a rising welt. He almost cast a spell to reduce the swelling and rid himself of the bruise that would mark him, but he did not. *That would be seen as a sign of weakness.*

A shadow fell over him as Ghislaine grabbed his tunic and hauled him to his feet. "Are you *mad*? What were you trying to do?"

"You asked me to kill a *tauroch*. I did it." Shoth met her hard stare. "You saw that."

"No, what I saw was someone who did something completely beyond reason." She jerked her head toward the dead bull. "I asked you to use a spell to kill it. I wanted it done at range, so no one would be hurt."

"No one was."

"You could have been killed."

"And you'd not have cared in the least."

Her head came up. "And that makes a difference to you?"

"No. Yes."

"Wait a minute." Ghislaine released him and pointed to the bull. "Keph and Irin, start butchering the *tauroch*. The rest of you go back and get our supplies. We will stay here today and tonight. Phark, you will pitch the wizard's tent and prepare his camp."

Her orders given, she guided Shoth back toward the rocky hillside he'd descended and sat him down. "What were you trying to do down there?"

"I was doing what none of you dared to do." Shoth looked down at his hands. "I wanted to earn the respect of your company, your people. I *am* Matarun, no matter how small and fair I may be, yet you treat me like some fish-gutter from the islands."

Ghislaine towered over him, her fists planted on her hips and a dark scowl on her face. "You're an idiot, Shoth. You think the Guards ignore you because you're not tall and you're not dark and your eyes are gray? You think they don't think you are Matarun?"

"It's obvious, isn't it?"

"No, it is not." She shook her head, letting her thick black braid flop forward over her left shoulder. "You have no idea what it takes for someone to become one of the Princess's Guards, do you? They have mastered more weapons skills than most people know exist. They train so they can run for miles without tiring, swim against strong mountain-stream currents for hours, track a shadow across stone and move without leaving a trace of their passing. There may be better individual warriors in the world, but none better as a class than these Mountain Guards."

Shoth looked out at where two of them were quickly reducing the *tauroch* to its component parts. "All the more reason for them to despise me."

"You fool, they despise *everyone*." She folded her arms over her chest. "True, they think you are clumsy, poorly conditioned, and they understand nothing of magick save that they can fall to it without being able to do anything about it. All they really know about you is that Princess Myat has sent you with us, and you are directing us on a search. So far that search has been fruitless, which makes them wonder if you have any idea what you are doing, but they don't despise you for an accident of birth. The fact that they've not abandoned you means they acknowledge that, at the very least, you *are* Matarun."

The sorcerer frowned. "Then I guess I'm missing something. Why did you order one of them to prepare my camp tonight, and never do it before?"

"Because they've had plenty to do themselves. I was letting you do your own share of the work, caring for yourself, so you'd not be a burden on them." Ghislaine laughed. "You think they don't like you now, you have no idea what life would have been like if they had to take care of you."

"Then why set my tent up tonight?"

She pointed at the *tauroch*. "You've done enough for us today. You've saved us hours of foraging for small game. What I want to know is, what did you think you were doing?"

Shoth sighed. "I was killing a *tauroch*. I *am* versed in some combat magicks, but primarily the kind that enhance the performance of others. I could, with a spell, put a magicked edge on the axes your people use, making the butchery much faster. While I am ranked as a Warder, I have not spent much time in Chaos. This you can tell by my eyes."

Ghislaine shrugged. "Matarun are not so easily affected by Chaos that we show it quickly in our eyes."

"My point is, I never learned the quick-death-at-range sort of spells that many Chaos Riders learn. My specialties run toward construction, concealment, and clairvoyance, with just enough curative and combat magicks to get by. In plain point of fact, Captain

Ghislaine, the spell I used to enhance my punch is the most powerful personal-combat spell I know. I did not feel I could risk using another spell and failing here."

"And the drama of killing the bull without a weapon, you could not resist that?"

"I've led your people from one empty place to another. The chance to prove I was not completely useless was not one I could pass by."

Ghislaine crouched at his feet. "I want you to understand two things. First, Princess Myat gave you over into *my* protection. If anyone is going to risk your life, it will be me, since I am responsible for it. Second, you are a vital part of our mission here, and, without you, we cannot complete it. If I have to cripple you and have you carried to prevent you from doing something this stupid again, I will. Am I understood?"

"Yes, Captain, perfectly."

One of the two butchers came trotting over, bearing a big, bloody blob of tissue in his hands. He stopped several paces away and nodded a quick salute to Ghislaine. "Captain, this is the *tauroch*'s heart. Warder Churgûn's punch splintered two ribs and drove them through a lung and the heart." The guard looked at Shoth. "I would know what you want us to do with the heart."

Shoth hesitated. Having been raised Matarun, he knew the slayer of a game beast was given the choicest cuts of the meat, and the heart was prime among them. To eat the heart of a kill was to take into yourself the most noble aspects of the animal that had been slain. As a child he had long dreamed of being given this honor, but as he became an adult and went away to study magick, that dream had died.

"I would have you prepare it in whichever way will

serve all of us, so we can share it." Shoth slowly began to smile. "We are here together, so this kill belongs to all of us. Sharing the strength and stamina of the *tauroch* will be good for all of us."

Ghislaine looked over at the guard. "There, Keph, you have your answer." As the warrior trotted back to the carcass, the captain gave Shoth a cautious smile. "That was a good choice."

"Thank you." The sorcerer looked down at his right hand and flexed it a few times. "Resting here tonight and eating well is probably our best bet because the area we have to cover in the next few days is likely to be very demanding."

The search pattern had begun at the spot on the Meter that had been disrupted but utterly untouched by the Chaos storm. Shoth had actually expected to find nothing there, but it was more convenient to check first because their entry point into Chaos put them fairly close to it, even though it would take them a day farther away from the other sites to be checked. The first night had been complicated by a brief run-in with a *Tsvortu* scouting party, but the Guards had driven them off in short order.

Ghislaine nodded. "From what you and the Princess said before the mission left the mountains, we will be traveling into an area recently visited by a Chaos storm. You have no reports as to what might be located there, so we don't know if we are going into a polar wasteland or strips of rain forest. And I still do not like the fact that we have no solid description of the person we are looking for."

"*That* cannot be helped, I am afraid." Shoth shrugged. "The few attempts to detect this person with clairvoyance magick have failed almost completely. I know he is out there—though I'm not wholly certain we are looking for a man, either by gender or species. There *are* two things I know about him, though. One is that he's out there and fairly close."

"You better hope so, or you'll be killing another *tauroch* before long." Ghislaine smiled. "And what is the other thing?"

"An impression, really, not much." Shoth frowned. He felt fairly certain Myat knew more about the target than she had ever told him, and the manner in which she crafted the part of the spell to summon him could also have contributed to the sense of the man that he got. The fact that Myat had not seen fit to tell him about any of this disturbed him a little, but he thrust his reservations aside.

"Our target is conducting a search himself." The sorcerer closed his eyes and tried to recapture the sensation he'd had the last time he cast a spell. "He's not certain what he's looking for, or why he's looking, but he's determined. Hunter and hunted, he's what we want, and, before long, we will have him."

8

Len shaded his eyes against the setting sun. This would be his third night wherever he was, and he wasn't looking forward to spending it out in the open. He'd seen a variety of fauna, and damned little friendly flora, with all of it being oddly mixed and matched creatures and plants. Most of them looked like the sort of fanciful monsters confused children drew after a visit to a zoo, which went a long way toward making Len think his brains had really been scrambled in his fall.

He laughed to himself and glanced over at where the fitting stool, now the size of a wolfhound, kept pace with him. "That's proof enough that I'm in a dream."

Jhesti sighed. "Are we back to that, again?"

"I'm not sure we ever got very far from it." Len trudged on, using the spear he'd captured as a staff. The war club hung from his hip, bumping gently along with each step. "It's gone on awfully long for a dream, but time functions weirdly in dreams. When I wake up, I probably won't remember any of this."

"Len, I've already told you how you can determine if you're dreaming or not."

The shoe clerk nodded in silence. Jhesti had reminded Len of a little factoid from Psychology 101— people in dream states cannot read printed words. The professor, in noting that some people have very lucid dreams in which they can exert some control, suggested anyone who wonders if he is dreaming should just move to where he can see a newspaper and actually see if he can read the words. If he can, he's not dreaming. Jhesti pointed out that Len could always pull out his wallet and attempt to read the text on a dollar or on his driver's license.

Len had resisted that temptation for a couple of reasons. When first reminded of what the professor had said, Len tried to take control of the dream and alter the reality to fit what he wanted. *If I'm going to be trapped in a dream, it might as well be one of those babes-from-a-beer-commercial dreams, right?* When that didn't work, he tried to at least rope Angie into his dream, but she didn't show up, either.

This inability to manipulate his dreams gnawed at Len. He'd done it a couple of times in the past, that he could remember, so his failure to do it here got him wondering if he was dreaming or not. Moreover, he usually didn't remember much in the way of his dreams, so the wealth of sensory data he was taking in shook his confidence as well. He knew he *had* to be dreaming because if he wasn't, he was either in a place far, far away from home, *or* he was seriously delusional and belonged in a rest home getting lithium by the boxcar.

Looking in his wallet would allow him to confirm or

dismiss the dreaming hypothesis, but he couldn't let himself even begin to think he was anything *but* dreaming. As long as he didn't know for certain, he could cling to the idea that he *was* dreaming. *Which means, sometime along here, I'll wake up and all this will be gone.*

He glanced down at the jester and saw it leaning back with ankles crossed and hands behind its head. The smug little smile just burrowed into his brain. "Look, you little petrochemical extrusion, I'll read what I want to read when I want to read it. I should just unfasten you and throw you away."

"Don't bother." Annoyance ran through Jhesti's voice. "I'm just trying to get you to look at the reality of the situation we're facing here. You want to believe it's a dream, go ahead, but don't expect things to function the way they would in a dream, okay? This dream of yours, for whatever reason, has its own ground rules. If you don't deal with that, you can get dead fast, and you know what they say about dying in your dreams."

Len laughed triumphantly. "Sure, they say if you die in your dreams, you die in reality. Think about it, though. *Who* had that experience and reported the result?"

The jester grumped. "Okay, point to Len. You're still way behind."

"Sure, 'cuz you're keeping score." Len came around the bend in the trail he was following and saw a little valley that narrowed to the dark mouth of a tunnel. Though the setting sun cast long shadows over the entrance, Len could still see that the stones around the entrance had been worked. Twin guardian statues stood on either side of the entrance. Both appeared to be large, anthropomorphic lizards. One bore an ax and the other a staff with what looked to be a crystal shard on the end. As he drew closer to the tunnel he saw a stone slab blocking it. Something gold gleamed in the darkness at the heart of it.

Len picked his pace up ever so slightly, then broke into a jog that the fitting stool matched effortlessly. "Another point for Len Fong, coming up."

"In your dreams."

"In my dreams, exactly." He stopped just inside the short tunnel leading to the stone slab. The gold he'd seen glinting consisted of an inlaid circle of gold with two lines, one off center to the left and one low, that met at a right angle on the left side of the circle. A bunch of other lines were contained by the angle formed by these first two, with some crossing and others just slanting back and forth. "There, clearly I'm dreaming."

"Okay, that's the play-by-play; now I want some analysis with it."

Len crossed his arms over his chest, but still let Jhesti peek out. "When I was a kid in school, some teacher wanted us to put together our own personal coat of arms. She was talking western heraldry, so I did it the way she wanted, but when I brought it home, my grandmother was angry. She showed me how to write my name in Chinese and made me practice it over and over until I had it right. Then, later, on a lark, I created this design. See the L on the side there? That's for my first name, and the other stuff is pretty much a compilation of the symbols for Fong."

Jhesti laughed. "So, you're telling me you're reading that here, right?"

Len hesitated for a second, then frowned. "Not at all. This is just an abstract symbol, and dreams are all in the realm of symbol, which is why I recognize it. And I remember putting it together, which is why I can tell you what it is. You're missing the bigger point, however."

"And that is?"

"If I'm not dreaming, if this isn't being born straight out of my brain, how can this symbol that I created and only I know about appear here?"

"Good question." Jhesti sounded almost bored. "So, genius, tell me *why* it's here?"

Len's frown deepened. "I created the symbol as my own personal crest, so perhaps its presence means this is the threshold of my rediscovering myself. Maybe if I get past it, I'll return to consciousness. You know, I have felt kind of pulled in this direction—nothing strong, but somehow coming this way always seemed a better choice than any of the others. I think I am meant to be here."

"Okay, how do you get past it?"

"I don't know."

"It's *your* dream, remember." Disgust tinged the jester's words. "How do you think it should be opened?"

"I'm not sure." Len reached out and touched the black stone with his left hand. The smooth surface drank in the warmth from his fingertip—not quickly like some vampire, but slowly, as if the rock were slightly cool water. As he dragged his hand along, it seemed as if his fingertips penetrated the black stone as though it were actually a fluid. Then his fingers bumped against the island of the gold circle.

He felt a sharp tingle and jumped back. The black stone began to flow like water and melted down into the ground. The gold crest slowly floated up to the tunnel's ceiling. There it clicked into place and began to glow softly. Beyond it other golden lights came up along the tunnel, illuminating a stairway heading up.

Len glanced contemptuously at the jester, then started into the tunnel. "Either we wake up now—see the stairs are leading *up* toward consciousness—or we'll have a dry place to spend the night."

"Maybe they'll have room service. Doesn't look wired for cable."

Bearing the spear in both hands, Len entered the tunnel cautiously. He started up the stairs, alert for any sort of danger, but saw nothing at all he could describe as even remotely threatening. In fact, he began to grin as he hit the first landing. "Yep, definitely a dream, no doubt about it."

The stairway, fashioned from black marble with white veins, came up into the front third of a massive room, two and a half stories tall. While the hillside outside had been made of the red stone he'd seen in all of his travels, the room itself had been carved from the same marble as the stairs. In the steeply pitched roof, small lights glowed like stars in the night sky. Back at the far end of the room another stairway headed up, then split at the wall, going right and left, up to hallways and other rooms.

The great room itself was nothing short of spectacular. Off to the right, in a slightly sunken area, a fireplace dominated a section set with blocky wooden furniture. Closer to him than the fireplace Len saw a massive oaken table, with seats for fourteen, set out as if for a feast. He sniffed the air and imagined roasted turkey and mashed potatoes lurking beneath the covered serving dishes in the center of the table.

To the left, back in the corner, he saw another fire pit and a variety of surfaces and shelves appropriate for a kitchen. While he saw nothing reminiscent of modern plumbing in terms of pipes or faucets, there were dual sinks over there and a vaned area that would naturally serve as a draining area for dishes.

At the very front of the room, on the left, stairs led down to an area that had been dug deeply enough that a railing warded it from the rest of the room. Countless shelves had been excavated from the stone walls and were filled with volumes of various sizes and bindings. They alternated with a variety of weird things, from crystal balls to what looked to Len, at this distance, to be dried remains of animals, some bones, odd shiny stones, and the occasional bit of pottery.

All of this, however, paled in comparison to the relief carving at the head of the landing where the stairs split. Excised from a single slab of marble, twelve feet tall and flanked on either side by boarspears mounted to the wall, the black stone revealed someone who looked frighteningly similar to Len. The figure wore his hair longer, so it flowed down over his shoulders, and had a few more muscles than Len, but the resemblance was quite clear. The medieval clothes the figure wore gave the image an archaic sense that fit well with the surroundings.

Len let his laughter fill the empty chamber. "Oh, man, this is better than I remember."

"You remember this?" Jhesti sounded piqued. "How is that possible?"

"When I used to play D&D, I designed this place for my character's home. I even drew it up using a CAD program on a buddy's computer. We scanned in a picture of me that we took at a Renaissance Faire and made it into that relief."

Jhesti laughed. "So, you took the picture while you were wearing the Death Boots."

Len craned his head forward and looked at the statue's feet. *The Death Boots! But that was long before I ever went to work for Dancing Joker Shoes.* "Well, because the boots were part of my injury, they're clearly on my mind, and that's why they're here. And I did play a magicker with magick boots, so that's why the boots are there."

"Cute. Rationalizations 'r' us. So, did your character have magick dishes that prepared him food, too?"

"Fong the Magnificent had a lot of things, but I don't recall magick dishes." Len wandered over to the dining table and pulled the huge silver turtle off the biggest serving dish. Steam erupted from it, carrying with it the scent of perfectly roasted turkey. Len's mouth immediately began to water, and the fact that the turkey had three pairs of legs didn't bother him too much.

"I always preferred dark meat. And the stuffing looks like that walnut stuff my mother makes."

"Great. Let's just hope the gravy boat doesn't have her gravy in it."

"Right, good point." Len picked up a carving knife and sliced into the bird. The crisp flesh parted cleanly, and clear juices ran from the breast. "Oh, man, this will be great."

"I'd be careful if I were you, Len."

"Why's that? This is a dream." Len pointed the carving knife at the bird and the other dishes. "My dream, my favorite meal. It's pretty clear."

"And after you stuff yourself, you'll just trundle up and off to bed?"

"You have a problem with that?"

"Only a slight one." The jester sighed. "The door's open."

Len glanced back at the stairs. "Meaning what?"

"Meaning there are things out there that can smell what you're smelling, only they can smell it from a lot further off. If you can't close the door, they can come join your little feast, and I bet they won't balk at taking a bite out of the host. Imagine some slavering wolf—or whatever passes for one here—coming in to snack on you while you're slumbering away."

"That's it!" Len snatched the plastic device from his shirt, tearing it, and slammed it down on the table. Jhesti lay flat, looking a lot like a fly that had just been swatted. "This is my dream and you're the voice of my subconscious and you've just injected a dark element into this dream, which means it's going to be nightmare time again. I don't like it, and I won't have it."

"Then close the door. You designed this place."

"Yeah, but I didn't have a door like that." Len frowned. He definitely knew he'd not worked his personal crest into the CAD design on the computer. And Fong the Magnificent had never had magick dishes because he had those two twins who were ever so grateful to him for rescuing them from the dragon . . . *Wait, don't need to start thinking about dragons. Talk about a nightmare!*

Glumly Len sat down, pulled a leg off the bird, and tore a piece of meat from it. "Okay, look, you don't do this nightmare thing to me tonight, and I'll do what I can to get us out of here. I know this place is significant, but I'm not sure why."

While Len had not been looking at him, Jhesti had rolled up onto his side and rested his head on his left hand. "Go ahead. Eat, don't stuff yourself. I can stand watch while you sleep."

"Thanks."

"And, Len . . ."

"Yeah?"

"I mean this from the bottom of my little plastic heart." The jester wore a smile. "I hope you have pleasant dreams."

9

Nagrendra slept until dawn of the day following his surgery, which came as no surprise to Tyrchon. Two days spent with a spike through his leg, doing everything he could to take care of Xoayya would have taxed anyone's strength. What *did* surprise Tyrchon was how quickly the Reptiad rolled to his feet and began walking.

"Isn't it a bit premature to be moving around?"

"You know as well as I do that remaining in one place in Chaos can be dangerous. This is the start of our third day in this cave." The sorcerer plucked his green woolen cloak from the ground, shook it out, and fastened it around his neck. "*Hobmotli* found us a day and a half ago, today it might be *Tsvortu* or *Drasacor*. We have to be moving, and my leg needs to hold up."

"I agree." Tyrchon pointed at Xoayya's sleeping form. "Do you think she's capable of a long march?"

"More so than I am, I think." A clear membrane nicti-tated up over Nagrendra's eyes and back down again. "She has some steel in her, Tyrchon. She fervently believes she will realize her destiny out here. From what she has said, she *sees* less in the way of visions and is, instead, relying on what *feels* right out here."

"You think she has the instinct for Chaos?"

The Reptiad opened his mouth in a smile. "More than many of those Chaos Riders who have claimed to have it in the past."

"Good, that makes her even more valuable." Tyrchon sighed and glanced up into the sorcerer's *Chaosfire* eyes. "You and I never met before this expe-dition, so you don't know me that well, if at all."

"A few things, perhaps, by reputation." Nagrendra nodded. "And your bid to join us in the Umbra was memorable."

"I'd hate to think that is the last anyone remembers of me." Tyrchon shook his head. "I've told Xoayya, and now I need to tell you and, I guess, ask your advice. After you vanished, I was wounded, left in a slow zone and healed up by Fialchar."

Nagrendra's tongue tasted the air. "Fialchar does nothing without exacting a price for it. In fact, I have a hard time imagining him actually *healing* anyone of any-thing."

"Doesn't quite fit the image, does it?" Tyrchon shiv-ered and made no attempt to hide it. "He wants me—and since he pointed me toward you, I assume he wants *us*—to scout out a place here in Chaos that is the site of something odd. He said a Chaos storm came through the area, hit this point, and went away. Now this is a place that he finds painful to go near, so he can't investi-gate it himself. He was vague enough about it that I don't think he knows much at all concerning it. It probably works as a big blind spot in his vision of his realm."

"I can understand why he would want it investigated." Nagrendra rubbed a hand over his scaled muzzle. "The storm went away, did he say?"

"That's what I recall. That point seemed to perplex him."

"No doubt." The Reptiad began to pace around the cave. "Chaos storms contain a lot of energy and generally wreak havoc until they dissipate. There *is* a fair amount of magickal energy contained in them, which is why they are able to make the changes to the landscape and things they touch as they go along. Things born in Chaos only suffer the effects of the physical energy, but anyone from the Empire would be overwhelmed by it. It would be a lot like the wave of Chaos that washed over Fialchar when he shattered the Seal of Reality, and you have seen how it left him."

"I've always taken cover when I saw the boiling purple clouds on the horizon."

"As have I, but I've also lost friends who were not as cautious as either one of us." Nagrendra crouched for a second, then stood again. "Energy just doesn't go away. If the storm hit a certain point here in Chaos and vanished, then something absorbed that energy. That *something* would have been very powerful. Fialchar is a very powerful sorcerer, to be certain, but I think most of his power comes from his longevity and ability to work complex spells. Something that could suck in a Chaos storm might not be as skilled a magicker as Fialchar, but might be able to overwhelm him with the sheer raw energy of an attack."

The wolf-warrior stared out into the valley. "What could it be?"

"I don't know, but there are ample spells capable of capturing energy. I would suspect it was some long-standing enchantment that survived off the magick inherent in Chaos itself, which suggests it was cast by an Imperial sorcerer."

Tyrchon turned and looked back at the Reptiad. "Chaos storms aren't rare, and we see their track throughout this region. I would have thought another storm would have caused this situation before now."

"That may not be the right question to ask." Nagrendra shrugged. "It could be that no storm ever did pass through the area before or that other spells were in place to conceal the first one. The power in the storm could have been sufficient to overwhelm any concealment spell, though a storm of that intensity in this area would be rare. Something spectacular must have happened to kick it off."

Tyrchon smiled. "Did I mention that the Necroleum was destroyed?"

The sorcerer shook his head. "That could have done it, or could have contributed to damaging conceal-ment spells. If the sorcerer who cast the spell had done so using stone markers to delineate the field of the effect, one of the stones could have been dam-aged when the Necroleum was destroyed."

The wolf-warrior nodded. "That makes an odd bit of sense. As I recall Locke explaining to us, discovering the location of the Necroleum had been difficult. If there had been concealment magicks in place in the area, Chaos Riders would have been hard-pressed to get a good fix on the location."

"So, the Necroleum comes down, triggers a storm, and damages concealment magicks over a particular location in Chaos. The storm courses through there and is absorbed. Fialchar can't see into it, can't investigate it . . ."

"He said it actually hurt him to be near it."

"So he enlists your aid to find out what is going on."

"Right." Tyrchon drew his sword and pressed the tip into the earth at the cave's mouth. "He also gave me this. I ask it to point me toward where we need to go to complete the mission, and the sword's shadow points the way."

Nagrendra looked down. "You mean shadows."

"What?" Tyrchon glanced at the ground. He saw three distinct shadows on the ground, though none of them was particularly dark. One pointed straight out from the mouth of the cave, indicating a place due north. A second pointed to the northwest and overlapped at the base of the sword with the first to form a fat little triangle. The third pointed off to the east. "Hmmm, haven't seen it do that before."

"Do what?" Xoayya yawned and stretched as she sat up.

Tyrchon looked at her, then turned away quickly. Sitting there in the golden glow reflected from the valley's far hills, Xoayya seemed radiant to him. The bags under her eyes had gone away, and while she still had dirt on her face, something about her wide-eyed smile made her very beautiful in his eyes. In his conversations with her the previous day he had found her to be thoughtful and innocently alive, which was a trait seldom found among Chaos Riders. He had enjoyed speaking with her, and thought of her fondly, but had not expected to find himself the least bit attracted to her.

He recovered himself quickly. "The shadow is split. I mean, it shouldn't even be pointing north, since all the light coming in is from that direction, but two points of it are, and a third shadow is pointing east."

"I see." Her voice came quietly. "Is there something you Chaos Riders know that makes this significant? Will you share it with me?"

Nagrendra boomed out a sibilant laugh. "Tyrchon's sword indicates with a shadow which direction he is to travel to complete his mission for Lord Disaster. Right now we have three choices, but nothing to indicate which one is the correct one."

Tyrchon crouched to look at the shadows, yet an ear cocked itself back to listen to Xoayya's approach. He caught her scent as she got close, then felt a hand rest lightly on his right shoulder. That touch, though barely felt through his armor and jerkin, had the tangibility of a knife slicing through his flesh. It came with no pain, but neither could he ignore it.

"It strikes me that with two shadows pointing north, we should go that way."

Tyrchon didn't dare look back at her. "That takes us away from the Empire."

"And?"

"You're relatively inexperienced in Chaos, Nagrendra is injured, we have no supplies, and are underarmed for this trek. We could return to the Empire, get provisions, and get you to safety."

"I appreciate your concern, Tyrchon, but I have seen us walking together, and I think we are heading north." Her hand gave his shoulder a squeeze. "I think that is the direction we should go."

Nagrendra stepped up into the cave mouth. "I concur."

Tyrchon nodded and stood, feeling every bit of Xoayya's hand trailing down his flank. "I'll take a quick tour around this area and see if I find any sign of hazards, then we can be off."

He trotted out of the cave and started a long circular

loop around the camp. He moved carefully, sniffing, listening, watching for Chaos demons or other forms of harmful life, but could not fully concentrate on what he was doing. He deliberately snuffled some dust and sneezed to get Xoayya's scent out of his nose.

What are you thinking? Despite all the grand stories of heroes and heroines finding love and adventure in Chaos, the reality was hardly that glorious. The Lost Prince and Mira Vilewolf might well have roamed and trysted in countless places before the *Drasacor* killed her, but that was one of the few lasting romances he'd ever heard of among Chaos Riders. There were affairs aplenty—the unpredictable climate in Chaos and unrelenting terror of some expeditions made snuggling up with someone most appealing. Coupling among Chaos Riders was hardly unknown, nor was it considered shocking; but few, if any, of those relationships lasted beyond a return to the Empire.

Most Chaos Riders—*if* they were inclined to embrace a life that could even vaguely be considered normal—sought the stability of a partner who knew little of Chaos and had no desire to visit it. Since everything in Chaos was mutable, having an anchor that would not change helped many Riders cope with the unforeseeable events that unfolded in Chaos. And an Imperial partner chosen wisely was one who accepted change in the Rider and managed to ease the transition back into Imperial society for him or her.

There were, of course, Imperial citizens with a taste for the exotic who didn't even dare dream of venturing into Chaos. For them, instead, the Rider enclave in various cities became a haven. In Herakopolis, the Imperial capital, the Riders called their haven the Asylum, yet only at its core could one avoid all contact with those who had never left the Empire. Several well-known places catered to citizens who wanted to indulge their fantasies, and there always seemed to be Riders willing to oblige them.

Tyrchon had availed himself of such companionship in the past and noted that the Riders who did were usually very new to Chaos or had had *Chaosfire* burning in their eyes for a long time. The young ones usually went because they, as he once had, felt as if their forays into Chaos made them heroes. He and his kind were all that stood between the Empire and sinister plots to bring down the Ward Walls. The women he met at one such place, the Arch, seemed to thrill in his status and greatly rewarded the sacrifices he was willing to make on their behalf.

He stopped going to the Arch when he realized that these citizens were incapable of understanding what it meant to be a Chaos Rider. In these trysting places they used him as much as he used them, and both sides knew it. What drove him away from the company of those who had never left the Imperial womb was their failure to realize just how truly dangerous Chaos could be. Certainly, Chaos could change a man's physical appearance, but it also changed him inside. Walking into Chaos was walking into a war where the enemy could strike at any time, without warning, and in numbers that most people failed to comprehend. Strolling through the most vile section of Herakopolis seemed very peaceful by comparison to Chaos, but this was a point no citizen seemed able to grasp.

One other time he had gone back. It was after the cowl and cape had become part of him. He knew, as far as changes Chaos could make in someone went, it was a fairly benign one, yet it distanced him from normal people and even other Chaos Riders. Citizens just found him peculiar-looking, daring only to sneak glances at him from afar. They never realized he could hear what they were saying and smell the fear on them. Chaos Riders who had been misshapen and twisted into parodies of human beings resented how normal and symmetrical his change had been. Those who had not been changed as much as he had saw him as an example of what not to do. While many could hide scaly flesh, or bone spurs, or tiger stripes beneath a robe—enabling them to pass as normal in society—there was no hiding his change.

He felt inhuman, so he returned to the Arch, hoping for human contact. A touch, some kindness, joining with someone in the exhaustion of lovemaking—those were what he sought, and he found a willing partner. Unfortunately, what she wanted was the touch of inhumanity that he represented. While physically compatible, their purposes conflicted, leaving him frustrated and feeling very alone.

But alone he had been before, and he came to accept it as the way of things. He looked at himself as a man, but a man who had made certain sacrifices for the good of others. While he did feel lustful from time to time, and had shared the billets of other Chaos Riders with similar desires, he'd managed to stop looking for anything more than physical satisfaction.

Then Xoayya appears. He shook his head. He knew the two of them could never be together. First off, she was but a child. If she was even half his age, he would have been surprised. Second, and directly to the point, she'd want nothing to do to him. She rested her hand on his shoulder the way she had petted Roarke's wolfhound, Cruach. *If I had asked her to scratch behind my ear, she would have gladly done it.* Third and finally, an expedition like theirs was far too dangerous in time and place even to contemplate courting or romance. Tyrchon had to focus on keeping them on track and alive. Indulging fantasies that could never be was simply a way to get all of them killed.

He completed his circuit, having seen a few *Hobmotli* tracks but nothing more dangerous than that. He returned to the cave and saw his companions ready to leave. He sank his sword into the ground again, sighted along the northern shadow, then pointed toward a gap in the hills across the valley. "Through there, my friends, and we can take another sighting. We'll keep going until we find what we're supposed to find, then I'll have this blade show us the shortest route home, and our adventure will be at an end."

10

Len Fong's dream hadn't been the most pleasant he could imagine, but it hadn't been that bad, either. It involved Angie searching for him, anxious to find him. He recognized Wizard of Oz imagery in it—no flying monkeys, but he did see Angie gazing into a crystal ball. It reminded him of the point in the movie when Dorothy fell asleep in the field of poppies. Equating sleep with danger that way caused him enough anxiety that he woke up with a start.

He sat up in bed and sighed. He'd ensconced himself in the master bedroom, of course, luxuriating in the massive bed he'd dreamed up for Fong the Magnificent. The mattress seemed stiffer than he normally liked, but Fong never would have complained after so many nights spent curling up on hard dungeon floors or spent under the stars.

Len threw back the bedclothes and stumbled to the bathroom. His friends had given him endless grief about how nonperiod a bathroom was for a wizard's domain, but some quick research had turned up promising indications that the Minoan culture could have invented flush toilets, and the Romans were well-known for having water piped into their homes. Jhesti had been right that the place wasn't wired for cable, but it beat most motels all hollow for luxuries beyond that.

He stepped into the shower stall and immediately got hit with two sprays of water, both heated to the temperature he preferred—not too hot, not too cold. Len couldn't see any soap, so he just scrubbed himself with his hands as best he could. *If I get down at least one layer of grime, I'll be happy.* He let the water blast over him for a good long time, then decided it was time to step out, at which point the water stopped.

He shook his head, flicking water from his hair, then smiled as he stepped out of the shower. From a variety of places warm little zephyrs swirled around him, drying him off. Including captive air elementals in the bathroom to do that had been one of his better innovations, he thought, and was pleased to see how well it worked. *Too bad there's no such thing as a deodorant elemental.*

He walked over to the wardrobe and opened it. Hanging there on pegs he saw his Dancing Joker Shoes uniform, along with his socks and Jockey shorts. The clothes looked freshly laundered, and the hole in the shirt where he had torn Jhesti free had been repaired. As he pulled the clothes on he remembered he had just left them on the floor the night before. While Fong the Magnificent had relied on the twins to do all of the caretaking, in their absence it seemed invisible forces managed to perform the duties of a valet and cook.

"Nice innovation. If I ever play D&D again, I'll include it in a redesign." Len closed the wardrobe's doors, waited for a second, then opened them again. The wardrobe remained empty, and this surprised Len. As best he could recall, the one thing he had specified about the wardrobe and its magick was that it would always provide Fong with exactly the appropriate apparel for whatever adventure he was heading out on. *If I was going out, it would give me a cloak and my City-trekkers, wouldn't it? I guess I stay here today.*

He shrugged, closed the wardrobe a second time, then headed out toward the front room. Descending the stairs, he caught the scent of bacon and pancakes with real maple syrup. A crystal goblet at the head of the table appeared to be full of orange juice. Len smiled. "No cable, but I like the breakfast service."

Jhesti stood in the middle of the table brandishing a fork like a gladiator with a trident. "Think you can convince one of those dishes to create a couple of nicad batteries for me? I'm feeling a mite peckish."

"You can have the battery from my watch."

"Thanks, but I don't like eating Japanese. I was thinking of something in a nice copper-top, perhaps?"

"I'll work on it." He glanced around the room. "Where's the fitting stool?"

"Went out grazing, I guess. Everyone's hungry this morning."

"No arguing with that." Len tucked himself in at the table and lifted the dome from his food. He breathed in deeply, closing his eyes and sitting back rapturously. "Yeah, this is the kind of dream I like having."

"Pretty much decided it's a dream, then?"

Len opened his eyes and found Jhesti perched atop

an unlit candle, looking at him eye to eye. "Evidence keeps piling up and leaning in that direction, yes."

"Okay, so what are we going to be doing today in your little dreamworld?"

"I *o no*," Len mumbled around a mouthful. He swallowed, then picked up a perfectly crisped piece of bacon. "I thought I'd look around here and see what's up."

"Gonna hit the library?"

Len hesitated, then nodded. "You think I'm afraid because I'll see I can read things and know I'm not dreaming, right?"

"Hey, twelve hours of sleep have your synapses firing again, good."

"Well, the answer is that, yes, I will look around in the library." He crunched his bacon. "I might find some maps and stuff that would be useful."

"So this isn't the conduit to consciousness you thought it was, then?"

Len ignored him while he sliced a triangle of pancakes free with his fork, stabbed them, and sailed them back and forth through a lake of amber syrup. "Look, at least we're on turf I recognize. That's better than where we were before."

"Okay, you're right." The jester figure's chin now rested in his hands. "I'll let you eat in peace."

"No, wait, one thing." Len frowned at him. "I never see you move, but you're always in different positions and stuff. And you're getting to be a bit more three-dimensional. What gives?"

Len watched Jhesti closely, and in an eyeblink the figure went from having its chin in its hand to a shrug. "Don't ask me; this is your dream, remember? Maybe it has to do with my being an advertising tool: I show folks what they expect to see. Don't expect me to start being some Claymation Gumby, though, and don't start dreaming that. I'm plastic, I have my pride."

"Cool, Jhesti. I'd just as soon have you the way you are."

After breakfast Len wandered over to the library and descended the steep steps into the pit. It almost felt as if he were climbing down into a mine shaft, but here the ore to be mined was knowledge. On a wall he found a weathered parchment map showing continents in configurations he'd never seen before. Central to it was a twisted peninsula that reminded him vaguely of Greece. While he recognized some of the symbols for cities and roads—which were, in fact, fairly obvious and intuitive—he couldn't understand any of the words used to label the various sites.

He glanced over at where Jhesti stood perched on the page of an open book as relief washed over him. "See, I *am* dreaming. I can't read any of the words here on this map."

"What words?"

"The words right here, next to the cities. Their names, I suspect."

"I don't see any words. I don't see any there or any here."

"What?" Len frowned and walked over to the book. Even from where he was standing he could see ink tracery on the pages. As he grew closer he saw he couldn't read them, but there definitely were words there. "There are words on that page."

Jhesti had tucked himself into the book's gutter like a bookmark. "Looks blank to me. Maybe my plastic eyes just can't see the stuff."

Len's mouth went dry, and he sat abruptly in the middle of the floor. The sense of well-being he'd felt just a second before had vanished, and uncertainty smashed down into him like a pile driver. "Oh, man, I wish you hadn't said that."

Jhesti stood at the edge of the bookstand and looked down. "What's the matter?"

"Okay, remember I said this was all from my D&D playing days?"

"Days misspent rolling dice, scarfing down Doritos, and wondering why you couldn't get a date?"

"Yeah, something like that." Jhesti's joke could neither raise a laugh nor inspire ire in Len. "We played with a guy, Bobby Larson. Larson was always taking credit for stuff others had done. I'd work out some new spell for Fong, then Larson's character, a cleric that was pretty much a televangelist, would be casting something similar. He said his character read the spell from my spellbook, then his god let him cast something similar. It was pretty lame, and I didn't like it.

"Brandon, our gamemaster, and I talked about it, and I came up with a solution. Brandon turned the solution into a house rule for the world we played in. He said wizards could write things down in their spellbooks using a spell that was keyed to a code word. If you didn't know the code word, you'd know something had been written there, but you couldn't read it. If you were a warrior, you'd just see blank pages, which meant warriors were always hauling around books they couldn't read, hoping to sell them to some wizard who could read them."

"So you could read these if you could come up with the wizard's code word."

"Maybe." Len shook his head. "No, that's impossible. I can't read this stuff because I'm dreaming. That's it."

"Yeah? What was Fong's code word?" The jester had

his arms crossed over his chest. "Say it, invoke it, and see if you can read this stuff. I mean, if your rules are true, then you must be magickally inclined. Maybe one of these books has a spell that can get you home again."

Len hung his head. "When I was playing D&D there was a lot in the news about computer security and how a hacker could compare a list of encrypted passwords to a dictionary encrypted with the same algorithm. Once he had a match, he decrypted things and had your password. For that reason I used a randomly determined sequence of letters and numbers for my spellbook password. I wrote it down on my player sheet, but I can't remember it."

"Great, just great."

"Hey, I don't like it any better than you do, you know." Len looked up and felt the weight of the books pressing down on him. "I gotta get out of here. I have to go for a walk."

He ran up the stairs, only slipping once near the top. That reminded him he had no boots, so he continued on up further to the master bedroom. He got to the wardrobe and opened it. It contained a cloak, but no boots. "This is very weird." He grabbed the cloak and swung it around his shoulders, fastening it closed with a simple button and hook.

Suddenly a piercing tone keened through the building. Len reflexively glanced toward the ceiling, looking for a smoke detector. He realized there was none and a half second later figured out where the sound was coming from. *Jhesti! There must be trouble.*

He sprinted from the bedroom in his stocking feet. He bounced off the corridor's opposite wall, almost fell as he fought for traction, then raced to the head of the right-hand branch of the stairs. He pushed himself off the railing and started down as fast as he could, only slowing as he reached the landing. *Maybe getting down here fast wasn't the best idea . . .*

A hulking creature with long gray fur and three eyes stalked up the entryway stairs toward him. She wore a belt and a scabbard, with the drawn saber held in her right hand. Though the thick fur hid details of them well, Len could tell the creature was female by her breasts. *Kinda like a creature from* Cats *on steroids, suffering from* PMS.

She snarled something at him, and slashed the air with the saber.

Len held his hands up. "I want no trouble."

Jhesti's wail stopped. "Len, she can't understand you, and her stomach is rumbling."

The creature glanced back at Jhesti, and snarled.

Len took the moment of distraction to snatch one of the boarspears flanking Fong's monument from the wall. A sharp metal blade about a foot in length topped a wooden shaft taller than Len himself. At the base of the blade, where the metal was joined to the wood, a stout metal crosspost had been set in place to prevent a boar from riding all the way up the spear and goring the hunter who had stabbed it.

"You don't look like a boar, but this should stop you plenty fine." Len gripped the weapon tightly in both hands and made a couple of gentle thrusts at the cat-thing. "You don't want a piece of this, sister."

The cat-thing's return growl sounded contemptuous to Len, but he knew he had an advantage since he was on the landing and she had to come up the stairs at him. He read intelligence in the creature's trio of eyes, so he knew that she knew killing him was not going to be easy. The fact that the creature continued to approach him meant she felt confident she could beat him. *She's got to be fast. Parry me wide once, and she's in. I'm dead.*

His only choice, then, was to kill the creature. *Too bad I'm not Fong. He'd have nailed her with a spell that would have had her outsides covering a dozen plush toys before she knew what hit her.* He forced himself to take a step forward and jab tentatively again toward her.

The creature brought the saber forward in a guard position. Len didn't put everything he had into the jabs. He wanted her to think he was slower than he really was. He wasn't going to underestimate her, but he'd invite her to underestimate him. *In reality, I've got one shot. If it doesn't work, it's all over.*

As she approached he caught a musky scent that he didn't find wholly unpleasant. He also got a good look at a mouthful of teeth that looked decidedly sharp to him. The talons on the creature's hands and feet didn't look very pleasant, either. One swipe with a paw, and he'd be kitty vittles.

He jabbed twice more, weakly, and the creature batted the spearpoint aside. Len recovered, set himself, and lunged, realizing only at the last second that his attack had been anticipated. The creature's right arm had come back, the blade raised for a head-high cut that would slice through his neck, while the creature's twisting body would make him miss his lunge.

Then Len's feet, clad only in white athletic socks, slipped on the polished marble.

He felt himself falling forward into a split, with his left heel riding painfully over the edge of the top step. Len's groin muscles protested, so he rolled over on his left flank to get the pressure off. As he did this, the saber slash passed over his head, missing him cleanly. More importantly, though, his roll and attempt to regain his balance brought the spearpoint around to where it stabbed deep into the creature's flank.

The saber came back around in a slash that chopped the spear's shaft in half and almost caught Len's fingers into the bargain. The snarling creature leaned back against the banister and slid down several steps, then yanked the spear from her side and threw it away. Her left hand probed the wound and came away stained with indigo blood. Len thought he saw a hint of blue begin to drip from her nostrils as well, indicating a lung hit, but if the monster's bellows were any indication, the wound wasn't slowing her down at all.

"Oh, shit." Len scrambled to his feet. He turned to run, intent upon heading back up the stairs, but again his socks betrayed him. He stumbled to a knee, then saw the creature rising up above him, ready with a strike that would split him from top to bottom. Having no other choice, he threw himself to the right. He braced for impact with Fong's monument, hoping he was clear of that first slash. *Not that the second won't get me.*

Suddenly he felt a jolt run through his body, then the world went dark. He heard a faint scream of rage that he attributed to the creature, and wondered why it wasn't more triumphant. *I'd be triumphant if I'd killed my enemy.* Len let his momentum carry him through a roll and to his feet, then marveled at his own agility.

"Not bad for a dead man." Holding the haft of the spear in his right hand, he ran his left hand over his body, checking for blood or a wound. "I'm clean, and I seem to hear pretty well for a dead man, too."

Slowly his eyes adjusted to the darkness, allowing him to look around at the small room in which he found himself. Ten feet wide by twenty deep, and with a ceiling he could not make out in the scarce light, the room appeared featureless except for a big block of marble forming an island in the center of it. The island itself was four feet wide and twelve long, making it a tight fit on the sides, but only as tall as a coffee table. Len looked around intently, trying to see if spiders or other potential hazards lurked in dark corners, but he saw nothing.

He thought for a moment and did his best to recall what was behind the monument in the home he'd designed for Fong the Magnificent. The plans had left ample room for something, but he'd never put anything there, as best he could recall. He'd toyed with putting a treasure trove in that place, but had chosen instead to locate it in the library behind one of the shelves that would swing out.

Len bounced the heel of his hand off his forehead. *That's why I knew this place was significant. The secret door must be the way out. It leads through riches, which is a symbol for my job, which is where I was hurt. It's so obvious.*

He glanced back at the wall he'd come through, but only saw unbroken stone. *That's weird. Likely to be another way out, though. A secret passage or something.* He worked his way around the room, running his left hand up and down the walls. He didn't feel anything shift under his hand, nor did he hear anything click. He used the stick in his right hand to tap high up on the stone, listening for any hollows, but got nothing there, either.

He'd worked three-quarters of the way around the room, when he turned and looked at the island. On the narrow end, facing him, he once again saw the golden crest sunk into the stone. "Of course, it's so obvious." He leaned over and touched the gold, once again feeling the tingle he had when he opened the door to Fong's Sanctuary.

The thick top slab on the island evaporated slowly,

and something moved within the depths of the black fog. As the mist drained away, Len's heartbeat quickened, and he retreated as fast as he could. He bounced off the chamber's back wall and raised the spear haft like a baseball bat. A shiver shook him from head to toe, and if the creature outside hadn't convinced him, what he saw now made him certain he'd slipped into the realm of nightmare fully and totally.

The black fog drained away to reveal a skeleton's bleached bones. All the clothing it had worn had long since rotted away, and Len couldn't see any metal to suggest that jewelry or tools had been buried with the person. He squinted, then took a step forward, trying to guesstimate the skeleton's sex by its pelvis. He wanted to say the person had been male, but he knew that was, at best, wishful thinking.

Another step brought him to the foot of the bier and gave him another shock. "The Death Boots." Len looked down and saw the skeleton wearing the very boots that had kicked him into unconsciousness. "Oh, man, my brain's really screwed up."

The rattle of bones brought Len's head up. The skeleton began to sit up, its right arm reaching for him.

Panic shot through Len, and with it came a curious detachment. Intellectually he knew his body was kicking into the "fight or flight" reaction that characterized the behavior of creatures in life-threatening situations. He wanted nothing more than to run, and the fact that there was nowhere to run heightened his panic. His adrenal glands started dumping adrenaline into his bloodstream, filling him with a chemical courage that, as a byproduct, cut him off from most rational modes of thought and left him acting almost entirely on instinct.

Had Len been a trained warrior—his martial experience pretty much consisted of a year's worth of tae kwon do at the YMCA and his D&D gaming—he might have reacted in a heroic manner. John Carter of Mars would have just whipped out a sword and picked the skeleton apart, but John Carter had been trained for that sort of thing. Not only had Len not had that sort of training, he also didn't have a sword.

Fortunately for Len, human beings are very adaptive. They excel at seeing patterns and adjusting behaviors to cope with new patterns by employing old behavior modes. As the skeleton sat up from its stone coffin, Len's eyes recognized a pattern, communicated it to his brain, which analyzed it, found a similar pattern, and sent his body into action.

As far as Len's body was concerned, the skull was nothing more than a fat, slow-pitch softball coming in high and outside, where he liked them. Len's right leg came forward, his body uncoiled, his wrists snapped, and the spear haft connected solidly. The blow crushed the left side of the skull, then sent the whole bone globe flying off toward the wall. When it hit, the skull shattered into hundreds of fragments, leaving a powdery starburst where it had hit.

The rest of the bones just came all apart and clattered down against the coffin, creating a hideous din. Arm bones tumbled out of the stone box, with finger bones and wristbones scattering like dice. Len struck at them with the stick, blasting them back away from himself, then he threw the stick down. It cartwheeled off to the farside of the room, cut off from sight by the stone island.

Len sank to his knees and rested his head against the gold crest. "This is too much. This is very weird and too much. All these symbols—it's a big puzzle, and I can't figure it out." He felt his whole body shaking, and he knew, in part, that was because of the adrenaline. He also knew he felt himself coming apart at the seams. "What if this isn't a dream? What if?"

He shook his head sharply. "There is no 'what if.' This *is* a dream, and that's final."

Raising his head, he looked into the coffin and saw the boots. Shrugging, he reached in, shook the bones out of them, then sat on the edge of the island and put them on. It kind of surprised him that they fit. His feet weren't particularly large—and, in fact, were on the small side for a man—but he'd always thought the boots were actually sized for a woman. *That's just because the only customers you heard of being interested in them were women.*

He stood and looked down at the boots. "Why would a woman want these? They'd always be looking up her skirt." He laughed, then his laughter caught in his throat.

The eyes on the toes of the boots, both of them a bright emerald green, winked at him.

Something inside Len snapped. Monsters that wanted to kill him, talking plastic pins, magick dishes that made his meals, and even a fitting stool traipsing around after him, somehow that had all been manageable. It seemed benign or expected. Jhesti really was just talking, which is what it was supposed to do. At the store they'd occasionally had fitting-stool races, galumphing the things around the store when all was quiet. Monsters? He'd seen countless monsters in movies and computer games and had slain them by the score.

But the boots, the boots were different. They were something he knew and understood, and even feared. They weren't supposed to be winking at him. Staring, sure, but winking? Of all the things he had experienced, somehow that was the most unbelievable and the one that destroyed his ability to cope.

Len turned and started to run. The absurdity of trying to run away from boots on his feet never registered with him, he just knew he had to get away. He was two steps beyond and through the chamber's back wall before he realized he should have been smashed flat against it. He heard gravel crunch beneath his feet and realized that, somehow, he had gotten outside. The continued darkness meant it was night, but the significance of that fact meant nothing to him.

Then, suddenly, he found himself running through a thick rain forest. Leaves and branches struck at his face. Roots tried to trip him. He smelled flowers and heard the hoots of animals. That such plants and animals had no place in the area he had been in did make an impression, but it just further unhinged him. He plunged on through the underbrush, then found a narrow trail. He darted off onto it, then lost it again when it turned sharply to cut across the face of a hill.

Len ran straight off the top of the hill and slammed into a sapling that bowed under his weight. He fell from the tree, dropping ten feet to the ground, and hit hard. He started to roll, then tried to regain his feet, but his cloak snagged on something and yanked him down again. He found himself tumbling head over heels down the hillside, bouncing from thick trees and off rocks. Finally he crashed into a fallen log that gave him a chance to right himself.

He did, getting to his feet with an agility and ease that surprised even him. He smiled and shivered, then looked back up the hill at the course of broken branches and crushed bushes that marked his passage. *God, this is going to hurt in the morning.*

Then he remembered why he'd been running. He looked down at the boots, daring them to wink at him, then saw a tree stump on which he could sit to remove them. "You come off now!"

Len took one step forward and felt something brush against his face. It felt like a spiderweb, only stronger. It stopped him in midstride, giving birth in his brain to images of giant spiders. Before he could panic yet again, the invisible web flared a neon blue. Just for a second Len decided he knew what it felt like for a bug to be trapped in a bug-zapper, then, mercifully, the world went black.

11

Shoth Churgûn trotted forward through the maroon twilight at Ghislaine's heels. Behind them four of the Mountain Guards acted as a rear guard while, up ahead, four had secured the entrance to the tunnel. The remaining four had already entered the tunnel and relayed a message saying there was no danger within.

As he got closer to the opening, Shoth slowed, then stopped. Ghislaine turned and frowned at him. "We want to get inside and to cover. It's not safe out here." Thunder cracked, and golden lightning flashed on their backtrail to underscore her point.

He nodded. "I know, it's just that . . . well, this is incredible."

Ghislaine grunted. "Nice carvings out in the middle of nowhere. I'm just thankful we found something because I don't want to be caught in the open with the *Tsvortu* stirring things up."

Shoth nodded because he knew from her tone she expected him to. Still, her words meant little to him as he stared at the golden crest at the top of the tunnel. He stepped closer and extended a hand toward it, but did not touch it. He idly traced the lines with a forefinger, then folded his arms around himself.

The Guard captain glanced at the crest as she passed beneath it. "Probably not solid gold, so don't even think of looting it, Warder."

"No, no, of course not." A rivulet of outrage trickled through him at her suggestion. *Does she not know how significant this might be?* He shivered as cold fingers walked up his spine. *How can she? No one here knows save me, and sharing the secret with them would be as foolish as it is unnecessary.*

Still, the presence of the crest made a surprising amount of sense to him, though it smacked of serendipity. *I can scarcely believe it.*

He moved into the tunnel and up the stairs, avoiding the splashes of indigo blood that stained them. "Is it *Tsvortu* blood?"

Ghislaine nodded. "Looks like it, and a lot. One of the Storm demons got hurt badly in here. Half the spear that did it is over there. I suspect her injury is what has upset them, and that they're heading here." She smiled carefully. "No matter, this looks like a good place to defend."

"It is, believe me. Call your people in here."

"Why?"

Shoth pointed at the crest. "I can close the door, I'm fairly certain, and that should keep them out."

"Really?"

"Really."

The Guard captain smiled. "Warder Churgûn, you are

full of surprises." She ran down the stairs and bellowed orders that brought the rest of her command running.

Once the entire squad had entered the chamber, Shoth squeezed past Ghislaine and studied the crest from the back side. Again he traced his finger through the air, mimicking the sigil, then nodded. "This should work." His hand glowed blue, then he touched the crest.

The crest floated down to the center of the circular doorway, then shadow bubbled up like water filling a narrow channel. The slight breeze that had been blowing through the doorway began to whistle sharply as the opening contracted, then silence fell as the door shut fully.

Ghislaine pounded her fist against the black stone. "Nice trick that. How did you manage it?"

Shoth shrugged. "The full explanation would take too long. Suffice it to say, the crest gave me a clue as to which spell would work here. We should be safe enough now."

She gave him a quick smile. "And you think it was the person we're searching for who opened it?"

The sorcerer shifted his shoulders. "All of the divinations I cast today pointed us in this direction. I think it is very logical that he headed here."

"He? I thought you said before you didn't know if our target was a man or a woman." She posted her fists on her hips. "What makes you so certain now?"

Shoth smiled and pointed at the carved figure at the landing in the back of the room. "I believe *that* is the person we seek."

Ghislaine squinted. "Something wrong with his eyes."

"I suspect it's a mere fold of flesh. Rather benign, given the changes Chaos could make in one." Shoth trotted up the steps and looked around. He spotted the library immediately and headed for it. "I want to check some things, but right now I think that our target, this Dashan, used to live in this place. It makes sense that he would return here when he found himself in the area." He purposely avoided suggesting Dashan had been summoned from afar—there *were* details that would do the captain no good to know.

He descended the stairs into the library and saw an old Imperial map. *Pre-Chaos.* The map looked fairly new, yet had to be more than five centuries old. *In Dashan's absence, a lot of magick must have been used to preserve this place for his return. That amount of power is incredible, but, then, he was one of the sorcerers who survived the Shattering.*

Just looking around made a thrill run through Shoth. From the moment he'd seen the crest he knew the mission had been successful, and in more ways than even Princess Myat could have anticipated. Not only had they succeeded in bringing Dashan back to the world, but his reappearance provided Shoth with a chance to move beyond his current understanding of magick and into the next realm, which would make him very powerful indeed.

Within the City of Sorcerers students were taught that all magick broke down into eight branches. Students were instructed in the basics of all branches, then tended to specialize in a branch or two for which they showed an aptitude. There were core spells thought to be vital for each branch, but once these had been mastered, students were allowed to deepen their studies within their branch, even getting to the point where they learned how to fashion their own spells.

The Ward Walls had been erected to drive back the forces of Chaos once the Seal of Reality had been shattered. All the lands inside the Ward lines had a sense of order imposed on them by the magick, and society itself reinforced this to banish Chaos from the Empire. Imperial magick, however, had to distort this order to create the desired effects. Spells, whether those taught in the City of Sorcerers or those a mage created on his own, really invoked and sought to control Chaos to achieve their planned results.

Controlling Chaos was by no means easy. It required a lot of mental discipline, and that was just for the spells most magickers learned. Those crafted by individual magick-users also tended to be somewhat idiosyncratic, since part of the caster's worldview became worked into the spells. One of Shoth's instructors had likened it to songs sung by different individuals. There were some songs that almost anyone could sing, but they tended to be fairly simple. The tougher ones, the ones bards composed and sang themselves, were songs that might suit only one throat in the world.

So it was with spells. The common catalog of them almost anyone could cast. The specialized ones often included the necessity to understand what the mage who created it intended so the spell would work right. To facilitate this understanding, most mages created tools to aid in concentration. It might be nothing more than a word, or might require a pebble of a specific size or a wand or the casting mage to hop up and down three times and spin around. These aids were as varied as could be imagined.

In doing his researches in the City of Sorcerers, Shoth had run across the crest on the door. He could find no records indicating who had created it, but its complexity intrigued him. Of the spells that were to be focused through it he had only dim reports, many of which he thought were hyperbole. Still, in looking at the sigil, Shoth had always felt he had a glimmer of understanding and hoped that, someday, it would lead him to be able to unlock those magicks and use them himself.

His quest to unlock the meaning of the crest had been his secret. Inquiries he'd made were discreet and casual—not the sort of thing that would have attracted attention in the City of Sorcerers. He had continued his search after leaving the city to rejoin his cousin, Myat, but his researches had tailed off as he worked more and more with her. What she wanted became paramount in his life, subordinating his own desires, and yet satisfying many of them.

I have learned from her, and now I shall learn from Dashan. If he could get to know the sorcerer, he felt that his understanding of the crest would expand. Myat was looking to use Dashan to destroy Lord Disaster, but with a fuller understanding of Dashan's symbol, *he could be the one to oppose Fialchar. And if Dashan proves to be as rapacious as Fialchar, I will be in a position to oppose him.*

"Warder, we have need of you."

Shoth looked up at one of the Guards—Keph, he thought it was. "What?"

"The captain has something she wants to ask you about."

The sorcerer mounted the stairs and crossed over to where a large banquet table had been laid out. He caught the aroma of a spicy stew and fresh-baked bread. Shoth quickly cast a low-level diagnostic spell and saw the various serving dishes glowing a light blue color. "What's going on, Captain?"

"That's what I want to ask you." Ghislaine waved a

hand at the table. "Fourteen places set, and food we've not smelled since we left the mountains. Do you think it is safe?"

The sorcerer shrugged and lifted the cover from the tureen of stew. The reddish brown stew looked good to him. He saw bits of carrots and celery floating in it. He picked up a spoon, dipped it in, and tasted it. "It seems fine to me. You might want to have your people eat in shifts, just in case there's a problem, but I sense no harmful spells here. Just very utilitarian ones."

The captain's expression eased, so Shoth saw no reason to point out that an enchantment that created matter out of nothing required an incredible amount of energy. In addition to that, it required a fantastically skilled mage to create and cast the spell. While he himself could cast spells that would take water and flour and transform it into something resembling bread closely enough to be choked down, those spells were considered inefficient to the point of being used only in a dire emergency. It was simply easier, in most cases, to make bread and bake it, exchanging time and hard work for the magickal energy needed to make the spell function. There simply was not enough return for the cost of the spell to make it one that was widely employed.

The energy is probably coming from Chaos itself. Shoth decided he would turn the serving platters over after dinner and see if he could find the crest etched into them anywhere. *If Dashan can cast such a spell, Princess Myat's dreams are answered.*

Ghislaine complied with Shoth's suggestion and only let half her people eat at any one time. Shoth seated himself at the foot of the table and demanded the others leave the head of the table open in honor of their host. Most of the guards ignored him, but a few thanked him, as if he had conjured the meal himself. He kept directing the praise to Dashan, and everyone left the table satisfied.

Ghislaine sent half the Guards to the upper rooms to get some sleep, leaving herself, Shoth, and a half dozen Guards in the main area. She joined him in the library, leafing disinterestedly through various books. Part of Shoth wished she'd go away and leave him alone to see what he could discover about the crest, but another part wanted her there. Dashan's abode awed Shoth and seemed to cow Ghislaine somewhat, so their companionship meant neither of them had to be alone and overwhelmed by where they were.

"I have to ask you, Shoth, when you think this Dashan will return here?"

"I don't know." He ran a hand over the rough stubble on his chin and did his best to ignore the storm booming outside. "I cannot imagine he was the one who wounded the Tsvortu. Dashan is too good, too powerful a mage to have to resort to using a spear on such a creature. This thing is built in the side of a hill, and we don't know how far it extends back. He could have some secret sanctum, a retreat, where he is recovering from his journey. For all we know a Hobmotli wounded the Tsvortu, then fled; or some poor Chaos Rider found this place and was ambushed by the Tsvortu."

"How do you think he will receive us when he finds us here?"

"That is an excellent question." Shoth smiled carefully. "I think, because I was able to close the door here, he will find me reasonable and will be willing to listen to what I have to say. When things are laid out for him, he'll join us."

She nodded slowly. "I hope so. I am getting the

impression that he's as tough a foe as I would ever face in this incarnation, and opposing him would be a quick way to move on to my next. I think I would rather avoid that, if at all possible."

Without warning the earth shook incredibly hard, pitching Shoth forward into Ghislaine's arms. Before he could disentangle himself from her, a sharp thundercrack sent another tremor through the stone. In its wake came a third vibration that rippled through him and left him colder than the first two. *Magick! The Tsvortu are attacking.*

"Captain, get up here." Irin appeared at the railing and pointed toward the stairs to the doorway. "I think that was lightning, *Tsvortu* lightning."

Ghislaine immediately mounted the steps. "Anyone hurt?"

"No, Captain, not yet." Irin shook her head. "But the door, it's cracked, and it's not going to hold."

12

"Come now, Tyrchon, you can't be afraid of a little rain."

Tyrchon half turned and gave Xoayya a walleyed stare.

The woman blushed. "There is nothing as normal as rain out here in Chaos?"

Nagrendra moved to the head of the narrow pass between the hills and pointed off to the northwest, where red-gold lightning flashed through the sky. "There actually can be normal rain out here, Xoayya, but what we are seeing is no normal storm. The thunder we've been hearing and the lightning we're now seeing has been moving on an east-southeast track, which runs counter to the prevailing winds."

"It's not natural, then?"

Tyrchon shook his head and waved Xoayya forward. "Notice anything unusual about the valley we're going to enter here?"

The petite woman stepped past Tyrchon, and he resisted the desire to rest his hands on her shoulders. "I take it you're referring to the fact that we've been marching through bone-dry, red-rock canyons, and now we're coming into a lush valley full of a rain forest?" She turned to look at him and smiled. "Track of the Chaos storm, right?"

Tyrchon nodded. "Very good. Somewhere out there in Chaos, in the middle of a rain forest, there's a swath of red-rock desert carved through the middle of it. This valley channeled at least part of the storm." He looked out over the expanse of greenery and saw it extended well off to the east. "This much stuff got moved, it was a very strong storm."

"True, but look at the west end of the valley." The Reptiad pointed off in that direction. Forest goes right up to that pass, then it's red rocks again."

Xoayya frowned. "Is that unusual?"

"It is in that the storms normally fade, so the transplanting becomes spottier as things go along. There's always a transition zone that's very mixed. The fact that the change there is so abrupt confirms the idea that the energy got sucked out of the storm all at one time." The wolf-warrior shrugged. "How that happened I don't know."

Xoayya walked forward on the path they'd been using and stopped at the edge of the forest's growth. "How long will this forest stay here?"

Nagrendra's tongue flickered out and back. "Barring another Chaos storm, the desert should encroach over the next few decades, and it will be gone."

"Unless the *Firknu* decide to move in."

The Reptiad's eyes half shut. "The chances of that are slender, don't you think, Tyrchon? I've seen none

of them in this area ever before. I thought the
Bharashadi had hunted them to extinction."

"So the story goes. Question is, were any of the
trees the storm transplanted a broodtree?"

"You have a point there."

Xoayya looked from Nagrendra to Tyrchon and back
again. "Could you please tell me what you're talking
about?"

The sorcerer nodded. "The *Firknu* are creatures that
came through Chaos to this world at roughly the same
time as the Chaos demons. They're also known as Tree
Spiders, but they're really eight-limbed apes that get
as big as a human five-year-old. They have the intelligence and disposition of the little dogs fashionable
matrons carry with them. They're not smart enough to
use tools, but they will harass anything moving
through their territory."

She glanced back over her shoulder at the forest.
"You don't think the storm brought any through with it?"

Tyrchon shook his head. "We'd be hearing the
howls if they had. Only way any made the transition
would be in a broodtree. From what I've heard, the
females lay eggs in trees. The young feed off the tree,
hatch, and form a band of their own. Here, with no
predators to feed on them, the population would
overrun the area in no time."

The redheaded woman frowned. "So, what are we
going to do?"

"We only have an hour or so of sunlight left, so we
ought to make camp."

Nagrendra leaned on the *Hobmotli* spear he'd been
using as a walking stick. "You don't want to try to push
on to the other side of the forest?"

"I don't think so." Tyrchon pointed down into the

middle of the valley. "I'd like to make camp down there."

"But if you think the Storm demons are close enough to attack, why allow them to have the high ground?" Xoayya opened her hands. "That's not wise, is it?"

Nagrendra patted her on the shoulder. "Under normal circumstances, no, but with the Tsvortu it is not a bad idea. Their magickers—males, as I understand it, one and all—are capable of creating lightning and other storm effects. The forest will insulate us from that sort of thing. Lightning bolts will hit trees as easily as they will us, and anything we can do to make ourselves hard to spot will help protect us."

"But the underbrush will make it more difficult for you to cast spells to hurt them, won't it? And that sword, you can't go swinging it in a thick stand of trees."

Tyrchon dropped his jaw in a smile. "Agreed. We'll set our camp up in a place where we have a good killing ground. The storm over there isn't so nasty that I'd guess they have more than a couple dozen warriors and maybe four magickers. It's just a small band, and they're clearly not hunting us. We'll be careful and quiet, and we'll get through this."

Down in the heart of the valley, near the base of the far upslope, they located a good spot to make camp. Three trees had long ago fallen into a rough triangle, into the middle of which they set their camp. Twenty paces away a little seep provided them with water, and Tyrchon managed to kill a snake that made for a good, if meager, supply of meat.

In surveying the area, Tyrchon selected what he thought were the most defensible areas around the camp and used his sword to clear enough brush to give him full play with it. The blade slashed through the undergrowth as if it were no more substantial than spiderwebs. Not yet having employed it against a living target, he did wonder how well it would function in combat. *If it goes through armor the way it does this brush, none will stand against me.*

The second that thought coursed through his mind, he hesitated and glanced at the blade again. "I bet that's just what all the others that have ever wielded you have thought. They draw you, they use you, they come to think of themselves as invincible. Nothing stands before them. All challenges bow to you, except for that last challenge. It crushes them."

He crouched down and purposely nicked his left thumb on the blade. He let blood well up in the cut, then streaked it down both flats of the blade. The blood showed red for a moment against the gold tracery, then the sigils drank the blood in. "With my blood I anoint you and name you Restraint. Every time I draw you, I will be reminded why I should not draw you the next time. You are a sword, not a mirror that reflects glory on me, or allows me to bask in vanity."

"Do you often speak to your sword?"

Tyrchon whirled and held the quivering blade pointed at Xoayya's chest. He blinked and lowered Restraint, surprised that she had gotten within ten feet of him, and he hadn't noticed. "I'm sorry."

"I shouldn't have sneaked up on you."

Tyrchon stood and resheathed his blade. "You shouldn't have been able to. I guess I just don't reckon you as a threat."

She smiled. "Good, I like you, too." She caught herself. "I realize that isn't exactly what you said, but . . ."

"I understand." He rested a hand on his sword and marveled at how what little sunlight made it through the forest canopy managed to ignite golden highlights in her hair. "And, no, I don't usually talk to my weapons, but this blade and I, we needed to have a conversation."

"Does it speak to you?"

The Chaos Rider barked a short laugh. "No, at least, not yet. I decided I needed to give it a name."

"Restraint."

"You heard."

"I did." Xoayya reached up and unbound her curly red hair. "Why did you choose that name?"

"It has to do with what Fialchar told me about the blade. He said every hero who had borne it before was faced by one final challenge against which the blade would not be of any use. I chose Restraint to remind me to think first, before drawing the sword."

"Your hand, it's bleeding." Xoayya stepped forward and took Tyrchon's left hand into hers. "It's just a small cut. I can spell it closed."

Tyrchon gently lifted his hand away. "Save your strength, you may need it later. Has Nagrendra taught you any combat magicks?"

"Would you think ill of me if I said I didn't want to learn any?"

He thought for a moment. To be in Chaos without combat spells was as stupid as being here without weapons. Not only did it deprive Xoayya of the ability to defend herself, but she could not help her fellows in the midst of combat. While curative spells, which Xoayya did possess, were vital for survival in Chaos, there were times when a blast of sorcerous fire would finish a battle even before it started, preventing the need for healing spells. Choosing not to learn combat spells was a decidedly selfish thing to do, and most

Chaos Riders would have abandoned Xoayya once she made that announcement.

"I know that decision should strike me as wrong, but, for you, I don't see it that way. Knowing the spells doesn't mean you'd ever find yourself willing to cast them, which makes learning them rather useless." Tyrchon shrugged slightly. "I don't see you as someone who is a killer."

"Do you think I should be here in Chaos?"

"Ha! There are plenty of killers in the womb that I don't think should be in Chaos, so that's not a fair question." He gave her a firm nod. "I'm not sorry you're here. You've not complained about the pace I've set."

"But it's not the pace you'd set for yourself."

"True enough, but I've slackened it for Nagrendra, not you. I could see . . ." He stopped in mid-sentence, his mind overriding his mouth. *I was going to tell her I could see adventuring far and wide with her in Chaos! That's insanity. She'll laugh politely and blush and walk away.*

"You could see?" Xoayya smiled openly and innocently at him.

"I was saying that I can see how you have taken to Chaos. Few do as well as you." Tyrchon opened his mouth in a lupine grin. "You seem stronger."

"I feel it, too. Not physically, of course, but I just feel more alive and energetic." She glanced down. "With the changes Chaos makes in everyone, I wonder what it will do to me." Her eyes came back up, and a look of horror passed through their blue depths. "I didn't mean anything by that . . ."

"I know." Tyrchon turned away from her. "I've had a long time to become accustomed to the way I look. I wasn't comfortable at first, but, well, there are advantages to it."

"I think it makes you look terribly heroic . . ." Tyrchon turned back to smile at her, but saw her looking back toward the camp. ". . . As do the changes Chaos has made in you, Nagrendra."

The Reptiad sketched a little bow. "You are most kind, Lady Xoayya. I've gone ahead and set up two perimeter rings of spells. I think they will slow the Tsvortu down. If they decide to push the issue, I think we can deal with whatever gets through."

Xoayya frowned. "Something will get through? The spells you used against the Bharashadi slew multiple dozens. How can Tsvortu get through them?"

"Tsvortu couldn't, but I didn't use those spells here." Nagrendra smiled carefully. "Those spells would take a lot more energy to set up, especially to surround the camp, and they are not well suited to dealing with the Tsvortu threat."

"What do you mean by that?"

Tyrchon pointed off in the direction of a thunderclap. "The Tsvortu have a very strong family structure and loyalty system. The band out there is likely made up of sisters and cousins, and the sorcerers with them are brothers or breeders. They're all related and sworn to care for each other, or to avenge each other. If one of Nagrendra's spells kills a Tsvortu, they will be sworn to hunt him down until either he or the whole related bloodline is dead."

The Reptiad nodded. "And the way they intermarry, at this point, all Tsvortu would have to be dead to solve the hunting problem. If, on the other hand, the spells just hurt one of the Tsvortu, her kin will try to rescue her." He pointed at the little clay discs Tyrchon wore around his neck. "The similarity in design on those tokens shows that the Tsvortu Tyrchon killed were all of a family, and any Tsvortu with direct ties to that family would consider it the highest honor to kill him."

Xoayya frowned at Tyrchon. "Why wear them, then?"

He shrugged. "Any Tsvortu that gets close enough to see these tokens will already be trying to kill me, so it hardly matters."

Nagrendra laughed aloud. "Wearing them shows others what he's survived. It's a better indicator than healed scars."

"Proving how tough you are?" Mild scorn rode through Xoayya's voice.

"No, just reminding me how lucky I've been." He gave Xoayya a gracious bow, then pointed back toward the camp. "Let's get something to eat and set up watches."

Because they had the trees to break up the smoke, they risked a small fire to cook the snake. Tyrchon let his portion of the meat cook until the outside was charred, but both Xoayya and Nagrendra went for something a bit more juicy. No one complained about the taste, though Xoayya did ask Nagrendra if he minded eating snake.

"Why? Because I am a Reptiad?" The sorcerer leaned forward, an elbow on his right knee. "Even if I were descended from lizards that Chaos had changed into humanoids before the Ward Walls reached the islands, I'd still have no problems with it. Snakes eat lizards and lizards eat snakes all the time. Since we are men who were warped to survive in the islands more easily, my tastes run along those of other men. Tyrchon, if need be, you would eat a dog, wouldn't you?"

Xoayya held a hand up to forestall Tyrchon's answer. "Not a fair question, is it, since he's not really a wolf."

"He is as much a wolf as I am a reptile." Nagrendra's tone of voice remained light, but Tyrchon caught the hint of an edge beneath it. "We are both men who were changed by Chaos, though the change came to me through ancestors subjected to Chaos years ago. Where I would balk is at eating humanoid flesh. A Tree Spider, maybe, but never a humanoid."

Tyrchon shook his head. "Humans need too much spice. Aelves, on the other hand, are tender, as long as you get them young."

Xoayya stared at him, wide-eyed. "You haven't!"

"No, I haven't." The wolf-warrior swallowed a mouthful of snake. "I was kidding, but there is a point to it. Once you have the *Chaosfire* in your eyes, once folks know you've been out here, they will think you capable of all manner of things. The question you asked Nagrendra about eating snake makes sense, from an Imperial point of view. Within the Empire it's easy to see Reptiads as having more in common with reptiles and snakes than humans or Aelves or Dwarves. Out here, on the other hand, we're all of a kind."

A sharp crack of thunder shook the ground. Nagrendra looked out beyond the circle of firelight. "Getting active."

Tyrchon's ears flicked forward. "But not closer. Wait, I hear something crashing through the brush." He stood and drew his sword. Nagrendra came to his feet and picked up the spear. The crashing ended abruptly, then, after a couple seconds of silence, a sizzling sound ended with a pop. "It hit one of your walls?"

"Sounds like. This way." The Reptiad headed out the north side of the camp, then cut off east. At a bush with a broken branch, he went forward again, then cut west. "Not very far."

Tyrchon followed exactly in Nagrendra's steps and waved Xoayya along after him. "Stay on this path. When Nagrendra set his spell walls, he let them overlap so we'd have a gap to get out through if we needed to."

By the time they caught up with the sorcerer, he was already on one knee looking down at a man wearing very peculiar garments. Tyrchon could see no armor, and the crest on the tunic was one he'd never seen before. It looked like a shield being held by a court fool. The shield had two shoes on it. "Is there a guild for making Fool shoes?"

Nagrendra shook his head. "I don't know. I'm not familiar with this crest design."

Xoayya dropped to her knees beside the young man. "Is he hurt? Have you fixed him?"

"My spell wall would have stunned him, nothing more. The cuts and bruises are from his running through the forest here."

"Running from the *Tsvortu*, most likely." Tyrchon sniffed the air. "He doesn't smell like he's been in the wilderness for long. He must live nearby."

"There may be others; I'm going to try to wake him." Xoayya looked up at the Reptiad, who nodded to her. She pressed her hands to the man's head, then leaped back, stumbled, and went down.

Tyrchon reached her side in an instant. "What happened?" He took her arm to help her up, but felt her trembling, so he lowered himself to his knees and hugged her to his chest.

Xoayya clung to him tightly. "I . . . ah, I . . . when I touched him, I got flashes of his life or lives. I . . ."

Tyrchon stroked her hair. "Take it easy." He nodded to Nagrendra, so the Reptiad sorcerer touched the man and cast a spell on him. The man's body twitched twice, then he began to moan.

Xoayya looked in his direction, then closed her eyes.

"I saw many things. Things I can't begin to describe, all past and present jumbled together. Before, at best, I might get a hint of a past life with someone, but never like this. Many lives I saw."

The man rolled over and got onto his hands and knees. He glanced over at Nagrendra and recoiled from him, then stared at Tyrchon and Xoayya. "Who are you?"

"Doesn't matter who we are right now. Were you running from the Tsvortu?"

The man's mouth worked a bit as he pondered Tyrchon's question. "Tsvortu?"

"Storm demons? Big, gray fur?"

"Yeah, I stabbed one with a spear in Fong's Sanctuary."

"That explains why they're attacking." Tyrchon glanced back up the hill. "Up there is the Sanctuary? Is there anyone else there?"

The man glanced down at his chest, then looked back up and blinked. "Just Jhesti."

"Jhesti?" Tyrchon stood and pulled Xoayya to her feet. He drew his sword and pointed it at the man. "Lead us back there. If Jhesti is in trouble, we have to save him."

13

The desire to save Jhesti made perfect sense to Len. He struggled to his feet and started after the trio of figures moving through the forest and up the hillside toward the Sanctuary. He marveled at how easily the wolf-guy—he mentally tagged him Beowulf—moved through the forest without making much in the way of noise. The big lizard following on his heels also ran effortlessly. *If Captain Kirk had run up against him in that old Trek episode, the Gorns would rule the Federation and Shatner would be best known for having a lousy hairpiece.*

The redheaded woman intrigued him. She was small, like Angie, but had that wonderful head of fiery hair and eyes that were a bit icier than Angie's. She'd been taking shelter in Beowulf's arms when he first saw her, and she had been watching him with a shocked expression on her face. Len felt guilty for that, but he couldn't remember having done anything to her. *I guess I'll have to figure out what happened and ask her.*

It wasn't until Beowulf crested the hill and drew his sword that Len started to question why anyone would be rushing into battle to save a little plastic merchandising thingamajig. *And how do they know who Jhesti is and why do they care?* Len blinked as he topped the rise himself. *Unless they're more constructs of my unconscious. That's got to be it.*

And quite the constructs they turned out to be. From his position Len saw the narrow valley that led up to the front door of Fong's Sanctuary. The door had been blasted open, as a scattering of debris made painfully clear. A dozen and a half of the Storm demons drove toward the door, while behind them, three smaller creatures with golden fur—clearly Storm demons and probably male—stood in an aura of red-gold energy. One of the *Tsvortu* warriors screamed a warning, the troops at the door split aside, and from the trio of magickers a golden globe shot toward the doorway. It floated like a knuckleball pitch, dancing around quite a bit, and burned with a red fire that gave it a cometlike tail.

The gold ball burned its way through the tunnel, then detonated. Len couldn't tell what sort of damage it had done, but the bright flash of light, the thunderclap, and a rush of heat that he could feel even forty yards away told him it had been very hot. *Jhesti's going to be a puddle of plastic.*

Coming in from the flank, Beowulf and the lizardman lit into the overwhelming Storm-demon force. A blue-white light wreathed the lizard-man, then pulsed off his hands in a gout of fire that blasted the centermost *Tsvortu* magicker off his feet. The fire ignited the Storm demon as it knocked him down. The air filled with the acrid scent of burning fur. The flaming magicker writhed in agony, screaming in a high-pitched voice that echoed throughout the small valley.

His screams brought the rearmost ranks of Tsvortu warriors around to see what was happening, while their compatriots poured into the Sanctuary. Beowulf was there behind them, his long slender blade held in two hands, ready to greet them. A quick slash parallel to the ground sent one warrior spinning away with a slit belly. Beowulf parried an overhand blow high, then rotated his hands and cut down, cleaving a Tsvortu from shoulder to breastbone. He ducked beneath a cut aimed at his head, then slashed one-handed to the right. His blade swept through a Tsvortu's leg at the knee, dropping that warrior to the ground. Coming up from his crouch, Beowulf slid past another Tsvortu saber cut, then whipped his blade from right to left, catching a Tsvortu in the head and spinning her to the ground.

Len watched all this, his mouth agape. The blood, the smoke, the stink, the screams—he'd imagined it countless times in games, watched it in movies, read it in books, but now, here, it seemed very real. For a dream, this was the most realistic dream experience he'd ever had. *Then again, how do you know what is real? Aside from sparring in the year of tae kwon do classes you took, what do you know of combat?*

Before he could continue along that line of thought, he noticed two things that deflected him. One of the Tsvortu magickers flicked a hand at the scaly mage. Three red daggers appeared and sped from his hand toward the lizard-man. The reptilian sorcerer quickly conjured a defense in the form of a blue-white disc that stopped two of them, but the third slipped below the shield. It caught him right over the left hip, whirling him around and to the ground.

The redhead ran toward the lizard-man, her hands glowing white. The other remaining *Tsvortu* magicker watched her for a second, then turned toward Len. He waved a hand in Len's direction almost dismissively, launching a trio of red daggers at him. The creature snarled something as he did so, then ended the comment with a laugh.

Oh, God, he's attacking me! Fear bubbled acid into Len's throat as he watched the daggers cross the twenty yards that separated him from his attacker. Len started to twist to his left and back away from the daggers' line of flight, but he knew he'd never be fast enough to dodge them.

Yet somehow he was, or fast enough to dodge most of them. One of them raked a line of fire across his belly, shredding his shirt. Len slapped his right hand against his stomach and it came away black with blood in the night's dim light. The wound stung, and even though he knew it wasn't serious—*or real*—adrenaline jolted through him. He saw his nemesis preparing to cast another spell, and even though twenty yards separated them, Len wasn't about to give him another shot. *No monster from my id gets to hurt me like that and live.*

Len started to sprint toward the *Tsvortu* magicker, prepared to dodge if he got off a spell before Len had closed with him. In a heartbeat, Len found himself at top speed and only a couple of yards from the Storm demon. Len reacted reflexively, leaping into the air off his left foot, extending his right foot, and flying at his enemy with a kick aimed at his heart.

Even before he had his right leg fully extended, his kick landed on the Storm demon's breastbone. The creature *whuffed* as the kick drove the air from his lungs. Bones shattered, popping like wet sticks in a fire as the Tsvortu flew back off his feet. His hands grasped at Len's leg, then indigo blood began to well up around Len's foot. They landed together at the feet of the remaining Tsvortu sorcerer.

Len and the gold-furred sorcerer stared at each other for a half second, then Len hauled off and hit him square on the snout with a right jab. Len heard something pop and hoped it was the Storm demon's nose, but a growing ache in his hand told him he'd broken something. The Tsvortu, who had reeled back, leaked blue blood from his nose. He snarled at Len and started toward him when another jet of blue-white fire tumbled him back and set him on fire.

Len tried to dance back away from the burning Tsvortu, but his right foot remained trapped in the other sorcerer's chest. He stomped down hard, gushing blood back up his pant leg, then twisted his foot and pulled it free. It actually came unstuck a bit faster than he had anticipated. He hopped back and tried to regain his balance, but failed utterly and landed unceremoniously on his butt.

The golden globe's explosion had knocked Shoth back all the way against the railing in the library. The blast had toppled Mountain Guards like chesspieces on an overturned board. Two who had been nearest the head of the stairs reeled away, screaming, their clothes on fire. Others moved to help them, and Ghislaine came to her feet shouting orders. Shoth could barely hear them because of the ringing in his ears, but he knew what she wanted.

The Tsvortu boiling up the stairs made that abundantly clear. The majority of the Storm demons rushed up, overpowering the Guards coming to block them, while others vaulted railings and spread out in a flanking maneuver. The Mountain Guards, armed with big double-bitted broad-axes, closed on the head of the stairs, stopping the headlong Tsvortu rush temporarily.

Shoth concentrated for a second, then thrust his hands forward and opened them. A whitish spark flew from them and arced over toward the head of the stairs. When it reached its target, it flared brightly for a second, then a gap opened between the second and third Tsvortu ranks. The third rankers clawed at the gap, but the invisible wall he'd spelled into place held them back.

Two of the Tsvortu that had come up over the side immediately oriented on him. They dashed forward with big bounding steps, then one stopped abruptly as Ghislaine swung her broad-ax around in a huge arc. The blade caught the Tsvortu in mid-leap, crunching through ribs and lodging solidly in the demon's breastbone. The Tsvortu twisted with the force of the blow, tearing Ghislaine's ax from her hands, and landed solidly on the floor. The body bounced once, then lay there, oozing indigo blood.

The second Tsvortu leaped at Shoth, her blade raised high for an overhand strike. Shoth felt his mouth go dry, but he worked a quick spell. A spark shot from his hands and hit the marble floor, flashing like a reflection from it. The Tsvortu's war cry pierced the ringing in his ears, then ended suddenly as the Tsvortu slammed into the invisible wall he'd raised between himself and her. She glanced off it, her arms and legs flailing, and fell into the library well.

Ghislaine tugged her ax free of the Tsvortu corpse and shrieked at him. "Don't use walls to block them, *flatten* them!"

Shoth stared at her for a moment, then nodded. He eyed the width of the stairwell carefully, then cast the spell. The spark he sent out brightened above the Tsvortu's heads, then the invisible wall crashed down on them. The Storm demons, being incredibly strong, resisted being crushed by it, but had to devote all of their attention to keeping it up off them. *But my wall now shields them from our fighters' attacks.*

Fighting raged between Tsvortu and Guards all over the grand chamber. Matarun bodies lay scattered about, some in pieces, but Tsvortu bodies lay along with them. The Mountain Guards fought with a ferocity that surprised Shoth. Because they had all been fairly quiet and stoic on their journey, he never would have thought them so implacable and savage in combat.

Suddenly a roaring torrent of fire exploded in the stairwell, sending blue tongues jetting out between the balustrade's railings. Tsvortu screams mixed with the fire's cacophony, and, for a second, Shoth thought another Tsvortu lightning ball had accidentally exploded among the warriors. Then he realized, from the color of the flames, that the spell causing them was Imperial magick, which meant it had been cast by an ally.

He pointed at it and began to shout, then felt something grab his ankle. He tried to pull free, but claws pierced the leather of his boot. He looked back over his shoulder and saw a bloody-faced Tsvortu clinging to a railing post with one hand and his boot with the other. The Storm demon yanked hard, pulling Shoth from his feet. The mage slammed into the stone floor on his right flank and twisted around to face the Tsvortu as she shifted her grip and yanked again. She succeeded in pulling Shoth forward, slamming his groin into one of the stone posts.

He screamed and doubled over in pain, clutching himself. He tried to concentrate enough to cast a curative spell, but he could not. Another tug by the Tsvortu, and his hands got rapped against the stone. He cried out again, this time more from terror than pain, and the Tsvortu chittered out a horrible laugh.

Shoth heard something go bump behind him and looked back to see Ghislaine reeling away from her collision with the invisible wall he'd created. The Tsvortu laughed again, louder, and started to tug sideways on his leg. She quickly trapped his thigh between two posts. A little more pressure and his thigh would snap, or his knee would be shredded. He looked at her, seeking any glimmer of mercy in her three agate eyes, but he saw nothing but a spark of silver in one of them.

A fork with a little humanoid thing on it—a thing dressed in green-and-black motley—stabbed down into the creature's centermost eye. The Tsvortu squealed in agony and clapped both hands over her damaged eye. Without her handhold, the Tsvortu started to fall, but it seemed to Shoth to take forever for her to drop from sight. He heard her hit with the sort of crisp, wet sound made when a ripe apple is thrown hard against a wall, then a wave of nausea washed over him.

He vomited for what seemed to him to be an eternity. Tears rolled from his eyes, and sobs racked his body. His limbs quaked as his guts rebelled. He tried to close his mouth and just breathe through his nose, but the cloying scent of burned fur and the pungent one of vomitus would cause him to heave yet again. A shudder rippled through him, then he spat as best he could to rid his mouth of that horrible taste.

Shoth finally pushed himself away from the puddle that had been his dinner and slid his leg free of the balustrade. He looked up and noticed that he seemed to be the only thing moving in the room. Very shaky, he crawled around the edge of his invisible wall and used the railing to pull himself to his feet. He felt dizzy for a moment, then steadied himself and waited for the sensation to pass. It did, quickly enough, so he staggered to the stairs. He dispelled the walls he had raised and picked his way through the charred or bleeding Tsvortu bodies. Finally, he stumbled out into the night and sank to his knees in the middle of another battlefield.

Shoth looked up at the figures assembled there. Ghislaine and the half dozen Guards he recognized easily. Three of the others, from the Chaosfire glowing in their eyes, were Chaos Riders of one sort or another. The girl looked fairly young to be in Chaos, but the hint of fire burned in her eyes nonetheless. The other two, the Reptiad and wolf-warrior, bore a few cuts and scrapes from the battle, but they appeared to have given better than they got.

The last figure, once Shoth got a good look at him, captured his attention completely. The hair was shorter than he expected it to be, and the man didn't seem quite as rugged as Shoth had hoped. The apparel was strange in the extreme and torn open across his stomach. The crest on the shirt was not one Shoth recognized and didn't seem to be anything that could possibly be associated with magick.

Any question about this man's not being the person he had come seeking died aborning when Shoth saw the boots. One was covered with blue gore, but the eyes made it unmistakable. One of the eyes winked at him, and Shoth smiled. He bowed forward, touching his forehead to the ground, then straightened up again.

"It is I who summoned you here, Dashan, and I am pleased you came back to this place to save us."

14

Len stared down at the blond man on his knees. "What's a Dashan?"

The blond man's jaw dropped open. "An honorific, not a name? Of course, I should have seen it. Forgive me, Dashan, I didn't realize."

The awe in the man's voice took Len completely by surprise. The man seemed completely cowed by him, terrified that his error would bring some sort of retribution. *He's not hearing what I am asking him. He's just hearing me question him.*

Though Len could puzzle out at least part of the man's problem, it raised another problem for him. Up to this point he'd been able to place everyone and everything as being a product of his imagination being funneled into his dream. The guy he had tagged as Beowulf fit exactly the sort of image that name had conjured up in Len's mind when Len had first been exposed to the epic poem in school. The lizard-man looked like a Gorn from *Star Trek*, though he did have a tail. The warriors, the women, all of them had come from TV shows or comic books or some fleeting memory of the beach or campus life or the store. Everything fit except for this guy and the word "Dashan."

The small redhead stepped forward from Beowulf's side and offered her hand to the big woman leading the folks who had come out of the Sanctuary. "Introductions are in order, I believe. I am Xoayya. This is Tyrchon and Nagrendra. We are late of an Imperial expedition into Chaos to deal with the B*harashadi*."

The tall woman eyed her suspiciously as she quickly shook her hand. "The three of you are a long way from the Ward Walls."

Tyrchon rested his hands on his sword and let the tip bite into the ground. "We have other business to conduct in Chaos. I hope you didn't mind our interference here."

The tall woman smiled despite the blood besmirching her cheek. "Not at all. I am Captain Ghislaine of the Mountain Guards. These are some of my people." She pointed to the man on his knees. "This is Shoth Churgûn, a Warder."

They all turned to look at Len, but it took him a second to realize what they were waiting for. "Oh, me. I'm Len Fong. Pleased to meet you all."

Xoayya looked from Len to Shoth and back again. "You two have never met before?"

Len shook his head, then shrugged. "Well, I guess, since you are all figments of my imagination, trapped here in my dream, he's a construct the same way you all are. I guess I know him, then."

She looked at Shoth, but the blond sorcerer shook his head. "No, we have not met."

"Do you have any idea what he was talking about?"

Shoth again shook his head as he rose to his feet. "His confusion is not to be unexpected. He has come a long way to be here, but there is no doubt he is the Dashan."

Nagrendra inclined his head toward Shoth. "You said you had summoned him?"

"Did I?" Shoth hesitated, the same sort of hesitation Len caught in folks when they said they'd be back to buy shoes after thinking about them, but they never returned. "Researches indicated the Dashan was a powerful mage from the time of the Shattering. With Lord Disaster becoming more bold, it was decided a weapon was needed to oppose him. The Dashan here can be that weapon, or can provide us with such a weapon, since he is very wise and strong in the ways of magick."

Len laughed. "Me, a magicker? I don't think so. I've played one, and I've fooled around with tarot cards and stuff, but magick? Nope."

Nagrendra's tongue flicked out. "But you were able to use the magick in those boots."

"Huh?"

The lizard-man pointed back toward where the *Tsvortu* corpse with a staved-in chest lay. "You invoked the power in the boots to cross the distance between yourself and that sorcerer, then you kicked your foot through his chest. It was a fascinating display that showed contempt for your enemy and much courage."

"Right." Len raised his right hand and displayed the swollen and discolored middle knuckle. "And I broke my hand on the other one."

The small, redheaded woman came over and took his hand in hers. He tried to jerk his hand back as she applied slight pressure to the broken knuckle. It hurt for a second, then a whitish glow spread from her hands and covered his. It tickled for a second, then numbed the injury. When she pulled her hands away, the swelling had gone down, and he was able to wiggle his fingers without pain.

Len stared at her, his jaw open. "Oh, man, that was great? Can you teach me how to do that?"

Xoayya frowned at him, then turned to face Shoth. "I thought you said he was a great mage. How can a great mage not know how to cast such a spell?"

Shoth shook his head again. "The summoning process may have left him confused."

Len looked up from between the fingers of his right hand. "Maybe it's like air travel—all my baggage didn't make it."

"Perhaps." Xoayya walked over to Shoth and held her hands out to him. "May I have your hand?"

The blond sorcerer gave her his hand. The woman stiffened for a second, then stumbled back. Tyrchon caught her, and she leaned heavily against him.

"Are you all right?"

Xoayya reached a hand up and patted him on the shoulder. "Yes, I am. I thought I had braced myself for it, but I still found it overwhelming."

Ghislaine folded her arms across her chest. "What did you find?"

"Wait." Tyrchon recovered his sword and pointed toward the tunnel into Fong's Sanctuary. "Let's get inside first. I can smell food in there, and I'd just as soon not be standing around in the night in case more Tsvortu decide to avenge those we've slain."

"Good idea." Ghislaine detailed her warriors to gather up the Tsvortu bodies and pile them together so Nagrendra could burn them later. "Follow me. We'll need to clean up inside, too . . . What?"

Len had stepped in behind her and glanced past her at the Sanctuary. Though he had seen a bunch of Tsvortu clogging the stairs when Nagrendra blasted them with his firespell, he saw absolutely no trace of them now. Not a charred bit of bone, not a smoke smudge on the wall, not even a sword scar on a stair or the hint of burned flesh in the air. "Interesting. I didn't anticipate this effect."

The tall woman turned on him. "What are you talking about?"

Len slipped past her and climbed up the stairs. The room looked as clean and untouched as it had the first time he saw it. "The place is maintained, kept clean, and I would have thought it would take a long time to clean the place up, but I guess it doesn't."

Shoth came halfway up the stairs past Ghislaine. "This is what you intended?"

"Well, not exactly. When I designed the place I had two servants who kept the place clean, but they were both magickers, too. Maybe they added the spells that kept the place clean when they weren't around."

The blond sorcerer smiled. "But you remember designing this place. This *is* your stronghold."

Len nodded. "Yes, but it's not like you think. I designed this for a game."

Shoth's gray eyes grew wide. "You designed this for *play*?" The sheer wonderment in the man's voice sounded one step shy of orgasmic. "You did this for recreation?"

"You're making it sound like more than it is." Len opened his hands helplessly. "I designed this, yes, but I didn't make it. Do you understand?"

"I'm not certain either one of you can understand." Xoayya came up the stairs, letting her right hand trail along the marble. "There is much of you in this place."

Len frowned. "Me?"

Xoayya half turned and pointed back at Shoth. "Him as well."

Shoth frowned. "What are you talking about?"

"An idea I have." She paused and looked up at the Fong monument. "The boots, where did you get them?"

"Why do you ask?"

She clasped her hands together and looked back at both Len and Shoth. "I am, in the eyes of those in the City of Sorcerers, a feral mage."

Len blinked. "A what?"

Nagrendra pushed past Len and started up the stairs toward the monument. "She is naturally adept in one of the schools of magick. In her case, it is Clairvoyance. She is able to see things past, present, and future. Her ability is natural and not always easy to control. When she first touched you, Len, thinking to heal you, she got visions about you, terrible and confusing visions."

Xoayya nodded. "And some of them included Shoth, but Shoth alone. And visions of you, of course, alone and in a place I cannot begin to comprehend." She pointed a hand at the monument. "Even a few of the visions featured him, exactly as I see him in the carving."

Shoth frowned. "So, when you asked to touch my hand, you were seeking visions as well?"

"I was, and I got them. Most of you, some of Len, and a few more of this individual." She shrugged and topped the stairs. "Perhaps we shall refer to him as the Dashan?"

Len walked over to the dinner table, pulled a chair out, and sat. "What do these various visions mean, then? Why did you see me when you touched him?"

"I cannot be certain, but if I judge what I saw with

each of you as I would anyone else, I would have said I was looking at scenes from past or future lives."

Len glanced at Shoth. "But if I'm his future, or he's mine, we couldn't be here at the same time, right? I mean, reincarnation works with a soul getting recycled into new bodies, right?"

Ghislaine came over and sat at the opposite side of the table. "I am no priestess, but this is what I understand of how that works."

Xoayya nodded. "I agree, which means something extraordinary is going on here. I think each of you possesses half the soul of the Dashan."

Len frowned. "What? That's impossible, isn't it?"

"Not exactly, Len." Jhesti appeared on the table at his elbow, looking a bit more like some child's toy soldier than the flat piece of plastic he had been before. His limbs had been rounded, and his body had taken on more depth. Len still didn't see him move, but in an eyeblink the figure seated himself. "The two of you look pretty much the same to me."

Shoth stared at the small figure. "You can mistake him for me?"

Jhesti laughed. "I did earlier, didn't I? You think these fake little eyes work very well for seeing? Don't bet on it. What I sense about you—seeing isn't quite it, but close—is nearly identical. It is as if you two are identical shields with different devices painted on them. If not for that overlay, you'd be the same."

Len shivered. "And that overlay is *this* lifetime?"

"It's shallow enough, in your case, to be true."

"Thanks a lot." Len looked up and around at the others. Somehow it did not surprise him that they all could see and hear Jhesti, but they watched and listened to him as if nothing were out of the ordinary.

"So, then, we'd both be the reincarnation of the Dashan, right?"

"Correct." Xoayya nodded. "You are the reincarnation of the magicker who created this place. Both of you seem to have memories from his previous life lodged in your minds. Certain things, symbols, ideas, may have bled through to your consciousness and have taken on significance in your lives."

Shoth nodded slowly. "The crest."

"But I created that . . ." Len stopped as he went absolutely cold. He had rested his dream defense on a foundation that consisted of his recognition of what he had imagined and created. Because he knew he created it, he knew why it was in his mind and why it figured in his dream. What Xoayya had just suggested, however, was that he might not have *imagined* things, but *remembered* them from the Dashan's lifetime. *That would mean this place is real and I am trapped far from home, or I'm completely delusional.*

A shiver shook him and almost unseated him.

Ghislaine leaned across the table and grabbed his arm. "Are you sick, Len?"

"Oh, God, I hope not." Len swallowed sour saliva and centered himself in the chair. "I should be okay." *I'm just a bazillion miles from home in a place with magick and demons and stuff. Talk about your nightmares.*

His chin came up. It occurred to him that his dream defense had not wholly eroded. *I could just be dreaming that I didn't create this stuff. Before I had too much control over the world and environment, but who has that much control in life? Things happen, variables intrude. These people and the demons, they're like getting notice of an IRS audit, or having a rent check get lost in the mail. Maybe I am still dreaming, but now just dreaming harder or something.*

He clung to that explanation, even though it sounded weaker than he felt, and refused to let the seeming reality of the situation impinge on him.

Nagrendra walked around to the head of the table and peeked beneath one of the silver covers. "Haven't had that for a long time." He lowered the cover again, cutting off the faint scent of oranges that Len caught on the air, and looked over at Shoth. "You said you did the summoning of Len. Was this a choice you made yourself, or were you chosen for the job?"

"What do you mean?"

"What I know of conjuration is limited, but I always thought that having an affinity for the target would be a benefit. If you felt compelled to summon Len because of your connection to him, it would make sense that you did so." The scaled sorcerer shrugged. "Or perhaps you were chosen for the job because of your affinity for him."

Shoth thought for a moment, then slowly shook his head. "I was given some very basic information about the Dashan so I could understand the spell I would be casting. I did modify it a bit, of course, and I was involved in the casting, but the link between Len and me—*if* it exists at all—was pure happenstance."

"Then quite lucky." Xoayya smiled cautiously. "So, Len, did you come with the boots?"

"No, I found them there." He pointed at the monument. "There is a room back there that had a body in it wearing the boots. The skeleton tried to attack me, but I defeated it."

Xoayya walked up the stairs to the monument and touched the slab. "How did you open it?"

"I didn't. I just walked through."

She waved him to her. "Come, show me how you did it."

Len got up and climbed to the landing. He took her right hand in his left, then touched the stone with his own right hand. His hand sank into the stone's surface as if it were no more substantial than shadow. He walked into it, and she came with him. "It will take a moment for your eyes to get used to the dark."

"Actually, I can see fairly well in here as it is." Len heard the rustle of her skirts as she walked past him and into the main part of the room. "The skeleton here is the one you destroyed?"

Len saw her outline as she moved past the island. The top slab had not been returned to it, and the skeleton lay in the stone enclosure the way it had before it had tried to kill him, save this time it did not have the boots on. "Yes, that was it. I crushed the skull."

Xoayya reached into the box and brought her hands up full of a skull. "*This* skull?"

Len shrugged. "I don't know. Are skulls that easy to recognize?"

"I should think this one might be for you, Len." Xoayya smiled at him. "After all, for many years, this is where your soul resided."

15

Shoth Churgûn leaned against the stairwell's stone railing as he watched Xoayya and Len disappear through the monument. Even thirty feet away he could feel the magick radiating from the boots and Len and the wall, and it stunned him with its complexity. For him it was akin to hearing an incredibly involved song played by a dozen minstrels. One simple exposure to it could not allow him to understand the whole of it.

Still, he *did* understand pieces of it, and that surprised him. He knew his limitations as a magicker, and the subtle bits and pieces of the spell should have escaped him. While he was an excellent practitioner of magick, and could even see ways to refine spells to make them easier for him to cast, it took someone like Myat or the Dashan actually to create complex spells that were able to account for and deal with all the variables that could interfere with the magick.

And Len, he says he made this place as a game. Whether that is him remembering what the Dashan remembered having done, or is some exercise he engaged in, he, too, must be one of the complex thinkers that I am not. Shoth frowned for a moment. *Perhaps that is something contained in the part of the soul I do not have. My affinity for and partial understanding of the crest and the spells it marks could come from my having part of that soul.*

This made perfect sense to him, and even began to bring parts of his life into sharper focus. While born and raised in the mountains, he never felt part of the mountains. The Matarun and he seemed incompatible. Moreover, he had never felt fully complete. His friendship with Princess Myat had helped fill some of that void in his life, but he was always missing something. He seemed to have an abundance of fears that kept limiting him, and, indeed, only his fear of failing Myat and disappointing her had kept him going.

He truly treasured her friendship and cherished the memories of the time they had spent together. Shoth had been afraid when, on a return from the City of Sorcerers, he had found Myat fully grown into womanhood, and she had evidenced a desire for him. It hadn't been that they were cousins—that relationship was distant enough to be acknowledged without triggering any sort of taboo. Instead, he had not felt he was worthy of her, or that she should demean herself by showing an interest in him. And yet, when she had finally pursued and cornered him, it had been wonderful, and all of his fears vanished in her confidence and strength.

Shoth, for all his caution, or perhaps because of it, was not a stupid man. Something Nagrendra had asked came rolling back around through his mind and made him feel a touch uneasy. While he had not known about his link to the Dashan, was it possible Myat had? He didn't recall telling her of the crest or his studies, but she was intelligent enough to have perhaps read some of his notes, or to have inquired of others about what he was studying. He had heard enough of her planning after their trysts to know she was fully capable of putting him into a position where he cast the spell to summon Len without knowing fully what he was doing.

But, is that what she did? He couldn't be certain, and he certainly didn't want to believe it of her. *No, if she had told me everything, it would have made the summoning easier. She had no reason to hide from me information that would have increased the chances of our success.*

He brought his head up. "What was that you asked, Nagrendra?"

"I asked what your plans were now that you have found your Dashan."

The blond sorcerer came up to the main floor and over to the table. He seated himself next to Ghislaine, then shook his head. "My original expectation was to find him and bring him back to the Empire."

Ghislaine looked over at him. "And that is what we will do. That is our mission."

"I agree, Captain, that *was* our mission." Shoth stared at his oblong reflection in one of the serving-dish covers. "Our mission was to bring forth someone who could fend off Lord Disaster. I don't see that in Len, and I don't know if there is something here or something in Chaos that will make him able to do just that."

"We have our orders."

"So I understand." He looked over at Nagrendra. "Was there a purpose to your question?"

"There was, but I think Tyrchon can explain it better than I can." The Reptiad looked over at the wolf-warrior as the latter topped the stairs. "The bodies are all in place to be burned?"

"They are. Some of the Matarun are scouting around to see if we have other *Tsvortu* lurking in the area." Tyrchon tapped his own snout with a finger. "I suggested there was no need for that, but they wanted to make certain for themselves. Your troops are quite good, Captain Ghislaine."

"Thank you, Tyrchon."

Nagrendra pointed at Shoth. "I asked if they had plans now that they have found their man here. I was thinking we might want to enlist their help in our quest, and I will leave you to explain it to them as I go start the pyre."

Ghislaine kicked back the chair at the end of the table. "You can sit here, Tyrchon."

The wolfman nodded to her once, then sat and fixed Shoth with a *Chaosfire* stare. "The expedition of which I was part left me in Chaos in a slow zone. I had been wounded by a *vindictxvara* and was dying. Our expedition's leader tricked Fialchar into having to heal my wound, which he did."

Shoth blinked. "Lord Disaster committed an altruistic act?"

"Hardly. He also set upon me four *Tsvortu* while I was unarmed. I killed three of them, and he eliminated the last one. He suggested that he would set more of them upon me and my friends unless I agreed to help him with a problem." Tyrchon held up a hand to forestall a protest from Ghislaine. "Please, hear me out. With your mission to bring someone in to hurt Lord Disaster, you will find this information very useful."

Shoth laid a hand on Ghislaine's shoulder. "Give him a chance."

"I don't like even entertaining the idea of working for Lord Disaster."

Tyrchon's jaw dropped in a grin. "Neither do I. There was, several days ago, a huge Chaos storm that rolled through this area. Part of it made it right up to the ridge-line of this valley, then it stopped suddenly. Lord Disaster indicated that the storm died without warning. He said he had gone to explore the place where it had vanished, but he found the area painful to be in. It hurt him; therefore, he asked me to go, see what it was, and report back to him."

The Matarun sorcerer sat back in his chair. "He said it *hurt* him?"

Tyrchon nodded slowly. "He considered the Ward Walls a mild inconvenience by comparison."

"And part of the storm came almost to this point. I wonder . . ." He closed his eyes to concentrate. "If the storm died prematurely, perhaps not all of the pieces of the Dashan that Len needed were implanted into him. I mean, if you look at him, Len is almost the image of the Dashan, but not quite. Perhaps the storm still possesses some of his essence and has it trapped wherever the energy from the storm was trapped."

The Matarun warrior-woman toyed with her black braid. "I don't understand."

"The process of summoning the Dashan here may not have been instantaneous. A loaf of bread does not bake all at once, it takes time. Perhaps, as he was summoned, there was not enough time to complete the job. Len arrived at one point, the boots at another, and perhaps his acumen with magick is yet elsewhere. And that else-where may be where the storm's energy got captured."

Ghislaine looked over at Tyrchon. "Do you have a proposition for us?"

"One you should like, I think. You have six of your soldiers left, which would be more than enough to get you back to the Empire, but not back in the direction from which you came. Tsvortu will be moving into this country now that the Bharashadi are dead. The place we are going is east-southeast of here, which means we will be moving farther away from the Tsvortu as we go. We travel together, letting our strength complement yours. I am no match for six of your Guards, mind you, but Nagrendra is a powerful sorcerer and quite adept in the ways of combat magick. And Xoayya has certain talents that we could all find very useful on a dangerous journey like this."

Ghislaine flicked her braid back over her shoulder. "You would have us travel east-southeast? How many days?"

"Two or three at the most, I think."

Shoth consulted his mental map of Chaos, opened his eyes, and nodded. "That would be very close to a place where the storm became quite active. It would not surprise me if we find what you are seeking there."

The Guard captain slowly stretched. "I would normally not even consider this possibility. We are Mountain Guards and do not fear all the Tsvortu in the world. However, in this case, prudence is not a bad thing. Getting the Dashan, or what there is of him, back to the Empire will be difficult, and I would appreciate the aid. You must understand, though, I am in charge of this operation. I will accept your advice, but my people will not take your orders."

Tyrchon held up both hands. "I have no quarrel with your leading. Consider me a fighting scout. You'll find

Nagrendra and Xoayya are quite hardy." He looked around. "Where is she?"

Shoth pointed at the monument. "She had Len take her inside there. Behind that stone is where he found the boots and, he said, a skeleton that animated and tried to kill him."

One of the wolf-warrior's ears flicked toward the monument. "When did they go in there?"

"Half an hour ago?" Shoth shrugged. "I doubt they are in any danger in there, since Len said he had destroyed the skeleton when it attacked him."

Tyrchon nodded. "I saw what he did to the Tsvortu sorcerer out there. I doubt any skeleton could stand up to such treatment."

Nagrendra reentered the great chamber and came over to the table. "The bodies are burned to ash and will be scattered to the winds." He tossed a set of the Tsvortu clan necklaces on the table. "Captain, you might as well have these. If you sell them in the Empire, the money can go to the families of the people you had slain here."

She accepted them and tucked them into a pouch on her belt. "That was thoughtful of you."

"It is a kindness to the survivors of those who die in Chaos. Those of us who survive out here should never forget those left behind on either side of the Ward Walls."

Shoth felt a chill run down his spine. *Were my parents to be given gold earned from the sale of such things to pay them for my death, they would refuse it. Even though I labor in the service of Princess Myat, they barely acknowledge they have a son named Shoth.*

He brought his head up. "Do you have family you left behind in the islands, Nagrendra?"

"No one who would remember me." The Reptiad

uncovered a dish, pulled out what looked to be a bird leg, and sucked the flesh from the bone. He crunched the cartilage merrily, then swallowed. "I left the islands early on to travel to the City of Sorcerers for training. I became a Master of Magicks, but never quite got to your rank of Warder. From there I became a Chaos Rider. I've never returned to the islands and never truly get homesick for them. Of late I have taken to living in Herakopolis and was enjoying the holidays there when I accepted an Imperial medallion and went out on this expedition."

Nagrendra set the bone down on a plate. "I recognize the fact that my life could have been different, but I accept that it was not. Xoayya is a firm believer in destiny and would tell me that everything I have done in my life was precisely to get me to this point, and that my getting to this point was so I could move to the next point. I don't agree with that view of life, but, in looking back over my life, it would be very difficult to say that it isn't true. I think, however, at least the *illusion* of free will is what keeps me willing to accept the responsibilities of venturing into Chaos."

Shoth smiled carefully. "You believe we have a responsibility to venture into Chaos? There *are* those who think our expeditions into Chaos are what keep the forces in Chaos intent on destroying us."

Tyrchon raised an eyebrow. "This is a curious place to bring up that point."

Shoth nodded. "I know, and clearly I don't accept that point as a general rule. If I did, I'd not be here. By the same token, this is my longest foray into Chaos and not one that I'd care to repeat. Because of that I find Nagrendra's use of the word responsibility rather curious."

The Reptiad gnawed the meat off another leg, then waved the bone about. "I see it as a responsibility to be out here. I know this is not a view all Chaos Riders or even a majority of them hold to be true. There are those of the younger generations who view my thoughts as curious, and ancient even. For them Chaos is a place of grand adventure, but I've lived beyond that stage. In coming into Chaos I can see how different it is from the Empire, and I have no trouble visualizing how terrible things would be if the Ward Walls were to fall."

"Is that because your people were so changed by Chaos?" Ghislaine leaned forward, resting an elbow on the table. "Or is it a more personal observation?"

Nagrendra tipped his muzzle down toward her. "All peoples of the Empire were changed by the time it spent in Chaos. Some of us more, many of us less; some of us physically, but *all* of us mentally. The reality the people had known before the Shattering went away, and from that point forward they had to guard against its ever happening again."

The Reptiad sorcerer ran a taloned thumb down the edge of his cloak that bore his rank badges. "Why do we wear these? They are worn to show others that we conform to what they expect. We have created symbols to quantify and represent reality so we can spot that which is abnormal and destroy it. We have defined ourselves to be the opposite of Chaos, and it is this rigid attention to details that has allowed us to survive.

"Now, however, there are those who do not believe in all this so fervently. Chaos overswept the world five centuries ago. Lord Disaster might well have appeared at the Emperor's Bear's Eve Ball, but that doesn't mean the Ward Walls are coming down tomorrow or next week or next year or next century."

Nagrendra shrugged. "In light of such ignorance, I do feel a responsibility to keep Chaos at bay. If that means going out and discovering lost artifacts of power so they can be denied to Chademons or Lord Disaster, I'm more than pleased to do so. If I do not, then I will have allowed Chaos to get one step closer to washing over the world again."

Shoth nodded emphatically. "Even though I do not share your desire to adventure in Chaos, I agree most heartily with your philosophy. None of us wants Chaos to hold sway, so, for that reason and all those Ghislaine has pointed out, we will join our forces with yours and see what it is that causes Lord Disaster so much pain."

Tyrchon nodded. "And once we have it, we'll figure out how best to use it against him."

16

L en looked at the skull and shook his head. "If you say that used to be my skull, I guess I'll believe you." He had a hard time believing he was saying those words, but the simple way in which she delivered the statement made it easier to accept. "How do you know that?"

Xoayya laid the skull back down in the box. "I get enough of an impression from the bones to link it to visions I had of your life as the Dashan. These bones have long been stripped of flesh, but there are sufficient clues to tie them to you and Shoth."

Len walked over to the stone coffin and leaned against the side opposite her. The skeleton looked peaceful and whole, not the ruined mess he'd left behind. "How long has he been dead?"

"Five hundred years or so. There are hints of a cataclysm in your past life that I would guess was the Shattering of the Seal of Reality."

"What?"

The small woman smiled and clasped her hands together on the edge of the coffin. "Five centuries ago a debate rose between two groups of sorcerers. One maintained it was impossible to create an item that could encompass all aspects of reality. Think of the device as a mirror, but one such that, if it is broken, so is that which it reflects."

Len nodded. "Got it. We have a superstition about breaking mirrors that starts from pretty much that same idea."

"Another group of sorcerers disagreed with that idea and set about to create what they called the Seal of Reality. There were a dozen of them, all very intelligent. They succeeded in making the Seal, then a thirteenth sorcerer, named Fialchar, shattered that Seal. It broke reality, and Chaos swept over the world. Where we are now is land still under the sway of Chaos, which is why you can have rain forest and desert mixed so closely, for example."

Len pointed a finger at the skeleton. "But the Dashan survived this Shattering?"

"I believe so." Xoayya frowned. "His memories are very powerful in you, less so in Shoth, but nonetheless there in fragmentary form. I got many impressions from the both of you, and there don't seem to have been any intervening incarnations to muddle things, but sorting them out is difficult."

"Wait a minute. You said there were no intervening incarnations? Why not? I would have thought, in five hundred years, we could have lived a half dozen lives."

"I would like to tell you that such a thing is unusual, but I don't know enough about reincarnation to make that statement." She shrugged. "The fact that each of you only has a portion of the Dashan's soul may account for it. From what I have seen of your life, you come from a very strange place very far away. It could be that both portions of the soul had to be reincarnated at the same time, and traveling to wherever you were took a lot of time."

"But is that possible?" Len frowned. "Do souls get ripped up at death?" He hesitated, recalling all sorts of news stories and books about individuals with multiple personalities, in which each personality wasn't a whole being, but just a fractured part of a whole. *What would happen if such a person died? Would his soul be whole or would it be broken up into parts and sent out to find new host bodies?*

Again, Xoayya shook her head. "I don't know." She patted the coffin edge with the palms of her hands. "I can tell you this, however. In this chamber I can sense residual magick that I think was probably the last spell the Dashan cast. I'm not good at identifying spells, but I think it combined aspects of construction and conjuration, but they were reversed. I think, when he laid himself down to die here, he purposely sundered his own soul and sent it out and away."

Something in what she said sounded hauntingly familiar to Len. He couldn't place it, though, and that began to worry him. It wasn't a spell from some game, and he couldn't remember having read it in a book. He didn't even think he'd heard such a thing mentioned when he'd watched Pat Robertson railing against games or alternate religions on the 700 Club. It wasn't even the sort of thing his New-Agey friends had talked about, primarily because it sounded negative, and they avoided any negativity as if it were the karmic equivalent of herpes.

Yet familiar it was, and he couldn't help but think that

he might be picking up on the final memories of his life as the Dashan. Shredding his own soul likely had delayed his reincarnation, and sending part of it so far away made the odds of the pieces ever being rejoined all but impossible. This had to have been the Dashan's goal, and Len couldn't see it as being anything but self-sacrificial. While he knew that observation was pretty clear, destructive acts are usually seen as decidedly selfish. *But a selfish man wouldn't deny himself another chance at life—he would do whatever he could to maximize his chance at life.*

He looked at Xoayya. "This act of breaking up his soul, it must have been to prevent him from being reincarnated. If he were a murderer or something, I could see him doing this as he repented. He would be guaranteeing that he could never again commit the acts that he thought were so horrible, but I don't see the Dashan as being that sort of person."

"Not at all—at least, not from the impressions I have."

"Good." Len peered down into the skull's empty eye sockets. "This magick stuff is complex, and you said, or Shoth said, the Dashan was very powerful in magick. Could he have created a spell that only he could cast, and he wanted to make sure it would never be cast again?"

"Possible, *or* . . ."

"Or?"

Xoayya toyed with a lock of her red hair, coiling it around a finger. "Or perhaps he meant to be reincarnated, but only at a specific time, when that spell or something else required his attention. He didn't want to undergo the normal cycle of reincarnation because, when the right time came, he didn't want to be cut off from the memories of his previous life. He couldn't prevent his coming back, but he delayed it until the time was right."

Len leaned his elbows on the coffin's stone edge. "But that would mean he cast a spell in which he took into account all the variables that would be necessary to trigger things at the right time, allowing the bits of his soul to come back. He had to be looking into the future from five centuries earlier to pick a point when he'd have to return, then he had to let the dispersed parts of his soul reincarnate twenty to forty years earlier, allowing the pieces to mature so that they could reunite." He rubbed his hands over his face. "I don't even want to begin to think about that."

"If you are right, that would have to be the most complex spell I've ever heard of." She smiled carefully. "Still, if it was his destiny to return here and now, there was no way the spell could fail."

Len arched an eyebrow at her. "You believe in predestination?"

Xoayya nodded. "I do. What about you?"

"I took a philosophy class, and we covered it. I don't believe in it for one simple reason."

Her chin came up. "Really?"

Len smiled at the doubtful tone in her voice. "Look, you're welcome to believe whatever you want. I don't want to challenge your belief system."

"And you think you can?"

He nodded. "I can, but I don't think you want me to do that, do you?"

"Perhaps I'm destined to have you do that."

"Well, you have the free will to make that choice, don't you?"

Xoayya laughed. "Actually, I don't. Why don't you believe in predestination?"

"It's kind of simple, really." He shrugged. "If there is no freedom of choice, there is no reason to live. If predestination is true, then the final outcome of every-thing is already known, and this presupposes an entity that figured it all out since it is *known*."

She narrowed her eyes. "I'm waiting for your argument."

"Okay, here it is: at some point this entity that knows everything had to choose to know all or not to know all. This means a universe of predestination was born of free choice. Where free choice once existed, it can exist again. The entity can choose to forget that he knows all."

"But what if this entity is bound by her own rules concerning predestination?"

"If she is bound by predestination, those rules were predetermined for her by a yet greater entity." Len opened his hands. "At the top, there is always an entity that had free choice. She or he may *choose* to abide by the choice of predestination, but to be *bound* by it means there never was a choice in the first place, which means that entity is not the entity at the top."

Xoayya looked at him. "There is something wrong with your argument, but I cannot pick it out at the moment."

"I'll be happy to discuss it with you whenever you figure out what's wrong with it." Len smiled broadly. "I did ace the philosophy course, though . . ."

"I have no idea what you are talking about, but I gather that was a warning of some sort. I consider myself warned." She came around the edge of the coffin and walked toward the monument slab through which they had entered. "We had best get back to the others."

Len pointed at the slab. "I couldn't get back through it before. I went out through that . . ." He glanced at the chamber's rear wall, but it appeared as solid as the slab. "I thought there was a door there."

"Did you have the boots on when you left?"

"Yeah, I did." He walked over and stood beside her. "You think they will get us out?"

She took his hand. "After you."

Len approached the slab and found that his hand passed through it easily. He led her through and saw that the grand chamber's lights had dimmed. A couple of the guards stood at the doorway, while others had wrapped themselves in blankets and thrown themselves on the floor to sleep. He saw no trace of Shoth, Nagrendra, or Ghislaine, but Tyrchon stretched and roused himself from one of the dining table's chairs.

Xoayya freed her hand from Len's and wandered down the stairs to the table. "How long were we in there?"

"Five hours or so." Tyrchon stood and offered her a crystal goblet full of wine. "I gather it did not seem that long to you?"

"Ten, fifteen minutes." Len descended and joined the other two at the table. "I guess we lost track of time in there."

"Probably a slow zone." The wolf-warrior's ears flicked forward, confirming for Len that the cowl was more than a garment. "If that place were meant to house valuables, making time run slower in there would hinder decay and, if a thief got in, it would give those on the outside more time to notice the intrusion and react to it."

"Makes sense." Len lifted up a serving-dish cover and saw a platter full of tacos. "What, no hot sauce?"

A crystal container filled with salsa slid over to bang into the side of the serving plate. "All you want there, Len." The little plastic jester pointed toward the salsa like a model on a game show pointing out prizes.

"Thanks, Jhesti."

Tyrchon's nostrils flared as he caught the scent of tacos, then he glanced at the little jester. "*That* is Jhesti?"

"You were expecting someone else?" Len sat down, shoveled a couple of tacos onto a plate, and anointed them with salsa. "He came with me."

The wolf-warrior lowered his torso until his nose was two inches from Jhesti. "Are you really Jhesti, the Lost Prince?"

"I'm lost, yes, and my name is Jhesti, but I don't think I'm a prince." Jhesti's voice betrayed uncertainty. "Safe to say I'm a fool, however."

Len crunched a taco and had the rest of it disintegrate onto his plate. He swallowed and laughed. "So much for magick tacos. They fall apart like the real thing."

Xoayya picked a taco up and inspected it. "It seems they are designed to fall apart once you bite into them."

"Yeah, but, you know, in a dream I would think one could hold together."

Tyrchon oriented on Len. "Dream? This is the second time you have suggested this is a dream."

Jhesti laughed. "You're in trouble now, Len."

How do I explain to figments of my imagination that they are just that? He nodded. "I think I'm dreaming all of this, that I'm remembering things I created, and now, because of a fall I took, I'm in a coma. While I'm sleeping I'm dreaming, and you're all in it."

The wolfman straightened up. "Did you dream up Jhesti here?"

"Yes, sort of. He's based on something I was given."

"And he has been with you, helping you, since you arrived in Chaos?"

Jhesti laughed. "If not for me, he'd be a dozen times dead."

"Dream on, clown." Len frowned. "Don't *you* think it's a little unusual for all of us to be seeing and hearing this little thing here?"

Tyrchon shook his head. "There are stranger things to see in Chaos, Len, much stranger. You dreamed up his name, too?"

"I guess so. I mean, he told me what it was." Len looked up at him. "Why?"

"You don't know who Jhesti is, do you?"

Len shook his head. "Nope. I'd guess he's a lost prince, right?"

Tyrchon nodded a little salute in Len's direction. "Very good. Jhesti was in line to become the Emperor, and because he knew the responsibilities he would face then would leave him no time for pleasures, he became something of a wastrel. The Imperial nobles decided they had no confidence in him and urged his father to declare one of Jhesti's younger brothers to be the heir. The Emperor refused, and instead went to Jhesti and told him of the nobles' concerns. Jhesti decided to prove he could be serious and vowed to beard Fialchar in his own lair. He set out for Chaos, and no trace of him has been seen since."

"Officially," Xoayya added.

"Officially?" Len sipped from a goblet of milk. "What do you mean by that?"

Tyrchon folded his arms across his chest. "It's said Jhesti succeeded in bearding Fialchar and that Lord Disaster refused to maintain his beard lest the missing lock show and embarrass him. I've met Fialchar, and he has no beard."

Len narrowed his eyes. "And?"

Xoayya smiled easily. "Legend has it that Jhesti still lives and wanders both Chaos and the Empire. A stranger helping a stranger is often referred to as Jhesti. Children born to unwed mothers are often called 'Jhesti's Get.' Most of all, however, Jhesti is known for saving the innocent or foolish who blunder into Chaos."

Tyrchon pointed at the little jester. "Just as your Jhesti has done."

"So, what, you think your Lost Prince had his soul fragment like this taco, and part of it lodged in this piece of plastic here?"

"Not at all, Len, not at all." Tyrchon arched an eyebrow at him. "I just wonder how it is that you dreamed for your little friend here a name and a role that fits *our* legend?"

Suddenly no longer hungry, Len rubbed at his eyes. "I don't know, Tyrchon. But dreaming I am. No question."

"If that is what you want to believe . . ." The warrior shrugged. "Then why don't you get some sleep. We're heading out early tomorrow and, if at all possible, I'd like you to dream up a safe passage for us."

17

Tyrchon rose with the sun and set about making preparations for their trek. From the Sanctuary's closets he took blankets and odds and ends of clothing. He tucked them into the spare gear left over from the guards who had died. He also took one of the serving dishes outside the Sanctuary to see if it would provide food while they were on the road, but the magick seemed to diminish rather quickly when away from the Sanctuary. Returning to it, he let himself imagine all sorts of wonderful road rations and discovered, to his delight, that they did not fall apart once he took them outside.

All the others seemed to wake slowly, but they looked refreshed and ready to go. Len came downstairs in the clothes he'd been wearing the day before, but the cut in the tunic had been repaired overnight. The cloak he had worn the day before had been rolled up with a blanket to make a bedroll, which he wore slung across his back. On his right hip he had an oversize pouch that hung from a shoulder strap. It looked like it contained something heavy. On the other hip he had a canteen. A pair of curious-looking shoes tied by the laces hung over his right shoulder. A quilted jacket of green homespun fabric, an odd, wide-brimmed hat, and the all-seeing boots completed his outfit.

Len smiled at him. "I know the outfit is kind of *Kung Fu* and *Raiders of the Lost Ark*, but it was the best I could do. The magick here doesn't seem to get the idea of Gore-Tex and nylon."

As Tyrchon did with many mages who spoke to him of things arcane and unknowable, he just nodded and did not ask for clarification. Len's talk of dreaming had disturbed the warrior only because of a few past ventures into Chaos on expeditions with mages who had no practical experience of the world. The City of Sorcerers, while a splendid place for magickers to ponder mysteries of the world, hardly trained them for the rigors of Chaos. That Len had survived several days on his own did count in his favor, but the last thing Tyrchon wanted was for trouble to start and Len to spend valuable time trying to dream a solution to the problem. Ultimately, if he felt they were nothing more than dream-denizens, he would have no reason to do anything but act as a spectator in whatever adventure unfolded for them.

Despite that reservation about him, Tyrchon found himself inclined toward liking Len. Unlike Shoth, Len had an openness about him that Tyrchon had never seen with any other mage. That didn't make him exactly guileless, but he did lack the air of superiority that many mages sought to project. Tyrchon remembered quite well that after Ghislaine had already decided the group would travel together toward the east, Shoth felt it necessary to reconfirm that decision, projecting the image that he was somehow in charge of the guards' expedition.

Jhesti clung to the pouch's strap, a hand raised to shade his eyes. "I know you'll be scouting, Tyrchon, but if you need a spare pair of eyes, I'm available."

"Your offer is appreciated, Jhesti."

Len smiled. "Say the word, and he's yours."

"I'll leave him with you for now, Len." Tyrchon smiled, then turned and bowed to Xoayya as she descended the stairs. "Good morning to you, Lady Xoayya."

She smiled broadly at him, causing his stomach to tighten a bit. "And to you, Tyrchon. I feel wonderful this morning."

"Good. I can see you found new clothes for the journey."

"I did, with Len's help." She had changed into clothes a bit more practical than those she had worn to this point. From somewhere she had found a good pair of walking boots that encased her legs in leather up to the knees. A bright blue blouse, a bit big for her, had been cinched at her waist with a thick belt. The blouse hung beneath it, covering the top of black pants. A green kerchief covered her head like a skullcap and was knotted beneath a thick red ponytail. "A wardrobe he has up there will provide you with the clothes you want for a journey. It even included this kerchief, but that's not what you called it, is it, Len?"

The black-haired man smiled. "It's a do-rag, but kerchief is fine." Len looked at Tyrchon. "You can go try it if you want."

"Thank you, but I'm fine." The wolf-warrior's jaw opened in a smile. "Whatever magick you wove into the place managed to repair the rents in my mail."

"We should be good to go, then." Len looked over toward the doorway. "What's going on?"

"I don't know." Tyrchon raced past him and outside as the surprised shouts of some of the Guards reached him. He came out into the little valley before the Sanctuary and immediately drew his sword. He held up a hand to forestall Len and Xoayya from following him any farther. "I don't know what it is, but we'll deal with it soon enough."

Two of the Guards brandished axes and were taking wild swings at a metal beast with four legs and an impossibly flat, wide neck. Though Tyrchon could see no eyes on the creature, nor a head for that matter, it somehow managed to sense the ax blows coming in at it and dodged away with incredible agility. In the wake of one missed cut, the beast lashed out with a black-capped hoof and knocked one of the Guards flying.

Tyrchon started forward, but Len grabbed his sword arm. "Wait, don't hurt it. Get back from it."

The standing Guard looked at Tyrchon, then retreated a step. The beast also backed off a bit, then took a tentative step toward the Sanctuary. It lowered the end of its neck to the ground and pushed a little mound of red earth forward, then came up and began to bounce around like a happy puppy as Len approached it. The thing lowered its front end, then leaped up and ran around in a circle.

"Easy, now, boy, easy." Len held his hand out toward the thing. "I never did give you a name, did I? You're a fitting stool. What name fits?" He got a little closer, then laughed. "Fitz? That works. C'mere, Fitz, calm down."

Tyrchon watched the beast slink on its—*well, it doesn't really have a belly, does it?*—anyway, slink toward

Len, then come up, bringing its red body beneath his hand. The creature came up to Len's chest, with the neck rising six inches or so above his head. The wolf-warrior glanced over at Xoayya, but she just shrugged.

Len looked back at them. "Fitz here came through with me and Jhesti. He saved my life when I ran into this little six-limbed thing about so tall—Fitz was more the size of a dog then."

"It killed a *Hobmotli*?"

"Fitz helped. He stopped it from stabbing me, then I kicked it, and it fell partially into a fast zone—I guess that's what you would call it, right?" Len smiled sheepishly. "I guess Chaos killed it. Anyway, Fitz here went out grazing about this time yesterday and just got back. That's good, too, because he can haul some of our equipment, or let Xoayya ride if she gets tired."

Xoayya looked closely at the thing, then shook her head. "Not me, I think."

"Having the help will be a big advantage." Tyrchon reached down and helped the kicked Guard to his feet. "Let's get everyone else rounded up, and we're off."

Tyrchon started out leading the way, but by midafternoon Ghislaine sent two of her people forward to replace him. He returned to the group's main body and dropped back to where Xoayya walked, keeping pace with Fitz. Len and Shoth walked ahead of them, while Ghislaine and Nagrendra trailed behind. Two of the remaining Guards made up the rear guard and the other two warded the flanks.

"Not convinced it's time to ride yet?"

Xoayya gave him a sidelong look that would have incinerated him were it not accompanied by a smile. "Are you suggesting I can't keep up?"

"That you are able to is obvious, but the journey

will be wearing. No one would fault you if you did ride."

"I know, but I'm not going to." She lifted her chin. "I've not seen myself riding, I don't feel I should be riding, so I won't."

"That's interesting."

"What is?"

Tyrchon scratched at his throat. "It occurred to me that your belief in predestination parallels Len's belief that all of this is a dream."

Her blue eyes became narrow crescents of color. "I don't see it."

"Your belief says that because all the choices have already been made, you are absolved of any responsibility for your life and actions. With Len, because all of this is a dream, he isn't really responsible for any of it. It is all a fantasy, entirely unreal, so what happens is beyond his control. For that reason he doesn't have any responsibility here."

"I can see how you made the connection." She glanced up at him, her eyes searching his face for something. "It's a very interesting thought. I don't think I agree with it, though, because I *do* feel responsible toward you and the others. I don't know all of what will happen to me, but I know there will be sadness and regret in my life. How can I not feel that sadness if I don't feel responsible?"

"Or, if you *do* feel that sadness, how can you truly live a predestined life?"

Xoayya blinked at him. "What?"

"Back in the cave you said that you had chosen to live more of your life, to become more involved and engaged with it."

"I remember."

"Good." Tyrchon frowned as he gathered his thoughts. "So what is the purpose of emotion in a life where every choice is already made? If life is already plotted out, and we can do nothing to change it, what is the value of regret or remorse or anxiety? I can understand the idea of positive emotions being rewards to us for enduring a life where we can make no difference, but why the negative? Is it to punish us for things over which we have no control?"

Xoayya pressed a hand to her lips. "Or are the negative emotions goads to prevent us from repeating mistakes, and positive emotions reward to encourage us to continue making the right ones?"

"That idea seems to make a lot of sense to me, Xoayya."

She shook her head. "You're thinking emotions are for *us*, but perhaps they serve another purpose. Suppose the gods feed off our emotions, and all the conflicting ones provide a meal as varied as those we had back in the Sanctuary."

Tyrchon thought for a moment, then nodded. He conceded her point because it was perfectly valid. Looking at things from his own point of view, emotions had to be important to him. For Xoayya, they could be god-food or any number of other things unrelated to her directly. "Yours is an excellent point."

"As were your points." She smiled at him. "I'd not have thought a philosopher existed beneath that fierce exterior."

"No, I don't imagine many would think that. Including myself." Tyrchon nodded and looked ahead as the trail took them up along a ridgeline. He realized that until he had begun to think about Xoayya he had packed away most of his emotions. All of them, save those necessary for survival, had been stuffed back into the recesses of his mind. *I lowered myself to a more primal level and thought only about those things that increased my chances for survival. Debating questions of philosophy are not necessary for survival.*

Shutting down his emotions had also enabled him to travel alone through Chaos. His detachment from others freed him of all sorts of anxieties and distractions. It wasn't until now, talking to her, that he recalled he was once capable of more intellectual pursuits. He had tricked himself into thinking this gradual shutting down of his emotions was really just the death of idealism as realism and cynicism grew in him.

He felt Xoayya's hand on his shoulder. "It is a new side of you, Tyrchon. I think it is a good side. You should have shared it with the world before."

"I did, once, but that was many journeys into Chaos ago." He shrugged. "Discussing the fine points of philosophy is seldom a pastime when you're waiting for Chademons to ambush you."

"Locke and I managed to discuss it a bit on the trip here."

"The two of you are young and were excited about your journey." He looked down at her and flashed a little tooth. "After you have been in Chaos a while you certainly can be surprised by things you find here, but mostly you get a feel for the absolute hatred everything here has for you. It tends to settle you down into thinking about tactics and how you're never coming to Chaos again if you survive this one last expedition."

"I can understand that, I suppose." She looked up at him. "And forgive me for saying I never expected to hear philosophy from you. I never thought you were stupid, and I know that's how that sounded."

He barked out a laugh. "I do not bleed; therefore, I am not wounded."

"Good, I wouldn't want to hurt you."

"Nor I, you." His ears flicked forward as he heard something running hard toward the group. He looked along the ridgeline and saw one of the two Guards making her way back to the group's main body. Tyrchon studied the scout's backtrail, but saw no sign of anything chasing her. Nor did he see any sign of the other Guard scout.

Ghislaine jogged up toward her scout, and Tyrchon followed on her heels. "Irin, report."

The blond woman bent over, hands on her knees, and struggled to catch her breath. "We found something. Yrl is still up there, where the ridge dips down. The valley, it's all shiny."

"Shiny?" Ghislaine eyed her guard closely. "Care to be more specific?"

Sweat streaking her face, the woman looked up. "It is shiny, as if the Reptiad's scales were spread all over it. It's a small valley. Hillsides look as if they have had silver poured over them. Down in the center there are spikes and crystals. It is the most incredible thing I have seen in Chaos."

Tyrchon squatted, then looked up at her. "Any movement? Any sign of life?"

Irin shook her head, then knit her brow. "I didn't see anything, but the crystals; they looked like they could have grown there. There seemed to be a pattern, so I don't think it was an accident. I also don't think the place is peaceful. Just the look of it is upsetting."

Ghislaine looked down at him. "What do you think?"

"Nothing beyond the obvious." Tyrchon shook his

head. "Whatever it is, I'm willing to bet it's our goal. When I started out, the thought of something that hurt Lord Fialchar made me feel good. I'm fairly certain what we're going to run into over that rise will make me rethink that position a whole bunch."

18

The valley spread out below him took Len's breath away. The narrow valley's high walls met at both ends, providing neither entrance nor egress for a river or glacier or anything else that might have carved it out of the ground. Its appearance almost suggested that some heavenly pickax had gouged the valley into life. *This is not a natural formation.*

Viewing it as a wound in the flesh of the planet made a lot of sense because the valley itself seemed formed of scar tissue. Glass covered it, every little bump and hole, every crack and crevasse. The sun's dying rays flashed maroon-and-gold highlights from peaks and edges. The valley looked to Len, for the most part, as if molten glass had been sprayed over it, then artisans had gone in and had cut away the excess so the glass reflected the land it covered, but only in very precise, angular forms.

He could have found the whole thing indescribably

beautiful except for the cluster of crystalline towers at the valley's lowest point. Tall and sharp, they jutted out at all angles, like a tangle of crystal thorns. The light other surfaces reflected tended to concentrate in and run through them like blood running down a sword. A phalanx of glass spears, the bristle of glass seemed to be anger and fury made physical.

Worse yet, the breeze wending its way through the valley made the crystal hum. Len recalled with delight running a wet finger around the rim of a crystal goblet to make it sing, but these towers shrieked and moaned. The sound they produced would have formed the perfect sound track for a film about human misery, running from Nazi death camps to the killing fields of Kampuchea or mass graves in the Balkans.

He closed his eyes and would have clapped his hands over his ears, but he could feel the mournful humming resonating through his chest. "This is horrible."

Tyrchon crouched beside him. "Is this something you dreamed?"

"This would qualify as a nightmare, no doubt about it." Len sat down beside Tyrchon. "As it is, though, I do recognize aspects of it."

The wolf-warrior flicked an ear in his direction. "What seems familiar?"

Len pointed at the crystal towers. "Where I come from we don't have magick, but we have found ways to do things almost as evil as the Shattering. We have industries that produce weapons and other things that are deadly poisonous, and will be for tens and hundreds of centuries. Some of them are so lethal that a droplet on your skin would kill you in seconds."

Tyrchon turned and looked carefully at Len. "Seconds?"

"Yes."

"Why would anyone produce such a weapon?"

"The Empire and Chaos each hate each other; so it is between groups of nations in my world." Len shook his head. "Anyway, there are disarmament movements that want to get rid of these sorts of things—and not all of them are weapons. Some of it is just radioactive waste—um, sort of like concentrated Chaos that's really bad for you. They wanted to find one place, in the middle of nowhere, to store all of this stuff, but they also realized that because it will be deadly for twenty-five thousand years or more, they needed to be able to post some sort of warning that people would understand even if they couldn't read."

He pointed again toward the towers. "They suggested a design of towers that looked like thorns, but all twisted and odd and forbidding. They wanted anyone who looked at it to know this was a bad place. The lights down there, looking like blood as they slide down the spikes, and the sounds, that's really good stuff to add. I don't know about you, but I don't want to go down there."

Ghislaine walked over and worked her way down-slope enough to keep her head at a level with Len's. "We are going to have to go down there anyway."

"Did you miss what I just said? That's a very bad place."

"I heard you, but that doesn't really make any difference." The tall woman crossed her arms over her chest. "We have to determine what's down there and what sort of threat it might or might not pose to the Empire. We have a responsibility to do that, since this could be something even more dangerous than the B*harashadi* or even Lord Disaster. I've been through this area before and, I would swear an oath that I've even stood right here, but I never saw this valley."

Tyrchon picked up a couple of small rocks and tossed them farther down the hillside. "I've scouted this area, and I *know* I've never seen this place before. If what Fialchar said about it is true, the Chaos storm came to this point, then all of the energy in it was pulled into this area."

Nagrendra came up behind them, casting his shadow over Len and Tyrchon. "I shall add another thing for you to consider. You've noticed how the light is reflected toward the towers, then bleeds down them?"

"Oh, man, I should have seen that." Len smacked his forehead with the heel of his hand. "This is a big solar collector. It's pulling in the sunlight and feeding it down into the heart of the valley."

Nagrendra's heavy hand landed on Len's shoulder. "Very good, Len. My point is this: there are enchantments that use the energy of the sun to help them work, the same way other basic elements like wind and fire might be used. Something is actively going on down there, and it would be irresponsible not to note that the reddish color shown in the light is commonly associated with Chaos-based spells."

Len looked around and back at all three of them. "So, knowing there is danger there, you're just going to wander down there? You're going to risk death because of what might be a trick of light?"

Ghislaine shook her head. "We're not stupid, Len. I will leave two of my Guards here to watch us and report back to the Empire if we do not return. We will explore because we must."

Tyrchon arched another stone out to where it bounced off glass mounds. "And it is not really a risk to our lives. Yes, we could die; but what we learn might prevent others from dying. There have been plenty of people who have ventured into Chaos at the risk of their lives so that we would have a chance at a future. Now it is our turn to hazard making the sacrifice for others. And it is not that we don't love life or don't want to continue living, it's just that we don't choose to live as timid creatures waiting for something to happen to us."

Nagrendra laughed. "We would prefer to happen to it."

Their earnest declarations hammered Len and impressed him. Here he was, in his dream, creating characters who had more convictions when facing a life threat than he'd ever evidenced when dealing with the most trivial of decisions. *I equivocate when trying to figure out if I want Junior Mints or Raisinets at a movie. None of these guys would, nor would they let Corbett steal their ideas.* "I suppose you want me to go down there with you?"

Tyrchon nodded. "You were able to understand how the valley was collecting sunlight, which means to me you're intelligent and/or some of your memories from before are coming through and you remember things about magick."

Len frowned. *What is it that my subconscious wants here? If I'm to return to life, do I need to actually live a life, take some chances? Am I in a coma because my whole life has been a coma? Or am I simply searching for anything that looks like an escape route from this whole weird fantasy? Does it matter?*

He couldn't answer any of those questions, but it was pretty certain an answer did matter. "I guess I can go down there. I'd make one suggestion, though."

Ghislaine raised an eyebrow. "Yes?"

"If the valley truly is funneling energy into that centerpoint, we'd best go in when the sun is down."

Tyrchon slapped him on the back. "Smart. We'll see what's down there, what's happening, and maybe, if we're smart enough, we can figure out what it means to the Empire."

As she said she would, Ghislaine left two of her Guards behind to carry news of their expedition back to the Empire while the rest of them descended into the glass valley toward the crystal spikes. Even with the sun having set, the crystalline towers still pulled in starlight and channeled it down into the ground. The march down to the valley's center took longer than Len would have expected, and the glassy spires ended up being far taller than he had thought they would be.

And his sense of foreboding grew proportionately.

It seemed to Len rather obvious that they weren't supposed to be there. Everyone appeared to be hyperalert, and Len couldn't help feeling he was being watched on the journey. This feeling was aided and abetted by warped and fragmentary reflections from the multifaceted landscape. He would catch a quick glimpse of himself, then his face would race along like a rabbit through the glass. Each time it did that he felt as if a little piece of his soul had been nibbled away.

Tyrchon led the way into the forest of crystals. Picking a path through them was not easy. The mineral spikes had edges sharper than razors, and Shoth hissed as a casual brushing of his arm past one opened his sleeve and traced a bloody red line across his flesh. Len got the impression that Shoth would have turned and run at that point, but to do so would have torn him apart before he got five steps. The blond sorcerer calmed himself and kept going forward, but he took incredible care slipping through tight spots.

To Len the forest almost seemed like a winter won-derland, but without the cold. Regardless, he felt chilled, as if the crystals were willing to accept heat instead of light and were sucking it out of him. Even the blinking eyeballs on his boots seemed to be reacting sluggishly, as if falling asleep because of the chill. *If magickal energy is as good as sunlight, perhaps we're all being drained.*

The trail opened out into a small ledge that overlooked a deep hole. Crystals lined all sides of it, such that falling into it would guarantee a wholesale butchering before the person reached bottom—*however far down that is.* The image struck Len as the sort of thing he imagined a garbage disposal to be, though this was far larger and beautiful. *Chances are I saw something like this in some comic book and am only now remembering it.*

Given their location, however, that was not the most curious thing about the ledge. In the center of it stood a crystalline podium. A square base upon which a speaker might stand to address a crowd supported a slender crystal pole that stood about three and a half feet tall. The top of the pole widened out slightly into a disc. The flat disc had been incised with the crest Len had created.

He crossed to the podium, with Shoth trailing in his wake. Len noticed two faint impressions in the top of the base unit and traced a finger around the heel imprint of one. "This matches the boots I'm wearing." He glanced at Shoth. "Think I should stand here?"

The Warder's gray eyes narrowed. "I don't know. I would be careful."

"We know I'm going to do it at some point." Len straightened up and mounted the box, resting his hands on the crest. He felt a little tickle in his palms, and saw a jagged golden trickle of lightning sink through the podium shaft, but nothing more happened. He stepped back off and shrugged. "Nothing happening here."

Xoayya pointed at the podium shaft. "Not exactly nothing. I saw the light."

Shoth leaned forward and looked at the crest. "What did you try to do when you touched the crest?"

"Try to do? I didn't try to do anything, I just touched it." Len frowned. "What should I have tried to do?"

"Cast a spell."

"Do you want to try it?" He sat on the edge of the base unit and tugged his right boot off. "You're welcome to give it a go."

Shoth shook his head. "I don't think so. My feet are bigger than yours."

Nagrendra lumbered over. "We can squeeze your feet in there, just for this."

Len shook his head and fished his shoe sizer from the pouch he wore. "Not going to happen, Nagrendra. Trust me, I do this for a living. Shoth, take off your boot and bring your foot over here."

The Warder did as he was told. Len fixed his heel in the cup, adjusted the width indicator, and moved the toe-knuckle pointer to the right place. "See, he's an 11-D, I'm a 9-B." Len put the boot on the sizer to show how much smaller it was. He adjusted the width and length indicators down to 9-B, fitting the boot perfectly, then brought it up to 11-D. As he did so, the boot grew to the appropriate size. "Now that's different."

Xoayya crouched and looked at the resized boot. "It occurs to me that the Dashan may have created this podium as a locking mechanism that only he could open. Len, you are only one half of him, as is Shoth. Perhaps if you both stand on it, each of you wearing one boot, and touch the crest, Shoth can cast a spell and you can help power it. The device might recognize the both of you as the Dashan."

"Not a bad idea." Len smiled and tucked the sizer away in his pouch. "I'm willing to give it a go."

Shoth remained very still for a moment, then reluctantly nodded. "I will try." He slipped on the boot and stepped onto the podium base. He placed his right foot in the appropriate impression. Len stood beside him, grabbing Shoth's belt at the small of his back to steady himself. Shoth did the same to Len's belt with his left hand, then, together, they touched the crest.

Whereas before a thin tendril of lightning wormed its way through the post, now the whole crystal became a shaft of golden light. It sank into the ground for a moment, then shot out to form a disc hovering above the central hole. The two of them stepped back from the podium, but the disc remained in place.

Tyrchon glanced at the disc and the hole beneath it. "I believe we are meant to ride this down."

Nagrendra waved a hand through the air, causing the gold disc to glow with a blue light for a moment. "Simple conveyance magick. I trust it. It can carry all of us."

Ghislaine sketched a mocking bow. "After you."

Everyone piled onto the disc, including Fitz. Len was last to get on and slowly shook his head.

Xoayya smiled at him. "Something wrong?"

"No, not really, I guess." He shrugged. "I'm just remembering a story I read about a girl going down a rabbit hole. I'm wondering if that's what put this in place."

"Was it a bad story?"

"No, a classic and well loved." Len smiled. "Should make for an interesting trip if it is the source."

Shoth raised an eyebrow. "No danger, then?"

"Not really." Len hesitated. "Then again, if the Queen of Hearts wants to play croquet, run. It'll save time later."

19

A shiver ran through Shoth Churgûn as the golden disc began its stately descent into the hole. He looked up and watched the crystals lining the tunnel slowly strangle the night sky. Shoth had never thought of himself as afraid of small dark places, but descending through the tunnel made his flesh crawl. He wasn't certain why it made him so uneasy, but he had the unsettling feeling his fear was based on something he remembered from the Dashan's life.

Distinct bits and pieces of things did not come back to Shoth per se, but he had impressions that bordered on familiarity. In some ways he could see in the arrangement of crystals in the tunnel some of the nuances he'd read in the crest. He could not remember having created the tunnel or having placed the gems, but he recognized his own handiwork.

Below the disc the spikes retreated into the walls to allow passage, and above it they grew back in again.

They looked to Shoth like so many teeth prepared hungrily to gnaw apart anything that did not have the right to pass through here. *There is no doubt this was meant to keep people out, but it also serves to keep something in.*

He looked over at Len. "You've been here before, haven't you?"

The black-haired man shrugged. "I've seen things like it, but I can't say I was ever here." He hesitated, then looked down. "Can't deny it, either, I guess."

Shoth nodded and hugged his arms around himself. "Not a place I think I want to visit long or again."

Len nodded. "Yeah, this is kind of like a ride you'd expect to see in a punk Disneyland."

Shoth smiled indulgently, getting meaning for the sentence from tone and context. "That sounds unpleasant."

"Hardly my idea of fun." Len held his hands out, grabbing the shoulders of both Xoayya and Shoth as the disc came to an abrupt stop. "Whoa, looks like we're in the basement."

The company filed off the golden disc, Fitz's clanking footfalls echoing through the hall as he worked his way down a set of stone steps. The stairs brought them into a reasonable-sized room that could have housed several times their number without difficulty. No windows allowed them to see out, but a circular doorway fitted with a black stone slab suggested there actually was an outside to be seen. Shoth approached the door and saw the crest worked into the heart of it.

"I believe I can open this, if you wish."

Ghislaine nodded. "If you please, Warder."

"Wait." Len held up a hand. "Since we don't know what's out there, and we might just have to run, can I get my boot back?"

Everyone laughed, and Shoth felt somewhat relieved at getting the boot off his foot. Len resized it and pulled it on, tossing the boot he had previously worn back to Shoth. The Warder put it back on, then traced his right index finger along the crest. Finally, he ran his finger around the circle to the right, and the door rolled away to that side.

"Oh, my," gasped Xoayya. "I never would have thought anything could be so beautiful."

Shoth nodded all but unconsciously as he stumbled out and onto the ivory path that split emerald fields. The path itself seemed truly to be made of ivory, one long piece without a sign of joinery anywhere. The ivory seemed to give a little with Shoth's steps and push back slightly as he stepped forward. It added spring to his step and made him feel a bit more energized.

He knelt at the path's edge and peered closely at the green grasses waving with unseen breezes. That near to them he saw they were not truly plants, but thin slivers of a verdant crystal. The grasses swayed fluidly, mimicking their botanical counterparts as far as the eye was concerned. Shoth wanted to reach out and touch the plants, but the slender nature of the leaves suggested they would cut even more cleanly than the thorn that had gouged him above.

Glancing back up toward the surface, he saw a limitless sky above him, all blue and wonderful, the way it was back in the Empire. The building he had just stepped from had been fashioned after a gatehouse, with crystalline ivy wending its way up the towers. Over the top of the tower he saw nothing but sky, but then he looked a bit more closely. The blue scales that made up the skyvault likewise coated the tunnel through which they had descended, hiding it from all but the most diligent scrutiny.

Tree groves flanked either side of the fields through which the pathway ran. In the distance they appeared to be perfectly normal, with a fine combination of pines and oaks and scrub brush, but Shoth felt certain they, too, were crystal simulacra of the real things. He also suspected that somewhere in their depths were the walls of the cavern in which they stood. *The place is huge, but must have its limits.*

The question of exactly what those limits might be dwindled as Shoth peered further down the pathway and saw what had to be the most magnificent structure he had ever seen. In general shape it appeared to be a massive castle, with towers and battlements, flying buttresses and crenelations, but there ended its familiarity. The building had been constructed with a lattice of crystal beams and blocks. Amethyst and ruby, sapphire and diamond, the castle could have been some mad jeweler's plaything, but only if it remained on the horizon and small enough to fit in the palm of his hand.

Shoth straightened up and looked at the others. "You've all realized by now that we're inside a giant cavern."

Tyrchon lifted his muzzle and sniffed. "The air is fresh, with much of it coming in through the tunnel."

The Mountain Guards' leader pointed at the castle. "From here, I can't see if anything is moving in the castle."

The Reptiad started off down the road toward the castle. "Let us go get a better look."

"Hang on a minute, Nagrendra." Len stood in the middle of the road with his arms crossed over his chest. He would have looked very heroic, had Fitz not laid himself at Len's feet. "You may look as if you belong in their realm, but I have the distinct impression I'm a little less than welcome."

Tyrchon barked a laugh. "You're in Chaos, Len. You should always feel that way."

Xoayya nodded. "I do not think we have that much to worry about right now. I have seen Tyrchon, Nagrendra, and me walking in surroundings that look like this. We were in no distress."

One of the troopers joked, "So the three of you are safe."

Nagrendra shook his head. "Practical point, people: if we can see the castle, anyone there can see us, and that's not the only way they might know we are here. For those of you who are not magickally inclined, this place all but oozes magick."

Ghislaine smiled. "The nature of the path and the grasses tipped me to that fact, Nagrendra."

"Good, then think about this: anyone who created this place, or can maintain it, would have been powerful enough to slay us where we stand." The Reptiad waved a hand toward the castle. "I would hate to see what happens if our host thinks we are not approaching with suitable alacrity."

Although the castle was still a half mile away, two details about it stunned Shoth. The first was its size. The palace in Garikopolis had never been described as small—save, perhaps, in comparison to the Imperial Palace in Herakopolis—but it would have easily fit inside the walls of Castle Corona. That name had come to Shoth as they drew closer to the structure. While he could find no sun in the false sky, the building itself seemed to glow with radiated light. The aura it projected seemed to shift with perspectives, yet focusing on it remained hauntingly difficult.

The second thing that impressed Shoth was the nature of the work being done on the castle itself, and the workers being pressed into service. The workers resembled oversize ants made of crystal that, he assumed, would come up to about waist height on him. They varied in color, with most of it carried in their abdomens. In fact, it seemed to him, their color depended upon their diets, and that diet, in turn, determined the color in which they worked on the project. As nearly as he could tell, the crystal blocks and beams were not quarried somewhere, but spun by the workers out of slender threads they tugged from their abdomens. Their heads worked back and forth so that their powerful mandibles could massage the threads into place. *Once it hardens, you have this stone.*

The crystalline nature of their bodies made it difficult to spot them in the distance, but up close they seemed to swarm everywhere over the castle. Some tore down bits, while others built back up, making things bigger and more complex. They worked quickly and, it seemed, flawlessly.

Nagrendra led the way into the huge gate and courtyard beyond it. The manor house rose high enough to top the tallest wall, but only just barely. Archways at either side allowed ingress to the courtyard beyond it, but a broad stairway narrowed to the front door a good twenty feet above the courtyard itself. Crystal creatures that looked like a cross between a lion and a mantis warded each side of the stairs. In the Empire, Shoth would have assumed they were just carvings, but here he wondered if they were not living sentinels.

More of the construction workers moved through the yard, and seemed to be the only living creatures in the courtyard. Shoth saw a number of other crystalline creatures—all resembling bugs or creatures Shoth had seen in the Empire—but none was an exact match or mobile. The insectoid creatures looked more natural to him than any other, but they tended toward angles and unusual body types well suited to being rendered in crystal. Other things, like reptiles and birds, also did not suffer much in translation. Mammalian life, however, seemed trapped in the stone. A glass cage held a ruby bear, but the stone could not seem to capture adequately the beast's pure power and majesty.

Shoth looked around to see if he could find any human constructs, but he saw none at first. Then, at the head of the stairs, he saw a woman who appeared so normal to be jarringly out of place. Tall and fit, with long golden hair that fell to her waist, she smiled openly and began to descend toward them. The dress she wore bore the unmistakable pattern of a sea-python's skin, but the creature that gave up its flesh to make that dress would have been large enough to swallow a small boat. The pattern, which had undulating indigo lines running up and down the dress, with lighter blue defining the midline of her body, did not allow for the dress to have been fitted together of pieces. And the boots she wore, which disappeared beneath the skirt at midcalf, had likewise been fashioned from the same skin.

"Welcome, my first visitors, welcome." She opened her arms as she approached. "Though it seems as if no time at all has passed, I know I have been without company for too long. Welcome to my sanctuary."

Nagrendra bowed at the foot of the stairs. "You honor us to welcome us into your home."

She stopped and regarded him carefully. "Those words, you are from the islands. I was from Thas."

The Reptiad nodded. "It was my home as well."

"Very interesting." She watched him, her eyes glowing with *Chaosfire*. She blinked, then smiled at the rest of them. "Forgive me, but I pondered the chances of meeting a Thassian in my first assembly of guests. I am Spiriastar, late of Thas—I suspect very late of it."

The company introduced themselves, and she graciously welcomed everyone, leaving Len to introduce himself last. "I'm Len Fong. I'm from San Rafael."

She lifted a pert nose. "You look the image of someone I once knew. My Dashan."

Len blinked. "Dashan?"

Shoth smiled. "Perhaps, Mistress Spiriastar, you could tell us about the Dashan."

"*The* Dashan?" She laughed delightfully. "He was not the only Dashan, just the last and most promising. And you needn't breathe so much reverence into that word."

The Warder frowned. "Dashan?"

"Yes. It's simply old Thassian for 'aide.'" She pointed at Len. "He looks the image of my last apprentice. He even wears the same sort of boots."

Xoayya looked from Len to Spiriastar and back. "You are telling us that your Dashan was an apprentice? When was that?"

Spiriastar shook her head. "I have no way of knowing, child. I don't recall seeing Dashan after the Shattering."

Shoth's mouth hung open. "You were there?"

"Of course, I was there." She smiled proudly. "I helped create the Seal of Reality. I dealt mostly with the aspects of time that were woven into it. The key to my work was discovering how one moment related to the next, so the sequence and speed would remain unbroken and constant. When it was shattered, I wondered what would happen to time."

"It yet exists, Lady Spiriastar." Nagrendra's tongue

flickered out through the air. "In Chaos it passes differently in different zones, but it still exists. On Thas, when it was still under the sway of Chaos, it moved swiftly." He pressed a hand to his own chest. "This is the change it wrought in us."

The sorceress smiled carefully. "Some of us theorized that in Chaos men would learn of their own true nature. Is that what happened, or is it too soon to tell?"

Shoth narrowed his eyes. "The Shattering occurred five centuries ago. We've pushed Chaos back from some of the Empire—most of the core provinces anyway. Many people were changed by it, and some yet are today. This we have long known as true."

"Five centuries?" She said it with an air of nonconcern that surprised Shoth. *She has less concern over the passing of five centuries than Myat would have of being five minutes late for a rendezvous.* Spiriastar's smile broadened. "If it has been five centuries, I should think you will have much to discuss with me over dinner. In the last five hundred years dinner has not been abolished, has it?"

"By no means, my lady." Nagrendra started up the steps and extended his arm to her. "And Thassian hospitality is still legendary, so this is a dinner to which all of us shall look forward and enjoy."

20

The number of things that struck Len as odd in Spiriastar's realm quickly rose into the tens and approached the hundreds. It seemed to him as if every little thing was wrong, yet when he tried to examine any *one* thing, the *wrongness* of it would, at best, be considered trivial. He didn't like what he was seeing, but until he mounted the manor-house steps and began to ascend, he wasn't able to put his finger on the core problem.

The core problem, he decided, *is that I don't recognize any of this*. Up to this point he had been able to rationalize his whole experience as being a dream because he could pick out things here and there that he knew from the real world. Even the question of whether or not he had invented things or was remembering things from a previous life faded in importance when he recognized it as an added twist on *The Wizard of Oz*. The movie certainly left the existence of Oz in question, but the whole of the novel series did not. *And this whole adventure wouldn't play well to Pink Floyd's* Dark Side of the Moon *anyway.*

Spiriastar's realm provided him no clear clues to where he might have seen it before or thought of it before. There were plenty of stories of whole realms being found in caves that looked like the out-of-doors, but none was exactly like this. There were ant-creatures in many stories, but none like the ones running around in this realm. There were magnificent crystal castles in stories, but none exactly like this. And none of that would have bothered him, but he found the whole of the place chillingly familiar. The sense of déjà vu would not leave him.

His ability to recognize and place things had been the lifeline binding him to the idea that he was dreaming. He admitted that his consciousness of being in a dream state had all but vanished. He was, for all intents and purposes, living in this, his fantasy world, but the concept of its being all a dream was his safety switch. Whenever things got nasty he could just step away and note it was a dream. It didn't matter.

Except to those people here who are my friends. The realization that he considered Tyrchon, Nagrendra, Xoayya, Shoth, and the others friends surprised him. He hadn't spent much time with them, but their open acceptance of him was something he had not expected. Len had always thought himself too ordinary to attract much attention. While he always had friends, they tended to be situational: there because of school or work or the neighborhood. Few of those friendships had survived separation, however, leaving him alone to make new friends.

For a half second it struck him as completely odd that he could consider figments of his imagination friends. After that, the whole idea seemed very right, and certainly within his normal experience. He'd felt as if characters in books and movies were friends—or, at least, he felt friendly toward them. Len knew very well the difference between fantasy and reality, but the fact was that characters and people who exhibited all the traits and behaviors one wants in a friend produce that same mental reaction to them, whether they are real or not.

And he couldn't shake the impression that the people he had met here were real. *And that means* . . .

Further erosion of his dream defense ended as Spiriastar conducted them into her manor, and its sheer scale stunned Len. The main doorway opened onto a broad walkway that arched over series of plateaus descending into the earth. The whole of the main floor appeared to have been laid out like a chessboard, with squares sinking ten, twenty, or thirty feet in a haphazard pattern. Travel between levels was facilitated by stairwells carved inside the tallest towers and the massive pillars that blossomed upward to support the ceiling. Had the floor shifted so all squares became even, no sign would have been left of the previous arrangement.

He was pretty sure he would have pegged it as nothing more than an Escheresque maze, but the riot of colors and variety of alcoves that housed works of art made it all seem like a vast museum. The walkway carried them above the main floor at a distance that didn't allow him a close look at anything, but the layout and lighting meant the displays were there to be seen and admired. He stopped and tried to make out detail, but Fitz nudged him so he'd catch up with the others.

The other end of the arch ended at a gray-marble landing. Beyond it stood two doors made of bronze that had to be at least thirty feet tall. Len couldn't imagine the antlings having eaten copper and tin, then spinning the doors into existence, but it seemed as if anything might be possible in this realm. As they approached the doors, two of the portals retracted slowly and in a very stately manner into the walls themselves. Beyond them Len saw a banquet room that at first glance seemed simply enormous. As they got closer to it, however, the room appeared to shrink to more intimate proportions.

The dining room seemed to impress the others as they filed in and made their way around the table. Various nooks and alcoves housed a variety of artifacts, from urns and other items of pottery to a bust of a woman. Around the bust's neck hung a necklace fitted with one exquisite baroque pearl. Len almost thought it was the same piece he'd admired in the window of the jewelry store next to Dancing Joker Shoes, but this piece had a halo of opals surrounding it, and the pearl was as big around as the last joint of his thumb.

The table itself had been set for twelve, and Len found himself being waved to the chair that sat opposite the head of the table. Spiriastar smiled beneficently at him. "Seeing you there makes it possible to believe no time has passed since I last saw my Dashan."

Len nodded and looked down to break eye contact. He noticed the place settings and serving dishes seemed identical to those in Fong's Sanctuary. He could even see the crest worked into the engraving on the utensils and serving-platter covers. "A gift from the Dashan?"

She nodded very serenely. "He wanted me to be certain to be sated when I was hungry. Now I can share his largesse with you. Please, be seated. You shall eat, and in the meantime I shall make certain my servants have prepared proper resting chambers for you."

The meal went well for the most part. The only real negative came when one of the antlings tried to pour wine from a pitcher into a goblet. The antling seemed unable to judge flow rate and sufficiency, causing the wine to spill across the table and into Irin's lap. Spiriastar apologized and, with the most casual flick of a finger, cleaned the mess up. They poured their own wine after that, and Len imagined the antling being assigned to some hideous duty for punishment.

Because of the nature of the Dashan's serving dishes, everyone got what they most desired and had fun sharing different things. Len took great delight in remembering some of the best, really hot Thai meals he'd ever had. The lemongrass soup left his lips numb and could have etched steel. Shoth tried it and immediately broke out into a frightful sweat, while Tyrchon was left panting. Len toned the fire level down as others refused to try things, which injected fun back into the party because Imperial cuisine was not terribly experimental or spicy as far as Len was concerned.

The wine, a deep red that wasn't as dry as Len expected, flowed freely, and tongues became loosened. Everyone took turns sharing stories that were funny or heroic. The one that caught everyone by surprise was Ghislaine's relating of Shoth's killing the *tauroch*. Tyrchon nodded his admiration to Shoth, and Nagrendra applauded him. Spiriastar studied the blond mage for a moment, then raised her cup toward him.

"Your heroism and daring belie the life path you have chosen, Shoth Churgûn."

Shoth blushed. "It just proves I can be as foolish as anyone else." He looked around at the rest of his companions. "Please, don't relate this story of me any-more, lest others come to expect me to repeat that act."

Xoayya smiled sweetly. "You would have us take mercy on the *tauroch* population?"

The blond mage nodded thankfully. "Exactly, Mistress Xoayya. That is what I wish."

An antling rose on its two hind legs like a trained dog and balanced itself against Spiriastar's chair. A sweet scent—terribly complex and gone so quickly Len never had a chance to identify it—wafted down from the head of the table. Len would have thought he was imagining things, but he saw Tyrchon sniff at it and frown.

Spiriastar glanced at the creature, then turned to her guests. "I have been told that chambers have been prepared for all of you. It is late, and I imagine you will want to rest."

Nagrendra, seated at her immediate right, raised a hand. "Did you not want us to tell you of what has hap-pened since the Shattering?"

"I do, very much so, Nagrendra." She took his hand and squeezed it, her alabaster flesh a sharp contrast against his gray-green. "The truth of the matter is that having so many of my own kind here, in one place, is somewhat overwhelming for me. I sought to shield you from my fatigue, lest you think you have over-taxed me."

The Reptiad nodded. "And we have, of course."

"But I enjoyed every second of it. I have longed for such bright companions for an eternity." She smiled at them all, and Len felt a tightening in his belly. "I do want you to tell me of the Empire and Chaos, all you can and do know. Tomorrow, though, when we shall all be refreshed and suited to the exchange."

"Of course, Lady Spiriastar." Nagrendra looked around the room. "We thank you for your hospitality and will do all we can to repay it tomorrow."

An antling led them to their various rooms in an upper level of the west wing. Len had the distinct impression that during dinner the interior of the castle had been shifted around to create these rooms. The steps had been cantilevered into the walls, allowing them a vista of the museum below as they ascended to their accommodations.

Len gaped at everything, since the jewel-like blocks from which the building had been constructed were arrayed in a grand mosaic that reminded him of Mandelbrot patterns. It didn't strike him as at all unusual that he was seeing things associated with chaos theory here in a place called Chaos. It helped reinforce the idea that he was dreaming, but the patterns were pretty much the only thing that did.

Len started toward the doorway the antling indicated was his, but Shoth held a hand up. "What do you want?"

The Warder smiled guardedly. "A word or two, if I might."

"Sure." Len followed Shoth into his room and found himself impressed. While the room itself seemed a bit small, it did so because of the abundance of furnishings and art objects. As with other parts of the castle, alcoves and recesses housed statues and murals, pottery and jewels. The furnishings themselves would have been dismissed as being blocky and primitive, but each appeared to have been woven by an antling artisan from pure silicon. Len had seen Christmas ornaments and delicate crystal animals that had been created from drawn glass, but never of the size of a four-poster bed or a big desk. *They look like wickerwork, but made of glass.*

He crossed to the bed and ran a hand over the coverlet. It had the feel of silk or wool. Len didn't want to know what the antlings ate to produce the softer fibers, but he had no doubt antlings had indeed been the source of the fabric. "At least we'll be warm in these beds."

Shoth hugged his arms to himself as if he was freezing. "I'm not certain I believe that." He stood opposite Len on the other side of the bed. "This is far too big for me ever to warm up."

Len smiled and fished the shoe sizer from the pouch. He pointed it at the bed and worked the length indicator down. "Hmmm, didn't work."

Shoth winced. "Actually it did. My shoes are a lot tighter now."

"Oops, should have realized you were in the line of fire." Len readjusted the size, and the pain on Shoth's face eased. "I guess it doesn't work on beds."

"Magick doesn't always work the way we want. At least you know it works on shoes." The blond magicker gave Len a brave smile. "That's not what I wanted to discuss with you, however. I wanted to ask you, what sort of feelings are you getting from our hostess?"

Len shrugged. "I don't know. There's something a little off-putting about her, but I think that's because she has this little tone in her voice when she looks at me and uses the word Dashan."

Shoth nodded. "You're not afraid of her?"

"I don't think so."

"Maybe it's just me, then."

Len put his shoe sizer away and frowned. "Want to explain?"

Shoth sighed, then pulled a chair away from the

table against the wall. "I have spent my whole life being afraid. I have done it so long I am very used to the feeling. I am a coward—and cowards are not allowed among the Matarun. Even my eyes and hair mark me as a coward and terribly unlike the other Matarun."

The sorcerer laughed and plucked at his clothes. "These rank badges, we use them to proclaim our skills and strengths within the Empire. To wear badges to which you are not entitled is a fraud punishable, in some cases, by death. Yet I am even a greater fraud because I should wear a coward's badge to show my true self, but I do not."

"What are you talking about, Shoth?" Len pointed off in the rough direction of the dining room. "I heard Ghislaine describe your killing of the *tauroch*. That was about as brave an act as I've ever heard of. That took huge stones to do that."

"I think you're confused, Len, I didn't use stones at all."

"And you're confused if you think I'm talking about rocks." Len shook his head. "I know, to kill the *tauroch* you used your bare hands."

The Warder shook his head, and a blue glow engulfed his hands. "No, I used magick."

"Ghislaine said that."

"But she only understood the half of what I did." Shoth looked down at his hands. "She saw the spell I worked on my hands to kill the beast. What she didn't see was the *other* spell I used." His left hand flicked at Len. "This was it."

Len felt a tingle, then saw that the chair Shoth had been sitting in was empty. Five feet to the right, Shoth hovered in the air in a sitting position. His hands still glowed, and his mouth moved when he spoke, though the words still seemed to come from the area of the chair.

"You see, Len, the *tauroch* saw me being five feet to the right of where I truly was. It's a simple concealment spell. It's not very useful on a foe that can think, or relies on a sense of smell or hearing. The Guards didn't know I'd cast it. I slipped past the *tauroch's* horns and killed it. It was hardly an honorable death for so noble a beast."

Len blinked, then shook his head. "It still took a lot of courage even to approach the creature. You could have been hurt."

"But that wasn't courage, it was just a greater fear winning out. I feared death less than I feared being scorned by the Matarun." Shoth clapped his hands, and his image returned to the chair. "My fear of being discovered to be a coward motivates me to do many things. In your sanctuary I created invisible walls to save myself from the *Tsvortu*, but in doing so I almost doomed myself. One of my walls prevented Ghislaine from being able to save me. If not for your Jhesti mistaking me for you and plunging a fork into the eye of a *Tsvortu*, I would have been slain."

Len looked down at the plastic figure clinging to the pouch's shoulder strap. "You did that?"

"Desperate times call for desperate measures."

The shoe salesman nodded, then raised his head in Shoth's direction. "What is it about Spiriastar that scares you?"

"It's nothing specific that I can point to." The mage knit his brows in concentration. "This is why I wanted to ask what your impression was. I am getting the feeling that my unease with her stems from impressions I still carry of the Dashan's time here. I do feel as if I have been here before. Do you?"

Len slowly nodded. "I do, but I can't recognize anything specific." He thought for a moment, then scratched at the back of his neck. "Something isn't right, but I suspect everyone save Nagrendra gets that message."

"He *does* seem to be quite taken with her, but it is said that Reptiads become rather single-minded when a female from the islands is fertile and preparing to produce a clutch."

"Short skirt and a cute smile will do it for me." Len held his hands up. "Regardless, I think you're being a bit hard on yourself on this coward thing. The fact is, you might have been afraid of all sorts of things, but when it came time to act, you acted. You had no way of knowing if your spell would really work on that *tauroch* or not. You faced down two fears at one time, right then and there."

"That's kind of you to say . . ."

"Believe it, Shoth. At least you know you're afraid. That beats most other folks by a country mile." Len pointed a finger at him. "And your fear is going to mean that you and I need to check some things out tomorrow. We need to do some fact-finding and see if we can recognize something. The Dashan clearly set the warning markers around the tunnel. We want to know why, and see if there is anything we can do to make sure his original intentions aren't violated."

"Good idea." Shoth's head came up quickly. "But what if just by coming here we've already violated those intentions?"

Len shook his head. "Then we damn well better hope we can undo what we've done and set everything to rights again. As powerful as we think the Dashan was, Spiriastar was his boss. If he wanted her bottled up here, I don't think her getting out will do anyone any good at all."

21

Tyrchon awoke more refreshed than he would have imagined possible. He recalled sleeping fitfully because of an incredible number of high-pitched squeals that rang through the building during the night. He suspected that none of the others had heard them—the benefits of the wolf's hearing turning out to be a curse in this case. The incessant shifting of walls in the castle created all manner of unusual sounds, but eventually they stopped, or he grew used to them enough to allow him to drop off to sleep.

At the foot of his bed he found laid out for him some new clothes. He pulled on the green silken pants and tucked them into knee-high boots of black that had a flap rising to cover his kneecaps. A white shirt went on over his upper torso, though the thickness of his pelt pulled the collar back enough that he had to loosen the throat lacings or choke himself. He didn't tuck the shirt into his pants and fastened on his sword belt. He felt a touch odd to be carrying Restraint with him in such a place, but he'd lived in armor and with weapons for so long that wearing only a sword made him feel practically naked anyway.

He stepped from his room and sniffed the air. He caught the scents of his companions coming from their rooms, and the hint of the complex scent used by the antlings. He assumed it was the means by which they communicated—a concept that hardly seemed alien to him since his wolf senses allowed him to understand how effective a medium it could be. Still, wolves tended to use it for very simple communications, whereas the antlings produced scents infinitely more complicated than those wolves used to mark territories.

The scents of Nagrendra and food mixed most strongly, so Tyrchon backtracked his way to the dining chamber they had used the night before. On his way he saw that much of the castle around the pathway they'd used had changed. *Our territory has remained the same, but everything else shifts. This is very odd.* He frowned, wondering if, with all the changes, he could find his way back out of the castle.

Nagrendra dabbed his mouth with a napkin, then bowed his head to Tyrchon.

"Good morning. I trust you slept well."

"I'm rested." Tyrchon lifted a serving-dish cover and smelled braised liver swimming in a spiced sauce. "I take it Lady Spiriastar slept well, too."

Clear membranes nictitated up over Nagrendra's eyes for a second. "What are you insinuating?"

"Your attraction to her was rather obvious, and she seemed taken with you, as well."

Nagrendra's forked tongue flickered out to taste the steam rising from another dish. "I believe she is intrigued by me. We spoke for a while after everyone retired. She loves puzzles and riddles, so we spoke of them, and then of philosophy. This concept that man reaches his full potential under the influence of Chaos is one she wondered about as the Seal was being created. She said she had any number of interesting conversations about it with her peers, but no conclusion could be reached. Now, after five centuries, she wanted to know if the theory had been proved true or not."

The wolf-warrior served himself some liver and sat across from the Reptiad. "That concept is one of the main precepts of the Church of Chaos Encroaching."

"It is rather interesting that what was once a cause for speculation among sorcerers has become dogma for the Black Church. I don't believe, however, that she had anything to do with the Church's formation." Nagrendra fished a roundish lump of something in a steaming green sauce onto his plate. "As nearly as I can tell, the time since the Shattering has passed in an eyeblink for her."

Tyrchon forked a piece of liver into his mouth and chewed it slowly. "Do we know if she truly was one of the mages who created the Seal?"

Nagrendra shrugged, letting light flash from his stony scales. "The names of those individuals are hardly revered. The sorcerers in the cabal that said creating such a Seal was impossible were the founders of the City of Sorcerers and, though they lost their argument, they fashioned themselves the victors in the battle because they saved what they could of the Empire. I had always heard that everyone save Fialchar died when the Seal was shattered; but his survival suggests others could have survived as well. Clearly Spiriastar did, though, again, I have no proof Spiriastar was there, nor that if she was, that *this* Spiriastar is she."

"Yet she seems powerful enough to have been one of Fialchar's peers."

"Fialchar's *peer*?" Spiriastar swept into the room, this time wearing a dress fashioned from scales that made her look a match for Nagrendra. "Fialchar was ever just an ambitious apprentice. He had some talent, and we certainly underestimated him, but even my Dashan was his superior in magicks."

Her voice grew a bit cold as she looked at Tyrchon. "Did Fialchar survive the Shattering?"

"After a manner of speaking." The warrior set his fork down. "Chaos has not been kind to him, but the last five centuries have afforded him a long time to learn from his mistakes. He has had rivals for power in Chaos from time to time, but they have not succeeded in destroying him or taking over his realm. The *Bharashadi* were the most recent and potent threat, but Imperial forces eliminated them."

"The Empire still exists, then?"

Nagrendra nodded. "As we were just discussing, the sorcerers who didn't believe a Seal of Reality could be created became a potent force in holding Chaos back. They created the Ward Walls and, over the centuries, the walls have been expanded to reclaim territory from Chaos. Most citizens never venture into Chaos, but Tyrchon and our companions, save Len, do brave Chaos to oppose threats to the Empire."

"Brave men, then, you both are." She nodded toward Tyrchon. "That sword you wear, it has an enchantment or two woven into it."

"So I understand." He stood. "Would you like to see it?"

Spiriastar smiled and swept locks of golden hair past a shoulder. "I have seen it before. I knew one of the warriors who bore it before you. She was a very good friend, and a superior fighter. I wonder if you are better than she was?"

Tyrchon shrugged. "I do not know, and I fear there is no way of knowing now."

"Actually, there is." Spiriastar waved her left hand past Nagrendra and toward the doorway.

Tyrchon heard the high-pitched shrieks of stones rubbing one against another. By the time he came out from around his side of the table and could look out through the doorway, things had shifted so that four arched walkways rose to meet at a stepped disc suspended high above the main floor of the manor house. The disc itself had a dozen steps leading up to what he assumed would be a flat landing.

"If you will join me there, and if you are willing to display your skills, we can settle this question."

"As you wish, my lady."

Spiriastar accepted Nagrendra's hand and allowed the Reptiad to lead her up to the disc. Tyrchon trailed behind and wondered how it would be possible for him to test himself against someone who had died at least five centuries previous. Stepping up to the disc, he got the first glimmering of his answer. Waiting there for them were two crystalline antlings and a pile of bones.

The sorceress gestured casually at the antlings, limning them in blue. Their angular edges seemed to soften. The two of them melted together like candles and poured in a glistening mass over the bones. Ivory swam through the fluid crystal, then a figure rose from the floor. Facing him across the disc stood a perfectly formed and very beautiful woman who wore the crystal like flesh over her bones. That he could see her skeleton made the experience rather disconcerting, but invisible muscles and organs distorted enough of the bones that he could focus more on the whole person.

Spiriastar smiled. "This is Zin Anzal, or as close as I can get to her now. These are her bones. While animating her in this fashion will allow some access to her fighting skills, to get more out of her would require the presence of soft tissue, like muscles or heart or brain. Unfortunately, none of that has survived her death."

Tyrchon frowned. "I feel uneasy about fighting with the bones of your friend. I would hope to treat the remains of another swordbearer with more respect."

"Your sentiment is appreciated, but Zin has gone on to other incarnations now." She smiled indulgently. "Besides, she made the mistake all of you swordbearers make—she drew the blade in response to a challenge where the blade would do her no good. Her death was the price she paid for that error."

The warrior shifted his shoulders. "It is a price I hope not to pay."

"Good luck to you, then. Have you named the blade?"

"I have. Restraint."

The sorceress nodded carefully. "Zin had called it 'Invincible.' It wasn't, nor was she, I am sad to say." Spiriastar pressed the tips of her fingers to her lips, then blew a kiss to the crystal warrior. Tyrchon caught a scent, then saw a four-foot-long blade grow out from the simulacrum's right hand. Zin's statue set herself, her breasts swaying slightly as she did so, then slowly advanced.

Tyrchon drew Restraint and squared his shoulders to his foe. He wrapped both hands around the blade's hilt, spread his legs to shoulder width, then dropped his left foot back ever so slightly. With small steps he moved to his right, circling carefully. He wanted to let Zin make the first strike, so he could get a measure of her speed and strength before he decided what he would do to attack her.

Zin came in hard at his left, slashing low at his leg. Pushing off with his right foot, Tyrchon lunged back to the left and brought Restraint around in a block that had his sword's point directed at the ground. Then, pivoting on his left foot, he whipped his right leg around and caught Zin behind the left knee. She started to go down, but posted up on her left arm, then rolled her body forward and stabbed her blade in at him.

Tyrchon continued his pivot, giving her a momentary glimpse of his back. Her lunge passed behind him, but he spun fast enough to parry her blade as she tried to slash down and hamstring him. He took her blade high enough that he could duck under it, then tried to bring Restraint around in a slash that would open her from groin to throat. She threw herself flat on her back, letting the metal blade slice through the air an inch above her flesh.

As the sword passed her without causing damage, she rolled to her feet and set herself again. Tyrchon saw her jaw work and her lips move, but heard no words. Instead he smelled something familiar and comfortable, almost friendly. It seemed one part each old leather, campfire smoke, and ale.

The wolf-warrior dropped his jaw in a smile. "Yes, I respect your skill. Well met."

Tyrchon took a quick step forward and feinted a cut at her left leg. As Zin brought her sword down to block him, he shifted his wrists and hauled Restraint up and over her parry. His slash back to the left traced a thin line across her left cheek as she twisted her head out of the way. Then Tyrchon felt a solid thump against his right flank that trailed up toward his armpit. He spun away, but felt her blade kiss the underside of his arm.

Coming around, he nodded a salute to her. "I should be bleeding to death with an open artery right now."

Her blade, which had become rounded and dull where it hit him, sharpened again. Zin passed a hand over the cut on her face, smoothing it into nonexistence. She smiled at him, then raised her blade up and back by her right ear. A scent Tyrchon associated with the nervousness of combat wafted off her, but he knew it was not her fear, but an invitation to join in a great battle.

He nodded and closed with her. He blocked a cut high left, then ducked beneath its twin and tried to slash her across the belly. She bent herself around the circle of his cut, then attacked in at his left again. He blocked her again, weakly, then scythed his blade down and around toward her legs. She leaped well above his cut, then brought her blade down on his left shoulder. The glass sword blunted itself again, but hit hard enough to sting him.

Tyrchon windmilled a series of blows in at her head, trying to overpower her blocks. He didn't know if her present strength was the equivalent of what it had been in her lifetime, but she absorbed the blows more easily than he ever would have expected. She retreated quickly before him, always circling to his left, stepping back when he brought a cut around low. Her ripostes would force him to parry as best he could, and more than once he felt the fabric of his shirt tug where her cuts grazed along his ribs.

Back and forth they worked, trading offense and defense. It almost struck Tyrchon as a dance of sorts. She had more experience with a blade, especially in fencing than he did, but his strength and speed compensated for that. While Zin was by no means as small as Xoayya, nor was she as large as Ghislaine, which meant Tyrchon had a hard time with getting as much of her with his cuts as he wanted. All of the wounds he inflicted scored flesh only, while hers would have had him bleeding from a dozen cuts and several of them would have been arterial.

Zin aimed a lunge at his left flank that came a bit more slowly than Tyrchon had expected. He brought Restraint up to parry and rode her blade down to the cross guard. Their swords became bound there, and both fighters pushed forward until mere inches separated their faces. At that distance Tyrchon was easily able to read the enthusiasm on her face. He knew it mirrored the exhilaration he felt, for finally he had been matched against a foe who was not only his equal in ability, but in spirit and heart as well.

Then the expression on her face shifted from joy to profound sadness and despair. She peered up at him, and through her transparent eyes he stared into the depths of her empty eye sockets. He felt his heart catch in his throat, then her lips formed words. She was imploring him to do something, but he remained puzzled for the half second it took for the scent to reach him.

Her request bore the stench of a battlefield the morning after a daylong war. Blood and mud, the greasiness of roasted flesh and the musky odor of carrion beasts mixed with the stomach-turning stink of rotting corpses. It made his eyes water and his mouth go sour, but it also conveyed in full what she wanted.

And it is what she deserves.

Tyrchon levered the hilt of his blade forward, catching her beneath the chin. That backed her up a step, giving him the room to raise his hands above his head.

He brought his blade forward and down with all his might, shattering the sword she offered to block the blow. Restraint's edge carved down through the crystalline flesh on her head, splitting her skull and carrying down to shatter the vertebrae in her neck.

The figure that had been Zin Anzal reeled back, then split in two and sagged to the ground. The two antlings began to take shape again, but neither could seem to form itself fully. They collapsed into shapeless pools that flowed viscously from the bones.

Tyrchon stared down at what he had done, then looked up and over at Spiriastar. "Forgive me, Lady Spiriastar. I meant no disrespect to your friend's remains. I . . ."

She held a hand up. "Do not concern yourself, Tyrchon. I wished to see who was better, and you are. When pushed, you are willing to kill. In a swordbearer, this is not a bad trait."

"Thank you." With Restraint he saluted her, and then the lifeless bones.

Spiriastar laid her hand on Nagrendra's arm. "I would have you attend me, Nagrendra, to tell me more of the time since Chaos overswept the world. Will you indulge me."

"It would be my pleasure." Nagrendra looked at Tyrchon. "I beg your leave."

"Granted." Tyrchon watched the two of them walk away and would have trailed after as far as the dining room, but he didn't feel hungry anymore. Something about Spiriastar did not strike him as right, but even the oracle of tangled bones at his feet could not reveal to him exactly why that was.

22

In his decision the night before that he would sneak around the manor house and see what he could uncover to explain his uneasiness with Spiriastar, Len had envisioned himself alone, stealthily moving through the place. He could recall playing James Bond games with other kids in the neighborhood as he was growing up, and this was his chance to live it all out. *It might just be a dream, but I can have fun with it, too.*

Unfortunately for him, Jhesti and Fitz had decided he could not be trusted alone. "You can stand there with your hands on your hips and a pout on your lips for as long as you want, Len, but we're coming with you." Jhesti, having grown to that awkward action-figure height somewhere between a toy soldier and a prom date for Harlequin Barbie, stood on Fitz's back, aping Len's stance. "Your sense of direction isn't that good . . ."

"My sense of direction is fine."

"Sure, then you explain why you're so far away from San Rafael."

Len started to reply, then stopped. He glowered at the plastic man. "Keep this up, and I'm going to stick you on a car dashboard on a sunny day."

"Save the idle threats until we're somewhere they've heard of an internal-combustion engine." In an eyeblink Jhesti threw his arms wide. "This place is set up to entrance and defeat a visually oriented creature like you. I don't have your sort of eyes, and Fitz here relies on other senses to get around. We can get you back here, and that should be something you want with what you and Shoth were planning."

"Okay, okay, you win." Len shook his head. "Where do you think we should start?"

"As deep as we can get. Any secrets to be found here will be buried fast and deep, I think."

Len used his pouch's leather strap to secure it to Fitz's back. "Let's get going, then."

The fitting stool strode confidently through the manor house as if it had always been part of the furnishings. Though he did not feel inclined to admit it, Len knew he would have been lost in a matter of minutes had he been on his own. Corridors and stairwells looked very much the same, and even though he tried to count his paces and remember the turns, little treasures revealed in alcoves kept breaking his concentration. To make matters worse, he could feel vibrations from the shifting of blocks and, every so often, could identify a new feature, like the disc with walkways arching high into the sky.

Even if I had graph paper and a global-positioning-system receiver, I'd be lost. He thought a moment about how the journey might be a clue from his subconscious about how he could recover from the dream, but dismissed that idea. *Every time I've thought that previously, I just move from one puzzle to another. If there are clues here, I don't think they're going to have to do with my return to consciousness.*

The journey through the manor house's lower reaches carried Len through the heart of what he mentally tagged the "gallery district." Little cul-de-sacs were filled with works of art. He studied countless pictures painted in styles that he vaguely recognized as those of great masters, or a particular culture, but he recognized no one specific piece. For a moment or two it seemed him as if every lost masterpiece by a famous painter had somehow ended up here, in Spiriastar's sanctuary. "But if this is the repository of all lost items, then I'm going to turn the corner and find a metric ton of paper clips sitting on a vast cushion of singleton socks."

Jhesti ignored his joke. "Notice anything peculiar about the figures in the portraits and statues?"

Len looked again at a piece that looked as if it were a Rembrandt. "Looks relatively normal to me. Paint's barely cracked and"—he laughed triumphantly—"I can't read the artist's signature, which means I must be dreaming."

"Len, you're dreaming if you think you can read *any* artist's signature."

"You have a point there—a weak one, but a point." Len frowned, then glanced at another piece, and another. "Hey, these pieces don't have the emblems on their clothes that Shoth and Nagrendra do."

"And you make of that, what?"

"All these pieces were created before the Shattering?"

"I think you've got something there, boss."

But they don't look like they've aged five hundred years. Len shook his head and followed in the stool's wake. "This is quite a collection of items here. It would have taken forever to compile it."

"Not forever, Len." Jhesti lounged on the pouch. "You remember the stories told last night about expeditions into Chaos? Tyrchon said Chaos riders often went out to recover artifacts of the time before the Shattering. Magickal items are greatly appreciated, but that's not all they bring out. They are basically plundering and looting what used to be Imperial villas, and I would guess they're not the only ones. I think the antlings have been burrowing up to the surface and pulling things down throughout the time since the Shattering."

"I can understand the desire to amass wealth, but here?" Len shook his head. "Spiriastar has everything she needs here. Ample food of an infinite variety, a home that can be made to accommodate whatever she might want or need. The only thing she wants for is companionship, and all the art in the world isn't going to buy that."

"You're missing it, Len. The value of the art isn't in what someone would pay for it, the value of the art is intrinsic to it. Look at that picture and tell me what you see."

Len glanced at a large canvas painted in the style of Italian masters, with two rather plump naked women wading in a pool of water. Swimming toward them came a magnificent swan. The two women were smiling rather enigmatically, and Len found himself grinning back at them. "Okay, I see two women enjoying the guilty pleasure of skinny-dipping and admiring nature in the form of this swan swimming toward them."

"Okay, good." The little plastic figure had folded its arms across his chest. "Now what if I tell you that the piece is really about a myth of two sisters who fell in love with a godling who manifested himself as a swan. He's come to tell them that he can only turn one of them into a goddess, so they will have to bid each other farewell forever, but this they do not know yet."

"I'd say that sucks." Len frowned. "They don't know it and they're happy and he's going to ruin it."

"Agreed, it's bad. Now what if I tell you that the swan is an evil god who has kidnapped the twin brothers to whom the women are married. They plan to seduce the god and get him to lead them to their husbands so they can free them."

"Well, then, that's not bad, but not really that good, either." Len ran a hand over his mouth. "But all three of the interpretations of the painting are equally valid. We're discussing what the artist had in mind, and without the artist being here, there is no way to know if what we are thinking is right or not."

"Right, which means a single work of art here could keep someone distracted for minutes or hours or days. Even once a decision is made about it, more study can ensue to confirm or deny that conclusion. Or someone can just gaze upon the picture because they love it."

Len nodded. "Museums don't seem to lack for visitors."

"Exactly, and this is one big museum that is constantly changing, so no one can be sure they've seen everything."

The shoe salesman stared down at Jhesti. "You think this museum was set up to distract Spiriastar? Why?"

"I don't know. I think we'll find out down below, however."

Fitz seemed to sense Len's urgency, so he picked up the pace and deftly avoided the antlings swarming all over the place. Len focused himself as much as he could on the stool and found that the artwork no longer distracted him as much as it had before. It struck him that subtle enchantments could well have been worked into the whole of the building to make it easy to forget things that had been seen. *Everything would be even that much newer, which means there would be no simple way to make sure everything had been seen.*

He swallowed hard and started weaving together what Shoth had said with conclusions he was drawing. Both of them had experienced a sense of having been in this place before, and Shoth attributed it to memories from the Dashan slipping through into his brain. Len couldn't discount that observation, but he also knew he had not seen exactly what he was seeing now. *I feel as if I've been here before, or have thought about this place before, but I haven't experienced exactly this.*

Things began to coalesce for him. Five centuries ago Spiriastar had been at ground zero of a magickal cataclysm. Len had seen what a little Chaos had done to Tyrchon and Nagrendra, yet Spiriastar seemed singularly unwarped by Chaos. This, in spite of the fact that she had been living for five centuries deep inside the territory where Chaos held sway. *Perhaps the damage wasn't external, but internal.*

Somehow the idea that Spiriastar's mind had been warped by Chaos didn't make Len feel all happy and warm inside. What followed from that concept was her aide's creating this place for her. It would be a place that would force her to focus. It had things she could recognize and, more importantly, things that encouraged reflection on the human condition. If she had become as inhuman in mind as Nagrendra was in form, then a therapy based on resocialization by forcing Spiriastar to examine, reflect on, and draw into herself the lessons of humanity and its struggle for life would make perfect sense. *This thing is a big Skinner box that rewards exploration and helps modify her behavior.*

He frowned as he started down a dim stairwell. The only problem he had with that concept was that the Dashan couldn't have known what a Skinner box was. He wouldn't have known about operant conditioning or any of the techniques of psychology. Not only did Len have no evidence that modern medical sciences existed in this realm, but he sincerely doubted if, in a world where magick was available, they would be at all necessary. *Any spell that can knit bones or stop bleeding should be able to balance the neurochemicals in someone's brain.*

A shiver ran through him. *She referred to this place as her sanctuary. Another word for sanctuary is asylum.* If Spiriastar had been rendered insane by the wave of Chaos, then the Dashan might have trapped her here in a place she would never want to escape. The whole of the manor could be nothing more than one big roach motel. *It doesn't kill her because the Dashan respected her and hoped she might be able to be cured, but he never wanted anyone to find her and free her.*

At the bottom of the stairs Len cut to the right and went down a short set of steps into a very cool and dim chamber. The feeling of déjà vu slammed into him in full force in the small room. In the center of it he saw a black island similar to the one he had seen back in Fong's Sanctuary, in the hidden room. It even bore the crest on one end.

The difference between the one he had seen before and this one was that the top slab had never evaporated. It lay around the island in pieces, as if it had been shattered with single sharp upward blow. Whatever had been in the tomb had not been pleased to be trapped there, and the edges on the breaks looked very sharp, as if they were not particularly old.

"Not that there would be much weathering here." Len crouched by a stone shard and ran a hand along it. He glanced back at the corridor leading to the stairs and saw antlings pass in the distance, but none headed in their direction. "I don't like this at all, Jhesti."

"You want to take a guess at what was in the tomb?"

Len shook his head. "I think I know already. The Dashan imprisoned Spiriastar here. I think he also created the antlings and provided them with the mission of preparing this castle to house her. He had them go out and find all this artwork and set it up here. Given that none of it seems to have aged, the Dashan worked under Spiriastar, and she said her work on the Seal of Reality involved time, I think the Dashan null-timed this crypt and the alcoves. The distraction spells on the alcoves might also affect one's time sense, so you waste even more time when you're looking at a piece of art."

"Kind of like TV."

"Right." Len straightened up and sighed. "If I had to guess, I'd say the big Chaos storm hit the valley above, and all the energy was funneled down in here. It was enough to awaken Spiriastar or make her aware of the fact that no time was passing for her, or it just shorted the null-time spell on this room. I don't know if magick can be overloaded that way, but if it can, I think that's what happened. Spiriastar emerges from her resting place and finds herself in this castle. Right now she's content, still exploring, but I don't expect that to last for long. I'd guess the Dashan didn't think so either."

Jhesti wore a frown. "But if the Dashan had trapped her, why didn't she strike at you when she recognized you?"

"That thought's occurred to me, and I only like one of the possibilities. Could be she's forgiven the Dashan for what he did." Len winced. "I think it's more likely she's just in a very benign phase in some weird bipolar disorder. If she gets nasty, well, her curiosity about the nature of man being realized in Chaos could cause her to try to take the Ward Walls down and run the experiment for herself."

"Not really the sort of thing I want to see happen." Jhesti's voice grew solemn. "Even in a dream."

"Me neither." Len shook his head. "Well, I've dreamed us into this mess, now I better figure a way out of it again. If I can't, I'm not sure I deserve to wake up."

23

Tyrchon assumed it was midafternoon by the time he made his way out to the gardens at the rear of the manor house. His ruminations about Spiriastar and Zin and the fight had not gotten very far, but seemed to have taken him longer than he would have expected them to. He was accustomed to thinking about things, and often found that mulling over a point would make time pass faster than it seemed. Still, in this instance too much time passed too quickly.

The crux of the problem for him involved magick, and he admitted to himself he didn't know enough about it to know if the conclusion he had drawn was accurate enough. Spiriastar had said that Zin Anzal's bones should only have contained her skill and knowledge of fighting, yet his foe had congratulated him on his skill. After that, she had asked for death.

His two logical choices were that Spiriastar was mistaken, or there was something more at play. Tyrchon discounted the error idea because Nagrendra had not seemed surprised at what she had said. He would have expected the Reptiad to question Spiriastar if she had made a mistake, if only to expand his own knowledge of her abilities.

Tyrchon had not fought against the other sword-bearer's bones alone. Two of the antlings had been melded together to create his foe, and both of them died when he struck. The form of communication used by Zin was that used by the antlings. He supposed it was possible that the antlings had picked up on whatever essence of Zin had been left in the bones and had communicated her wishes. *I wonder, though, if the death wish did not come from the antlings themselves?*

The question then became one of why the antlings wanted to die. As much as Tyrchon felt that something odd was going on in Spiriastar's realm, he couldn't positively identify it. Moreover, he didn't know if his uneasiness was just his alone, or something everyone else felt. *This is not something I'm going to figure out on my own.*

The gardens at the rear of the castle stretched out much further than they should have. The castle wall behind the manor house had never been completed and sloped down from the towers to a wide walkway that led from one portion of the gardens into a veritable maze of shrubs and blossoms. Crushed white stones crunched underfoot as Tyrchon passed between shrubs with crystal bristles and cascades of glassine ivy. The flower blossoms, though made of crystal, seemed to have the delicacy of the real thing, and even bore the correct scents.

The bouquet of the flowers overwhelmed his ability to smell, and the riot of color made it difficult for him to focus on any one patch of blooms. He wandered through the garden, heedless of where he was going because he knew a glance this way or that would show him enough of the manor house that he could find his way home again. *I can be lost without being lost. With her love of puzzles, Spiriastar must find this garden a delight.*

Rounding a corner, he bumped into Xoayya, but caught her arms and prevented her from falling. "Forgive me, Mistress Xoayya, I should have been paying more attention."

The small woman looked up at him and smiled as he released her. She wore a simple, off-the-shoulder dress of white wool that fell to just below her knees. Brown boots that laced halfway up her calves and a simple silver necklace completed the outfit. Her red hair flowed over her bare shoulders. A bit more *Chaosfire* burned in her eyes, yet they still had the ability to look right through him. "You need not apologize. I had a feeling I would find you here, but was uncertain of the details."

"You had a vision of us here?"

"Not a vision, a feeling." Xoayya glanced down. "I have had more feelings than visions since entering Chaos, but here even they feel a bit muted. I don't find myself looking beyond the next hour or two. It's almost a welcome relief, but also unusual."

"Very little seems usual here, I think." Tyrchon dropped his jaw in a smile. "It's a beautiful place, almost an oasis in the heart of Chaos. However, that alone is enough to make it very unusual."

"It has given me time to consider other things." She smiled and stroked a hand over his shoulder. "I realized I have not thanked you for being as kind to and solicitous of me as you have been."

The soft tone of her voice seemed to incite his heart

to pound a bit harder. "I thank you, but . . ." He hesitated, then shook his head. "I was going to say I have done for you what I would have done for anyone else in Chaos, but that's not wholly true."

"Someone like Nagrendra would not need comforting." Xoayya toyed with the cuff of his right sleeve. "When I touched Len and got all those visions, you pulled me into your arms and held me. I was feeling very scared and vulnerable—I had glimpsed a world I could not comprehend, and I was at a loss to deal with it. Feeling your arms around me, your strength shielding me, I . . ."

She turned abruptly away and hugged her arms around herself. "I'm sorry, forgive me. I'm indulging in childish fantasy here. You are so strong and smart, capable of being funny and yet so serious in combat. You're a hero, a hero on the scale with the Imperial Warlord or Gavin Madhand or Locke's father, Cardew."

Tyrchon stepped forward and rested his hands on her shoulders. "Xoayya, hush."

"No, I'm sorry for embarrassing you. I . . . I don't know that you don't have a wife and children back in the Empire or if . . ."

The distress in her voice ran through Tyrchon in three distinct currents. One raised him to the heights of ecstasy as he realized she was interested in him. That was something he had never expected, and had never dared dream about. The second came in the form of a desire to spin her around and hug her firmly to him. The same arms that had given her comfort before could show her that he returned her affection.

The third current undercut the other two and trickled ice through his guts. *I want to crush her to me, to kiss her, but how can I? She named it a fantasy, but I am the reality—a man with a wolf's head and pelt. I am a Chaos Rider. What she wants I don't think I can offer.*

"Xoayya, hush. Look at me, please." He guided her around in a circle and held her out at arm's length. He bent at the waist, lowering his head and chest so he could look in her eyes. "You have no idea what effect hearing your words has on me. I remember you in the cave where we healed Nagrendra. It was as if I was seeing you for the first time. Your voice, your thoughts, your smile—I noticed them all and in a way I'd thought I'd cut myself off from. I found myself concerned for you and attracted to you."

She smiled. "You did a good job of hiding that fact."

He nodded slowly. "I did, but for a reason. Look at me. Look at what Chaos has done to me."

Xoayya shook her head and reached a hand out. She touched him in the center of his chest. "The form you've taken makes no difference to me. You comforted me when I needed it. You've made sure the trip has not been hard on me. I watched you stand and slay over a half dozen *Tsvortu* and never had any fear they would get past you and to me. I knew you would not let that happen. And you waited for me to return with Len from the Sanctuary's inner chamber. These things are the mirrors of your soul."

"But I think you have only seen a small part of the reflection."

"I have seen enough." She raised a hand and stroked his cheek. "I may be young, but I have seen enough of Chaos to know spending time out here calls for choices you might not otherwise want to make. Something as simple as your traveling alone in Chaos shows me that you have concern for others. You don't want to lead them into things that could get them killed. And, yet, when you learned of Locke's expedition to destroy the *Bharashadi* Necroleum, you did not hesitate to join what should have been a suicidal expedition. You take responsibility, even as you are trying to do here, by telling me that I should stay away from you."

"You're not going to make this easy for me, are you?"

Xoayya laughed aloud. The merry sound buoyed Tyrchon's spirits, but only caused a momentary flutter in the third current. "Tyrchon, what we are talking about should never be easy, but neither should it be hard." She opened her arms wide. "What I feel for you, what you feel for me, this is the foundation for a future together. If we do not find that daunting, we're fools. If we find it overwhelming, we're not worthy of it."

His eyes narrowed. "You've had a vision of us together, then?"

She frowned. "No, no I have not, but here, as I said, I'm not getting them. But when I had the feeling that I would find you here, I also felt happier. I hadn't realized before that I was unhappy, but just thinking of you made me happier."

Tyrchon straightened up. "And seeing you makes me happy. Last night, when sharing what we were eating, I did my best to recall dishes I hoped you would enjoy. I felt all nervous that you would not like them, and wanted to growl at Len when he wanted to try the last portion of something you seemed to like. But, with that said, I am a Chaos Rider . . ."

She pressed a hand to his muzzle. "You are the Chaos Rider I believe I love. Other details are superfluous."

He tilted his head to the side. "Even if I have children in the Empire?"

Xoayya pursed her lips for a moment. "How many?"

"A litter or two." He barked a little laugh. "I am joking, but those are the sorts of jokes you will endure in my company. What I have become revolts some people and scares other. Neither group is inclined to be kind as a result."

"Then we will have to do our best to avoid letting people of either group into our circle of friends." She took his right hand into her hands and raised it to her lips. "The strength of our feelings for one another will ward us against the unkindness of others."

Tyrchon raised her hands to his mouth and tried his best to kiss them. "There are things I cannot do for you that others could."

She shook her head. "And there are things you have already done for me that others would not. You care for me, you make me happy. All else can flow from this."

He pulled her forward and hugged her against his chest. Her hands went around his waist, and she held him tightly. He raised a hand to stroke her coppery hair, scarcely believing what he was doing. Part of him still wanted to pull away, to fend her off before she could get into a position where she could be hurt, but it lost to the parts of him that were luxuriating in the moment.

Besides, I'm not worried about her being hurt as much as I am worried about myself being hurt. Accepting her meant he accepted a vulnerability. Those who wished to strike at him could strike at her and hurt him. It was a tremendous risk, for him and for her. *But the rewards more than compensate for it. Erecting invincible walls around a heart may prevent it from ever being hurt, but it also has no room to grow. Do I live life, or just insulate myself from it?*

With Xoayya in his arms, the only choice he could make was to live life. He lowered his head, pressing his muzzle against her head. "I wish I could kiss you."

"Just that wish is enough for me."

Stones crunched and sprayed beneath Len's feet as he rounded the corner at a dead run. He swept past them, skidded to a halt, looked at them, blushed, and turned away. "Sorry about that. I didn't mean to intrude."

Tyrchon smothered a spark of anger. "You're in a hurry."

"I was looking for you, either of you."

Xoayya smiled and slipped from Tyrchon arms. She grasped his left hand in her right. "You've found us. What is it?"

Len frowned and lowered his voice. "I've spent most of the day looking around with Jhesti and Fitz. We've found some interesting stuff, and I think I know what it means, but I'd like some perspective. I was hoping to talk to Nagrendra, too. Is he here?"

Tyrchon shook his head. "Last I saw him he was in Spiriastar's company."

"Not good. I hope Jhesti and Fitz find him; they're looking now." Len looked up. "What do you know about Spiriastar?"

Xoayya shrugged. "Not much. She's a powerful sorceress. She knows nothing much of the world since Chaos washed over it."

The smaller man nodded. "Kind of like she slept through the whole thing?"

"Could be."

Tyrchon narrowed his eyes. "She's from the islands, and she likes puzzles."

Len's head came up. "Where did you get the puzzle bit?"

"Nagrendra mentioned it this morning when describing what he and Spiriastar had been talking about. I think the infinite variation of things here is a delight to her."

"Keeps her mind occupied?"

"Could be." Tyrchon scratched at his throat with his right hand. "I know she kept track of the bones of a friend who died five centuries ago. She used them as the basis for a sparring partner for me. And that partner, which was two antlings and the bones all combined, wanted me to kill it."

"Damn, not the sort of news I wanted." Len shook his head. "This is not good."

Xoayya reached out and grabbed his wrist in her left hand. "Explain, Len, so we can give you that perspective you want."

"Right. In my exploring I pretty much came up with two theories about this place and Spiriastar. Both start with the Shattering and the idea that it broke her mind. The Dashan, seeing she was broken, locked her away in a place that was null-timed—time just ceased to function there, so five centuries didn't even register as a second for Spiriastar. I think the Chaos storm's energy burned that magick out, freeing her."

Len opened his arms to take in the whole of the cave. "I think the Dashan knew that someday she might get free, which is why he created the antlings and set them to creating this place and recovering all sorts of artwork from Chaos. It was all put together in a big puzzle to keep Spiriastar occupied. One theory says he wanted to have her look at all this art so she would come back to her senses by experiencing the human condition through art."

Tyrchon frowned. "I'm not certain how well I would think that would work."

"Yeah, and you're the guy who says she's been packing bones around for five centuries. That makes me think the Dashan set this place up to occupy her mind, distract her, keep her trapped down here while she tried to solve the puzzle of this place. If you think antlings and a skeleton wanted to die, I'd have to guess that the Dashan didn't think Spiriastar would unlock the puzzle of controlling the antlings this quickly."

Tyrchon felt a shiver run through Xoayya's hand. "What you're saying, Len, is that this place was meant to be a prison for Spiriastar."

"Looks like it."

Xoayya shivered and leaned against Tyrchon. "By entering into the place, we've given her a new puzzle to solve, one involving Chaos and the Empire."

Len nodded resignedly. "The Dashan was the key to unlocking this place. When he died, he tried to guarantee it would never be opened again. In trying to figure out what he wanted to do, we've undone his work. And, I'm afraid, redoing it will take more of an effort than all of us combined can manage."

24

Len fell silent as one of the antlings happened upon the scene. It looked at each of them, and when it turned toward him, Len caught the scent of freshly buttered movie-theater popcorn. His mouth immediately started watering. He blinked once as he understood what the antling was trying to communicate. "I guess it's time for dinner."

The wolf-warrior nodded and licked his chops. "That is the impression I was given as well."

The three of them wended their way back through the garden, but as they approached the courtyard behind the manor house, they were surprised to see the dining table had been moved out to it. A slight breeze ruffled the tablecloth and guttered the candles burning there. The full formal service looked out of place out of doors to Len. *Just the sort of thing one might see in a Fellini film, I guess.*

Everyone else in their group filtered into the courtyard save for Nagrendra. His absence struck Len as odd, so when he reached Fitz's side, he spoke to Jhesti. "See if you can find Nagrendra, will you?"

"Think something is up, boss?"

"I'm sure he's just distracted, but given how he's been hanging around with Spiriastar, and she's here, he must be *very* distracted."

Jhesti laughed, his plastic hands firmly grasping the pouch bound to Fitz. "We'll find him and get him out here."

Tyrchon and Xoayya had already taken their seats along with Irin on the left side of the table, leaving the spots at the corner nearest Spiriastar open for Nagrendra. Ghislaine, three other guards, and Shoth sat on the right side, leaving Shoth at Len's right hand. Len could barely see Spiriastar because of the silver-and-wax forest between them, but he really didn't want to be looking in her eyes all that much, so he didn't protest.

From what Len could see of Spiriastar, his hostess was quite pleased. She wore a big smile, which he would have found reassuring, but it didn't seem to carry all the way up into her eyes. "In your honor, I have decided to have dinner out here, in the open. As magnificent as the manor is, there are times it really can be too confining. It's almost like a prison."

Len shot Tyrchon a glance, and the wolf-warrior acknowledged it with a nod.

Ghislaine smiled. "The manor is quite fantastic. It seems almost as variable as the world outside."

"Yes, the outside world." Spiriastar laid her hand on Ghislaine's wrist. "Nagrendra has told me much of the islands, how he loves them and what they mean to him."

Xoayya cleared her throat. "Where is Nagrendra, Lady Spiriastar, if you don't mind my asking?"

"He is resting, child. He found the afternoon rather exhausting." The sorceress's laughter rolled over the table. "He will join us later, but he wanted you to partake of dinner without him. I labored to produce the meal myself, so I hope you enjoy it." She waved a hand at the various dishes before them, and the silver covers evaporated in a blue fog.

Len stared at the vegetables in the dish nearest him. They looked to be green onions that had been marinated and grilled. They glistened with traces of the dark juice in the bottom of the dish. Steam even rose off them and smelled right. When his father prepared the same sort of thing on the grill for summer cookouts, Len couldn't get enough of them.

Even so, he didn't reach for a spoon. *The big difference between these onions and the ones my father makes is that his aren't glass.*

Everything else at the table, from the roast boar at the far end, to a mound of small fowl sitting between Irin and Shoth, looked perfectly delicious, but had telltale signs that it was crystalline in nature. As far as Len could see, the boar's eyes, for example, looked, well, glassy. And the ends of the leg bones on the fowl didn't seem to Len to be quite as rounded as they would have been naturally. While it all had the proper scent, any mouthful would produce nothing but glass splinters, and that was if it hadn't shattered teeth in the chewing.

Len smiled weakly. "This is all, really, too beautiful to eat."

Spiriastar looked down at the food, then blinked and smiled. "Of course, you cannot digest what is produced here. I can adjust your systems so you can."

Shoth held his hands up. "No, wait, there is no need for you to do that. We would not put you to the trouble. If the dishes the Dashan left you were brought out here, I'm certain we could reproduce this meal and enjoy it as you intended."

"Ah, yes, the Dashan's dishes." Spiriastar waved her hand again, sending a red-gold wave of light rippling down the table. As it passed, the items on the serving dishes began to shift and change. The boar got up on its feet, then drained itself of color, and re-formed itself into one of the antlings. Then the three fowls balanced one atop the others and melted together into an antling. One of the little game hens dove into Len's onions, then an antling pulled itself out of the sauce like a swimmer emerging from a pool. With it vanished the onions and all but the last bit of juice. The antlings all clambered down from the table and scurried off toward the manor house.

Spiriastar frowned. "It appears you will have to enjoy my Dashan's hospitality, not mine."

Shoth kept his voice soothing. "Lady Spiriastar, the kindness you showed us in your effort means more than all the food in the world."

"Yes, but relying on *his* things for sustenance here means you are in *his* debt." As she spoke, Spiriastar looked at Len, making him decidedly uncomfortable. "*He* provided this place, these servants, all that you see here. It is all because of him. I owe him a vast debt, and I will repay it." Her voice grew icy as she pointed a finger at Len.

"Wait, Lady Spiriastar, wait." Tyrchon stood and held his hands up to forestall her action. "Len is *not* your Dashan. He just looks like him."

"It is always like a swordbearer to take his side in an argument. Will you draw your blade against me?"

Spiriastar stood, her eyes blazing. "You recall what happened when you did that before, do you not?"

Len's mouth began to gape open. *It's late in the day, the collector above has been pulling in power all day, so she's at her strongest. The magick that keeps her befuddled is breaking down, probably because of all of us being here.* "Take it easy, Lady Spiriastar. No one here wants to hurt you."

"You think *you* could hurt me?" A golden nimbus began to surround her. "You always wanted to supplant me, your master, and you finally found a way to do it. But I have defeated your treachery. I see what is going on here now. Neither you nor your swordbearer will prevail against me."

A bright pulse moved through the nimbus, then gathered at her fingertip and launched itself in the form of a golden stiletto at Len. He instantly kicked back with his feet, intending to tip his chair backward, but a blue flash at his feet rocketed him into the air. He came up and out of his chair and saw the glittering blade dart in betwixt his knees. It exploded through the back of his chair, reducing it to charred splinters, and Len landed lightly within the cone of debris.

"Yes, the boots saved you, but not forever, Dashan." She raised her hands, but before she could cast another spell, a wall of blue slammed into her back and flowed down over her like a blanket. It pitched her forward against the table, then seemed to congeal over her. Tyrchon's first sword stroke glanced off it, so he brought the blade around for another strike, but a voice stopped him.

Clinging to Fitz, Nagrendra half slid down the stairs to the courtyard. "Don't, Tyrchon, you will weaken the spell."

Shoth looked up at Nagrendra, and Xoayya had

already started running toward him. "What happened to you?"

Whole patches of scales had been ripped from his chest, and black blood had oozed down over them. "She wanted to know of the outside world and was very persuasive."

Ghislaine pointed at Spiriastar. "What did you do to her?"

"I congealed the air around her, I froze it." Nagrendra closed his eyes for a moment. "It might have killed her, it might not. We have to get out of here."

Tyrchon brandished his sword. "Release her, let me finish the job."

"No! If she's dead, she's dead. If not, if I release her, she will be too powerful to destroy. She wasn't expecting that, and"—Nagrendra coughed wetly—"I can't do it again."

Shoth gestured at Spiriastar, and the table snapped at her end, looking as if something big had taken a bite out of the table. "There, I've encased her in an invisible cylinder. If she gets out of his spell, she has to work on mine. Move."

Ghislaine and her Guards started around through the archway leading to the castle's front court. Xoayya followed, helping balance Nagrendra on Fitz's back. Shoth, Len, and Tyrchon brought up the rear, and Len's last vision of Spiriastar showed thin, angry red veins running through the blue of Nagrendra's spell.

Tyrchon snarled as they ran through the milling crowd of antlings. "I should have killed her."

Shoth shook his head. "Did you miss what she said? She's dealt with someone who carried your sword before, and she wasn't dead because of it. You wouldn't have succeeded."

"I could have killed her, I could have."

"Might be true, Tyrchon." As Len ran through the castle's main gate, he glanced back and saw a gold flash light up the far towers. "And you might yet get your chance."

"I don't think so." Shoth's voice became very solemn. "Her attack on you, Len, was not usual. She rarely did her own work, which is why she had us, the Dashan, and why we gave her all the antlings to order about."

A shiver ran down Len's spine. Part of him knew that what Shoth was telling him was true, and yet he wanted to deny it. The dream was becoming too complex to be a dream, and that scared him. What scared him even more was that Nagrendra was bleeding, and a very powerful magicker was coming after them. *But we'll get away.*

Len's jaw dropped open. "Wait, we can't run."

Shoth glanced over at him. "Why not?"

"If we run to the gatehouse and go up through the tunnel, she'll know how to get out of here. We can't let her get loose."

"You truly *are* dreaming, Len, if you think we can contain her forever." Tyrchon slowed his retreat. "Ghislaine, get your people back here. We have to hold Spiriastar's troops off."

Len glanced back and saw light glittering off the backs of antlings as they poured from the castle. They descended the walls and swarmed out along the ivory road. They did not stampede forward, but came at a steady pace that promised to overtake the group before they could reach the gatehouse. A spirited defense might buy some time, but the antling force was too overwhelming to stop.

Unless I buy them some time.

Len ran up to Fitz and grabbed Nagrendra's shoulder. "Give me your cloak."

Xoayya looked at Len, horrified. "What are you doing?"

"Trust me. Give me your cloak."

The Reptiad nodded. He slipped the throat clasp, then helped tear it free of a couple of wounds where it had become encrusted. They began to bleed anew, and Len dabbed clean cloth against the wounds. "I hope this works, for all our sakes."

"Go, Len, but don't go too far." The Reptiad's tongue slithered out and tasted the side of Len's neck. "Good, you're calm. Go."

Len ran back to Tyrchon. "Stay close to Fitz. Go. I have a plan, and it should work. Go and set up defenses at the gatehouse. Now."

The wolf-warrior regarded him for a moment, then pulled back. Ghislaine and her Guards followed him, opening a twenty-yard gap between themselves and the antling lead element. "Good luck, Len."

"Thanks." He looked down at his boots and saw them wink at him. "This better work, or I'm meat munchies for glass bugs—and that entomology course was a waste." He wasn't at all certain that the antlings would react like real ants, but he hoped they would. *It's my damn dream, so they damn well better work like ants.*

Len dragged the bloodied cloak across the line of the antling's march rather slowly, then he reached the glass grass at the path's edge. "Okay, boots, now you do your stuff." He visualized himself running fast out into the field, dragging the cloak behind him and, suddenly, as he began to run, each step ate up yards. The cloak caught and pulled on the grass behind him, but it could not slow him down. In the blink of an eye he ran forty yards off the pathway and started a short curve back toward the castle. He outstripped the antling flankers and stopped long enough to see them begin to move after him.

Yes! They're following a scent trail, just like real ants! He set off again, running in a crazed pattern that would put the antlings through a confused course, then he tossed the cloak aside and sprinted toward the gatehouse. *Let's hope they fight over the cloak and don't follow my course.*

He caught up with his comrades as they came within a hundred yards of the gatehouse. The vast majority of antlings had swerved off the pathway, but a determined few pressed forward. Tyrchon and the Matarun attacked the scouts, but with mixed results. Tyrchon's sword sliced through the antlings easily, dropping them to the ground, where they spread out like puddles of gelatin. The Guards managed to hit the antlings at which they swung their axes, but other than shattering an antenna or cracking off a leg, they did little damage.

Len darted forward and toe-kicked one of the creatures trying to flank Tyrchon. The boots glowed blue as the blow landed, and the antling shattered like hammer-struck glass. Sharp shards sprayed back, raking the next two ranks. Pierced antlings fell, and others paused to investigate and skirt their viscous remains, buying the fleeing group a little more time.

"We're at the door." Shoth waved his hand before the black plug's crest, and it rolled away. Fitz galloped in and up the steps to where the golden disc had landed, taking Nagrendra and Jhesti with it. Xoayya raced after them. Ghislaine and the Guards followed, leaving Len, Tyrchon, and Shoth in the rear.

The wolf-warrior took the two of them in with a glance. "Go, now. It's been an honor."

Shoth shook his head. "No, *you* go, the both of you."

Len stared at him. "What? You can't be serious."

"I am, very."

"But what you told me last night . . ."

"Forget that, it's what *you* told *me* last night." Shoth smiled and exuded confidence. "This is the time to act, so I'm going to act! I can hold them off. Walls are my specialty, and I'm the only one here who has even the least little chance of making it back up through the tunnel, so *go*!"

Len rested his hands on Shoth's shoulders. "You want the boots?"

"And give her a chance to get them? No!"

Tyrchon looked down at him. "You're going to die, you know."

The blond Warder nodded. "Maybe. I've lived my whole life in fear, and, when I should be most afraid, I'm not. If I have to die in this state, I'll be happy."

Len felt a lump rise to his throat. The wolf-warrior tugged Len toward the stairs and spoke the words Len wished he could. "You may think, Shoth Churgûn, that you were a coward, but we shall always remember you as a man of courage."

At the top of the steps they found the gold disc waiting for them. The second they stepped on, Len visualized the top of the tunnel, and they began their ascent. As the disc rose, he looked down at Shoth and saw the Warder closing the gatehouse door. Len waved, Shoth waved back, then the edge of the tunnel stole him from sight.

Only the fact that Shoth had erected three invisible walls to further plug the doorway saved his life. For what seemed like forever to him he heard the antlings scurrying around on the gatehouse's exterior, seeking a way in, but they could find none. Then he sensed magick being employed against the doorway. The first spells were subtle, and with a quick little counterspell he managed to alter things enough to blunt Spiriastar's attempts to break in.

This is a game I can keep up for a long time. Shoth smiled, knowing that eventually he would tire and have to sleep, and she would come for him then, but he was confident his friends had escaped her. Though he knew he was going to die and had sincere regrets in that regard, he didn't feel cheated. *It might have taken these last moments for me to be truly alive, but I am, and that is worth all the pain that ever can be inflicted upon me.*

The black-stone doorway suddenly dissolved beneath a ferocious assault. A red-line grid carved it into chunks that blasted forward into the gatehouse. They blew through the first two walls he had created and still had enough strength to rip the last wall from the anchor points where he'd linked it to the structure itself. He leaped back to avoid the falling wall and got peppered with bouncing stone fragments. One clipped him over his left ear, sending him reeling to the steps of the landing pad.

Things went black for a second—he knew it wasn't longer than that—but when he awoke he found himself pinned down by a dozen antlings. He struggled against them, but their mandibles tightened, holding him still and filling him with pain.

Spiriastar strode through the ruined doorway, her eyes pulsing out dark *Chaosfire*. Her dress had become transformed into a clinging garment that almost appeared to be her flesh. It maintained the mica-scale pattern akin to Nagrendra's skin, but struck Shoth as being very armorlike. It rose to cover her throat and had grown down into fine-scaled gauntlets with rather thick talons on each finger.

She leaned down and grasped his chin. "It took me a while to recognize you, my Dashan. The other looked like you once did, but you bear the part of my Dashan that was his greatest weakness. You should have killed me five centuries ago. You failed, and you'll not get that chance again."

"Now you will kill me and get your revenge?" Shoth found himself smiling in the face of her fury. Memories of his past life boiled forth, and he felt as if another were speaking through him. "You have me at your mercy."

"And you know I have no mercy." She straightened up and grabbed an antling behind its head, lifting it from the ground. She held it over him and traced a single talon down over the creature's abdomen. "Just as you left me with a shadow existence, so I will do to you."

A thin, glistening fluid thread began to flow from the wound she'd opened in the antling. She moved the creature so the liquid struck Shoth on the forehead and slowly oozed down across his eyes and toward his ears. It ran further and started into his nose. He tried to snort it back out, but when he opened his mouth to gather a breath, Spiriastar squeezed the antling, gushing fluid past his lips and down his throat. He tried to vomit it out, but the thick liquid seemed to calm him—after a moment's distress of feeling it slide down the back of his throat from his nose, he felt blissfully numb.

"Yes, Shoth, you will die now, but I will have you live again, just as I do." The fluid over his eyes tightened his focus on her victorious smile. "Spiriastar will emerge from this crystal cocoon to take the world meant to be her own. And she will have a new Dashan with her who, *this time*, will do her bidding in all things."

25

Racing along through the night-shrouded landscape, Len stumbled and fell the very moment Shoth Churgûn died. Len's foot slipped on a narrow hillside trail, sending him somersaulting slowly through the air. The hollowness in his stomach, the nausea, he put down to the tumble at first, but it twisted down tight into his guts even after he hit the ground.

He landed hard on his right shoulder, then his back, and began to roll. Sparks exploded before his eyes as his head hit something. Rocks and sand, scree and pebbles all began to bounce around him. He tasted dirt in his mouth, felt blood flowing from his head. The sting of raw elbows and knees made it through the throbbing aches from the pounding of bigger rocks on his body.

Yet all that physical pain seemed remote, defying Len in his attempt to embrace it. He wanted to use it to fill him and push away the pain of Shoth's death. He didn't know how he knew Shoth had died, but the emotional turmoil felt as real as any he had ever known. The logical thought of his knowing of Shoth's death because they had once been one person seemed clear, but that suggested what he was experiencing was real, not a dream.

And if this is not a dream, I abandoned someone to die. I left him to make a heroic stand, to sacrifice himself so I could live. How could I do that? Why am I more worthy of life than he? This can't be happening.

Len's body slammed into a big rock and hung up there, his arms and legs spread out as little stones trickled down over him. He could feel warm blood flowing down over his left ear and knew he should stop the wound, but he had neither the energy nor desire to do so. *Let me bleed out, let me die.*

He heard the crunch of footsteps in the scree and saw Tyrchon's distinctive outline looming over him. "How badly are you hurt, Len?"

"Leave me alone. Go away." Len weakly flapped an arm at Tyrchon. "Just let me die here."

"Can't do that, Len." Tyrchon crouched and tried to lift Len into a sitting position.

Len pushed him away. "Shoth is dead. We let him die."

"Wrong. Shoth is dead because he decided to let us live."

"I don't want to live. This is all a dream, and it shouldn't hurt like this. I didn't ask for this. Go away."

The wolf-warrior grabbed Len's jaw in a firm grip and lowered his muzzle so their noses touched. "At the moment, I don't care what you think is happening, and I don't care how much Shoth's death hurt you. Those things are immaterial to me. All I know is that

I'm not leaving you here for Spiriastar or the T*svortu* or Hob*motli* to find."

"Go *away!*" Len tried to punch Tyrchon, but the warrior blocked the punch effortlessly.

A quick openhanded slap snapped Len's head around. "Listen to me, Len, and listen very carefully. You've lost a friend. You've lost a part of you. We've *all* lost a friend. Shoth made the choice he did so we could live. If you want to die, that's fine with me, but you're not doing it now. I won't have you tarnishing Shoth's sacrifice. Do you understand?"

"But he's dead."

"I know, but watering the ground in Chaos with tears for a fallen comrade is worthless. We save them for the Empire." Tyrchon hooked his hands in Len's armpits, then straightened up, hauling Len to his feet. "Nasty gash on your skull, but you'll live. We've got to get going."

Len let Tyrchon help him back up the slope. Once they reached the others, Xoayya cast a quick healing spell that clotted the wound and sealed it up. She offered to renew the spell later to prevent scarring, but said she was tired from helping Nagrendra. Len just nodded mutely at her and began to trudge along with everyone else.

He tried hard to put what he was experiencing into some sort of perspective, but it wasn't easy. While in Spiriastar's realm the whole dream thing had seemed to drift into the background, but any explanation he had for why that happened ended up being wrapped up in the idea that he wasn't dreaming anyway. He could have supposed that the part of him that was the Dashan had felt at home there, or that the enchantments meant to befuddle Spiriastar had likewise prevented him from being analytical enough to see the dream clues in her realm. Either way, what he was experiencing had to be real, and yet he could not accept that.

The anguish and loss he felt at Shoth's death shook him terribly. He tried to remember back to a time when the death of a fictional character had hurt him so. As a kid he'd seen countless sappy films where all his buttons got pushed and he cried. The death of a dog here, or an alien there, could choke him up. In a couple of books he'd experienced the same thing, but those emotions passed. It was as if the brevity of his time spent with that character limited the emotional attachments to it. Even the loss of some of his gaming characters—characters he'd created and played for months and years—hadn't hurt him this much.

The only death that had hurt in this way had been that of his grandfather. The old man had been in his seventies and fairly vital, then, *boom*, a stroke dropped him on his morning walk, and, by the time he got to the hospital, he was dead. The doctors assured Len's family that he'd felt no pain. At the time it occurred to Len that this meant all the pain of his death was left for his family to absorb. It had been a cold and cruel observation, but Len had been young and had spent a lot of time with his grandfather, hanging out at his house after school, waiting for his parents to come home.

His grandfather had been part of him, part of his world. He had always been there, and there was no warning that he would not always be. Similarly Shoth had been part of his world, and a part of it that opened up to him. Shoth's simple display of trust had likewise opened Len to the world. It *made me vulnerable, and now I've been hurt.*

Len shook his head. But *this is a dream, so Shoth wasn't real. What I felt for him was as real as what I feel for a character in a book. This will pass. It's not important. I'm wasting my time caring here because this is all make-believe. They must have me on some killer drugs in the hospital. Yeah, morphine. That's why I'm seeing all this weird stuff. I should have thought of that sooner.*

Ghislaine had been leading the company, and, as the sun began to dawn bloody and hot, she pointed out a cavern mouth down in a little valley. "That's where we are going."

Tyrchon crouched at the head of the trail. "This is the way your other two people went."

"And I'm glad to see they made it this far." The Matarun captain nodded confidently. "In there we will be safe."

Nagrendra rolled off Fitz's back and got unsteadily to his feet. "There is a rent in there?"

Ghislaine's eyes narrowed. "You know of this place?"

The Reptiad shook his head. "Not this one, but of others."

The Guard leader looked somewhat surprised. "I was led to believe there are very few of these points in Chaos."

Tyrchon stood and clapped his hands to rid them of the red dust. "Actually, they're rare on the Imperial side of things. In Chaos they're not terribly uncommon."

Xoayya frowned. "What is a rent?"

Nagrendra coughed lightly and leaned heavily on the fitting stool. "The Ward Walls on the borders penetrate the ground for a considerable distance to prevent Chaos demons from tunneling beneath them. Sometimes the nature of the stones it passed through causes a dislocation of magickal energy. If you will recall, when you passed through the Ward Walls, you did so as if walking through a veil of smoke. One moment you were on one side, and the next you were on the other."

The redheaded woman nodded. "These rents are not like that?"

"Oh, they function in the same way, but there is a far more vast distance between the sides. Imagine if you could enter a tunnel at one end and exit at the other, without having to travel the intervening distance, much as the spell that allowed us to get out of the collapsing tower did." The Reptiad shrugged uneasily. "I have heard rumors of rents that pass hundreds of miles from one side to the other. Where will this one take us, Captain Ghislaine?"

She shook her head. "The Empire. That's all I can tell you."

Xoayya regarded her carefully. "Why have I never heard of rents before?"

Tyrchon came around and rested a hand on her shoulder. "Rents are a closely held secret. In the City of Sorcerers they deny their existence."

"Not deny, exactly." Nagrendra forced a weak laugh. "They allow that, in theory, under highly unusual conditions, rents might appear. They also suggest they are unstable and unreliable and could vanish at any moment. Tyrchon's point, however, is correct. If all Imperial citizens knew that there were apparent gaps in the Ward Walls, they would begin to panic. As it is, the rents stop Chaos creatures from going through, so they serve their original purpose anyway."

Len scratched at crusted blood on his neck. "Great. Now do you want to stay out here in the open to talk about this, or do we get out of here and do it?"

Tyrchon nodded. "He has a good point."

Ghislaine sent Irin and another Guard running down to the cave. They entered it, popped back out again, and signaled the others that all was clear. The rest of the group came on slowly, keeping pace with Nagrendra and Len. All Len's bruises had begun to stiffen him up, but he still moved better than the Reptiad. He wanted to reach out to Nagrendra, to tell him he was sorry for what had happened to him, but he held back.

He told himself he did so because Nagrendra would just say it wasn't his fault and he couldn't have prevented it. Len would have countered that he felt responsible since it was his dream that was putting Nagrendra through all the pain, but that would reopen the dream discussion, and Len didn't have the heart for it.

He also knew that such reasoning was just a cover. He *did* feel for Nagrendra, and that meant he had another point of vulnerability to deal with. *If you let yourself be concerned about these people, you'll only be hurt again.* He suddenly realized that emotional withdrawal felt comfortable for him because that was how he dealt with everyone who could possibly hurt him or claim some obligation from him. *This is why friends you make on one job go away when you change jobs. You disengage—you never fully engage—for fear your life will be intruded upon. You hate that from people like Comrade Corbett, but you tolerate it because they are your bosses. Others you don't even give a chance.*

Their arrival at the cavern cut short Len's thinking. They worked their way in, having to shift to single file as the passage narrowed. After a turn that cut off the reflected sunlight, everything plunged into darkness. Len felt his way around another turn and saw a glowing from ahead. The passage widened again, and the party assembled in a circular chamber roughly twenty feet across and ten high.

The glowing came from a ten-foot-wide patch of light that shimmered like a curtain being teased by a light breeze. Though white predominated, red and purple highlights wove their way through, making the whole thing opalescent and beautiful. Len realized he'd seen the pattern before, in the *Chaosfire* in his compatriot's eyes. There it had power, but here it threatened to overwhelm, and yet he couldn't take his eyes from its beauty.

"This is a Ward Wall?"

Tyrchon nodded. "Very much like one, but the Ward Walls stretch from horizon to horizon and on up into the sky."

"Wow."

Ghislaine waved a hand toward the light wall. "Please, after you."

Battered, bruised, and covered with blood from his wounds, Len staggered toward the rent. He reached out with his left hand and touched the wall. He got a quick cold shock, like dipping a toe into the ocean in April, but he didn't pull back. He let the cold wash over him as he pushed forward, using it to extinguish some of the aches he felt. Then a warm tingle passed over him, and he started to smile. The warmth invited him onward, welcoming him into the Empire. In its embrace he felt safe and more secure.

On the other side he found himself in another small stone chamber like the first, but with two exceptions. The first was that it had another rent set in a wall roughly ninety degrees from the one he stepped through. The second was that Irin and a half dozen other Mountain Guards stood there to greet him. Len smiled at her and got a slight nod in return, but no reaction from the others.

Tyrchon, Nagrendra, Xoayya, Fitz, and Jhesti came through next, and only when Ghislaine and her remaining Guards brought up the rear did Len realize they had been neatly surrounded. He heard Ghislaine whisper, "This is just a precaution. We want no trouble."

Len turned on her. "Wait a minute! You can't do this."

Ghislaine shrugged. "I have my orders. Be calm, and everything will be fine."

He pointed at the other rent. "I've got half a mind to head out into Chaos again."

"And," said a voice from behind him, "because you have a fraction of a mind, you will die if you do that."

Len saw Ghislaine come to attention, then whirled. Facing him he saw a beautiful petite woman with long black hair and pale blue eyes. *Now I know I'm dreaming.*

The woman nodded to him. "Welcome, Dashan. It has been far too long."

Len's jaw dropped open. "Angie?"

"No, I am Myat. You are in my realm now. And you have the boots."

"You know about the boots?" Len frowned, then he nodded. "Of course, the Guards who came ahead told you."

"I'd known about them before. They are the reason you are here." Myat smiled carefully. "I also know Shoth is dead, and I knew that before it was reported to me as well. I knew it the same moment you did."

"That's not possible." Len pressed his hands to his head. "There is no way you could know. I only knew because . . ."

"Yes," Myat smiled, "I knew the same way. Five hundred years ago, when the Dashan tore his soul apart, he didn't break it in half. He tore it into three unequal parts, and now, finally, the most important parts are together again."

26

Tyrchon caught Len as the young man staggered back a step. The wolf-warrior laid Len down, then looked up at Myat. "You're saying you're host to part of the Dashan's soul?"

"The most important part." The small, black-haired woman touched fingers to her temple. "I possess his intellect. When I sundered my soul, I split it into three parts. I put all of my fears and concerns for the world in one small bit, and Shoth Churgûn was born with it. He was my conscience. He had some basic magickal skills and some power, but only a fraction of that which I had known in my lifetime. He was my conscience and served me well in summoning the remaining part of myself."

Tyrchon suppressed a growl as the woman explained herself, but he could do nothing to control the way his hackles rose on the back of his neck. He'd never met Prince Aloren's wife before, but had heard rumors of her venality and ruthlessness. If *she was born without a con-*

science, this would go a long way toward explaining why she is the way she is. The instant that thought occurred to him, he knew that was part of the puzzle, but not the whole of it.

Xoayya stood over Tyrchon and smoothed the fur on his spine. "You never told Shoth who and what he was, did you?"

Myat laughed a bit. "No. When I first met him, I recognized what he was. I knew how important he would be to the future. If I had told him even as much as I have told you, he would have balked at doing what needed to be done. But, please, this place is hardly conducive to our discussion. Follow me."

The request, though phrased as an invitation, came as an order. Tyrchon got Len to his feet and let him lean on Fitz. "Are you all right?"

Len blinked a couple of times, then his brown eyes focused. "I don't exactly know. Um, she looks like someone I know, and I do feel a connection. It's sort of like what I felt for Shoth as I got to know him. He was an old friend. She feels like . . ." Len fell silent for a moment, then his voice sank into a very low whisper. "She feels like a lover who is bad for you. Can't resist, but should, you know?"

"Sure. Come on." Tyrchon helped Len walk through the rough-hewn corridor which led fairly directly into a man-altered tear-shaped chamber with stairs leading up. The wolf-warrior sniffed. "This was a place where Shoth spent a lot of time."

Len nodded weakly. "I know. I can feel him here."

They skirted the smeared circular map painted on the floor and moved to the wooden chairs and table back against the far wall. Cheese, bread, some fruit, and wine had been laid out. Standing in the painted circle, Myat opened her arms to the bounty on the table. "I know your journey has been arduous. I would not keep you that much longer, but there are things you must know so you can make the right decision."

Nagrendra's eyes narrowed. "Right decision?" He glanced at Ghislaine, but the Guard captain shook her head. "You will explain?"

Myat smiled, but Tyrchon did not find that at all reassuring. "As I said before, your friend here—you call him Len, yes? Len possesses a portion of the Dashan's soul, as I do and as Shoth did. What I inherited was the Dashan's intellect. I have very little formal magickal training because I have no magickal power. I cannot manipulate the forces of Chaos well enough to cause spells to take effect. This does not mean, however, I cannot craft spells of an exquisite nature. The dishes in the Sanctuary that produced whatever you wanted for food, those were but an afterthought for the Dashan— mere whimsy. I crafted the spell which Shoth used to bring Len here, to Chaos, and even wove into it a compunction for Len to find the Sanctuary and open it. I wanted him to find the boots, which he has done. Congratulations, Len, you have served your purpose."

Jhesti appeared on Len's shoulder. "I don't think I like the sound of that."

Myat peered closely at Jhesti, and at Fitz lying like a dog at Len's feet. "Incredible. The proximity of these items to you has accelerated the effect of Chaos on them. They are animate and even possess a rudimentary intelligence. This is better than I could have hoped."

Tyrchon glanced at Len, taking in the droop-eyed sense of shock, then over at Myat. Reading the greed in her eyes was very easy to do. "If you have the Dashan's mind, what does Len have?"

"It should be obvious—he has the Dashan's power.

All the personal energy the Dashan used to create his spells, to manipulate matter and warp time, Len possesses it all. The boots function as a focusing device for such power, amplifying it and refining it for use in even the most complicated of spells."

Nagrendra swallowed a piece of cheese, then frowned. "And you summoned Len here to find the boots? I assume you want them; but if you have no personal energy for magick, what good will they do you?"

Myat smiled yet again. "With the boots I can tap the energy Len has to work magick. I will be able to defeat Lord Disaster and make the Empire safe once and for all time."

Len roused himself from the high-backed chair in which he sat. "What if I don't want to give you the boots?"

"You will. With them, I can send you home again."

Xoayya gave Myat a hard stare. "But then you would lose his magickal power."

Myat dismissed that suggestion with a casual wave of a hand. "Hardly. Because of our connection and with the boots, I can draw on his energy no matter where he is."

"Like a leech."

The Princess's blue eyes hardened at Xoayya's comment. "The relationship would hardly be parasitic. He would not notice the loss. He's not used the energy in his life, so it means nothing to him. Here, letting me use it, the power can keep our world safe from Fialchar."

Tyrchon barked a sharp laugh. "Fialchar is the least of your worries."

Myat cocked her head slightly to the right. "Are you suggesting *you* will oppose me?"

"Oh, I might, but only as an afterthought." He smiled carefully, letting his left hand rest on the hilt of his sword. "If you possess the Dashan's intellect, you also possess his memories?"

"Many of them. Most, in fact."

"Then what do you remember about Spiriastar?"

Myat staggered back as if she'd been punched in the chest. Her mouth opened and closed as if she were a fish out of water. "Spiriastar? What do you know of her?"

Xoayya took a step forward. "She's alive and well, and doesn't seem to remember you too fondly."

The Princess blinked a couple of times, then her face sharpened as she regained her composure. "How do you know this?"

"We've met her. We were her guests for a while." Xoayya folded her arms across her chest. "You knew Shoth died, but you didn't know she caused his death?"

Myat rubbed her left hand over her forehead and looked down. "This is not good. There were safeguards to keep her in her realm, trapped. What happened?"

Len eased himself forward in his seat and leaned heavily on the right arm of the chair. "The Chaos storm rolled over the valley where she had been hidden. It seems to have awakened her. We went into her realm—Shoth and I were enough to open it up. When you created it and enchanted it, you used spells that would confuse her and contain her, thinking you could go down there and trap her again. When we arrived, we taxed the spells you used, I guess, or we were enough mental stimulation for her to break through what you had done."

"She's free?"

"If she isn't yet, it's only a matter of time." Len shook his head. "She tortured Nagrendra here and likely would have done the same to the rest of us."

The Reptiad nodded. "We both came from Thas. She asked after her homeland and seemed to focus on it. When my answers proved unsatisfactory, she decided I was part of a plot to trap her. She began to question me more closely."

Myat shook her head, then shrieked. "You idiots; do you know what you have done? Have you any idea how much trouble you have caused?"

Len's eyes narrowed. "Hey, lady, we were there. We saw. We're the ones Shoth sacrificed himself to save."

"That may well be true, but you have no perspective." Myat's face darkened, and her voice took on an icy tone. "Even with five centuries of experience, Fialchar is nothing compared to Spiriastar. Of the Twelve who created the Seal of Reality, she could easily have been the most powerful. She certainly was the most brilliant, which is why she was given the task of weaving time into the Seal. She found a way to define it and quantify it so it could be made part of the Seal. If not for her, the Shattering would have been a gradual process that would have brought Chaos into the world in trickles, not the solid wave that passed over everything."

Myat's hands balled into fists and rose toward her shoulders. "When Fialchar shattered the Seal, Chaos blasted into Spiriastar and scrambled her mind. It left it in pieces. She loved puzzles and working their solutions, but after Chaos she began to view the solving of a puzzle as an exercise in time reversal. Instead of building the pieces back together, she saw it as a local manipulation of time to get the puzzle into a pre-scrambled state. Because of Chaos, she saw anything she could think of as a past state projecting itself forward. For her to make that reality come true all she had to do was strip away the layers of time until she got there. The past she imagined would become a future she could live in."

Xoayya hugged her arms around herself as if cold. "But the future is immutable."

"It could seem that way to you, child, but Spiriastar is a woman for whom past and present and future have no meaning. And if the future is built upon the past, and you change the past, do you not also change the future that might be built upon it?" Myat shook her head vehemently. "And now Spiriastar is free to remember a past filtered through her madness and to try to make it become real today. She will use the power of Chaos to crush the Empire so she can re-create what she knew. The past five centuries will be wiped away. That cannot happen."

"Agreed." Tyrchon patted his sword. "I'll go back there, find her, and kill her."

"No!" Xoayya and Myat spoke at the same time.

"I must."

Myat held a hand out. "I recognize the blade you bear, and I can tell you that you cannot kill her with it. Another tried and perished in the attempt."

Tyrchon frowned. "Zin Anzal?"

The Princess hesitated, then nodded. "Zin Anzal. She was Spiriastar's daughter and my wife. After her mother went mad, Zin tried to stop her and was slain. Zin and I, we had a child that I brought here, to the Matarun, to be raised in the mountains while I went back to trap Spiriastar and then destroy myself." She tapped herself on the breastbone. "Shoth and I are both descended from her, so the blood of the Dashan and Spiriastar runs in our veins. Spiritually and physically I am heir to those boots. Give them to me, and I can undo the trouble you have caused in releasing her."

Len sat back in his chair. "No."

"What?" Myat's mouth hung open in surprise. "You must, you *will*."

"No, no I won't." The young man scratched at the side of his neck, then regarded the dried blood dirtying his fingernails. "Where I come from, there is a saying: Power corrupts, and absolute power corrupts absolutely. You sent Shoth out into Chaos to find me, and you summoned me to find these boots, regardless of what could have happened to either one of us. You may even have been motivated by concern for the Empire, but I'm not feeling too sure about how pure that motive might be. If Shoth was our conscience, I'm not sure I want you possessing power without him."

Myat looked at Len coldly. "You know nothing of our world. You know nothing of the danger we face. A month ago, Fialchar appeared in the Imperial capital and said he would come inside a year to take it all away. And now you tell me you have unleashed a scourge that makes him look as dangerous as a mere footpad in comparison? You may well have doomed this world by your meddling, and now you even think of denying me the only means at our disposal for dealing with the problem?"

"And whose meddling was it that brought me here in the first place?"

The Princess snorted. "I did what was necessary to fulfill my destiny."

"Yeah, sure, but when you say that, do you mean *my* as in Myat's, or the Dashan's?" Len struggled from his chair and stood on unsteady feet. "I don't think the Dashan ever intended for his power to return to this world. His conscience, yes, so anything his intellect could come up with would be tempered by good judgment. And his intellect, yes, so that new spells could be created to preserve and protect the Empire. But his power? No, I think that was meant to stay away."

Xoayya shook her head. "The fact that you are here means this reunion was destined to happen."

"You could be right or wrong on that, Xoayya, but that still doesn't mean the Dashan wanted this to happen." Len looked around at everyone in the room. "This is your world, and you're the connection I have to it; but I'm not going to turn these boots over to someone who would use Shoth so coldly, regardless of the cost. I apologize to you, but this isn't what Shoth would have wanted. I can't do it."

Myat's blue eyes glittered like ice on a moonlit night. "You will have to be made to see how important this is. Guards, take everyone into custody. We will start with the woman, and her screams will make you change your mind, Len."

Tyrchon drew his sword and used his body to shield Xoayya from the Matarun. "If I have to slaughter every one of you, I will."

Myat laughed aloud and nodded toward the stairs. "You'll never fight your way clear of this place."

"Don't need to." Tyrchon nodded toward the tunnel leading to the rents. "I just have to cut my way clear to Chaos, and you, Princess, are in my way."

Myat smiled. "And the food and wine you've consumed was poisoned. You'll be dead in hours if I do not provide you the antidote. Even if you neutralize the poison with a spell right this second, the damage it's already done will destroy you in Chaos."

The wolf-warrior leveled his sword at Myat. "We are at an impasse, then."

"So it seems."

"I sincerely doubt that."

The word reverberated from down the tunnel leading to Chaos. Tyrchon saw no movement in it, then a shadow poured out into the round chamber. It thickened, then arms and legs grew out of it. As it congealed, Myat came slowly about, then stepped back off the central painting. The shadow figure usurped her position, then his metal flesh squealed as he smiled.

"How convenient to be in Chaos while out of it." Fialchar spread his arms to encompass the painting. "You would be Myat, the architect of the troubles we now face. What have you to say for yourself?"

"Not quite what you would expect, Lord Disaster." Myat's chin came up. "I would say, 'Like father, like son.'"

27

Fialchar's arrival and appearance left Len reeling. Tall and cadaverously thin, with metal flesh and ivory bone showing through in places, Fialchar was a creature of nightmares. In him Len could see bits and pieces from every scary movie he'd ever attended, yet somehow, in Fialchar, the elements combined in a most hideous fashion. *In films, at some level or another, the humanity behind the monster shines through. With him, there is none of that.*

Fialchar looked down at Myat. "Are you suggesting you are the fruit of my loins?"

She stared up at him, defiant determination on her face. "You were the father of Spiriastar's last aide so, yes, I am the fruit of your loins. My flesh is his flesh, generations removed, and my soul is his soul."

The monster pointed a skeletal finger at Len. "Yet the boots reside on *his* feet."

"He is part of me. His soul is part of my soul."

"You may, indeed, be in part my son, but you are far from the whole of him." Fialchar held his right hand out and into it materialized an ebon staff with a smoky quartz globe on one end. He glanced down at the painting on which he stood, then smiled. "I recognize the style. More of my son's handiwork?"

Myat nodded. "A piece that is now gone."

"Pity." Somehow Fialchar managed to say the word without the least trace of sympathy or regret making it to Len's ears.

The gaunt figure suddenly slammed the heel of his staff into the painting. Len saw a flash, but it was a flash of blackness, as if shadow exploded out from the point of impact. For a half second he saw everyone reversed out, with black skeletons instead of white bones. Everyone, save Myat and Fialchar, looked normal. She appeared to be taller, more massive. He couldn't quite figure out what Fialchar was, but it definitely didn't seem human.

Along with the flash came another sensation. Len felt squashed flat, as if trapped beneath the wheels of a semitrailer. A red-hot mesh seemed to slice his body into millions of little pieces, which oozed back together on the other side. The pains he had known before sank beneath this new feeling, but it ended quickly enough.

Then color leached back into the world, and Len found he was no longer in the subterranean circular chamber. He stood in a domed room with two sets of pillars that held up a circular gallery running around the room itself. Beneath the gallery, shelves lined the walls, each filled with countless volumes. The books varied in size and shape, with some lying flat, others leaning, and some jammed in so tight it would take a prybar to get them loose again.

Little tables and chairs, daybeds and bookstands occupied the space in the room's periphery. Len saw that one table had a chess set on it, with all the pieces ready to go for a game. Dust covered most all the other furnishings, giving Len the impression he had arrived in a building that hadn't seen use for ages.

The room's central feature, on the other hand, suggested that was not the case. A huge crystal globe hovered above a hole opened in the floor. A golden disc covered with odd serpentine sigils surrounded the globe and was supported by eight pillars that ended in dragon-claw designs clutching the floor. Weird images flitted through the globe itself, but Len was not close enough to see them without so much distortion that the pictures were rendered meaningless.

The room had been constructed out of emerald blocks, but it did not remind Len overmuch of Spiriastar's palace. The stones here had light playing through them in a most disturbing manner. Len recalled being instructed by a professor to look at the ice cubes in print ads for liquor to find the symbolic images hidden therein. The professor had said one could see a naked woman, which was a method used to suggest subliminally to men that to drink that brand of scotch would bring them sex.

Subtle and subliminal were not words that would be used to describe the images Len saw in these blocks. Stunningly holographic in quality, they depicted scenes from sick and twisted fantasies. They struck Len like the dreams of serial murderers such as Jeffrey Dahmer or John Wayne Gacy. One series of blocks seemed to reenact in exquisite details each murder committed by Jack the Ripper. While it did occur to Len that he might be projecting that imagery into the blocks himself, that made the images no less horrid.

Len tore his gaze from the blocks and looked at Fialchar. "I suppose you want the boots, too? Forget it. You'll have to kill me before you can have them."

Fialchar threw his head back in a laugh that sounded like cicadas buzzing their way in through Len's skull. "I know of those boots, and I know killing you to possess them would do me no good. If you do not give them of your own free will, they will be useless—and decidedly garish—footwear, nothing more."

Len looked over at Myat. "You knew that?"

She nodded.

"So you poisoned my friends and threatened to torture them to get the boots?" Len shook his head. "What a sad and pathetic creature you are."

Fialchar looked at Myat. "You didn't?"

Myat nodded. "I did."

The lich waved his staff through the air and a golden glow sank into everyone's flesh. Len immediately felt his aches and pains vanish and saw that Nagrendra had grown back his missing scales. Len felt his scalp over his left ear and realized the healing job Xoayya had started with her spell had been completed by Fialchar's magick.

"Your mistake, Myat, was in poisoning my servants." Fialchar opened his hand and left the staff hanging there in the air, then looked at Tyrchon. "You did as I requested? You discovered the disturbance that I could not penetrate?"

The wolf-warrior nodded. "The Dashan had imprisoned and hidden away Spiriastar. The Chaos storm appears to have affected the enchantments hiding her. She is awake and alive and apparently angry. She had nothing good to say about you."

"This explains many things." Fialchar drifted over toward the globe—Len would have said he walked, but he saw no feet nor any movement of the moldy robe that would indicate Fialchar was walking. "The area I could not see into had once been confined to a single valley, but now it has expanded."

Myat pointed at Tyrchon. "Your agents caused her prison to be opened. Had they not ventured there, she would still be contained."

"Perhaps, but I think not. Your effort to fix blame is misguided, for it is your fault that we face her now." Little gouts of flame licked up along Fialchar's forehead from his eye sockets. "The blame is yours—three times yours. You failed the first time when you did not kill her after capturing her. You failed a second time when you created a prison that could be reopened."

"But only by me."

"Yes, and you failed a third time when you summoned that part of you which could open the prison."

Myat shook her head. "But he was not supposed to go there."

"Immaterial." Fialchar glanced at Xoayya. "Tell her that such a thing was predestined."

"Is belaboring the obvious going to be productive?" Xoayya remained close to Tyrchon, but kept her chin up. "You know what the problem is, now a solution must be found."

Lord Disaster nodded, his flesh shrieking like twisted metal. "Pragmatic, how refreshing."

Len folded his arms over his chest. "Can anything be done? Spiriastar struck me as being very powerful."

Fialchar leaned on the gold disc, letting his head hang like a moon in orbit around the crystal sphere. "She is most powerful, but she also has her limitations.

Primary among them is a paradox: she trusts few people and prefers to control everything herself, but when she does find someone she can trust, she trusts him implicitly. This was how the Dashan was able to capture her even after she murdered his beloved wife. Spiriastar refused to see how he might hold the murder against her. He played to that blindness of hers, then sprang his trap."

Nagrendra frowned. "When last we left her, I did not sense in her a willingness to trust anyone or anything."

"Of course not, which means she will want to be in control of everything herself." Fialchar's head came up, and blue flames glowed in his eye sockets. "This means she will try to do everything herself. Powerful though she may be, she cannot manage every aspect of the campaign she will be required to launch against me."

Len frowned. "You think she will come after *you*?"

"Of course. My son trapped her. My efforts unhinged her mind. I *am* her greatest rival." The lich straightened up. "No matter what she wants to do, she will be vulnerable to my attacks, so she must eliminate me. If she were of a mind to, she might even strike an alliance with the Empire to destroy me."

Len slowly nodded. He'd always heard the phrase "the lesser of two evils," but had only thought it applied to presidential campaigns and scheduling choices at work. From all he had heard, Fialchar was a foe dedicated to destroying the Empire, but in the five hundred years he'd had to do it, he had failed. Spiriastar, who had been superior to him before, certainly seemed capable of doing the job he had not. *But will her elimination mean Fialchar will be that much more powerful for his attempts to destroy the Empire?*

It suddenly struck Len that Fialchar was not so

much fearful that Spiriastar would destroy him as usurp his place as the pinnacle of evil in the Empire. Len sensed a satisfaction from Fialchar concerning his position. He wasn't certain if it was memories of the Dashan for his father, or just Len's own experiences with bullies, but he recognized Fialchar's need to save face, to maintain his reputation and position. In this case, if it brought an end to Spiriastar and her threat to the Empire, it was to be praised.

What happens after that, however, will be very important.

Tyrchon waved a hand toward the globe. "You said you cannot see into her realm. What has she blocked from your view?"

Fire pulsed from Fialchar's eyes. "She has expanded north and west of her previous position."

"That would put her near the Dashan's Sanctuary."

"Correct, Tyrchon." Fialchar hunched forward over the globe again, allowing his shoulders to rise like mountain peaks to bracket his head. "It also extends her influence over what once was the Bharashadi Necroleum. I suspect she is heading there because of the residual magick left from when Locke destroyed it. However, I don't know this for a fact, and am reluctant to rely on speculation."

Lord Disaster came out from behind the globe, his hands hidden in the sleeves of his robe. "Before we can confront her, we need to know what she is doing. I need to have you scout out her position and relative strength."

"There's a suicide mission for you." Len shook his head. "She'll find us and destroy us in an instant."

"No, for I shall keep her occupied." Fialchar glanced at Myat. "You composed the spell that dragged your counterpart here?"

"I did."

"Good, then you will design more spells, and I shall put them into play. They will all be trying to penetrate Spiriastar's defenses, to ferret out her secrets. They will fail, of course, but she will be preoccupied defending herself against them."

A sly grin grew on Myat's face. "I will not need you to cast these spells when I have the boots."

"You're not getting these boots, sister." Len shook his head. "No way."

"I concur." Fialchar's smile writhed across his lips. "You may be able to compose spells of great power, but you have little experience of using same. While they are off scouting, you will be learning." He nodded toward Xoayya. "And you will be as well."

Tyrchon held a hand up. "I'm not leaving her here alone, with you."

"Your concern is touching, Tyrchon, but misplaced." Lord Disaster clasped his hands behind his back. "Tell him, Xoayya, tell him that you foresee no instance in which I will mistreat you."

"I don't 'see' such a thing, but my visions have been limited while in Chaos." Xoayya curled a lock of red hair around her finger. "But I also do not feel you will harm me. I think it is my place to remain here."

"You see? Your concerns are misplaced."

Tyrchon's eyes narrowed. "I would feel better if they had guardians. Bring the rest of Ghislaine's people here."

"The Matarun Guards might be formidable, but here they would stop little." Fialchar gestured almost casually with his right hand toward the chessboard. Four pieces moved across the table and leaped down to the floor. Once they hit, they grew up to become gigantic, with the horns on their helms touching the underside of the gallery. Two of the massive armored figures were black and two were red. Len could see no one inside the suits, and a reddish light glowed from within the black armor's helm. More unsettling, a shadowy vapor seemed to issue like steam from the faceplates of the scarlet figures. Each bore a huge sword, and all four wore red or black capes.

Fialchar's head craned around, almost turning a full circle on his neck, then he crooked the fingers of his left hand. That arm appeared very glassy to Len, as if it were formed out of seawater that had been trapped in that shape. Light refracted through it oddly, and Len found it unnerving to stare at the limb for any length of time.

From the corner of the room came four rats dancing on their hind legs. Len backed away because he seemed to remember such behavior indicated disease, but the rats seemed intent on Lord Disaster himself. The lich rotated his wrist once, then a red sphere engulfed the rats. It split into four parts that swelled to the size of a beach ball. Sharp claws then rent each from inside, and from within each came a muscular creature, devoid of fur, with a spiky ridge running down its spine. They looked vaguely feline in the body, but the earless head and wrinkled flesh reminded Len of Namibian naked mole rats.

"To you, Xoayya, I give the scarlet guardians. Myat, you shall have those that match your hair. They and their beasts will see to your safety at all times, so your companions here need not worry about you." Fialchar bowed his head toward Tyrchon. "Is this adequate protection for them?"

The wolf-warrior looked at the scarlet guardians,

then nodded slowly. "Know this: if Xoayya comes to any harm at all, I will hold you accountable."

"I would have it no other way, Tyrchon." The ancient sorcerer pressed his hands together. "I know this alliance makes you uneasy, as it does me. Still, without it, your realm and mine will be crushed. We have been enemies in the past, and shall be enemies in the future, but, for now, we can prevail only if united in our opposition to Spiriastar."

28

Tyrchon paused in the doorway to study Xoayya as she stood there on one of Castel Payne's grand balconies. The dawning sun sparked gold in her red hair. The gown she wore had an archaic look about it, being sleeveless, white, and gathered at her waist with a light gold chain. The hem nearly touched the ground, but he could still catch hints of sandal-sheathed feet on the stone. Xoayya stood there, at the emerald balustrade, facing outward, so he only caught her in profile.

Despite that, he knew he had never seen anyone in the world he considered more beautiful.

He took a step forward, but one of the scarlet guardians moved to block his path. The rat-thing it led on a stout chain snarled at Tyrchon. The wolf-warrior snarled back, and the watchbeast settled back down in a crouch.

Xoayya turned to face the doorway. A smile blossomed on her face. "Let him pass."

The guardian moved aside and yanked the rat-beast back with it.

She smiled at Tyrchon. "Forgive me. I said I wanted to be alone with my thoughts, and the guardian took it quite literally. What I really meant is that I did not want Myat around."

Tyrchon chuckled as he walked down a couple of steps and met her at the balcony edge. "I understand your reasoning. I can't really conceive of many situations where the words 'Myat' and 'friend' would be used in the same sentence."

"Save perhaps in a warning to someone, and with lots of negation involved."

"True enough." Tyrchon took her right hand in his and raised it to his muzzle. "You look radiant this morning."

She smiled and glanced away. "It comes from dreaming of you last night."

"You had a vision of us, together?"

Xoayya shook her head. "Not a vision, just a dream, but a dream I would rejoice in making come true." She stroked his cheek. "When you return from this mission."

"Then return I shall." He shot a glance back at the emerald walls of Fialchar's demesne. "I am still reluctant to leave you here."

"I know, and I love you for it, but I will be safe here." She turned away from him and rested her back against his chest. "When I was in the Empire the sorcerers in the City of Sorcerers rejected me as a student because I was too old and had no discipline. Since I have been in Chaos, I see the need for the discipline, and now I want to learn. While I have no doubt Fialchar will want to teach me things I do not want to learn, my becoming a better magicker could mean the difference between victory and defeat. Magick could save your life, so it is very important for me to concentrate and learn all I can."

"I recall your saying before you knew no combat spells and did not feel yourself inclined to learn any." Tyrchon's arms enfolded her in a hug. "Is that still what you feel?"

"Yes. I think, with Myat and Fialchar and Nagrendra with us, the need for offensive magicks will be more than met. I will be very content with a supporting role, providing aid and comfort as needed. And my clairvoyance skills will be helpful in determining where Spiriastar's forces are."

The wolf-warrior rested his chin on her crown. "Are you sure you want to try to spy out the future of this series of events?"

"You're going on a scouting mission to gather information I can get without putting myself or others in danger." Confusion crept into her voice. "Surely my ability to do that and communicate to you what is happening will be vital in the battle."

"It would be, but there is a difference in those two things. Our mission will be finding out what currently *is*. Your clairvoyance will be spying out what the future might or will be." He gave her a reassuring squeeze. "If you are right, that what you see is what will happen, and you see us losing, we are doomed. If what you see is mutable, then it has little value as information since it is not reliable."

She turned in his arms and looked up at him. "But I want to know that you will be all right."

"I will be, I promise." He looked out off the balcony and saw the red landscape extending for miles to the north. Occasional streaks of green broke it up like veins of disease eating into it. With Castel Payne floating over half a mile off the surface of the ground, the vista it offered could not have been equaled anywhere. *Pity that what I see is so barren.*

"I shall accept you at your word, then, but know I am uneasy about only four of you going on this scouting mission. Nagrendra is well enough now, and Ghislaine certainly knows how to take care of herself, but Len? The events of yesterday seem to have left him as confused as ever. He also has no experience for a mission like this."

"I agree with your assessment, but I don't want Len around Myat. She was willing to put all of us in jeopardy to get those boots on her feet. I have no doubt she can be more subtle, if needs be." A low growl rumbled from his throat. "More importantly, I think Len needs this trip."

"What do you mean?"

Tyrchon smiled down at her. "You recall how coming into Chaos made you more aware of your responsibilities?"

"Yes. You think Len needs that?"

"I do." The wolf-warrior brushed Xoayya's hair back over her left shoulder. "Aside from the time we spent in Spiriastar's realm, Len has been nothing but a body being dragged around. Even Myat admitted that she'd summoned him so he could get the boots for her. Only in Spiriastar's realm, when he was trying to figure out what was happening, and when he led the antlings off our path, was he truly alive and engaged in what was going on. As I noted before, you use your visions to prove everything has already been determined in the world. Len doesn't think anything matters, since this is all a dream. Both of you have a barrier to engaging with the world. You're overcoming yours, and Len has made strides, but Shoth's death and Myat's intervention have undercut his progress."

"And you think his engagement is important?" Xoayya frowned slightly. "You don't think he was summoned here just to be fuel for Myat's magick?"

"Myat said that she had the Dashan's intellect, Shoth had his conscience, and Len, all of his power. This is untrue, however, since Shoth could actually work magicks. He had some of the power that Myat says belongs to Len alone. And Len has been able to work with the magick of the boots to do any number of things, so even if he cannot consciously cast spells, something inside him allows him to make magick work."

The wolf-warrior sighed. "The Dashan, in rending his soul, wanted to prevent all he had learned and done from being misused. This determined the divisions he made of his soul. I find it significant that his intellect can only act in concert with others—others who can exercise their own discretion to prevent acts of evil from happening."

"So you think that Len has, in himself, the means to stop Myat from becoming a monster?"

"I think she may already be a monster, but he can stop her from becoming a powerful one." Tyrchon shook his head. "But he has to believe his work will make a difference. If he doesn't, he may not act when he really should."

Xoayya nodded. "I could speak with him, before you leave, if you wish."

"I have an idea of what to say to him, so, no, but thank you for offering. If I fail, you'll have your chance." He lowered his muzzle and kissed her on the forehead as best he could. "Be safe and be well. We'll return as soon as we can."

She slipped her arms around him and laid her head against his chest. "It will not be soon enough for me, Tyrchon. Hurry back."

Len did a quick check of his gear and felt very uneasy. From what had once been the castle's armory, Ghislaine had pulled a suit of leather armor studded with blackened steel buds. Similarly blackened greaves and bracers protected his shins and forearms respectively. A round pot of a helmet with a single, unicornish horn projecting from it had been strapped on his head, and he'd been given a relatively short and stout sword for his own protection.

He wore the boots, of course, and bore the shoe sizer on his left arm as if it were a shield. Jhesti rode on his right shoulder, and Fitz was carrying a full load of provisions. He felt like an extra in some fantasy movie destined to go straight to video and then straight to the discount racks. *This is ridiculous.*

He began to unfasten his helmet's chin strap, but a heavy hand landed on his left shoulder. "Don't do that, Len. We don't know what we will face out there."

Len looked up at Tyrchon. Unlike him, the wolf-warrior looked every bit the hero. His mail shirt fitted him well, and daggers peeked out from a half dozen sheaths. The sword he bore was clearly meant for combat, and seemed huge enough that only a true hero could possibly wield it.

Len shook his head. "I know what we will face out there—more id-beasts. Don't worry, though, I don't think I could dream up anything you couldn't handle."

"There's that word again."

"Which?"

"Dream."

"Right." Len glanced down at his hands. "It's the reality of this situation, Tyrchon. This is a dream—a sick, twisted dream, but a dream nonetheless. Myat is really Angie, I woman I work with. Fialchar is one part Terminator and one part villain from the film *Nosferatu*. Escher has an illustration that could explain this floating castle, and I'm even speaking to you and understanding you, but you have no reason to understand English. The evidence mounts up."

The wolf-warrior nodded and held his hands up. "You need not tell me all this. I will confess I don't understand it, but that does not matter. I merely want to understand you."

That brought Len's head up. "Understand me?"

"Yes." Tyrchon's stare hardened. "I, too, dream. In my dreams I am very active, as I am in life. If I were to judge you by the actions you take in *this*, your dream, I would have to say you are a man who prefers doing nothing. Granted, you have acted when faced with serious, life-threatening situations, but you do not act otherwise, it seems."

"That's not true." Len frowned, seeking an example to disprove Tyrchon's statement. "I stabbed a *Tsvortu* in the Sanctuary."

"To save your own life." The wolf-warrior cocked his head to the right. "In your world, what is it you do with your life?"

"I'm a shoe salesman."

"You were apprenticed to a cobbler and make shoes, then? This is your profession?"

"No, not exactly. I've been doing that for a year. Before that I was in school and worked delivering food for people. And I did telephone sales for a while, then worked stocking a grocery store, and I mowed lawns . . ."

Len stopped as the catalog of his banal jobs toppled over on him. "I guess Jhesti said it best when he told me that if I was hero material, I'd already have done something heroic with my life." *Like facing Corbett down over stealing the Gester idea.*

Tyrchon's jaw opened in a lupine grin. "Your Jhesti may be wise in many things, but not this. A hero is someone who takes action, decisive action in a place, at a time when action is required. It is true that someone can put himself in a position where those opportunities are more frequent, but until one of those chances comes up, no one will ever know if he has the stuff of heroes in him or not. That is a simple and sad fact of life."

The larger man folded his arms across his chest. "What concerns me more with you, Len, is that you seem content to let life come to you, then pass you by. You said you sell shoes—shoes someone else makes. What do you actually do?"

Len shifted his shoulders. "They come into the shop, they tell me what style and color they want. If they know the size, I get it, if they don't, I figure out what size they need with this thing." He patted his shield. "Then I bring the shoes to them, they try them on and pay for them."

"And you never see them again?"

"Maybe, depending. We have repeat customers."

"But fetching shoes is as active as you get?"

A cold hand squeezed Len's heart. "I guess so."

Tyrchon nodded slowly. "You have concerned yourself with whether or not you are in a dream. I would tell you that whether this is dream or reality, it does not matter."

"Sure it does."

"No, Len, it does not." The wolf-warrior opened his

hands and spread his arms wide. "What matters is how you act and react in this situation. If you want to remain passive and do nothing, this will work fine if you are dreaming. If this is reality, being passive will get you and others killed."

"But I was active in our escape from Spiriastar, and Shoth still died."

"True, but he also was active and took the action he knew no one else could take. Now, if this is reality instead of a dream, being active could make quite a difference in how things turn out. And even if this is a dream, being active will do no harm. Where you are and what is happening is not as important as how you deal with it."

Tyrchon clapped him on the shoulders. "Life can be *lived*, or it can just be experienced. When you live it, when you take control, you are able to do more things."

"But, if I do that, then Shoth's death is my responsibility."

"No, his death was *his* responsibility. That isn't to say his death wasn't a tragedy or that it shouldn't hurt. It was a tragedy. It *should* hurt. If it doesn't hurt, if it doesn't fill you with regret, you're a monster with no heart, or a monster that keeps his heart chained up."

Len sighed. "You're saying a life that isn't being lived isn't worth living?"

"In part. There are going to be times when things *are* beyond your control, or times when you relinquish control to others, but that isn't the same as never exerting control. And whether this is a dream or not, you still face that choice of exerting control or just remaining passive."

"But what if I make a mistake?"

"It won't be the first you ever make and probably won't be the last, unless it's a very *bad* mistake."

Tyrchon rested his left hand on the hilt of his sword. "Which is better, though, to be left with the memories of having done something that didn't work, or to know that if you *had* acted, you could have averted disaster?"

Len slowly nodded. "It's better to ask forgiveness than wait for permission."

"Well said."

"My father's line." Len suddenly wished his armor had pockets because he wanted to shove his hands into them. *How is it that Tyrchon can so easily get to the core of my problem? I'm passive because being more active brings confrontation. If I had claimed credit for the Dancing Joker pins, Mr. Corbett might have contested that claim, and I'd have to fight him. If I'd asked Angie out before she made it apparent she found me attractive, I would have risked rejection. I hold people off and back because to bring them in opens me to pain.*

The trick of it is this, though: pain is always going to be there. By stepping up and accepting responsibility for my actions, I determine how much pain I'm going to allow in, and I could shut some of it off before it ever gets in.

Len's head came up. "You think being along on this trip provides a good opportunity for me to begin to exert control over my life?"

Tyrchon nodded. "Probably no better opportunity I can think of."

"Okay, works for me." Len gave him a cautious smile in spite of feeling a bit giddy inside. "I've done nothing of import for twenty-three years, and that's gotten to be a rut. New day, new world, new Len Fong. Let's do it."

29

Xoayya stayed at the balcony's edge, hoping she would catch a glimpse of Tyrchon and the others heading down to the surface below. It felt very odd for her to be suspended so far above the ground. She would have thought such a thing would frighten her, but it did not. Part of the reason, she knew, was because the solidity of the castle itself, from the stout walls to the tall spires, suggested a permanence that belied a crash against the ground.

More importantly, she didn't *feel* she was in danger of falling. What might have been a hunch in someone else, or blind confidence, in her became certainty. She had learned long ago that she could peer into the future and that events she saw would unfold. While no vision had come to her concerning Castel Payne, what she *felt* was that the castle was very important to her and her life. She sensed nothing to cause concern, and, for her, that meant concern was a waste of energy.

A long shadow fell over her from behind. She turned, hoping it would be Tyrchon, but found herself facing Fialchar. The scarlet guardian who had tried to keep Tyrchon away from her had not moved to stop Lord Disaster, and the rat-beast cowered behind its red master.

Fialchar's face betrayed no emotion. "It is time for you to come with me, Xoayya. Princess Myat has determined it is time we get to work."

Xoayya arched an eyebrow. "She is deciding when we do things now?"

A metallic squeak betrayed the hint of a grin on his face. "It is perhaps a holdover from my son's personality, but she will not accept being told anything. When one tries to explain to her why this thing or that is impossible, she will demand it be made possible."

"So you told her it was impossible for us to get started this early in the day?"

"It's a simple trick, but one very effective against someone who does not believe she can be tricked." The tall lich's shoulder rose in a shrug. "If action must be compelled, I prefer to wait until I have no choice in the matter."

Xoayya crossed her arms and leaned back on the balustrade. "You mean to let her order you about so she will underestimate you."

"Is this something you have *seen*, or something you are supposing?"

"I've not *seen* it. My visions have been curtailed since my entry into Chaos." Xoayya shivered, then moved from beneath Fialchar's shadow. "She is used to commanding and does not expect opposition from those she considers underlings. How much of that is your son?"

Fialchar folded his hands together at his waist. "My

son, in temperament, is more like your Len. Myat's incisiveness and judgmental nature certainly speak to his reasoning ability. They also match his ability to hold a grudge over certain slights."

"Like shattering the Seal of Reality?"

"He did seem to have an adverse reaction to that event, yes." Fialchar's smile broadened a touch. "I was aware of his thoughts on that matter, though he never directly confronted me with them. I was otherwise occupied at the time."

She nodded. "And now you fear he may strike at you through Myat and Len?"

"I *fear* nothing, not Myat, not Spiriastar. They may once have been very powerful, but what I have learned since shattering the Seal makes me superior to them all." He turned on his heel. "Come, she will be impatient."

"You do think she will strike at you, however."

Fialchar stopped and looked back at her over his shoulder. "Think? I know. I could let you have a vision of the moment it will happen, if you wish."

Xoayya frowned. "'Let me have a vision'? How would you accomplish that?"

The tall sorcerer slowly turned back toward her. "You said your visions had been curtailed since you entered Chaos. Do you know why this happened?"

"You do?"

"Yes." Fialchar pressed his hands together, fingertip to fingertip. "In your Empire the number of variables that determine the future are relatively limited and, at best, have minimal effects on what will happen. The future is not so much determined absolutely as it has momentum in a particular direction. Someone like you has a relatively easy time seeing events that will come to pass, and by doing so, locking in values for all the variables that make that future happen. Chaos, on the other hand, is full of very dynamic forces and factors that make up the future. A *Tsvortu* smashing down a bird with a rock could deprive a *Hobmotli* shaman of a sign he needed to prevent a war between clans, which boils over into a battle that engages thousands of Chademons and forever shifts the balance of power within my realm. You simply lack the necessary techniques for being able to influence events to achieve your desired result."

"I *see* the future, not determine it."

"Yes, of course, child, that's what you say." Sparks danced from Fialchar's eyes. "Still, you maintain that the future you see is the future that will come about. However, if you have not seen it, then there is no true indication it will happen, correct?"

Xoayya hesitated. Her belief that her visions were true and immutable meant he was right: once she saw it, it had to come to pass. She smiled. "The problem with your premise is that I only see visions of times and places, but I do not always know what they are, nor how they happened. Say, for example, I see you, lying dead, in a pool of blood; I won't know how that happened, or when, I just know it will happen."

"That's very well and good for a hypothetical question, but there are times you will want to concentrate on a specific outcome, to see what will happen. Right now, you cannot, so that future is unformed yet." Fialchar shrugged. "It matters not to me, child, if you want your visions now or never again. I merely observe that I can provide you the tools to produce them here in Chaos. Whether or not you choose to avail yourself of them is your choice. Come, she expects us."

Xoayya fell into step with the sorcerer. "If you know she will betray you and strike at you, why keep her close, why help her?"

"Two reasons. The first is that Spiriastar bears her a greater grudge than she does me. Myat will be more than happy to take Spiriastar on, and I will be happy to let her." The lich led her down a circular stairway. "Second, by working with her I will be better able to deal with her when the time comes. I will learn her weaknesses."

"And she will learn yours."

"She may think so." Fialchar shook his head. "She will be wrong."

The stairway led to a short corridor and down into a long, narrow, high-ceilinged room cluttered with tables and benches. Dried clumps of plants, moldering animal carcasses, and odd lengths of coppery tubing hung from the rafters. The tables had countless glass beakers, pitchers, bowls, and an alembic or three scattered on them. Dust covered everything and rose up in a blizzard as Fialchar moved into the room. Xoayya sneezed once, then brought the neckline of her gown up to cover her nose and mouth.

Myat stood at a workbench at the far end of the room. She paged back and forth in a massive volume, the yellowed pages snapping crisply with her irritation. Xoayya's sneeze brought her around. She pointed a finger at Fialchar that trembled with outrage. "How can you expect me to work in a place like this? It is filthy, completely filthy, and this grimoire is useless. These spells are not fit for an apprentice to be learning, and they contain serious errors that could kill anyone attempting to follow the instructions."

Fialchar nodded. "So they do, but it is *my* grimoire. I know what the errors are, so I do not make those mistakes. I see no reason to reward someone who might slip in here and steal the book, do you?"

"No, I suppose not." Myat brushed her hands one against another to rid them of dust. Unlike Xoayya, she wore a black, hooded robe of the sort often seen in the City of Sorcerers, but it had no rank badges sewn into it. She gathered it at her slender waist with a golden cord, providing her outfit the same accents as the gilded black armor of the twin guardians Fialchar had created for her. "We should get to work, then. I will create for you the spells you want to preoccupy Spiriastar. You will cast them. The girl can clean up around here and do what we require to be sustained in our effort."

Fialchar nodded carefully. "I applaud your plan and agree to it with a minor alteration. You will prepare the spells to be cast at a very low and muted power level, one that will allow their effects to be contained here, in this room. Xoayya will cast them. Once she has effectively done so, I will modify the spells for a high power level and then I will cast them."

Myat's eyes widened. "You don't trust me."

"Should I?"

"We are united by the hatred of a common enemy." The Princess's eyes glittered coldly. "It would be foolish for me to strike at you during such a dire time."

"True, but mistakes will happen. I would hate to be discomfited because of a simple error. And I know you will work hard to make certain Xoayya does not die."

"Really? No offense, child, but you are nothing to me."

Xoayya felt her guts tighten. "Words are insufficient to describe my feelings for you, Princess Myat."

Fialchar laughed, a sound that had all the life and delight to it of the sucking wet noise made when a boot is pulled from thick mud. "This might turn out to be more interesting than I could have imagined. You will not hurt Xoayya, Myat, because Tyrchon would slay you."

Myat looked at Xoayya more closely. Xoayya felt the Princess's gaze rake her up and down, then the dark-haired woman shook her head dismissively. "I fail to see the attraction. She's a mere child, and he a beast. Still, I bear neither malice. I shall do my best to keep my spells simple enough for her to wield."

"Thank you, Highness." Xoayya mocked her with a curtsy, then looked at Fialchar. "My knowledge of spellcasting is limited, and all the spells I have cast are Imperial magick."

"Ah, yes, the famed dichotomy." Fialchar's features sharpened. "Time once was when what we now consider Chaos magick or Imperial magick were just magick, with the two approaches being as left is to right or north is to south. The same effect could be accomplished either way, and many magickers knew both methods for casting spells."

"Nagrendra explained that Chaos magick involves harnessing the very nature of Chaos to achieve a desired effect. Imperial magick breaks down the natural order of things to produce its effects." Xoayya smiled carefully. "This is not the way it always was?"

"The approaches are correct, but the sorcerers who established the Ward Walls forbade practitioners from using what is now called Chaos magick. They feel it is a threat to the Ward Walls. It would not surprise you to learn that magickers trained in the City of Sorcerers are inculcated into that tradition in a way that makes it all but impossible for them to jeopardize the Empire and the Ward Walls."

Xoayya frowned. "What do you mean?"

Myat snapped at her. "Did you not hear him? The way they are trained, they fail to learn those things they would need to know to unlock the Ward Walls. Imagine you are being taught to play and compose music, and you are told there are only eight notes in the scale. You will learn to create and play lovely songs with those notes. The Ward Walls, on the other hand, are spells that are composed on a scale that contains fourteen notes. Until a sorcerer rises to the rank of Warder, he does not know enough to raise the Ward Walls . . ."

"Nor can he bring them down." Xoayya slowly nodded. "Practitioners of Chaos magick suffer from no such inability, however. Why haven't you brought the walls down, then?"

"Aside from issues of motivation, the greatest problem in dealing with the Ward Walls is that they are not a single spell that, once cast, is maintained. They are multiple spells, all woven together. To take the walls down would require isolating a single line of a spell, destroying it, then finding another and another." Fialchar's finger plucked at the air as if he were playing an invisible harp. "It could be done, but would take so much time that the sorcerers would have a chance to repair the damage. As you have seen, both in Myat's domain and even at the Imperial Palace, the Ward Walls do not hinder my travel, so I see no reason to destroy them."

Xoayya looked over at Myat. "And you understand enough of the Ward Walls spells to be able to disrupt them, too?"

"I understand them, yes, but do not have the power to be able to bring them down." Myat fell silent for a moment or two, then continued. "And Fialchar's caution about the effort it would take is still valid."

But you never said you had no reason to refrain from bringing them down. Xoayya felt a chill run through her, puckering the flesh on her bare arms. Myat's willingness to use threats and coercion to get the boots had left no doubt in Xoayya's mind that the woman was dangerous. She could have easily put it down to the fact that Myat only received part of a soul, but two things argued against that simple an answer.

First was Tyrchon's noting that Shoth had possessed more of the Dashan's soul than Myat thought he did. The Dashan had taken great care in shutting Spiriastar away and in ripping his soul apart. There had to be a weakness in Myat that would leave her vulnerable, just in case the Dashan's intellect had been reincarnated under the influence of an unscrupulous master. Whatever that safeguard had been, Myat had been able to override it.

The second thing that argued against Myat's being blameless in her desire for power was the bit of herself that Xoayya recognized in the Princess. Xoayya had not been born into a politically powerful family, but her father had been rich enough that after her mother's death, Xoayya had been indulged in whatever she wanted. She had been spoiled rotten, but not beyond redemption. Her family had not just given her material things—which would have created an unending appetite for *more*, but had also given her time and experiences that forced her socialization. She had been taught how to act properly, and was disciplined when she did not.

Xoayya had grown up learning she was subject to rules, but Myat had been of a family that made the rules; therefore, she could be exempted from them. Xoayya had no doubt whatsoever that if Myat saw it as to her advantage to bring the Ward Walls down, she would do it. *If she had the power to do so.*

Xoayya clasped her hands together. "Will I be learning Imperial magick or Chaos magick, or both?"

"For now, child, it will be Imperial magick." Fialchar waved her forward to the workbench with his skeletal hand. "If things become desperate, you can learn Chaos magick. For all of our sakes, however, pray it does not come to that."

30

Having made the decision he did, Len felt better than he had in a long time. *For as long as I can remember.* He dimly recalled a philosophy professor positing that there was no actual way to prove if the world had existed for billions of years, or if it was only created that morning, and people and their memories with it. The professor had meant it as something of a Zen *koan*, to encourage his students to think in nontraditional manners, but Len had just taken the idea as confirmation of his inability to influence the world. *If it only started an hour ago, anything I did in the past didn't matter.*

In making his decision he had chosen to make certain that what he did actually did matter in some way. Tyrchon's point about whether or not he was in a dream or reality not mattering was directly on point. Len tapped his chest with a hand. *What's important is that I'm putting out an effort to make a difference. I might lose, but the only people who never lose in life are those who never take a chance at success.*

He worked his way along the corridor deep in the bowels of Castel Payne and came into a grotto that had been fitted with a crude approximation of railroad tracks made of wood. On them rested a fourteen-foot-long cross between a skiff and a mining truck. Nagrendra sat in the prow with his hands locked on to a big wheel. Ghislaine sat behind him, with Fitz and Jhesti directly amidships. He saw his gear laid into the boat near them, and Tyrchon's stuff in the stern.

Len frowned. "I don't see a rope or pulley system to lower us to the ground."

The Reptiad's tongue flicked in and out of his mouth. "We won't need one. Fialchar showed me the conveyance spell we need to control the descent."

"You've done something like this before?"

The Reptiad. "Something like it, yes."

Tyrchon helped Len into the boat, then leaped in himself. "Get yourself settled. It's likely to be a wild ride."

Len started to seat himself just as the boat lurched toward the grotto's mouth. He fell back on his seat, gripping it in both hands, and felt a pinch as Jhesti clung to his right ear. "Ouch."

"Sorry."

The boat gained momentum as a bluish glow drifted over it. Len could feel the wind playing across his face, then felt a jolt as the cart left the rails and fell from Castel Payne—leaving his stomach somewhere back in the emerald castle's grotto. The craft nosed toward the red earth, and Len suddenly noticed he was seeing more *falling* than *controlling*, and this did not please him. The blue glow vanished, and Len got no comfort from discovering he could still calculate the rate of their acceleration in his head.

And, in doing so, he figured they reached terminal velocity only 130 feet from Castel Payne.

Another magickal nimbus engulfed the craft, and Len started breathing again. The blue glow spread itself out into a long pair of wings that reacted to even the most subtle tug on the wheel by Nagrendra. The Reptiad banked the airboat around to the west and skirted mountains to the north. Len noticed that crystal spires rose from the mountains and hills, looking like upside-down icicles or needle-sharp teeth.

He pointed toward them, and shouted to Tyrchon, "Spiriastar has been busy."

"So it seems. I think she knows her realm is difficult to watch magickally, so the more she spreads out, the more area her enemies will have to scout."

"That would suggest she will have people about to keep folks like us away."

Tyrchon winked at him. "That's why we'll be very careful about being seen."

Nagrendra started the airboat descending more swiftly, then dropped it down into a valley. They flew the length of that valley, running little more than fifty feet above the ground. At the far end, Nagrendra threaded their way through a narrow pass, then brought the airboat down gently on the northern side of a watering place. They quickly disembarked, and Nagrendra cast one last spell. The boat rose from the ground and arrowed back through the sky toward Castel Payne.

Len frowned as he watched it go. "How are we getting back there? Long walk, and I don't think these boots will give me enough hang time to reach Fialchar's home with a jump."

Nagrendra smiled. "Fialchar will bring us back when

the time is right. He may not be able to peer into her realm, but he is fully capable of tracking us."

The shoe salesman looked at the Reptiad. "You trust him?"

"No, but I believe he would deny Spiriastar the satisfaction of destroying us. I trust in that."

Tyrchon looked around, scanning the ridgelines for any sign of the enemy. "Looks clear, but we'll keep it a cold camp. You'll want to get some sleep because we'll be moving mostly at night. And, yes, Len, I know you can't see that well at night. We'll bear that in mind."

"Sorry to be an inconvenience." Len shrugged. "I used to be good at sneaking out of the house at night, if that's a help."

Ghislaine smiled. "Any experience is a help. Tyrchon, let Len and me take the first watch. You and Nagrendra can sleep. Four hours or so?"

The wolf-warrior nodded. He lay down on the ground, shifted around a bit, then brought his pack over to use as a pillow. He removed his sword and laid it down beside him, then dropped off to sleep. On the other side of the camp Nagrendra had done the same thing.

Ghislaine led Len off to a trio of boulders and left him crouching in their shadow. She climbed up on one of them and let the largest shade her as well. "Don't stare at any one spot, Len. Try to open your focus up. What you'll see first is movement before you see detail, but movement is enough."

"Thanks." Crouching there, he removed his helmet and found himself reminded of the times he'd played paintball with some of his buddies. No matter how good the camouflage they wore, movement always gave them away. He'd learned to be very still and even patient. He had often volunteered to stay behind and guard the flag because he could lie in wait for the most adventurous guys on the other team to come to him. The few times he went forward with a raiding force, he got shot out.

Little bit more than paint can get shed here. He watched the reddish landscape and the twisted, spiky undergrowth that surrounded the water hole. He saw nothing moving, but wondered how easy it would be for the antlings to blend in, or to burrow beneath things. *They could come up from right below us, and we'd be in serious trouble.* Images of movies and scenes from science-fiction novels started dancing through his head, making him wish *he* was atop the boulder, not Ghislaine.

"Ghislaine, is it all right if we talk?"

She remained silent just long enough for him to figure the answer was actually "no," but then she replied to his question. "I don't seem to recall the antlings responding to sound. Even the creature she created from them to fight Tyrchon apparently worked with scents. Doesn't mean they can't feel vibrations from sound though. We should be careful."

"I agree." He raised his chin to look at something he thought he saw moving, but it was just a broken branch swinging in the breeze. "I have a question that might be personal for you."

"Really?" Amusement rang through her comment. "What do you want to know?"

"You've been with Princess Myat's Guard for a while, yes?"

"Four years."

"What do you think of her?"

"She is my mistress, my liege lord. My opinion of her does not matter."

"But it should, don't you think?" Len ran a hand across

his chin's raspy stubble. "Where I come from, my boss is a priggish sort of man who never gives others credit for what they do and acts like a tyrant all the time. He's not done what Myat did, poisoning us or anything, but when he learned Angie and I were going out on a date, he saw to it that we were never given overlapping schedules in the store again. I don't really like him at all."

"But you are sworn to serve him, so you remain." Ghislaine kept her voice low. "I do not approve of what Princess Myat did. Had Fialchar not intervened and prevented the poison from taking effect, I would have pressed her for the antidote."

"What if she had refused?"

"The situation did not occur, so speculating on it is futile." Ghislaine felt silent for a moment. "All of the Guards are sworn to her service, but we are also sworn to protect the Mountain Lords and to work toward the best interests of the Matarun."

"So, if you felt our deaths were not in the best interest of the Matarun, you would have done something?"

"In all likelihood, yes."

Len looked up toward her, but the edge of the rock above him hid her. "What about the loyalty you feel toward Tyrchon, Nagrendra, and Xoayya? That would have made no difference?"

He heard a scraping against rock, then found Ghislaine crouched beside him, yet still towering over him. "Why are you asking these questions?"

Len shifted his shoulders uneasily. "I'm not . . . I don't . . . Hell, something is not right about Princess Myat. Back where I come from, someone who operates without a conscience is called a sociopath, and you generally learn about them after they've murdered a bunch of people. She considers herself 'heir' to these boots and whatever power I possess. Her sending Shoth out here into Chaos to find me without letting him know how we were connected, well, she used him, and I think she wants to use me the same way. I don't intend to let her do that, and I don't want you to be caught in the middle of anything that happens because of my decision."

"I appreciate your concern, Len. I have a duty that binds me, but it is not one to which my soul is enslaved." She nodded toward where Tyrchon and Nagrendra slept. "There is also a bond among those who venture into Chaos together. Fighting our way free of the *Tsvortu* or Spiriastar's realm united us in ways that no one who has lived on only one side of the Ward Walls can appreciate. I think being brought to Lord Disaster's castle is the first time Princess Myat has ventured from the Empire."

Len smiled. "I'm not certain I can fault her reasoning for wanting to stay in the Empire."

Ghislaine gave him a puzzled look. "There are people among us, the Black Churchers, who work to bring Chaos back over the Empire again. Perhaps they would be these sociopaths you mentioned. They believe that people reach their full potential only under the influence of Chaos, and, in this, they are partially correct. Within the Empire, society determines what is acceptable and defines roles for everyone. The rank badges we wear proclaim all we are, and that determines our status. In Chaos, however, rank badges mean nothing. Here society is stripped away, and only by facing challenges can we determine who and what we truly are."

Len slowly nodded. "In Spiriastar's realm Shoth discovered he wasn't a coward."

"You did the same."

"Me?"

"Indeed." The Matarun captain gave him a warm smile. "You took Nagrendra's cloak and led most of the antlings off and away from us. Had you not done that, had you not taken that risk, we would have all died."

"But that wasn't . . . I mean, it didn't take courage, I just did it."

"Right." She reached out and tapped his forehead with a finger. "You took action that had to be taken. You didn't cringe or cower."

"But, before, when I was faced with the Dashan's skeleton and these boots, I ran from the Sanctuary."

Ghislaine's light laugh made Len blush. "There are times, Len, when running is the best strategy of all. When you were alone, you preserved yourself. When others had their lives at stake, you acted." She frowned. "But you must have done this before in your life."

He shook his head. "My life hasn't really presented me with very many of these situations." Through his mind flashed instances of bosses chewing out coworkers, teammates yelling at other teammates, and people just being rude, where he could have stepped up and helped the victim out. He knew that intervention might cause him trouble, but there seemed to be something wrong with not acting when he could. While in the past his default response to any situation seemed to be passivity, now he wanted to be more active. *Not violent or even confrontational, just taking a part in what goes on and helping others out.*

"Mine has, Len, and I have learned to cherish those individuals I can trust to safeguard my life as I would safeguard their lives. I count you among those individuals." She arched an eyebrow at him. "And that, my friend, is rare gift from a Matarun warrior, just so you know."

"Thank you, Ghislaine. I'll work to justify your trust."

Their watch ended uneventfully, and Len made himself as comfortable as possible on the ground. He didn't think he was really that tired, but he fell asleep fairly quickly. Tyrchon roused him gently as long, dusk shadows crept across the landscape. The wolf-warrior indicated that Len should toss his pack onto Fitz as Nagrendra had done, but Len shook his head and shouldered the burden. He adjusted the straps on the pack, then set off in the middle of the group.

The next two days took them steadily northward. They found very little in the way of signs of Spiriastar's activities on the first two nights of travel, but on the third they ran into a lot more crystal overlaying the landscape. Though Nagrendra said he caught no residual magick coming off it, they chose to skirt the areas by a wide margin. They also moved carefully, constantly checking their backtrail, to make certain they weren't being subtly herded into an ambush.

Finally, they crested a line of hills and saw very unusual activity in a deep, narrow valley running north to south. The landscape on the west side of it appeared to have been pulverized, as if some giant foot had just stomped it flat. The eastern edge rose up as high as the hills where they were perched, while the west side rubble sat a good five hundred yards lower.

A huge fire had been built up at the southern end of the valley, and antlings by the thousands swarmed over the rubble. They grasped huge pieces of debris in their mandibles and hauled them away. They looked like a living glass conveyor belt, mindlessly shifting a collapsed mountain from one spot to another.

Ghislaine looked over at Tyrchon. "This used to be

Bharashadi territory, and I never ventured this far into it. Any idea what they are digging at?"

The wolf-warrior's eyes narrowed. "I believe that is what remains of the *Bharashadi* Necroleum."

Nagrendra tasted the air with his tongue. "It does smell like a charnel pit. I know the Black Shadows were supposed to have buried vast treasures with their dead, but I fail to see why Spiriastar would want gold or jewels."

"She doesn't." Tyrchon exposed teeth as a low growl rolled from his throat. "To fight me she clothed a skeleton with antlings. I think she wants what's left of the Black Shadows themselves. She's digging out an army, and, if the duel I fought in her realm was any indication, it's one that won't be easy to stop at all."

31

Len glanced over at Tyrchon. "I don't doubt you're right, but I think we should get closer and make certain."

The wolf-warrior turned his muzzle toward Len. "I don't think you have any idea how dangerous that will be."

"I think I do, Tyrchon, and I wouldn't suggest it except for two things. First, the antlings seem to communicate and get around by their sense of smell. Nagrendra has said the whole place stinks of dead bodies, and that's a pretty powerful scent. It ought to cover us and our approach, and blunt any attempt to alert others if we're spotted. Second, since the antlings apparently can burrow in the dark to make tunnels, why the big fire down there? I don't think Spiriastar is there supervising, do you?"

Tyrchon dropped his jaw in a smile. "Your points are good. Ghislaine, Nagrendra, what do you think?"

The Reptiad looked up at the night sky, then nodded. "We have six hours or so until dawn. We can spend half of them getting down there and still have a margin of safety for our escape. Can't see that much from here, so I'm in favor of going closer."

Ghislaine smiled. "Now that Len brings it up, the fire does intrigue me."

"Me, as well, but I'm wondering if it isn't there to lure us into a trap. It's very easy to spot at night." Tyrchon shrugged. "Still, closing in and investigating makes sense. Ghislaine, you take point, Nagrendra and Len in the middle, Fitz, Jhesti, and me in the rear. Let's be quiet and ready to run."

Len couldn't help but smile as they worked their way down the hillside and closer into the valley. He'd made a suggestion, and everyone had agreed that it was a good one. This wasn't the first time something like that had happened in his life, but it was one of the few times it happened with people whose respect he wanted. He'd been willing to risk censure and hadn't been censured because his suggestion made sense. *They accepted it* and *accepted me. What's going on here is bigger than any of us and our ambitions—they see that and act accordingly, which are two things Comrade Corbett is incapable of managing.*

The descent ate up the better part of two hours, but put them in a sheltered position less than five hundred yards from the fire. The stench of things long dead—which smelled to Len like an overstuffed Dumpster being cooked by the noontime sun—permeated the area and had them all covering their noses with a hand. It was not a pleasant place to be in, but they were far from the most miserable individuals at the site.

Aside from the antlings busily moving rocks and

retrieving bones, Len saw two other types of creatures down in the valley. One set was exactly what Tyrchon had said he was afraid Spiriastar was creating at the site. Five antlings melted together over a pile of bones to produce a creature that Len thought of as a cross between an African lion and a professional wrestler. The hulking creatures had a decidedly feline cast to their features, from their long manes to whiplash tails. The hands and feet, though more humanoid, had long talons, and each of the creatures appeared to be very well muscled and lean.

They had gathered together a couple of dozen of their living counterparts, most of whom looked much worse for the wear. The black fur covering them flashed with blue highlights in a few places, and the crystal versions had not prepared Len for the pure gold of their eyes. Most of them wore full-flowing manes, but the biggest of them had shaved the sides of their heads, exposing their triangular ears. Those particular Black Shadows watched their captors carefully, suggesting to Len that they were warriors. Some of the others he took to be females and children, primarily because of their lesser size and the lack of manes.

The prisoners had been herded into a depression and remained there because of a red lattice that linked twelve stones standing roughly a foot high. The gaps in the lattice might have been large enough to fit a child through, but the operation would take so long that any of the Glass Shadows would be able to act and prevent an escape.

Len turned away from the fire and kept his voice low. "I think we can free the prisoners."

Ghislaine blinked at him. "What?"

"We can free them, get them away from Spiriastar's people."

Tyrchon shook his head. "They are B*harashadi*. They are one scourge I'm not sorry to see gone from Chaos."

Len frowned. "They're the enemies of our enemies, so they're our friends."

The Matarun Guard smiled gently. "Len, it is very admirable that you are taking an active part in what we are doing, but there is no reason to push it. Freeing them would be very dangerous and all but impossible."

"Will it?" Len looked at Nagrendra. "What would I have to do to take the grid down? Knock over a stone or two?"

The Reptiad thought for a second, then nodded. "That should suffice, but it will take time."

Len patted his boots. "These can get me down there fast. Can you, with a spell, douse the fire?"

"Completely? Not one that big."

"How about not completely." Len smiled. "I want as much smoke as possible."

Tyrchon frowned. "But you won't be able to see."

"More importantly, *they* won't be able to smell." Len reached over and plucked Jhesti from Fitz's back. "Smoke won't stop you from seeing, will it?"

"You mean you'd trust me to be your eyes?"

"Got no choice." He positioned the plastic figure on his helmet, with its arms and legs wrapped around the horn. "Hang on tight. I'm going to go down there, kick stones out of alignment, and get back here as fast as I can. I expect some of Glass Shadows will follow me, so you'll have to pick them off."

Tyrchon laid a hand on Len's arm. "This still makes little sense, Len. The reward is not worth the risk. Yes, on some grand level I can agree that I like B*harashadi* more than I like Spiriastar's creatures, but I don't like trading your life for their lives."

"I agree, but I think there's more to it than that, too." Len took in a deep breath and let it out with a sigh. "Spiriastar is not terribly patient. Right now I bet she figures these Glass Shadows are about the best she can do for warriors. If we free these Black Shadows, we will embarrass her. She might decide to leave the Glass Shadows alone and find new toys to play with. It will buy us more time to oppose her. Is that worth the risk?"

"Barely." The wolf-warrior shook his head. "This is completely insane."

"Which means it's the last thing she will expect." Len shrugged off his pack and fixed his shoe-sizer shield to his left forearm. "And it's only insane if it doesn't work. Otherwise, it's pure genius."

"Be careful, Len." Ghislaine smiled at him. "Remember, fools and geniuses can't be told apart by their corpses."

"Words to live by." Len worked himself into a cleft in the rocks. "Ready, Nagrendra?"

"Ready, Len. Go!"

Time seemed to slow for Len as he leaped from the cleft and dropped twelve feet to a talus slope. He raced down it, taking huge steps. He leaped over a boulder halfway down and reached the bottom of the slope about the same time the huge bonfire went from big, bright, and golden to the muted red glow of coals. Smoke began to pour off it in a dark cloud that curled down, cutting the valley in half. *So far, so good.*

Len sprinted the twenty yards to the edge of the prison pit and kicked one of the stones aside. The grid sputtered and died. "Quick, come on, get out of there! Move it! Go, go, *go*!" He waved the Bharashadi from their prison and pointed back down the valley. A smile split his face, and laughter rang in his voice. "Move it!"

About the time a female Black Shadow snarled at him, Len realized the rescue attempt wasn't the lark he had seen it being. Her scream was one filled with anger and outrage and fear. A hand flashed forward and caught him on the right cheek. Stars exploded before his eyes, and his jaw popped. His body followed his head, twisting around. His feet came up off the ground, then he crashed down hard in the talus. His right hand touched the side of his face, felt ruined flesh, and came away very wet, warm, and sticky.

He lay there in shock for a second or two. *Bharashadi* leaped over him and ran past, shrieking and shouting. The smoke rolled over him, then he saw a juvenile Black Shadow body go spinning through the air. It smashed into the rocks next to him and made a little mewing sound. Len glanced at the Chaos demon, then saw the crystalline warrior that still had blood on its talons stalking forward through the smoke to finish the job.

Len kicked out with his right foot, catching the Glass Shadow in the left knee. In the backglow from the fire he actually saw the joint lock, then snap backward. The creature's lower leg shattered into glassy splinters. The Glass Shadow fell to the left. As it went down, Len rolled over onto his right side, came up on his right knee, and brought his buckler around in a punch that pulverized the Glass Shadow's face.

The creature's body began to fall apart. Only one of the five antlings that had gone into its construction managed to reconstitute itself. It wiggled its antennae at Len, then lunged in to take a bite out of his left leg. Len fended it off with his buckler, then grabbed it around the neck with his right hand. He yanked it off the ground and started running with it back toward his waiting comrades.

"Give me directions, Jhesti."

"Right!"

Len made a quick cut to the left and realized his error even before Jhesti said, "No, you idiot, your *other* right." His left foot began to slip, then something solid loomed up out of the smoke and hammered his chest. Len bounced backward from his collision with a huge boulder, his ribs aching all the way, then he sat down abruptly. All around him, Glass Shadows moved through the smoke, and Len realized, without a doubt, any tributes he'd get to his bravery would be posthumous.

Tyrchon drained the goblet of brandy and dearly wished the warmth it kindled in his middle would get to his extremities. He set the goblet down on the table next to his chair, then flexed both of his hands. They ached and felt swollen, very much the way they would have if he'd gotten them frostbitten. He held them out toward the fire raging in the huge hearth, but they seemed impervious to the blazing heat.

He glanced over at Nagrendra. The Reptiad sat in a massive chair, with several blankets wrapped around him. The sorcerer moved very sluggishly and had done little more than flick his tongue into his brandy goblet for the better part of a half hour. Beyond the Reptiad, Ghislaine leaned forward in her chair, extending her hands and feet toward the fire.

The wolf-warrior shook his head. "It didn't hurt this way when Fialchar brought us to Castel Payne from Myat's tower."

Nagrendra screwed an eye around to look at Tyrchon. "Different circumstances."

Ghislaine nodded. "We were further away and in the heart of territory Spiriastar had secured."

The Reptiad's head drooped. "Correct. Every spell requires an expenditure of energy for it to work. Fialchar could not or did not want to supply all he needed to bring us back. He used some of our personal energy, which is why we are cold. We will warm again."

Xoayya entered the cavernous room with a crystal decanter in hand. "More brandy?"

"Please." Tyrchon extended his goblet toward her. "What can you tell us about Len?"

"He's resting comfortably. I've mended his face, but the bruises and everything else will have to wait." She refilled Tyrchon's goblet, swept past Nagrendra, and refilled Ghislaine's goblet as well. "Fialchar was well pleased by the capture of an antling. He and Myat have been going over it since your return."

Nagrendra's head came up. "Anything of interest?"

Xoayya pressed her lips together. "Perhaps. Myat seems to be able to reconstruct the spell the Dashan used to create the antlings in the first place. She took one look at the antling, touched it, smelled it, and started writing out the various formulae she used to make the things up."

The Matarun warrior shrugged. "That should not be unexpected, should it?"

"No, but something else is surprising." Xoayya set the decanter down on the table next to Nagrendra's chair. "Fialchar tasked her with figuring out how to unmake the antlings, and Myat can't do it. She tried hard, but something wasn't working there, so Fialchar is going to figure it out for himself. It was odd to watch her get frustrated in the attempt though. It was almost as if the portion of her brain that would do the unraveling of spells isn't there. She seems able to understand how such things work when they are explained to her, and she can repeat them back, but figuring them out is beyond her."

Tyrchon's eyes sharpened. "That's very interesting."

Ghislaine sipped some brandy. "What do you mean?"

"Xoayya and I were talking before our little expedition to the ruined Necroleum. Myat said that Len had gotten the Dashan's power and Shoth had his conscience while she had his intellect. It seemed to us, though, that Shoth clearly had enough power and intellect to work magicks. And Len, without knowing any spells, was able to open the Dashan's home and his resting place, so he's got more than just power."

Xoayya nodded in agreement. "The Dashan, when he split his soul, may not have divided it as cleanly as Myat thinks he did. If his purpose was to prevent his work from being undone, he might have divided things such that undoing what he had done would be difficult. Just as Shoth had some intellect and power, so Len might have some intellect and conscience. Given how he managed to unlock the Sanctuary and crypt, he might have the trick of undoing spells."

"Pity of it is," Nagrendra observed, coughing, "he doesn't understand how to control it, if it is true."

Tyrchon felt a shiver work its way down his spine. "There's a lot here that none of us know how to control. We better start learning how to do it, fast. If we don't, Spiriastar will glaze everything from Chaos to the Empire, and that is not something I want to see at all."

32

Tyrchon had intended to smile as he entered Len's sickroom, but the purple bruising over the right side of the man's face made anything but a wince impossible. Len lay in a large four-poster bed with a legion of pillows propping him up. Blankets swathed him, and Jhesti stood on his belly. Tyrchon caught the hints of a hushed conversation that died abruptly as he entered the room.

"How are you feeling, Len?"

The young man's uneasy shrug betrayed stiffness. "I feel like Mike Tyson's chew toy." Len clearly tried to muster a smile, but the bruised half of his face failed to comply. "I've felt much better in the past."

Tyrchon nodded as he entered the room and stood at the foot of the bed. "I owe you an apology. I never should have let you do what you did. I didn't like it, I didn't think it was a good idea, and I should have stopped you."

Len's face remained impassive. "Why didn't you?"

Tyrchon glanced down for a second. "I didn't because, I guess, I accepted your choice much as I would have accepted the choice of any other Chaos Rider. I had seen you in Spiriastar's realm leading the antlings away from us. I forgot how little experience you have in Chaos."

"You had accepted me."

The wolf-warrior's head came up. "I had. You have a hint of *Chaosfire* in your eyes, and you fit in perfectly on our expedition. It was my mistake and almost got you killed."

Len shook his head slowly. "Not your fault, Tyrchon. Short of restraining me physically, you couldn't have stopped me." He raked a hand back through his hair. "See, I had taken to heart your suggestion that whether this is a dream or reality, the difference doesn't matter. What that should have made me do was think and act and react as if this *is* reality. Instead, what I did was act as if it was a fantasy."

Len frowned. "What we were doing out there, what we're doing here, now, is stuff I've done countless times, in games. Fong the Magnificent was a character for whom rescuing the Black Shadows would have been a must. I knew Fong's abilities and knew that what I wanted to do was a piece of cake. I never imagined that a Black Shadow would see me as an enemy or strike out at me because of fear. Never happened in a game, mainly because my gamemaster didn't think that way."

Tyrchon didn't know what all the words he was hearing meant, but glimmers of meaning came through in context. "You underestimated the Black Shadows."

"I've underestimated everything here, except my abilities." Jhesti leaped clear as Len threw the covers back to reveal the boots. "I'm stuck with these boots that are full of power, but I can only make them work by accident. Without them, I'm nothing."

"You're wrong if you think that, Len."

Len held his hands up to stop Tyrchon from saying anything further. "Look, it's time for the truth here. One time we all decided that we would play ourselves in a game. We figured out what abilities we would have and our attributes and everything, and I came off really weak. I mean, I was able to credit myself with some fighting ability because of a tae kwon do class I was taking and a semester's worth of fencing, but that was it. Rolling up a character who was tougher than me would have been easy."

"Stop." Tyrchon pointed a finger at Len and put some growl into his voice. "You're forgetting two key things that I won't let you forget. First, it wasn't the boots that made you lead the antlings away, nor was it the boots that made you rescue the Black Shadows. That came from you. And it was also you who suggested the smoke might be a way to slow down the antlings and their ability to communicate. That was brilliant and is likely to be a key to defeating Spiriastar's forces in the future."

"Even a blind squirrel finds an acorn now and again."

"Stop it!" The wolf-warrior narrowed his eyes. "You have the same problem many Chaos Riders have when they first enter Chaos. They all come here with notions of what it is to be a hero. They see someone like me and decide it means being all muscle and blade. Or they look at Nagrendra and decide they have to cast incredible magicks. They're wrong, but this is what they think.

"The truth of the matter is that Spiriastar and the Black Churchers are not far off the mark: people *do* reach their full potential in Chaos. Either they use every tool at their disposal to survive or they become worm food." Tyrchon leaned forward on the bed's footboard. "You've got a good mind and a good heart, and you're tougher than you think. That slash by a B*harashadi* could have snapped your neck."

Len nodded slowly. "Okay, I'll accept that, but I want to ask you something."

"Go ahead."

"I was talking with Jhesti, which is when I realized I was treating all this like a game. I realized that was wrong. I now know I need more skills if I'm going to survive this thing. Will you help me? Will you teach me what I need to know to survive."

Tyrchon opened his mouth in a big grin. "It will be my pleasure. When do you want to begin?"

Len swung his legs out of the bed and pulled a purple robe from the chair beside his bed. "Soon as we can find me some decent clothes, I'm good to go."

"Good," offered Fialchar in a voice that sounded like gravel rattling around in an iron pot. He stood just inside the room's doorway, with the Staff of Emeterio grasped in both hands. "Both of you are required to go with me now."

The sorcerer spun the staff once, then an explosion of silvery light blinded Tyrchon. Thousands of talons shredded his flesh, then steel thorns impaled each little tidbit. Acid seemed to wash over him, then icy winds froze every piece. A shudder wracked him, then he opened his eyes as heat radiating up from glassy black rocks blanketed him.

Off to his side, Len swayed a bit, but managed to stay upright.

Fialchar's laughter filled the bowl in which they

stood. Tyrchon recognized the place as an extinct volcano, but he had no idea where in Chaos it was. The site had been modified, with a variety of odd sigils and runes cut into standing stones set into niches in the walls. The alphabets from which they had been taken appeared to have little in common with each other, and he saw nothing he recognized as being Imperial script.

He looked over at Fialchar. "Where are we?"

"It is known by many names. Council Mountain is likely the easiest for you to understand. It is a meeting place for Chademon tribes, and I have summoned some here. We will need an army to destroy Spiriastar, and the Chademons will provide it for us."

Two gold sparks shot from the quartz atop his staff. They flitted about like fireflies, then arrowed out to hit both men in the forehead. Len scrubbed at his forehead with his hand. "What was that for?"

"So you can understand them." Fialchar gestured with the staff. "Here they come now."

Four Chademons moved from the mouths of different lava tubes. Each bore a red pennant with the black silhouette of a volcano on it. They walked to the sigil that represented their tribe, planted their flags, then walked toward the center of the bowl. A *Tsvortu*, tall and with white streaks in her gray fur, came first. A hulking *Bharashadi* warrior came next, then a little *Hobmotli* wearing a saber sheathed on his back came third. Tyrchon thought he recognized that demon.

Finally came one of the *Drasacor*. Tyrchon had actually never seen one of the tall, skeletally gaunt demons before. Ragged robes with the consistency of cobwebs covered it from foot to crown, with a hooded cloak hiding all but its glowing purple eyes. The robes billowed out as if being teased constantly by wind, but Tyrchon couldn't feel even the hint of a breeze.

The Tsvortu looked right and left, then nodded at Fialchar. "You have summoned us. Why?"

"You are aware of the scourge upon the land?" Fialchar gestured at the Black Shadow. "He has seen it first paw. Dead Bharashadi clothed in glass, massing as an army."

The Tsvortu shrugged. "This means nothing to us."

"It will. I offer you a chance to oppose it and destroy it."

"Or?"

"Or I shall withhold my support for your efforts to save yourselves from it." Fialchar's flesh squeaked as he smiled. "Without me, you cannot stand against it. With me, with my assistance, you will prevail."

The Drasacor's voice came as haunting echoes. "And, without us, you would be threatened?"

"Inconvenienced. I could always take refuge in the Empire." The staff hung in the air as Fialchar opened his hands and spread them wide. "What happens in Chaos would be of little consequence to me. You will become my army and be commanded by Tyrchon here."

"What?" Tyrchon looked at the sorcerer. "I did not agree to this."

"There is another force you could lead to destroy Spiriastar?" Fialchar shook his head. "There is no other commander available. It will be you."

The Tsvortu walked over to Tyrchon and fingered the chits he wore around his neck. "You slew the sisters wearing these?"

"In single combat, yes." He rested a hand on his sword's hilt. "And since then I have slain more."

The Storm demon closed all three of its eyes, then nodded. "I will accept him as a commander."

Tyrchon blinked with surprise. "But I have slain *Tsvortu*."

"For which revenge shall be exacted at some point." The *Tsvortu* flicked a finger against the chits. "I know the mettle of those you have fought, so I can gauge your abilities. You will do."

The *Hobmotli* came forward on all sixes. "Fryl will follow Tyrchon."

The *Drasacor* drifted forward. "You fought the *Bharashadi* at Marrowcrack Pass?"

"A long time ago, yes." Tyrchon's eyes narrowed. "A hunting party caught my scent and pursued me. I slew a dozen of them and escaped."

The Mist Demon's eyes bobbed up and down as it nodded. "They had been on the track of *Drasacor*. Your intervention saved them. We will follow you."

Fialchar turned and looked at the Black Shadow. "Your people are limited in number, but formidable nonetheless. Will you join us?"

The *Bharashadi* warrior nodded. "We will, but we will not follow Tyrchon Shadowdeath." He pointed a clawed finger at Len. "Him we will follow."

Len's jaw gaped. "Me? What? Why?"

The Black Shadow's gold eyes became slitted crescents. "The bruises you bear came from one of my people, when you freed us from this crystal menace. You saved our lives and, few though we are, we acknowledge a debt to you. We are yours to command."

"I'm honored, I guess." Len brought his chin up. "I'll do everything I can to be worthy of your trust."

"And you will find no more ferocious troops available in all of Chaos."

Fialchar clapped his hands. "Wonderful. You shall gather your people in the valleys leading south in the

Rockfang Mountains. We will then bring you to us to inform you of our plans. You shall be ready within the week to attack. All you want or need shall be provided for you."

The D*rasacor* had drifted back a foot or two when Tyrchon caught a blur streaking over the eastern rim of the volcano. It appeared to be blue, but he could not be certain, for it hit the volcano's farside. The ground shook, and a bright light flashed, then a wave of heat blasted into Tyrchon. He hit the ground hard, then found himself rolling. He slammed into a boulder, then twisted himself around behind it.

Another blast came from the same direction, sending a tremor through the boulder. He heard a thundercrack in the explosions' wake, then the subsequent explosions sounded so distant the tremor could barely be felt. Tyrchon looked out as something moved through the sky again, and he saw a red streak sail through the hole that had been blasted through the volcano's wall. A final thunderclap followed that streak, then a distant explosion and faint tremor in the earth.

Only Fialchar had been left standing, and he had his right hand up and clenched around a blue gem that made his flesh sizzle and smoke. He gestured with his left hand, and Len rose to his feet from behind a rock where he had taken shelter. The Chademons slowly came to their feet as well, none of them looking too bad for the ordeal.

The T*svortu* crouched and scratched at a small piece of gemlike stone embedded in the ground. "What was that?"

Len shook his head. "Whatever it was, it was big and moving very fast. The thunderclap after it came because it was traveling faster than sound. That's why we didn't hear them coming in."

The staff came to Fialchar's left hand, and he waved it grandly. "This is of no consequence to any of you. Gather your people and prepare them to make war. We shall put an end to Spiriastar well before the month is out."

Light flashed again, and agonies soared through Tyrchon, then his vision cleared and he found himself in Fialchar's sanctum. Xoayya looked up from the huge crystal ball and Myat over from a desk where she was writing something out. Lord Disaster strode to the globe, casually tossing the staff aside to where it hung in the air motionless. "Did you see?"

Xoayya nodded. "I watched, as you asked. I don't know what it was that attacked you at the end."

"You will." He handed her the blackened, melted lump of blue glass, and she moved it gingerly from one hand to another. "This was a piece of the first one. You know what to do."

The redheaded woman nodded, then shot Tyrchon a brave smile and closed her eyes. She grasped the glass in her right hand, then pressed her left hand to the globe. A light blue nimbus played over her, limning her, then spread over the globe. "I have something."

Tyrchon stared at the globe as a scene came into focus. He couldn't see much other than some of the antlings in a blue haze, then they spun around and around and shifted out of sight. The light dimmed for a moment, then a series of bright lights flashed. They each formed a halo through the middle of which the viewpoint moved ever faster, then Tyrchon saw landscape streaking below. Ahead the volcano came into view, then a bright light burst from the globe, making Tyrchon raise a hand to shield his eyes.

As the light died, he looked over at Fialchar. "I don't understand."

Before Lord Disaster could say anything, Len spoke in a quiet and cold voice. "Xoayya, your vision showed us what was happening along the line of flight. Can you show it looking back in the other direction? Slowly, right after the light rings?"

Her eyes still closed, she nodded. "Give me a moment. There."

"Good, hold it." Len stepped closer and leaned on the railing. "Not good, not good at all."

Tyrchon frowned. What he saw was a tunnel angling up out of a square platform. A diagonal ramp angled down into the tunnel near the base and had four narrow, lozenge-shaped objects on it, all next to the tunnel. He could see some antlings near it and a man, but none of them very clearly. Even so, they provided scale, which told him the tunnel and base was no larger than the biggest catapult he'd ever seen. "I still don't understand."

"It's a rail gun, a magickal rail gun." Len sighed and hung his head wearily. "I did a project on rail guns for a physics class. I think the man there is Shoth, and whatever parts of our lives crossed, he drew the memory of that project and has converted it over to a magickal use."

Len looked over at him, but Tyrchon could only shrug.

Len sighed. "It takes big heavy things and propels them very fast, which means something the size of an antling can blast a hole in a volcano. The thing probably shoots twenty miles or so, which means we'll take a beating before we get to any battlefield where Spiriastar wants to meet us."

Tyrchon shivered. "A weapon like that could easily destroy our army."

Fialchar cackled wetly. "Then we shall destroy it first. I suggest, once I move my home beyond this thing's range, we have ourselves a long-overdue council of war."

33

Len found it slightly distracting that Jhesti had grown to approximately the size of a big G.I. Joe doll. The plastic figure stood out of all proportion with the scale of the map laid out on the table. Fialchar had used magick to construct it, so the map had depth and texture, halfway between a contour map and a holograph. The effect seemed weird to Len, and it made Jhesti's feet appear to be an inch or two underwater.

Central to the map was the valley beneath which they had found Spiriastar. Using the images Xoayya had taken from the projectile shard, they'd been able to locate the rail gun on a plateau roughly a mile north of Spiriastar's valley. It easily covered that valley and the new valley to the west, where the *Bharashadi* Necroleum had once stood. Castel Payne hung well off to the southwest of the rail gun and passed behind the Rockfang Mountains.

Looking out the window, Len saw the mountains drifting by. "In the images I didn't see any wheels or wings on the gun, and the model I used in my report was a stationary model, so Shoth might not have thought about making it mobile. If this map is accurate, though, there are few places where the gun can be stationed and still cover the targets she wants covered."

Tyrchon scratched at the back of his neck. "She could have had more than one of them built."

The flesh around Fialchar's eyes tightened. "I think not. She has Shoth powering the device. The images of him seem to show him being coated in antling, and both other parts of the Dashan reported Shoth had died. She is using him as a tool, which was always her way. After what the Dashan did to her, Shoth could never be fully trusted."

"That's all well and good, but let's not take it as guaranteed." Len shook his head. "First and worst mistake we can make is to assume the enemy is stupid or sloppy."

Myat laughed sharply. "Spiriastar is neither; nor is she that thoughtful. I doubt she will emerge from her hole unless forced out."

Nagrendra's tail slapped against the ground. "I do not look forward to going in to dig her out of there."

"That's a later concern." Len peered down at the map. "We have two immediate objectives. The first is the rail gun, and the second is destroying whatever army she has. Once we do those things, we are clear to go after Spiriastar."

Tyrchon glanced over at Len. "You are not thinking these objectives are pearls on a string, are you?"

If only it were that easy. Len slowly shook his head. "Nope. I'm figuring Spiriastar will protect the rail gun, which means we need her distracted. That means an attack on her army, with a lot of magickal support. That would be where you come in, Fialchar."

The lich's eyes flamed. "My power should be sufficient to oppose her."

"Good. While you do that, and Tyrchon takes his army of Chaos demons to attack her, I'm going to have to use my Black Shadows, Nagrendra, and Ghislaine to attack the rail gun." Len folded his arms across his chest. "Once we take it out, the army will have an easier time in its battle with the Glass Shadows. Once the army of Glass Shadows is wiped out, we close on Spiriastar."

Xoayya sat back. "That's a nice plan in general terms, but how will you execute it? To get to the rail gun you will have to move though and past the Glass Shadow army. And when engaging that army, *our* army will be subject to shots from the rail gun. And the magick—we don't know how effective Spiriastar's combat magick will be, nor that of Fialchar."

The wolf-warrior pressed his hands together. "We have the *Tsvortu* and their magickers, who can create a storm or two. Lightning may kill some of the Glass Shadows, and high winds and rain should help make communication between them more difficult. Of the *Hobmotli* the best that can be said is that there are many of them, and they take a lot of killing. Does anyone know for certain what special abilities the *Drasacor* have?"

Nagrendra nodded. "They have a piercing scream, which I've seen drive some men mad. I also think they fly."

"Not fly." Fialchar shook his head. "They are capable of leaping and gliding, and some are quite elegant at it. Unfortunately for us, their combat skills are rather limited. *Drasacor* consider the height of combat to be soaring out over an enemy and throwing rocks at him."

Tyrchon frowned. "Then why did you make them part of our coalition?"

The gaunt sorcerer shrugged. "I had a premonition they might be useful."

"Yeah, they just might." Len glanced at Myat. "You've been able to let Fialchar reproduce the antlings, right?"

"It was easy."

"Good. Look, crystal tends to vibrate, and the right sound can even make it shatter. I doubt we're going to be lucky enough that *Drasacor* songs will break up the Glass Shadows, but the vibrations could cause some problems. At the very least, if they're vibrating and someone hits them with something hard, it could set up a countervibration and shatter the Glass Shadow." Len sighed. "It's worth checking out, though I'd hate to think our effort here has to rest on that sort of serendipity."

The wolf-warrior nodded. "There is a lot here we have to think about. I don't know how many warriors I will have. I have to figure out how I want them arranged and whether or not they can fight in any sort of sensible order."

Fialchar waved that concern away with a flick of his hand. "Spiriastar's grasp of military strategy is minimal."

Tyrchon's eyes narrowed. "I won't underestimate her, and I don't intend to let my forces get slaughtered."

Lord Disaster lifted an eyebrow. "No? You'll just have to kill them later, you know."

"That could be, but not while they are my responsibility."

Len smiled. "I agree. I think we all need to sit down by ourselves, consider what we need to know, figure out how we can learn it, then go about learning it.

Where I come from, this sort of operation would call for months of planning and practice. We don't have that much time, so we better get things right out of the box. Let's get together a day from now and put together what we've learned."

Len sat alone in his room and studied the enlarged map of the plateau that housed the gun. Because of his being involved in role-playing games, he'd hung around gaming shops enough to eventually get wrangled into a few historical war games. He'd played a few ancient games—Romans versus the Gauls and the like—which gave him an appreciation for the sort of force Tyrchon would be leading. That fight would just be nasty, and even though magick provided some interesting additions to the weapons that could be brought to bear, bodies killing bodies would decide it.

Taking the rail gun out brought with it a whole host of other problems. The rail gun really was World War I– or WWII-type artillery, and he only had Iron Age weapons to employ against it. If it were a WWII game, he'd drop paratroopers on the plateau and hit it hard. While the flying skiff Fialchar possessed made that sort of plan vaguely feasible, Len had no idea how accurate the rail gun could be. If it hit the skiff coming in, the projectile would tear it apart and the fall would kill them all. *Moreover, since we will be using magick, Spiriastar might be able to track us and just cancel the spell that lets us fly.*

The door to Len's room creaked open, prompting him to turn in his chair. He saw Princess Myat in the doorway, holding a hand out to restrain her two black-and-gold guardians. They disappeared from his view, clearly moving to flank the door. She turned away from them, then smiled at him. "I hope you don't mind?"

Len shrugged. "Is there something I can do for you?"

"Perhaps, yes. No, no need for you to get up." She closed the door, then crossed to his side on very light feet. She wore a deep blue silk gown which didn't seem that low-cut to Len, but did reveal a fair amount of pale flesh on her throat and chest. Her collarbones stood out in sharp relief, and the shoulders of the gown clung to the tips of her shoulders with the tenacity of someone hanging on to a cliff by only his fingertips. A simple silver belt cinched it at her waist and matched the ribbon she had used to tie her hair back into a ponytail.

Len turned back to his map, well aware of her approach. He caught a whiff of her perfume and felt something jolt through him. It smelled enough like the scent Angie wore that he could imagine Myat to be his coworker all dressed up for a Renaissance Faire. Myat leaned against the back of his chair, the fingers of one hand pressing on his shoulder.

He glanced up at her quickly, then returned to studying the map. He leaned forward on his elbows, pulling his shoulder from beneath her hand. "What do you want?"

"You sound so accusatory. I deserve that, I suppose." He heard her gown rustle as she stepped to his side. "You must think I am a horrible person."

He did, but he heard himself saying, "No, not really."

"Good, because with the connection between us, I would hate for us to be at odds with each other." She moved to the side of the table and leaned over to study it. Her position provided him a better view of her cleavage, but Len ignored it. "And I know you are upset with me because of how I treated you when we first met. I apologize for that. I was wrong, but with Shoth's death . . . The pain I felt I linked to you. I know . . . believe me, I know you had nothing to do with his death. I am certain Shoth was very happy to have saved you. His mission was to bring us together, and he accomplished that, even in death."

"He did." Len nodded slowly. "Shoth was determined to complete his mission."

She turned her head and looked at him with those pale blue eyes. "You can feel the connection between us, can't you?"

He hesitated, then nodded. "Yes, I can." He couldn't put what he felt into words, but he knew he was drawn to her. It was sort of an outgrowth of the friendship he had felt for Shoth. Len couldn't deny that part of it was because they shared a soul, but there was part of him that wanted it to be more than that.

"Good. Shoth and I were very close, and, without him, I feel naked and vulnerable." She reached out with her right hand and rested it on his left forearm, giving it a warm squeeze. "Wait, I'm sorry. I didn't come here to talk to you about my problems. You're very busy—we all are—but I had a question I thought you could answer for me, help me with."

"Please, what is it?"

Myat straightened up and pressed her hands together against her chest. "Your analysis of what will happen got me thinking. If Spiriastar remains in her little hidey-hole when we come for her, she will have to be using magick to communicate with and control her troops."

Len nodded. "Command and control, two keys to warfare, if my military-history professors were correct. Break up communications, and the army will have trouble. We're hoping the *Tsvortu* storm might do that."

"I recall, and I think that is a good idea." She smiled

openly. "I was thinking, though, that we might be able to do more. Our specialty was communications magick—do you remember that at all?"

"No, I don't think so."

"Perhaps not consciously, but your ease with words, clearly it comes through." She glanced down for a second, then looked at him again. "I was thinking that, perhaps, I could prepare some spells that Fialchar could use to disrupt the spells with which Spiriastar commands her troops. Communications is not Fialchar's specialty, but he should be able to wield these spells and cause her difficulty."

Len nodded. "That should work. That's a great idea, in fact." He frowned. "Myat? Highness?"

The woman shivered for a second, then blushed. "Oh, forgive me. I'm sorry, I . . ." She raised a hand to her mouth, then turned away and took a step toward the door. "I shouldn't have come here, I . . . I must be going. You must hate me."

"No." Len stood and reached out for her, his hands landing on her shoulders. "Why would I hate you?"

"You would hate me because I do not have your strength." She leaned back against him, and tilted her head back until her cheek rested against his. "Shoth was my dearest friend in the world. Without him, I feel so alone. And now, with Spiriastar and everything, I am so useless. I can think of great spells, but I can do nothing to help the rest of you. Even Xoayya can defend herself with magick, but I am useless. Shoth would encourage me, make me feel . . . And I came here, thinking you . . . I feel so close to you, but . . ."

Myat turned within his arms and slid her hands up along his chest and around his neck. Her eyes closed as she raised her mouth to his. Her perfume filled his nose, the heat of her breath played on his chin and cheek. He tasted the wet warmth of her kiss and felt her body pressing against his. His arms went around her, and he held her close.

Myat kissed him again and nibbled at his lip, then pulled back and slipped from his arms. She took his hands in hers and smiled, then glanced over at where his bed was. "Come with me, Len, be with me. As we are one in spirit, let us be one in flesh." She gave his hands playful tug, then released them and slid her right arm from her gown. "Come to me."

Len stared, jaw agape, as Myat slithered from her gown. The silk garment puddled on the floor, and Myat casually stepped free of it. She turned away from Len, slowly, then let the ribbon fall from her hair. Her long black locks spread out over her back and shoulders, then slid off to her left as she folded back the covers on his bed and climbed into it.

Thoughts and fantasies exploded in Len's mind. Part of him thought going to her was the most appropriate thing he could possibly do. All the heroes of the stories he'd read bedded princesses aplenty, and none of them had the justification of their once having been one person. It seemed right and natural. She was lonely and vulnerable and in need of solace. He was alone and in a place he barely understood. They could provide for each other something that was lacking, and there was nothing wrong with that.

Yet before he could begin to shuck his robe and unfasten his belt, his thoughts jerked sideways. Part of him, a mischievous part, pointed out that since they had once been one person, really what he'd be doing is having sex with himself. Then he recalled one of those late-night-in-the-dorm conversations where a female friend had commented that there was nothing wrong with masturbation. "It's good," she'd said, "to be selfish now and again."

The word selfish began to resonate for him. From the very beginning he had thought Myat was decidedly selfish and self-absorbed. Though she claimed to be missing Shoth now, his death hardly concerned her right after it had happened. She had clearly wanted the boots he wore and was willing to torture and poison the others to get them.

Len blinked and looked into Myat's cold blue eyes. *She's read me perfectly. I sleep with her, I'll feel protective. She'll say she wants to do all she can to help me and the others, but she is too weak. She'll let me suggest she have the boots, and I'll given them to her because I'd feel horrible if anything happened to her. Then she would have the boots, and we'd be lost.*

He shivered, then shook his head. "No, I can't do this. I can't."

"Please, Len, you must." Myat mewed like a kitten and held the bedclothes aloft so he could see her. "I need you, Len. Only you."

"No!" Len swept past the bed and yanked the oak door open.

"You'll regret this, Len!"

He turned back and spitted her with a hard stare. "Until you said that, I just might have, Myat. No more." He stepped out into the hallway and slammed the door behind him, glad the oak proved stout enough to mute her laughter.

34

L en stalked through the castle and finally came
out into what might have once been a courtyard
garden, but had long since been overgrown with
weeds that had died and left desiccated corpses
standing about. The place looked about as appealing
as a forest after a fire, and wisps of clouds whipping up
over the edge of the courtyard did resemble smoke.
More, though, it reminded Len of fog rolling into San
Francisco, and very suddenly his emotions collapsed
into a sea of homesickness.

He walked to the edge of the courtyard and stared
down into the gray clouds. *Why am I here? What am I
doing? This is all nuts or I'm nuts.* He ran his fingers back
through his hair, then clasped his hands together at the
back of his neck. "None of this makes any sense."

The slow, rhythmic clapping of hands brought him
around. Ghislaine stood amid some shadows and nodded a salute to him. "You're a wise man, Len. Someone
as smart as you shouldn't consider jumping."

He stepped away from the edge. "I wasn't."

"Good. I would hate to lose you, even by accident." She crouched, picked up a stone, and pitched it over the edge. "The ground near the edge isn't as stable as you might like to think."

"Something I have in common with it." Len shrugged. "Didn't mean to disturb you."

"You're not." Ghislaine smiled as she stood. "I'm glad to see you here, in fact."

"Really? Why?"

"It means her plan to ensnare you didn't work."

Len's eyes narrowed. "You knew?"

The Guard nodded slowly. "She told me that you should be as easy to seduce as Shoth was. That's how she kept him gulled and in line, or so she says. I don't doubt it, though."

Len rubbed a hand over his jaw. "Shoth never said anything, never gave any indication."

"Nor would he. The Matarun tend not to speak much about such things."

"Then why tell me this?" The young man frowned. "Aren't you violating some confidence? Won't you get into trouble?"

Ghislaine shrugged easily. "You and I will be going on a trek to destroy this rail gun Shoth has created. I know enough about you to know I don't want you thinking about Myat when you should be thinking about our mission. I also consider you a friend, and I don't want to see a friend being twisted the way she would twist you. You deserve better than that."

Len listened to the tone of her voice, then shook his head sharply. "Forgive me, I'm clearly not tracking too well, thanks to Myat."

Ghislaine slid off the red bandanna that restrained

her hair and tangled the cloth in her hands. "What do you mean?"

"Nothing, really." Len blushed. "I was thinking that I could read into your tone and words an interest in me, but I know that can't be. Forgive me, I'll be over it in a minute."

Her head came up. "And why couldn't it be?"

"You're kidding, right?" He shook his head. "Look at me and look at you. You're tall and strong and gorgeous, and I'm puny. You lead a life of adventure, and I don't. Women like you are totally out of my league."

"But what if I were to tell you that you have nice eyes, and I like the way you laugh?" Ghislaine smiled. "What if I told you I admired how you wept when Shoth died and your courage in freeing the Black Shadows?"

The skin on his arms began to pucker. For the barest of moments he thought she might be trying to succeed where Myat had failed, but he dismissed that idea immediately. Something in her voice and her eyes told him that wasn't true. *She's bold enough and strong enough that if she wanted to kill me, she would stride right over and break my back. In this she hesitates and is being honest.*

"I guess I would have to tell you that I'm amazed. I . . . ah, I never would have thought . . ." Len glanced down at his hands. "Not the best of timing, is it?"

"No, not for either of us." She gave him a brave smile. "I *am* intrigued by you, but for either of us to act upon that now would be distracting. We have plans to make, and you have two very important decisions to make."

"I have a lot of them to make, but which two do you see as important?"

Ghislaine lifted a finger. "You know you were brought here through a spell that Myat created. You have to know that she can compose a spell that will send you home again. Your first big decision is whether or not you ask her to send you home."

Len nodded slowly. "I can see that. Yes, you're right, that's a big decision." He smiled at her. "Even if she could, I wouldn't ask her to do it before this business is finished. Maybe I'll have her compose it so someone could cast it if she's killed, but I'll see this little war against Spiriastar finished."

Len's smile grew as he spoke. *I'm taking responsibility for something I started, and that's good.* "What's the second thing."

Ghislaine frowned. "Second, you have to decide if you are going to give her the boots or not."

Len stared at her, his smile dimming. "Why would I do that? So I can get home again?"

She raised her face to the sky and pounded a fist into her hip. "Fialchar has boasted his abilities will be enough to hamstring Spiriastar, but he has so far been unable to succeed against her. He can't see into her realm. When he pulled us from her realm, his abilities were blunted, and we paid the price for it. He has said he has learned enough in the past five centuries for him not to be concerned about her, but he has continually used us to shield him from her wrath.

"You wouldn't give him the boots, and I'm not sure he could use them to defeat Spiriastar anyway. With the boots on, Myat becomes a second very powerful magicker to oppose Spiriastar. Spiriastar hates them both and could have trouble deciding whom to kill first."

He nodded. "Giving Spiriastar two targets is better than giving her just one."

Ghislaine sank to her knees. "You must think Myat planned this, wanted me to say this to you."

"No." Len shook his head, then gave her a quick grin.

"It would have required her to imagine she could fail in seducing me. I don't think that possibility ever occurred to her. Nope, what you're telling me is pretty obvious. I'd rather give them to Xoayya, but I don't think healing spells will help us much in the big battle."

"Not as much as blasting into Spiriastar." She looked up at him. "You see, tough decisions, aren't they?"

"I guess." Len walked over to her and extended his right hand. "With the counsel of good friends, though, I'll make the right decision."

Ghislaine took his hand and stood. "And with the help of friends, we can execute them, can't we?"

"Better them than us." Len laughed. "When last the Dashan dealt with Spiriastar, he made the wrong choice. Time to make it right."

Peering into the crystal ball in Fialchar's sanctum, Xoayya watched Len and Ghislaine walk back into the castle. She'd not meant to spy on them, and purposely muted the sound of their words. The tone still came through, rather somber and resolute, laced with a fatalism that surprised her. They clearly knew their task of destroying the rail gun would likely result in their deaths.

Even with that realization, they face their fate without complaint. Xoayya shook her head. She dearly believed in fate and destiny, which absolved her of responsibility for her life. There was nothing she could do to influence the outcome; therefore, what had to happen *would* happen to her, and she would deal with the consequences as she was meant to deal with them. It gave her a detachment from life that dulled all the pains.

It also dulls the joy. In Chaos, the visions of the future that used to plague her had been blunted. They came only rarely, and that meant most of what she did came as a surprise. The insulation on her emotions had been pulled away, and she felt far more alive. She liked the feeling and all it brought to her, but it made the frustration she felt very sharp and painful.

She turned from the globe and walked between the twin towers of her scarlet guardians. In their planning meeting, everyone else had been given a task to perform. Myat would be helping figure out the vulnerabilities of the Glass Shadows. Fialchar would be opposing Spiriastar. Tyrchon would be leading an army, and Nagrendra would be with Len and Ghislaine destroying the rail gun. The Chaos demons would be fighting the Glass Shadows.

"And me, I will do nothing."

She spun angrily on her heel and came up short as Fialchar appeared behind her. "Oh!"

The sorcerer snorted once, then turned from her. "I am surprised to find you here in my domain, Xoayya. I would have thought you would be off doing . . . something."

"I have nothing to do." She eyed his back, for the first time noting the bumps on his spine. "I have been given no duties, and I have not been told what my part will be in the final battle."

Fialchar drifted around the crystal ball until he faced her over the top of it. "I had thought you would aid me. Your healing skills might be of use."

"I am afraid they will be far too useful, and that there will be far too many who need them."

"It is a war, after all."

"It is." Xoayya stepped up to the crystal ball and traced a finger across it. "Earlier you said you had a premonition about the usefulness of the D*rasacor* in the battle."

"I did say that. It's true."

"So, you have peered into the future, and you know the outcome?"

The scream of metal warping accompanied Fialchar's smile. "I do not have your facility for clairvoyance, Xoayya. What I saw came in snippets, barely impressions. A second here, a moment or two there. Would you care to see for yourself?"

"Yes, no!" Xoayya clutched at the golden railing encircling the crystal. "I cannot."

"Afraid what you will see is unalterable and irrevocable?" The lich slipped his hands into the opposite sleeves. "Poor Xoayya. You would love to see what the future holds, but only if it is good news. If it is bad, you fear your friends will be locked into it. If it is good, you could not tell them, for fear they might do something to change it."

"But they cannot."

"No?" Fialchar shrugged. "The dilemma upon whose horns you find yourself is one that has tormented countless before you. Destiny or free will."

She arched an eyebrow at him. "Do you know the truth of it?"

"I do not, though I have an intriguing theory."

"Tell me."

"I think destiny holds true for those who believe in their souls, and free will does as well for those who believe in it."

Xoayya frowned. "Impossible, for those things would be mutually exclusive."

"Perhaps, but perhaps not. If you see something, perhaps people are locked into your ordered future because you have made it so. On the other hand, they may have come to it in a variety of manners, and may depart from it in a variety of manners. You control points, but they control the passage between points." Fialchar held out his skeletal hand. "You know I could let you look into the future."

"I know, but I cannot."

"What if I were to tell you that you would be pleased by the outcome?"

"Ha!" Xoayya felt proud of herself for having laughed at his suggestion. "And I would believe you? Why?"

Lord Disaster's eyes became dead black holes. "This battle is as much for my realm as it is for your friends, child. Do not forget that."

Her head came up, and she met his stare without flinching. "You want me to look into the future and see success. You want my belief in a victorious outcome to guarantee it. Are you a coward that you cannot face the future without knowing?"

"I am merely pragmatic, child." The volume of Fialchar's voice failed to drown the outrage at having been found out. "If the outcome you see is not to my liking, I will take steps to change it. You may see points, but I can control all else."

"No, I don't think I wish to see the future, thank you."

"Cast the fate of your friends to the winds, then."

Xoayya started to speak, then bit her lower lip. *Could he be right? Could he affect things to make certain we win? Perhaps I will see victory anyway. Is it better not knowing?* The thought of seeing Tyrchon dead and the guilt that would haunt her if she had done nothing to prevent his death suddenly choked her.

She looked up at Fialchar. "I will look."

He nodded slowly, then held up his left hand. The Staff of Emeterio floated to it. Fialchar touched the staff to the gold ring, and it immediately started to

glow. Xoayya felt the stinging pins and needles of a
sleeping limb play up her arms, along her shoulders,
and up her neck. At the base of her skull it stabbed
deep into her brain, and she felt herself falling.

The world around her dissolved and battle exploded around her. Her consciousness expanded like a
bubble and seemed almost that fragile. Xoayya
exerted control to rein it back in. Images and sensa-
tions washed over her as she did so. By the time her
consciousness had begun to retract, the battle against
Spiriastar was long over. The plan, their plan, had succeeded—not exactly the way they had intended, but
they had won. She didn't know details and could remember few specifics, but she felt no pain of loss.

Suddenly the world contracted and she found herself firmly rooted in the future. All around her she recognized the Imperial capital, Herakopolis. Back behind
her she saw friends: Locke and Marija, Kit and Eirene,
Roarke and Nagrendra, even Len and Ghislaine. *They
live! We won and they live and I am back in the Empire!*

She looked up and into the eyes of a most handsome man. *Chaosfire* filled them, but the constant shifting of the light had slowed, leaving them a deep blue
with gold tracery slowly drifting about. Square-jawed,
with sharp cheekbones and a strong nose, he smiled
at her, and she read undying love in those eyes. His
white hair lay heavy on his shoulders, yet shone with
golden highlights from the sun.

She heard words being spoken to her from her right.
She turned and saw a priestess from the Church of
Pleasure standing there. The woman smiled and finished her sentence. "Do you, Xoayya, enter this contract
of marriage with all your heart and mind free of encum-
brance?"

"I do," she heard herself say, then she blinked and found herself on the floor, looking up at Fialchar. She shivered and tried to get up, but her head swam.

"What did you see, child?"

"You knew, didn't you?"

The sorcerer opened his hands innocently. "I had to hope you would confirm what little I had seen."

"I don't believe you. Not for a second." Xoayya fought the dizziness and got to her knees. "I will tell you two things, one good and one bad. First the good—our effort to destroy Spiriastar will succeed. And I have seen far enough into my future to know my friends survive."

Fialchar smiled. "Very good. And the bad?"

She gave him the hardest stare she could manage. "In the future, I didn't see you at all. Take that omen as you will, Lord Disaster."

"I shall, Xoayya, have no fear." His smile did not die. "And you remember this. Your belief in the future may lock in details, but others might alter that which you cannot recall. Be careful what you say to others, lest you influence them to make choices that will change things. For me, given that I am not seen in your future, caution is in order. And I do not think any of the others would be remiss in adopting this mode of behavior as well."

35

Tyrchon found what Len was saying hauntingly familiar. He sat back, listening carefully to what the young man had to say. Len's animation and enthusiasm, emphasized by nods and smiles from Ghislaine and Jhesti, buoyed Tyrchon's spirits. Along with what he was thinking about his own planning, what had seemed to be a suicidal campaign yesterday now became a war to be prosecuted with a reasonable expectation of victory.

Len smiled broadly. "Then, last night, when I was talking with Ghislaine, everything became crystal clear for me. In this world here we don't have paratroopers, but we do have the *Drasacor*. When you told us that they leap, glide, and throw rocks at their enemies, you didn't mention they were huge honking rocks." He spread his arms apart. "They're capable of lifting hundreds of pounds, and that's what I need them to do."

He leaned forward and pointed to the plateau on

the map. "What we do is this: we run an airboat out as a decoy, so Spiriastar can track it by magick. We'll be running a big platform, above and behind the skiff, with our B*harashadi*—I'm looking at forty or so, I think—in addition to our D*rasacor*, me, Ghislaine, and Nagrendra. I want the skiff as magically obvious, while clearly being hidden, as you can make it. Spiriastar will direct the rail gun at it and destroy it, or she'll nail the magick on it and bring it down. When she does that, we abandon the platform and let the D*rasacor* float us down to the plateau. We want to come in here, on the north side. This little depression will give us cover and, if they turn the rail gun and use it to sweep us off the plateau, they won't be using it to nail Tyrchon's force. If they don't, we assault the rail gun and neutralize it."

Fialchar clapped his hands once, which sounded much like rotten fruit dropping on cobblestones, then looked at Tyrchon. "And what have you to report?"

The wolf-warrior stood, shifting his shoulders as a shiver ran down his spine. "As with Len, inspiration struck last night. I could see the battle clearly in my mind. I'll organize the force into fourteen divisions. Eight will be T*svortu*, four will be H*obmotli*, and two will be D*rasacor*—and, yes, I can spare Len the Mist Demons he will need. My H*obmotli* divisions will be the front line in the center and on each wing. The T*svortu* will back them, and the D*rasacor* will function as flanking units. Because of the nature of the valley and those valleys that feed into it, I have a unique battlefield situation."

He pointed to the map on the table. "The central basin here runs west to east, and this is where Spiriastar will be staging her army. We'll be coming in here, through the pass from the valley connecting from the northwest. The fact that the basin narrows into our valley is a concern because, clearly, the battle will have to be fought here. This limits our ability to maneuver, but Spiriastar's troops are limited as well. If they come up into our valley, they will be out from under the protection of the rail gun. While it might be able to lob shots into the valley, the high ridge sides will protect us from what Len has called direct fire.

"The only real concern I have in all of this is this southern spur, here. This is where Locke intended to approach the Necroleum. It's choked with debris, but Spiriastar's troop-harvesting may have cleared it out. It's on our flank and, at least for the initial part of the attack, we will be very vulnerable to an assault coming through there."

Lord Disaster's eyes flared. "Your southern flank will be vulnerable throughout the battle."

"Not really." The wolf-warrior opened his jaw in a smile as he traced his finger along a line to the northwest of the spur. "As you can see, right here the terrain begins to rise in elevation. The slope from the basin down to this point is very gradual, but the rise is fairly steep. We will engage the Glass Shadows well inside the basin, then fall back. Spiriastar should issue an order to her troops to advance as we retreat. Once they reach the low point, we have the *Tsvortu* sorcerers hit them with a serious storm. The winds and a driving rain will isolate the front lines from the troops in the back. As they come forward, they will be compacted, which will allow the *Drasacor* rock assaults to be far more effective. At that point, of course, the southern spur no longer threatens our flank. Even if they reinforce through it, they'll just tighten things up, and that's to our advantage."

Ghislaine frowned. "Unless the Glass Shadows break your lines and surge forward."

"Agreed. I'm keeping the tactics simple to avoid confusion, but if the Chademons can't defeat the Glass Shadows, everything is doomed anyway."

Fialchar stood, flames licking up over his forehead. "Very well. I am prepared to play my part as well."

Len held a hand up. "I think we have a change to your plans."

The lich sorcerer cocked his head. "Explain."

The young man took a second, then nodded. "All this planning has been done with us doing our best to avoid underestimating Spiriastar. Nothing we've done so far would come as a surprise to her, but her construction and use of the rail gun did surprise us. I get the impression she does not like surprises at all, and we have one for her that ought to give her a lot of trouble."

He raised a foot up and parked it on the tabletop. The boot's eyes blinked and stared at everyone. "With these boots, Myat becomes a viable force to employ against Spiriastar. This will give her two targets, two people she's disposed to hate. This will divide her attention and make the rest of us have a shot at getting our jobs done."

Myat shrieked with delight. "Yes, the boots! They are mine again. Spiriastar will pay! Give them to me, now."

Len shook his head. "No."

"What!" Myat's balled fists pounded the tabletop. "You must."

Len's foot disappeared beneath the table as he came out of his chair. "No, I don't have to do anything right now. Take the rest of the week and whip up the nastiest combat spells you can think of to deal with Spiriastar. Get them right, make them perfect. Fialchar can help you test them, but there will be no inkling that we have another magicker of Spiriastar's caliber here among us. That's part of the surprise. I'll give you the boots right before we depart, no sooner. Put the frustration you're feeling right now into those spells you'll use on her, and we'll do fine."

"I hate you."

"Yeah, well, here's something else you'll hate." Len held a hand up. "The first thing you will do is write down a spell that will send me back home after this is all over. I want it written down in case you die. When we get out of this, you're going to send me back home, got it?"

Myat's face darkened. "It will be my pleasure."

"I bet."

The Princess graced Len with a venomous stare. "And as for the spells you want, I have them created already. We should attack now."

Len shook his head. "No, I need a week. I want Tyrchon and Ghislaine to walk me through some combat basics so I won't be a liability out there."

Myat waved a hand toward Fialchar. "Conjure up for him some magickal sword or something that will take care of things."

Tyrchon shook his head. "That won't matter. We need a week to gather our troops. They're just filtering into the staging areas now. I'll need that time to bring them together and train them."

The Princess remained adamant. "But each day Spiriastar grows stronger."

"As do we." The wolf-warrior posted his fists on his hips. "You might be ready to go the second those boots land on your feet, but the rest of us need preparation."

Xoayya reached out and laid a hand on Myat's arm. "A week. We go in a week."

"We don't need . . . *ouch*!"

Xoayya's grip had tightened on the Princess's arm,

and a resolute edge had entered her voice. "A week. No sooner, no later."

Myat tore her arm out of Xoayya's grasp. "A week so you can try and find something to do?"

"My part in this is clear." Xoayya stood abruptly and stalked out.

Fire shot in twin jets from Fialchar's eyes. "You may think your spells are ready, Myat, but I have not reviewed them. A week, no sooner, no later. The rest of you similarly have details to work out. See to it. If there are problems, let me know, and they will be resolved."

Tyrchon found Xoayya in the dead garden. He paused in the castle doorway, gazing down at her as she stood near the edge. She looked so small, he wanted to leap down to the courtyard and sweep her up in his arms, to keep her safe and warm, to let her know she was loved, but he held himself back. In the past day he had been preoccupied with his planning and had seen little of her. In retrospect he could see she had been distant, but he couldn't think of anything he had done to cause it.

He cleared his voice. "I would not intrude, Lady Xoayya. If you wish me to leave, I will."

She slowly turned around and wiped tears from her face. "No, Tyrchon, that is the last thing I want." Her mouth opened to speak again, her lips quivered, but she said nothing.

Tyrchon slowly descended the half dozen steps. "What you said back there, a week, no sooner, no later . . . Fialchar repeated your words exactly. You looked into the future, didn't you?"

She nodded mutely.

"You saw what will happen."

"Not in detail. I know some things, but I am trapped by them. I cannot tell you."

He cocked his head to the side. "Why not? You believe the future is determined, so nothing you could tell me would change that."

Agony washed over her face. "I know what I believe, but if you ask Locke or Len, they will tell you they believe equally in free will. Fialchar says that perhaps whoever believes the most strongly will hold sway, and I know you believe in free will fervently. Would what I tell you allow you to change something, or have you refrain from doing something because you don't feel it is necessary? I don't know that, I can't know that. What I saw of the battle and its outcome was good for us, but I didn't see enough details to cast things as immutable."

His mouth opened in a grim smile. "Then you don't really know how things turn out."

"Oh, I do. I've thought about this a lot." Xoayya looked up at him with red-rimmed eyes. "You see, I think I wanted to see a vision that was vague. I wanted to do that on purpose. I wanted to see a future where free will—*your* free will—could be used to make the best of the situation. I didn't want to trap you. Go, do what you will to the best of your abilities, and you will win the day."

He opened his arms and approached her. "That's wonderful, that's perfect. You were brilliant in what you did."

Xoayya turned away from him. "Not really. There was a price I had to pay. If I loosened destiny's grip in one place, it freed destiny to hold on tighter elsewhere. I saw something else, something I didn't want to see."

A cold dread began to seep into his belly. "What?"

"My wedding." She hugged her arms around herself. "It was not to you."

"Oh." The hackles on the back of his neck rose.

"I saw everyone there. Len and Ghislaine, Nagrendra, Locke and Marija, Roarke, Kit and Eirene—she was pregnant, I think."

"That's good news." The words tasted bitter in his mouth. "Wait, you didn't see me there?"

"No."

"Did you see the ceremony end?"

"No."

"There, then, that's it. Perhaps I come riding up before it can be sealed and sweep you away." Tyrchon forced a laugh and clapped his hands. "I'll apologize now for being such a boor, and for being such a fool as to ever let you get away. I'll . . ."

"Stop it!" She turned and looked up at him. She reached out toward him with her right hand, then let it fall limp to her side. "I have thought of all these things, but I know none of them are true. When asked if I enter the marriage with my heart and mind free and clear of all encumbrances, I answer 'I do.' And I mean it. I have no doubt about it. I . . ."

Tyrchon tipped his face skyward and closed his eyes. "Then I shall apologize for having let you . . . for disappointing you . . . failing you."

"No, Tyrchon, you have not failed me." Her voice, which came soft, threaded thorny vines around his heart. "I failed you. I did not trust that you and the others could succeed. I sought the future so I would know what we needed to do. I hoped I was strong enough to influence things, but I failed. I fell back on believing in you and the others, which is why the balance is once again in your hands. I pay for my weakness, and I make you pay for it, too. I am so sorry."

"No." He opened his eyes and let a growl rumble

from his throat. "You did what you had to do. You contributed your part, using your abilities, to what we are doing. If I had been smart, if I had not feared the future, I would have asked you to do just this. I guess, deep down, I knew I would lose you. I think I will love you forever, and not regret that you have found better than me. I would have the best for you, always."

He turned away from her and began to walk off, then he felt her hand on his back.

"Tyrchon, wait."

He held up his right hand and refused to turn around. "No, Lady Xoayya, I cannot wait. You realized what you are and did what you had to do to guarantee our success. I am a warrior, a Chaos Rider, and I will be leading an army of Chaos demons into battle. Because of you, I have the freedom to win this battle, and this I will do."

Tyrchon relented and looked back at her over his shoulder, one last time. "What we have lost was probably never meant to be. Its sacrifice will save many from Spiriastar's tyranny. Our pain will be as nothing to what their pain would have been, and in this we should both find some comfort. Farewell, Xoayya, truly fare well."

36

Tyrchon departed Castel Payne and spent the remainder of the week in the company of Chaos demons. At first it seemed odd for him to find himself alone in their midst. Three-eyed creatures, six-limbed monsters, and things that looked like wind-blown rags, they all looked so bizarre in his sight that he could scarcely believe where he was. *Tsvortu* and *Hobmotli* had been enemies for years, which served to heighten his sense of dislocation. He had no doubt that the *Tsvortu* especially would hunt him in the future because he had killed some of their kind, but while they were united in their effort to oppose Spiriastar, the *Tsvortu* became his champions, appointing themselves his honor guard and helping to keep the other demons in line.

Litviro controlled the *Tsvortu*, and she ruled them with a mercilessness that invited little discussion and no insubordination. He had expected this would make her most difficult to deal with, but she listened to his plans very carefully and asked questions that made it clear she understood everything. While he had known the Tsvortu were highly organized socially, it had never occurred to Tyrchon that such organization might have required more intelligence than instinct. From the first he decided he could count upon the Tsvortu to hold against the Glass Shadows.

The Hobmotli, led by Fryl, made up for with enthusiasm what they lacked in intelligence and reasoning ability. Since they would be in the front line, it was important that they understood the concept of a false retreat. If they fell back, then did not stop and stiffen resistance at the right point in the valley, the Glass Shadows might develop enough momentum to keep pushing on. While the Tsvortu would certainly hold the middle, and their sorcerers would hammer the Glass Shadows with a fearful storm, a Hobmotli collapse would allow a Glass Shadow surge to envelop the center and crush it.

An individual called Shawa led the Drasacor, but Tyrchon could not be certain whether it was a name or, like Dashan, a title. He had the distinct impression that he met with more than one individual running under that name or title, and found himself constantly reexplaining details that he thought the Drasacor understood from previous meetings. They seemed more than pleased to be given their traditional combat role and even seemed elated at being able to be the force to spring the trap on the Glass Shadows. Tyrchon further honored them by asking a legion of them to watch over the camp in general, searching out and destroying the antling spies Spiriastar dispatched to see what he was doing. He also tasked them with monitoring the southern spur during the first part of the attack, so they could warn him of any Glass Shadow reinforcements coming through there.

If the Glass Shadows did bring troops in through the spur, he'd pull that right wing back as fast as possible and allow them to advance into the valley along that flank. That would simply accelerate the retreat as well as put Glass Shadow troops in danger of being hit by the rail gun's projectiles. He had no idea if that would prevent Spiriastar from using the weapon in the fight, but he hoped so. *If not, perhaps she will do as much damage to her people as she does to mine.*

In addition to planning the attack, reviewing troops, and overseeing the supplying of the *Hobmotli* with weapons, Tyrchon also became involved in helping train Len and his task force. They discovered, early on, that a single *Drasacor* could carry Len or Ghislaine; but the *Bharashadi* and Nagrendra required two of the Mist Demons to convey them successfully to the ground without harm. The only real difficulty with getting the *Drasacor* to understand what they were doing was in having them realize that they weren't supposed to drop the *Bharashadi* as they would stones.

Len's training went better than even Tyrchon would have expected. The young man wore the same studded-leather armor he had on the reconnaissance mission, though he had shifted to a helm that covered his face. Len chose a straight sword with two edges that he kept razor-sharp. The blade had a simple cross hilt, and Len fixed to it a red tassel. He was able to wield the blade effectively with one hand and use his peculiar buckler in the other.

From the way Len moved and fought, it appeared obvious to Tyrchon that Len had once had some fairly basic training with a sword. The wolf-warrior and Ghislaine acquainted Len with the cuts that would slice into arteries that ran close to the surface, though they all agreed that the Glass Shadows were unlikely to bleed to death. Still, a solid enough blow to one of the areas covered by an antling seemed sufficient to destroy that part of the Glass Shadow.

Tyrchon smiled at Len and waved him forward for another pass as they crossed swords in a sparring match. The Bharashadi flanked Ghislaine and backed Len, while Tsvortu, Hobmotli, and Drasacor completed the circle in which they fought. Len set himself, his eyes hidden by the shadows cast by his helm. He kept his buckler out and away from his left side. He had turned to the left, to present his right flank, which he covered with the blade. The red tassel danced in the light breeze, then jerked as Len advanced with a quick step.

His lunge came in low, and Tyrchon went to block it off down to the right. Len brought his blade up and over the block and continued to come in. Tyrchon pulled his left leg back and twisted his body, letting Len's blade skitter along the ringmail protecting his belly, then whipped Restraint up and in at Len's mid-section. The blade clanged against the buckler and bounced away.

Len cocked his right wrist, flicking the tip of his blade up in an arc. As he began to pull back, the blade tracked past Tyrchon's throat, but the wolf-warrior had anticipated the attack and had pulled his head back. Tyrchon pushed off his left leg and attacked as Len recovered himself. The wolf-warrior smashed his fist into the buckler, driving it back into Len's chest. The lighter man staggered back a step, gathering his feet beneath him, then leaped up into the air in a spinkick. His right foot a blur, Len brought it around and caught Tyrchon over the left ear.

The kick landed hard and spun Tyrchon to the

ground. He saw shimmering balls against a black backdrop, then saw a bareheaded Len leaning down over him as his vision cleared. "Are you okay, Tyrchon?"

The wolf-warrior rolled from his side to his back and laughed. "Very good. I saw it coming, but could not escape it. I doubt any Glass Shadows will, either."

Kiphlo, the leader of the Black Shadows, came walking over and crouched beside Len. "You have trained our leader well, Shadowdeath. It is no wonder those who fashioned *vindictxvara* in your image have died."

Tyrchon rolled up into a sitting position. "You make certain Len remains safe and his mission is completed. You will do that, won't you?"

"Our dead have been desecrated by Spiriastar. We will do all we can to enable you to destroy her." The Black Shadow flashed needle teeth in a hideous smile. "Fear not for our mission."

Len patted Kiphlo on the shoulder. "Go get the others ready to return to Castel Payne. Find Welas and have him get his *Drasacor* prepared as well. We go tomorrow and need to finish the platform."

The Chaos demon grunted and ran off. Len extended a hand to Tyrchon and helped him to his feet. "Thanks for not slipping that kick. I think it put some confidence in my, ah, people."

Tyrchon shook his head quickly, then stopped when a little pain started. "I didn't. You got me." He slid Restraint home and settled an arm over Len's shoulders. "You have changed a lot during your time here in Chaos. You have become . . ."

"More focused." Len smiled thoughtfully. "I think, through my life, I've been seeking a way to find out who I am. I know that can sound weird, because it should be obvious, but it wasn't. I tried a lot of different things seeking those that felt right for me, but I abandoned them because I didn't want them to define me. I kept people away from me because I didn't want them molding me into what they thought I should be.

"But here, whether this is a dream or not, I was cut off from everything that established who and what I was. Without those things I used in the real world to shield me from looking at who I was, I was forced to see what was left behind. I got a chance to look at the person who had grown up while not wanting to grow up. What I've found isn't perfect, but it's also not that bad."

The wolf-warrior nodded slowly. What he was so thoroughly defined him that he'd never been given a chance to wonder if he knew who he was. Xoayya's entry into and departure from his life did make him question if he was pleased with the person he had become. He wasn't certain of the answer, but he did know he was the best person available for the position into which he had been thrust. *For now, that's enough.*

"Who do you think you are, Len?"

"I think I'm smarter than I would have given myself credit for, and I think I have more guts than I ever expected." He shrugged. "I'm likely more stupid than I'd like to think, too, but not as stupid as someone like Myat would like to think I am. I think, ultimately, though, my time here has shown me that if I apply myself seriously to a problem, I deal with it. In the past I just avoided them as best I could because I didn't want to fail. Now, with this, I am facing it head-on because I don't want to fail."

"A wise man once told me there are only two types of fights to fight: those you *can* win and those you *must* win. Takes brains to sort out which is which." Tyrchon rapped knuckles on the helmet Len carried under his arm. "Fortunately, I think you are smart enough to figure all that out."

"Thanks." Len glanced over at where the skiff was landing. "I have to head back. When you're in position, we'll go. The *Tsvortu* storm should give us some cover, then we go in. When you see the skiff go down, you know to put on the pressure."

"It will be done. Good luck, Len."

The younger man nodded. "Any message you want me to carry back to Xoayya for you?"

Tyrchon did his best to ignore the tightness in his chest. "Tell her I wish her all the best tomorrow. And forever."

The wolf-warrior spent the rest of the day and early hours of the night in consultation with his commanders. They went over the battle plan again and again. He emphasized the meaning of particular patterns of thunderclaps and the nature of the maneuvers they heralded. He stressed the need for immediate and complete compliance with all orders. "If we do things the right way, we will win."

Fryl thumped four fists against his piebald chest. "*Hobmotli* will hold *Glazashari* back, Tyrchon."

"But only at the appropriate time. You hit, you hold, you retreat, then hold again, so they can be smashed."

"I know. Troops know."

He exchanged glances with Litviro but could read little on her face. "If we do not do this correctly, all of Chaos will fall to Spiriastar."

Litviro nodded. "It is understood. The *Hobmotli* will comply, as will the *Drasacor*."

Shawa's voice sounded distant. "The *Tsvortu* are our spine. If they do not break, we will succeed."

"We will not break."

"Good." Tyrchon patted Litviro on the arm. "Return to your people and get some sleep. Tomorrow we move at dawn."

Fryl clapped his hands together. "Tomorrow glass and bones left on stones."

"Agreed, my friends." Tyrchon nodded as he pointed them to the door of his tent. "Glass and bones."

The trio of Chademons left him alone in his tent, and the pang he felt at their departure surprised him. He wouldn't have ever expected to consider them "friends," but he knew he did. Able to communicate with them, and willing to show them the respect they deserved, he had created a bond with them. He had no doubt that it would last only as long as it took to destroy Spiriastar, but he doubted they would be able to think of an Imperial in the manner they had before their association with him. Likewise, he would not be able to see Chademons as mindless murder incarnate in the future. He didn't think that would make him more vulnerable to them on subsequent expeditions, but he knew it would change how he approached adventuring in Chaos.

We see them as having encroached on our world and now, after five centuries here, they see us as trespassers in their world. They are fighting to defend their realm against invasion much as we would. In the future, I will be more careful in choosing my fights in Chaos. I will only fight those I must win. The others can wait.

The next day dawned hot, and Tyrchon was up with the sun. The absolutely clear sky allowed him to see, off to the west, the green towers of Castel Payne floating in the air. Toward the east, on a high plateau, the sun glinted brightly off something he assumed to be the rail gun. On the ridges around him he saw Drasacor pickets, and their inactivity suggested no more antlings had attempted to infiltrate his camp during the night.

Clad in his ringmail coat, with Restraint slapping his left hip with each long stride, Tyrchon stalked through the camp. He tossed greetings to the Tsvortu warrior women as they stretched and donned their armor. He paused and exchanged best wishes with Alkurri, the leader of the Tsvortu sorcerers. There would be no problem, Tyrchon was told, in clouding up the sky and starting a ferocious storm by noon. The wolf-warrior heard that news happily, then continued to move through the camp. He joked with Fryl and stood in silent contemplation of the host they had raised with the Drasacor, Shawa.

Before and below them the army took shape. Each of the divisions broke down into ten legions, and each of them was comprised of four companies. Brilliant pennants rose above each Tsvortu company, proclaiming its proper place in the army, while the Hobmotli managed to paint their heads with various pigments to mark their company and legion. The Drasacor used no external sign that Tyrchon could see to differentiate their units, but somehow he knew who was whom and where they belonged.

Twenty-eight thousand Chaos demons waited for his command to advance. In all his time adventuring in Chaos he had never seen such a host assembled. He'd heard rumors of vast wars, of the Blood Titan tribe being wiped out by the Black Shadows, and of wars of extermination waged against Tree Spiders, but none of those tales had conjured up the barbaric splendor before him. The Hobmotli in position to lead, the sunlight glinting from the razored edges of Tsvortu spears, the Drasacor masses writhing with an unfelt breeze.

Tyrchon looked over at Alkurri and nodded. The sorcerer flung one arm toward the sky, and a rolling crack of thunder echoed through the valley. The Tsvortu began to move forward, and after a moment's hesitation, the Hobmotli led the way. The smaller Chademons moved at a steady but slower pace than the Tsvortu would have favored. The Drasacor, being used to leaping and gliding, advanced in great hops, securing the flanks.

It took the better part of an hour to march the two miles to what would be the jumping-off point. Two sharp thundercracks halted the advance at the line where the Hobmotli would be asked to hold after their retreat. Fifteen hundred yards separated them from the low point in the valley, and another thousand yards beyond that sat the vanguard of Spiriastar's force.

Tyrchon's first sight of them took his breath away. The crystalline host glittered and glowed in the morning sun. It sparkled like sunlight fragmented on waves. Her troops had been arrayed in divisions much as his had been, though each division's troopers were uniquely colored. A rainbow barred the advance of his army, the soldiers themselves breaking down sunlight, as dazzling and cold as ice.

He tore his eyes from them and nodded again to Alkurri. "The storm, bring it up and blot the sun. This will be a dark day, but it is *our* darkness, and it will be *our* day."

37

Len waved at Nagrendra, hopping from the landing skiff and walking over to the farside of the grotto where the assault platform lay. The craft had been fashioned by antlings that Fialchar conjured up based on the magicks the Dashan had used to create Spiriastar's servants. Lord Disaster's little workers seemed to be made of onyx, and sported hooks and barbs that made them look decidedly more ferocious than the antlings, and since they could fly for short distances, Len had taken to calling them roaches.

The roaches had spit-spun a landing craft that resembled a huge leaf. The central rib formed the keel, with the supporting ribs angling up at forty-five-degree angles from the ground, giving the craft a tight V-shape. A strong but very thin webbing linked the ribs and formed the sides of the craft. Len hadn't liked it, but he'd been unable to cut it with a knife, so he figured it would do.

Up at the stem end of the leaf, Nagrendra stood over the yoke-and-wheel-design controls. As he worked them forward and back, left and right, various parts of the leaf curled up or down. By augmenting the ship with magick, Nagrendra would be able to control the platform's flight to a certain extent.

"Think you have everything working?"

The Reptiad nodded. "While you were down there with Tyrchon, Fialchar and I ran over how we will approach the plateau. To avoid detection, we will put all the conveyance magick on the skiff and allow it to tow the platform. When the skiff is destroyed, we will be able to glide a bit further, then the Drasacor will have to bring us to the ground. We are hoping that the Tsvortu storm will put enough magickal energy into the air that picking out and hitting the skiff will be difficult until we've closed range."

"What if we get hit further out than we want?"

The magicker shrugged. "Fialchar has taught me the spells needed to keep the leaf flying. We will be vulnerable to detection at that point, but we have to get to the plateau."

Len nodded. "Think we'll make it?"

"I won't allow myself to think we won't."

He slapped Nagrendra on the arm. "With you at the helm, I'm sure we will make it, no problem."

Sidestepping a knot of roaches, Len left the platform and ascended the steps into the castle proper. At the first landing, he met Jhesti and Fitz. "Len, everything looks good to go for tomorrow's assault." The little plastic figure had become fully mobile and gave him a thumb's-up. "And Fitz and I are going with you."

Len frowned. "I don't recall that as part of the battle plan."

"It was in the fine print. Trust me, kid." The Dancing Joker smiled. "Look, we'll be as useless as an ethics consultant in the Gingrich campaign if you don't take us. Myat, Fialchar, and Xoayya won't need us. We're up here, so we aren't going to be helping Tyrchon. Clearly we're meant to go with you."

"I don't have *Drasacor* assets to carry you to the ground."

"Not to worry. I'm going to be riding with you. Fitz here, he's a bit more shock resistant than organic life-forms. I also had one of the roaches whip him up a parachute—or, at least, something that should slow his descent a bit. We gotta be there, trust me."

Len topped the stairs and entered the long hallway that would lead to the area where the roaches provided food for the commando force. "Okay, you're in. Just remember, the objective is to neutralize the rail gun. That's more important than me or anything else, got it?"

"Got it." Jhesti patted the fitting stool's back. "C'mon, Fitz, let's get you into that parachute. We're going to war."

Len couldn't suppress a smile as the fitting stool went galloping off. The enthusiasm in Jhesti's voice came from a thousand old war movies, most often offered by the earnest but green young lieutenant trying to inspire his battle-hardened veteran troops. It was all full of the romance of war, and had nothing to do with the realities of it.

The Vietnam War had ended before Len was born, with Grenada and Panama being news blips when he was a kid. Like everyone else he watched coverage of the Gulf War, but found it confusing. The soldiers sent over there seemed to be pretty clear about their mission: they were in place to stop a tyrant from taking over another nation. They were fighting for freedom, pure and simple, and were willing to lay their lives on the line for it. That sort of commitment impressed Len, but the fact that Kuwait was anything but a democracy meant the freedom for which blood would be shed would be very limited.

The press seemed determined to turn the Gulf War into Vietnam, part II. Len's history studies, war-gaming experience, and ability to read weapons-systems evaluations told him that short of Iraq popping some nukes, or massive use of biological or chemical weapons, the Allied forces weren't going to lose. He hadn't expected so one-sided an effort, but the press's disbelief at the results marked their pursuit of their own agenda. He recalled one Pentagon spokesman, when questioned about the deaths of Iraqi soldiers who had been bull-dozed and buried in their bunkers, saying, "There is really no good way to die in a war."

That was the truth of the whole thing, right there in a nutshell. The justifications, the suspicions, the obfuscations, none of them mattered when one got down to the bottom line: There is no good way to die in a war. The fact that the foes he faced were magical constructs consisting of bones from Black Shadows covered by antling flesh meant little in this regard. They might not be alive, but his people were. *Before this is over, a lot of blood will be shed, and a lot of lives will be ruined*.

He didn't want to think of any of his friends being dead, which seemed like a fairly obvious thing to him until he realized he'd not faced up to the logical consequences of what would be going on. Ghislaine could lie broken, Tyrchon torn to bloody shreds, Nagrendra smashed flat as the result of a fall. He shivered. *No, I won't let that happen!*

Len smiled at himself. "As if you can make the difference." He had grown pretty certain he wasn't in a dream, yet he had refused to look at his driver's license to confirm that conclusion. He clung to the idea of the dream less as armor for the sanity than as a game he played with himself. *I may be nuts, but if I can lie to myself and know I'm lying, then I'm not that far from sane.*

"Are you feeling well, Len?"

He smiled at Xoayya as he entered the dining room. "Yeah, just thinking."

The small woman nodded, and Len noticed dark rings beneath her eyes. "Everyone is fairly pensive now."

"Things are coming to a head." Len gave her a confident smile. "Tyrchon asked me to convey to you his best wishes, for tomorrow and forever."

Her face closed up for a moment, then she nodded. "Thank you."

Len frowned. "I thought you two were . . ."

"It was not to be." Xoayya's head came up. "And you have Ghislaine have spent a fair amount of time in each other's company."

"Strictly friends."

"For now."

Len arched an eyebrow. "That a guess, or do you know something?"

Xoayya shook her head. "You believe your future is your own to determine. Have confidence in that belief, Len. Let no one take it away from you." Her voice sank into a whisper. "Don't let yourself be trapped by someone else's future."

Before he could ask her to explain, she turned and walked from the room. He wanted to go after her, but refrained since she clearly would not explain herself further. Xoayya seemed like a friend of his who always read the last chapters of books first, so she would know which characters she should become attached to as she read. *Knowing something of the future is great when it's something that will make you happy, but frustrating when it isn't, and you can't do anything about it.*

He shook his head and plucked what looked like a plum-colored pear from a dish. "Doing something about the future is what tomorrow is for."

As storm clouds gathered over the valley to the east, Len took a final head count of his people on the platform, then nodded to Fialchar. "We're good to go."

Myat stamped her foot. "You are forgetting something, I think."

Len gave her a big smile to let her know he'd not forgotten at all. "The boots." He pointed his buckler at her feet. The width and length indicators adjusted themselves to reveal her size to be 4-B. *Four-B, always tough to fit.* "You realize these only come in one color."

She glowered at him in reply.

Len sat on the ground and pulled the boots off. When he pointed the buckler at them, it shifted out to a 9-B, his size. Keeping the buckler on target, he slid the sizer down to 4-B, and the boots shifted size appropriately. "There you go."

Myat had kicked her slippers off and held a foot out toward him, with her toes pointed and foot arched. Len groaned, but slipped the boots onto her feet. Given that she was wearing a sky-blue gown, the boots clashed horribly with her outfit, and a couple of the eyes seemed to wince as Myat wiggled her toes around.

"They're mine, finally mine."

"Remember our bargain."

Myat stopped and looked at him for a second, her

eyes a complete blank. Then she nodded quickly. "Of course. Fialchar has been given a copy of the spell that will send you home, in the unlikely event I fail to survive. Where he will get the power to wield it, I do not know."

A puff of flame from his eyes silently answered her comment.

Len gave her a hard stare. "Promise me, Myat."

"I promise, Len. I will enjoy sending you home."

Barely satisfied with her answer, Len pulled on his old City-trekkers and laced them up. *Just what the stylish commandos are wearing this year.* He stood and tossed a ragged salute to the magickers. "I'd wish you luck, but we'll be needing all we can get."

Fialchar laughed. "If random chance is your only ally, you are doomed."

"I'd rather be lucky than good." Len hopped into the leaf and sat beside Ghislaine. "Fortunately, we're both."

He slipped into the harness that bound him to a *Drasacor.* The *Bharashadi* sat along the central rib, with the *Drasacor* to whom they were bound sitting higher up on the V. The plan was for the *Drasacor* to just begin to glide when it came time to disembark. The platform would drop away beneath them, and they would drift down to the plateau.

A gout of golden energy surrounded and suffused the empty skiff. It rose from the grotto floor and floated out into the air, taking up slack on the cable linking it with the platform. Once the slack ran out, the leaf began to slide forward and actually started gliding before it had exited the grotto. Once it hit the open air it rocked a little, but Nagrendra's steady hands on the controls kept it level and flying thirty yards above and behind the skiff.

The clouds below had gathered with a vengeance and provided few glimpses of the forces below. Through a couple of breaks Len could see lines of troops marching forward. Lightning flashes and rumbling thunder drowned out any chance of hearing any noise from below.

Then, in the distance, Len saw five very bright lights strobe one right after another. He saw brilliant explosions track across a valley wall below, then heard sonic booms in the missiles' wake. Varicolored bursts of light burned through the clouds. Through a cloud gap he thought he saw the reddish glow of molten rock, and given the mass and velocity that the projectiles were traveling, that result did not surprise him in the least.

Len peeled back the cuff of his gauntlet and looked at his watch. He counted the seconds until he saw more flashes and the resulting explosions below. "Twenty seconds. Notice how they come in groups of five?"

Ghislaine nodded. "The loading ramp allowed for five projectiles to be ready to roll into what you called the breech."

"Right. Nagrendra, any idea how much energy it takes to launch those projectiles?"

"I have no way of knowing, but if the time interval between shots rises, I would have to guess Shoth would be tiring."

Jhesti, perched on Len's right shoulder, pointed at the watch. "Twenty-five seconds so far."

The light on the plateau flashed again. Out in front of them, the skiff became an incandescent ball of roiling gold fire. Even before the craft's explosion could rock them, four more projectiles shot through the fireball. Though they missed the platform, the shock wave of their passing battered the craft. The right side came up sharply, and the platform almost inverted. Clutching the rib where he had been seated, Len turned and saw that a quarter of the Black Shadows and their *Drasacor* had fallen from the platform. *Too far; they can't make the plateau now!*

At the leaf's stem end Nagrendra fought the control and leveled the platform out. "Redistribute the weight, balance it."

Len stood to relay the order. He felt Ghislaine take hold of the back of his sword belt, for which he was grateful. He shifted a half dozen Black Shadows to the left, and the platform righted itself. He turned toward Nagrendra and cupped his hands around his mouth. "How far?"

"Too far." A blue nimbus played over Nagrendra, then rippled over the leaf. "I will power our flight here for a bit." He cranked the wheel to the left, banking the platform, then shoved forward, and it began a steep dive into the clouds. Wind whipped over the platform, making Len's eyes water. Nagrendra pulled back, bringing the leaf's stem up, then the blue spell cut out.

"Better get ready to go!" Nagrendra pointed off toward the front of the platform. "Our target should be there, less than a mile."

In the direction he pointed, light flashed dimly through the clouds. Light built in intensity, then faded, chased by sonic booms. The platform rocked a little, but the projectiles had missed cleanly.

Len felt a cold chill run through him. "He was tracking our descent. That shot led us and would have hit us if you'd kept flying us."

"Right." A clear membrane nictitated up over Nagrendra's eyes. "I can fly this thing for a bit yet before I'm tired. Deploy now. I'll give him glimpses of a target."

"That could be suicide."

"I'm more mobile than the guys on the ground." The Reptiad stabbed a finger off toward the rail gun. "Go, now. Finish him."

Len turned and waved his hands upward. "Let's go, we're on target now. Go, go, go!"

Len's harness tugged groin and chest as his *Drasacor* spread his arms and caught the wind. Even though he only hung thirty feet below the Mist Demon, the clouds made it difficult to get a good look at him. Len had never actually seen wings on the creatures, but their arms and heads and bodies moved as if the *Drasacor* had a massive set of wings mated to their backs and they were just drifting in the breeze. Gulls floated through the air as effortlessly as *Drasacor*.

Below, he watched the platform sink out of sight for a moment or two. Then it lit up, bright blue, and shifted to the right. The light winked out, then flashed on again for a second or two. Nagrendra had transformed the platform into a giant firefly.

The rail gun flashed like a bug-zapper. The projectile boom came and went, then the projectiles slammed down to the ground in the distance. Len hoped nothing had been wandering around at ground zero, but he knew if it had, it had been obliterated. *And if that rail gun is turned on us when we land, we'll fare no better.*

He shivered. "Long way from a shoe store, isn't it, Jhesti?"

"That it is, Len, that it is." The plastic figure laughed. "No more waiting for something interesting to happen. We're interesting, and we're happening and, as bad as this might turn out, it's still better than selling shoes."

38

The very sight of Princess Myat rubbing her hands together with unbridled glee unsettled Xoayya. The sky-blue gown the Princess had chosen to wear would have been overdone at an Imperial ball. The skirts had many layers and spread out around her from the tight bodice like a bell. The neckline had been cut low, and the bodice pushed her breasts up high enough that the dress could barely contain them. A necklace of sapphire and silver, with earrings and rings that matched, added a sparkly element to Myat's ensemble. Lace chased the neckline and cuffs, and the boots, well, they just compounded the absurdity of the whole thing.

Xoayya herself had chosen attire more suitable to waging warfare. She wore an oversize blouse that she cinched at her waist with a thick belt. The blouse hung down over the tops of her black trousers, and they, in turn, tucked into the tops of her brown boots. She'd braided her hair and tied it with a green ribbon. It was her only ornamentation—the dagger hanging from her belt was well suited to war.

Fialchar looked long at Myat, then turned to Xoayya. "Are you ready?"

"I am."

The Princess nodded, then lifted her skirts and peeked at the boots. "More than ready."

"Good." Fialchar held a hand up. "First, I would have you deal with the problem of the valley where you hid Spiriastar. You are well aware of how it pains me."

Myat smiled easily. "I recall it well, *Father*." Contempt wove itself through her voice. "I had not wanted you disturbing Spiriastar's sleep. It is a minor matter to deal with that problem."

Myat opened her hands and in a reddish glow a scarlet bird materialized. It appeared, at first, to be a dove, but it quickly metamorphosed into a sharp-beaked hawk. The Princess lowered her face to it and whispered something, then kissed the bird on the beak. The bird screamed, then unfurled its wings and took flight. It soared out of the grotto, then seemed to flatten, as if it were a mere drawing on parchment, before it sliced into the air and vanished.

She brushed her hands one against the other. "There, you should already feel discomfort easing."

"So it is." Lord Disaster reached into a shadow and drew out his staff. He whirled it around his head once. The smoky topaz ball created a red halo that encircled them. Color ran like blood down from it, filling the hollow walls of an invisible cylinder surrounding them. When the color cut off all views of the outside world, Xoayya felt a lurch in her stomach, then the cylinder drained away into the ground, running through the glass like bloodstains through a wash-basin.

A hundred yards to her left she saw the thorn tow-ers that warded the entrance to Spiriastar's realm. Above her, black clouds gathered. Lightning linked them back and forth, with jagged fingers that clawed at the sky. In the distance she saw a gold spark wink at her from gaps in the clouds. "That must be the skiff."

"Indeed." Fialchar pointed to the north, where a flashing series of lights lit the undersides of the clouds. "And that is the rail gun."

"It doesn't matter." Myat pointed toward the towers. "Our goal is there."

"Come on." Xoayya ran past the two of them, care-fully slipping between the sharp edges of the thorns. She heard a few curses behind her and the sound of fabric tearing. She reached the clearing before them and was not surprised to see Myat's skirts hanging in shreds. "I guess the Dashan did not dress this grandly when he created this place."

"It matters not." Myat composed herself and looked around. "Yes, I remember this very well. Very well, indeed." She started to walk toward the podium that would summon the golden disc, but Fialchar inter-cepted her. "Yes, *Father*?"

"Be careful what you do."

"I was merely going to summon our conveyance." She shrugged her shoulders. "If you wish to do it."

"My pleasure." Lord Disaster reached out with the staff in his left hand and touched it to the podium's base. A burst of gold energy gathered around the quartz ball, then quickly shot back up the shaft and along Fialchar's arm. He screamed most horribly and reeled away. He crashed heavily against the wall, shattering the surface layer of crystal, then slid to the ground.

Xoayya ran to him and saw a face contorted in pain. Long crystal shards poked out through his robes all along his right side, but she got the distinct impression that he felt little or nothing from those wounds. His left arm, which had always seemed to be fluid, had stiffened and developed angular protrusions, as if the gold energy had frozen it solid. Likewise, his neck and the left side of his face had crystallized. Even the flames jetting from his left eye socket became abstractions of themselves, as if they were being viewed through a sharply faceted crystal lens.

His voice crackled with fury. "You knew that would happen."

"Did I?" Myat gestured casually, and the staff floated to her. She caressed its long black shaft, then brandished it like a sceptre. "You must have slipped in the past five centuries, Father. The Fialchar of old never would have been so careless."

"And my son never would have been so stupid as to cripple an ally before facing a most powerful foe."

"I do not fear Spiriastar. Don't you see, I left her alive because I knew she was no threat to me." Myat walked to the podium and stood upon it. She settled her feet into the slots on the base, then smiled back over her shoulder. "The Staff of Emeterio is very useful, Father. I hope you don't mind if I borrow it."

A hiss-snap-growl rolled from Fialchar's throat. "You are mistaken if you think I am powerless without it."

"I know why you are powerless at the moment, Father." She laughed lightly and touched the staff to the crest on the podium. Gold light filled the shaft, then shot out and formed the golden disc hovering over the crystal-lined shaft. Myat stepped back off the podium, then nodded at the disc, and it sank out of sight.

Xoayya looked at her. "You're going to bring Spiriastar up here?"

"Insane, isn't it? It would be except that down there she remains strong. The crystals here feed enough energy down into that realm to keep her healthy."

"That's what Len suspected."

"Of course, he knew, he just didn't know why he knew."

Off to the north the rail gun flashed again, and something in the air above the clouds exploded.

Mismatched fire jets shot from Fialchar's eyes. "The skiff is gone."

Xoayya shivered. She thought of Len and Nagrendra being torn apart, then remembered the vision of her wedding. *They* will *survive*, I *know it*. She turned to Fialchar. "What can I do?"

"For me?" The sorcerer coughed once, and a thick yellowish liquid dripped from the corner of his mouth. "It will take more than this to kill me."

"Sure, but Myat defines *more* right now, doesn't she?"

"Quite true." Fialchar pushed off with his skeletal arm, and many of the crystal needles withdrew at least partway from him. He then shifted to the right, shearing them off. He curled forward and sank onto his right knee. His left leg extended stiffly out to his side, and, where the robe lay against it, Xoayya saw the sort of blocky impressions that his visible flesh displayed. Crystal shards bristled from his back like cactus needles, but they quickly narrowed and fell out as if his body had just squeezed them free.

Fialchar coughed again and spat. "Better."

"I can cast a healing spell, if you need it."

Lord Disaster shook his head. "I need my staff."

Xoayya glanced over at Myat and saw the staff firmly in her grasp. Worse yet, the darkened hole brightened as the gold disc returned to the surface. Spiriastar stood in the center of it, clad in a dazzling ruby gown. It flowed as easily as silk when she moved, but froze into the same geometric edges as Fialchar's flesh when she stopped. Energy radiated off her, and a ruby staff grew out of nothing to link her two hands.

Spiriastar stared past Myat at Xoayya. "You I recognize as having been my guest, and *he*, though different than I last remember, is unmistakable." Her gaze shifted to Myat. "You I do not know, but to be in their company and do what you have done, you must be very stupid, or you have come to pledge to me your fealty."

"Wrong on both counts." Myat casually gestured at the disc with her staff, and it vanished.

Spiriastar spun her staff around, and, before she could descend more than a couple of inches, a diamond disc appeared beneath her feet and raised her a dozen feet. Her gown flowed back around her, covering her like a second skin, then expanded slightly into a ruby armor complete with gauntlets and a helm that raised her golden hair into horse-tail plume. "Dangerous games you play, child. You do not want to invoke my wrath."

Myat shrugged and suddenly her gown vanished and her jewelry expanded into silver-and-sapphire armor. "I have survived it before."

Spiriastar's eyes widened. "That look, that edge in your voice. You are my Dashan."

"The parts of him that count." Myat's voice became very cold. "The part of him that despises you for slaying his wife and, more importantly, the part that will kill you for just that."

39

A golden iridescence rippled over the Tsvortu sorcerers. For all of a heartbeat it expanded into a bubble of energy that suddenly burst. It became invisible as it did so, but Tyrchon could still feel it wash over him. In its wake the air cooled ever so slightly. With subsequent waves it became colder and colder and seemed somehow to pull moisture from the ground.

Wind began to rise, and clouds began to condense. At first he only saw slender strips of vapor, but they thickened and braided themselves together with other patches and tendrils in the air. As the puzzle pieces of clouds fitted themselves together, they swelled. Rising in the air, they began to billow and fill out. New, darker portions pushed out and down through white fluff, expanding to choke off the sunlight.

As the sunlight died, Spiriastar's army became less daunting and formidable. Without the sun's living energy pulsing through them, splitting apart to dazzle the Chademons with rainbow brilliance, the Glass Shadows lost some of their majesty. They still looked impressive, but no more so than some display of jeweled chess-pieces. Their crystal flesh seemed fragile, and though Tyrchon knew it was anything but, the positive omen was one he wanted very much to believe in.

Was this what Xoayya saw? Are her visions this clear, or will what I want to believe supersede what she saw? Tyrchon's face hardened. *Or will my belief simply provide her with what she saw.*

Raising a hand, he signaled Alkurri again. Another rolling thundercrack signaled the advance. The *Hobmotli* responded instantly this time, though a bit raggedly. They moved into the gap between the two forces unevenly, as if some of the legions were more anxious to close with their foes than others. He watched care-fully, ready to order a halt again to let things even up, but the problem did not become severe enough to require repair. *A ragged advance means untrained troops, and they are more likely to rout. This is not yet bad.*

The *Hobmotli* reached the lowest point between the valleys and started up the last thousand yards toward the Glass Shadows. Tyrchon braced for Spiriastar to send her troops forward in a running charge. The sheer weight of the Glass Shadows would blast them through the *Hobmotli* front lines. A concerted effort could crush his right wing and drive deep into his formation, or sever the left wing. A battle plan that had seemed so clear and easy before suddenly became muddled with countless new permutations.

Wait until there is something to react to.

Light flashed in the east, and Tyrchon scanned the sky for any sign of the rail gun's projectiles. On his right flank the valley wall rippled and exploded with five earthshaking impacts. A wall of heat slammed into him, then pieces of rock pitter-pattered down all around him. Huge clouds of dust rolled down from the valley side, revealing huge craters gouged from the stone. *Drasacor* fluttered around the area, with some dropping from the sky, and down below, as the dust settled, he saw *Tsvortu* and *Hobmotli* lying dead on the ground.

The stone fragments exploding back out into his troops hadn't killed that many, but he realized he'd grossly underestimated the power of the rail gun. The first shots had been high, but if they had been on target and plowed into his people, they would have been devastating in their impact. *I need Len and the others to destroy that thing, but I can't wait for them to do it.*

He looked at the *Tsvortu* sorcerer and pumped his left fist into the air twice. Alkurri sent two quick thunderbursts echoing through the valley. The *Hobmotli* in the front ranks greeted this with a savage cheer, then picked up their pace and charged up at the Glass Shadows. Behind them, but in better order, came the lead *Tsvortu* divisions.

Five more projectiles arced through the air. Three flew high, blasting into the canyon walls again. The dust and stone they sprayed out caught a few individuals in the rearmost ranks, but the charge had pulled most of the *Tsvortu* and *Hobmotli* forward of where they did damage. The fourth landed dead on target, hitting the ground in the midst of a *Hobmotli* legion. Where it hit, bodies just evaporated. The stone shrapnel cast up by the explosion scythed through the following ranks of *Hobmotli* and nibbled away *Tsvortu* front lines. Tyrchon heard screams in the explosion's aftermath, but they mixed with the *Hobmotli* war cries and became lost among them.

The fifth projectile tracked lower than the others and exploded in the air, above the Glass Shadow front ranks. Some of the constructs shattered, but more of the fragments sprayed out into the charging *Hobmotli*. It carved a swath through the center of a legion, cutting it in half.

The surviving Chademons closed ranks and kept coming. Tyrchon knew there had to be individuals in that mass who wanted to turn and run, but momentum carried them forward. They crashed into the Glass Shadow lines, and their charge carried four and five ranks deep into the Cobalt, Citrine, and Onyx divisions. Glass Shadows disintegrated beneath the assault as *Hobmotli* swarmed over them. He even thought, just for a moment, that his charge might crush the enemy's forward divisions, but the momentum slowed.

The Emerald and Ruby divisions on the right started forward to reinforce the Onyx division. On the left the Malachite division began to wheel toward the center to flank the *Hobmotli* troops attacking the Cobalt division. In the center the purple warriors of the Amethyst division began to filter into the Citrine division's ranks and push the *Hobmotli* back.

The rail gun flashed yet again, but an explosion high above and behind Tyrchon's position was the only casualty. *Had to have been the skiff, which means Len and his people are nowhere near in position yet. Have to play for time.* He pointed at his right wing and looked at Alkurri. "Right-wing *Drasacor*, now."

The *Drasacor* rose into the air like startled birds after three quick thunderstrikes sounded to their rear. The rail-gun missiles had clearly hammered them hard. Out of the full division he had on his right flank, barely three legions took to the air. They soared out over the Glass Shadow lines, dropping rocks into the Malachite and Beryl divisions. Glass Shadows fell, but only here and there. What should have been a devastating attack had been blunted.

Worse yet, the Serpentine division on that flank shimmered and contracted to become half as deep. At that distance Tyrchon couldn't be certain what had happened, then he saw Serpentine Shadows leaping into the air and unfurling bats' wings. Surprisingly agile, the Glass Shadows flew above the gliding D*rasacor*, then closed their wings and dove. The D*rasacor* turned and dodged as best they could, and some stooping Glass Shadows never came out of their dives and smashed themselves on the ground, but the D*rasacor* could not elude all of the winged constructs. D*rasacor* and Glass Shadows fell from the sky, but few D*rasacor* survived to make it back over the Chademon lines.

The Malachite and Cobalt divisions pushed forward, and the *Hobmotli* lines began to give. The Beryl division began to move out and around to the south, looking to roll up the edge of the Chademon line. Their advance would put them at the southern spur, and any reinforcements Spiriastar had lying in wait there could pour through. The only advantage that gave Tyrchon was to put Spiriastar troops in the direct line of fire from the rail gun, but with his forces flanked, there would be little reason to shoot.

It's too soon, but I have no choice! He looked at Alkurri, then pointed to the rear with his left hand. "Bring them, now, easily."

Three heavy thunderstrokes, long and rolling, crashed down over the armies. The *Tsvortu* stopped their advance immediately and began to withdraw. This opened a gap between them and the *Hobmotli*. The Hobs began to pull back in an orderly fashion, but when the rear ranks found they were no longer pressed by the Storm demons, they began to gallop to the rear. Each subsequent rank peeled off and ran, letting the front ranks get split by the Glass Shadows. Little pockets of *Hobmotli* warriors became engulfed, and though they fought valiantly, fell beneath the Glass Shadow forces.

Tyrchon shivered as he watched his line deteriorate. He had planned on a retreat, but the *Hobmotli* were making it look like a complete rout. The damage he had done to Spiriastar's forces was minimal, and the surprise he got from the Serpentine division's actions cast his entire plan into doubt. *If one division could do that, I have to assume more can and will. If just a quarter of her forces can do that, she will outnumber my flyers better than two to one. Once they're gone, the flying divisions land in my rear, and everything is lost.*

He forced his hands to open up. "It's not lost yet. When we get to the line, we hold. If we can't hold." He shook his head and rested a hand on Restraint's hilt. "This better not be the problem for which you are not the solution."

Len broke through the low cloud cover only a hundred feet above the plateau. He yanked on the straps linking him with his *Drasacor*. The Mist demon pulled up, slowing his descent, but Len still landed heavily and rolled. The *Drasacor* lighted easily beside him, shrugged off the harness, and leaped back into the air. He wondered at why the thing had departed so quickly, then a Ruby Shadow slashed a crystal saber at him.

Len parried with his buckler, skipping the blade wide, then kicked out with his left foot. He caught the construct over the right knee, but without his magick boots, the limb didn't break. The Ruby Shadow still staggered back a step, which let Len scramble to his feet and draw his sword.

An acrid scent poured from the Ruby Shadow's mouth as it charged him. The saber came up and around for a two-handed overhand cut. Len danced to his right, then whipped his blade around in a slash designed to hamstring the construct. If he could damage the antling forming one leg or another, that limb would collapse, leaving the construct at a severe disadvantage until it could find another antling to incorporate. Wounded and only semimobile, it would be easy to dispatch, though completely killing it would require destroying each of five antlings that made it up.

Len's slash missed the legs but managed to sever the creature's tail cleanly. As the Ruby Shadow started to turn, the antling making up the right side of its torso began to melt. The sword drooped and dripped away to nothing, while the arm fell away and right side of the rib cage flowed down over the right leg. The construct slashed at him with the claws on its left hand, but Len ducked it, and the missed strike left the Ruby Shadow unbalanced. Len slid to his right, then slashed his blade through the left side of his foe's chest.

The other half of its torso liquefied, dropping the head to the ground like an overripe watermelon. The legs collapsed and congealed into red antlings that scurried off. The one that had covered the skull limped away, dragging crushed legs after it.

"I should have already thought of this!" Len looked down at Jhesti clinging to his harness. "Spiriastar uses multiple antlings to create each Glass Shadow, but she bases the construct on the skeleton of a Black Shadow. The tail, and maybe fingers and toes or hands and feet, are very vulnerable. On a human a cut to the hand or foot would hurt, but it wouldn't kill, but with an antling, that's likely to be a nasty wound. We're not fighting one creature when we engage them, but five, and if we kill two or more, the thing falls apart."

Jhesti tugged on the harness. "There, to the left, Ghislaine and some of the B*harashadi* are fighting Glass Shadows."

Len cut the long straps from his harness, then sprinted off in that direction. About the time he felt the wind whipping through his hair he realized he'd left his helmet back in the leaf, or it had fallen out when the platform tipped. He felt stupid to be without head-gear—he'd never played a sport without a helmet, and had even worn padded headgear in his tae kwon do matches. *This is nuts!* he thought, then laughed aloud as he realized what he was thinking. *Being in the middle of a war is nuts, but here I am.*

Len sailed into the fray with full and complete abandon. He slashed the tail off an Emerald Shadow going after Ghislaine, then ducked beneath the saber slash of an Onyx construct. He caught the return slash on his buckler, then brought his own blade around and down to cleave through the thing's arm at the wrist. He felt pain in his back as the Onyx Shadow clawed him across the shoulders, but he let himself turn with the force and direction of the blow. As he came around he flicked his left arm out and smashed the buckler's edge against the construct's skull, crushing it and the antling sheathing it.

He caught a Ruby Shadow's slash on his blade and slid forward until their swords locked hilt to hilt. Len brought his buckler around and smashed it down on the red saber, snapping it against his sword's cross guard. The construct's arm began to melt, allowing Len's sword to flick forward in a quick slash that caught it in the side of the head. The Ruby Shadow fell to the ground in pieces.

Len heard something at his back and began to spin, but vertebrae from the Ruby Shadow rolled beneath his right foot. Len fell, dropping him beneath a cut that would have opened him from right shoulder to left hip. On his back, Len looked up and saw a Cinnabar Shadow rising above him, then he heard a loud *clang* and got a solid kick in the shoulder that tossed him back a couple of feet. As he turned and tried to gather his feet under him, he saw Ghislaine's ax flash down, beheading the construct.

Fitz scrambled out from beneath the Cinnabar Shadow's legs and reared up. It drove both its forelegs through the right side of the construct's chest. That side of it puddled away to nothing, and three antlings scurried away, abandoning the skeleton that had united them.

Ghislaine dropped to one knee beside Len. "Fitz took it down, I got the head, and he finished it."

"Good." Len looked around and saw a half dozen Black Shadow operational and four dead on the ground. "Where is everyone else?"

Ghislaine shook her head. "I don't know. Our D*rasacor* took off immediately."

"Mine, too." He stood slowly and looked around. "Rail gun should be over there, just over that rise."

The Matarun warrior rested her ax on her shoulder. "After you."

"Remember, lopping off pieces of these things are as good as some grand blow. Tail is especially vulnerable." Len pointed off toward the rail gun with his sword. "Let's move."

The adrenaline coursing through Len made him want to run, but without knowing what was over the rise, that didn't make any sense. *Of course, if there is a division of Glass Shadows between us and the rail gun, we're dead whether we walk or run.* Despite that cheery thought, he approached the rise carefully, then let Jhesti run ahead. The little figure hid behind two skull-sized stones, then waved Len forward.

Len topped the rise and scooped Jhesti up in his left hand. The plateau spread out before them, level and flat as a Martian plain. The rail gun just sat there, barely two hundred yards distant, with only Shoth, some antlings, and piles of projectiles around it. Beyond them, way to the south, he saw some light show going on in Spiriastar's valley. A few antlings roamed the plateau, and on the south side of the gun he saw Black Shadows fighting with some constructs, but the way to the rail gun was clear.

Brandishing his sword, Len began sprinting toward the rail gun. He hoped against hope that Shoth wouldn't have time to swing it around and fire at him. The antlings were relaying projectiles from mouth to mouth from an ammunition pile to the feeder ramp on the weapon. Shoth seemed more interested in them than he was Len—in fact, he gave no indication he knew Len was there at all.

As fast as Len might try to be, the Black Shadows were faster. One by one they outstripped him, the fastest among them a good thirty feet in front of him as they neared the rail gun. The leading Black Shadow raised a massive sword, preparing it for the strike that, forty feet or so further along, would allow him to split Shoth in two from crown to ground. Len almost wanted to cry out a warning to his former friend, but he knew that the old Shoth was dead and that this creature was under Spiriastar's control.

Then the lead Black Shadow hit an invisible wall. The wall seemed to give for a second, then an electric blue light played over it, revealing it to be a dome protecting the rail gun. The blue light sparked through a curious pattern of overlapping diamonds, which had been warped where the Black Shadow had run into it. The Chademon rebounded, its fur smoking.

The pattern, that was a chain-link fence, and it was electrified!

Shoth turned toward Len. "I did not want to use your memories in her service, but I had no choice, Len. She gave me no choice!" Shoth's voice resonated mechanically through the antling covering him. With it came the acrid scent of fear sweat. "Stay away, or I will have to destroy you!"

40

Xoayya shivered involuntarily as Spiriastar absorbed Myat's declaration of her identity and intent. The elder sorceress's eyes narrowed. "This would be the daughter you turned against me." Spiriastar's voice came in a cold hiss. "The one you made into a swordbearer. Her death, though at my hands, was at your instigation!"

Xoayya waited for Myat to strike, but instead the Princess touched the butt end of her staff to the ground and summoned a quicksilver disc that raised her into the air above the crystal-lined pit. "All the rationalization in the world will not save you." She opened her arms. "I will even allow you the honor of striking first."

Fialchar snorted. "Foolish little girl."

"Foolish?" Xoayya frowned at him. "Tell me what you want me to do, and I will do it."

"Not you, her." He pointed at Myat with a frozen finger. "She may have my son's intellect, but not *all* of it."

Spiriastar's staff came around with ruby energy pulsing up through it. A ruby spear leaped from the end of the staff and flew straight at Myat. The Princess's quartz ball flared blue, creating a round shield directly in the spear's path. Before the spear could hit the shield, the crystal shaft split lengthwise into a half dozen vines that grew ivylike out and around the shield. Thick thorns mounted like scorpions' stingers on each end curled inward to rake their way through Myat.

Myat's staff pulsed again, and the shield curled into a cylinder around the nexus point for all the ruby vines. It rolled forward, reeling them in until the vines wrapped around it like thread on a spool. The cylinder picked up speed and rolled through the air at Spiriastar. When it was barely five feet from her, she tightened her left hand into a fist, and the vines contracted, crushing the cylinder. Both spells died in a purple puff of energy.

The Princess leveled her staff at Spiriastar and cast a spell. A blue gout of flame shot out at the elder magicker, but before it crossed half the distance between them, each little licking tongue of flame became a blue dart. Nearly a third of them continued the direct flight in at their target, but the rest soared up and out, around and down, looking to attack Spiriastar from all angles.

Spiriastar immediately went to one knee and slammed her staff's heel against the diamond disc. The edges spread out, then curled up, engulfing her in a diamond sphere. The blue darts hit and skipped off, then turned and came back, relentlessly pummeling the sphere. The flame jet continued to produce them, and they swarmed the sphere, but none of them could dent it or chip it.

A hint of gold entered Myat's spell. The blue darts struck the sphere, but no longer bounced off it. They spread out over it, as if they were droplets of paint that had spattered it. The blue coat that soon covered the diamond ball vaguely reminded Xoayya of the spell Nagrendra had cast on Spiriastar. *Did anyone tell Myat about that?*

A massive golden hammer appeared in the air above the blue sphere and crashed down on it. The sharp blow echoed thunderously through the valley, and Xoayya felt it vibrate through her chest. The blue ball did not so much as move an inch, but being inside it had to be harmful to Spiriastar. Xoayya winced as the hammer rose to fall again, but Fialchar gestured weakly with his right hand and shielded them from the sound.

"How did you?"

Lord Disaster's eyes flared slightly. "Kill the sound? It is an elementary spell every sorcerer learns for when he wishes to study in peace."

Xoayya's eyes narrowed. "So the sound won't affect Spiriastar?"

His laugh sounded like bones breaking. "Hardly."

"But shouldn't Myat know her attack is useless?"

"She would if she were a sorceress, but she is not." The metal flesh around his eyes tightened. "She has recovered some memories my son had, the memories of his grand magicks. But, even as she could not undo the antlings, apparently neither can she recall undoing sound. In fact, her taking the offensive is uncharacteristic of my son. He was a great one for *disweaving* spells cast at him."

Xoayya's mouth hung open. "That would suggest . . ."

"Myat is overmatched, yes. Offensive spells cannot always be blunted by greater offensive spells.

Moreover, defense is often easier and, in this case, less taxing." He pointed at Myat's hammer. "She continues to power a spell that has failed to crack Spiriastar's defense once. Why would it succeed a second time?"

A chill stole over Xoayya. Though her experience with magick was severely limited, she was able to differentiate between the manifestation and the magick. The ruby spear Spiriastar had cast at Myat had been a simple attack spell, but it had manifested as a spear that split into vines because that was what Spiriastar wanted. It could have exploded into a flock of hawks or a swarm of bees without affecting the core spell being cast.

Good magickers did not fight spells based on manifestation, but on the basis of the magick. Simple counterspells could disrupt magicks, rendering them harmless or even turning them back on their caster. Dealing with a spell based on manifestation might be effective, and even showy. It often marked the contempt one magicker had for another, but it would never be considered subtle. *Not that Myat would ever have been taken as subtle.*

Xoayya shivered. *Spiriastar, on the other hand . . .*

A single diamond needle exploded from the blue ball and hit the gold mallet. Red cracks appeared in the gold, then the hammer exploded into a gold ball of fire. The blue magick coating the diamond burned away, then the sphere opened as Spiriastar straightened up. She stared hard at Myat, then shook her head.

"You are an amusing diversion, but you are not fully my Dashan."

"I am enough of him."

"No, quite simply, you are not." Spiriastar laughed contemptuously. "You are lacking the most important part of him."

"And that is?"

"The part that could kill me." With the speed of a striking snake, Spiriastar stabbed her left hand forward, and a thin, clear crystal layer formed like frost around Myat's throat. It began to thicken very slowly, and grow, with the serrated edges beginning to gnaw into Myat's flesh. "You have some interesting toys, but you lack the Dashan's power. You lack his subtlety. You cannot defeat me. Part of him is already under my control, and, soon, you will be, too."

Little tendrils of crystal grew up and began to inch their way into Myat's nostrils, mouth, and ears.

Fialchar tried to stand. "She cannot be allowed to succeed. Help me."

Xoayya passed a hand over her eyes, igniting a blue fire in them. "I know what I have to do." Fialchar clutched for her, but she slipped from his grasp and retreated toward the entryway.

The lich's eyes blazed. "You doom us all."

"I have to do this." She turned and fled.

Even though it was what he wanted them to do, Tyrchon felt his stomach lurch as the Glass Shadows started forward. The Beryl division led the right wing's advance, with the Malachite and Cobalt divisions surging forward to fill the gap between them and the retreating *Hobmotli*. The Hematite and Cinnabar divisions in the right-center of the Glass Shadow formation turned toward the south and began to march along to slip in back of and reinforce the right wing. The Diamond division likewise shifted south to reinforce the center right, then the center left began to push forward. The Glass Shadow left wing acted as the anchor as the whole line began a sweep.

Tyrchon's left hand tightened into a fist. *This was not what I had planned on happening.* The left-center advance would take it slightly north, eclipsing the left wing. Once it had disengaged from the enemy, the left wing would be free to move south and apply a push wherever it was needed along the line. What Tyrchon had wanted and hoped for would be a general advance that would compact the Glass Shadows, but Spiriastar's strategy would avoid that problem and allow her to mass troops to exploit any breakthroughs in his line.

Still, they're going to be moving uphill, so that is to our advantage. He walked over to Alkurri and pointed at the Hematite, Cinnabar, and Diamond divisions. "I want rain on them, now. They're all moving south, and if they can't get an order to turn west, it will cause problems. Can you do it?"

All three of the *Tsvortu* sorcerer's eyes rolled up into his skull. "Would I tolerate aught but warriors in my harem?"

"Do it." He squinted at the lines. "And be prepared to signal the halt when the *Hobmotli* reach the line."

"You will give me the signal."

Tyrchon shook his head. "No, I'll be down there." His stomach began to knot up. "Sound the halt until they halt."

"And an advance?"

"Keep your eye on me. You'll know."

The wolf-warrior drew Restraint and began to stalk forward. The company of *Tsvortu* warriors that had appointed themselves his bodyguards came trotting along after him. A large warrior came running over from one of the *Tsvortu* divisions, and Tyrchon tossed her a salute when she slowed to match his pace. "This is going to be it, Litviro."

"You commit yourself and your bodyguards too soon."

His eyes narrowed as lightning split the sky and sheets of rain began to lash the Glass Shadows. The right wing came on relentlessly, splashing their way through the low point of the battlefield. Three hundred yards separated them from the retreating *Hobmotli*, with the first of the retreating Chademons already reaching the *Tsvortu* formations. Many of the *Hobmotli* stopped as per their orders, but some individuals slipped into the safety of the Storm demon ranks.

To the south the Beryl division swept past the southern spur. The Serpentine Shadows pounced on a retreating legion of *Drasacor*. Tyrchon hadn't thought he had that many *Drasacor* capable of flight on the right flank, then he remembered those he had stationed to watch the spur. *They're coming back, which means they know they've been cut off.* He saw a small group of them—less than a company—fight their way past the Serpentine Shadows and work their way toward him. Their report, when he got it, would not be good news.

"Not likely there's going to be any good news here today." Ahead of him the Malachite and Cobalt Shadows broke into a run, charging up the hill at the *Hobmotli*. They closed the gap quickly, with some of the Serpentine Shadows preceding them and striking at stragglers. A few of the *Hobmotli* turned to fight, but most just galloped as quickly as they could toward safety, abandoning weapons and comrades alike.

Two heavy thunderstrikes sounded the halt, but the *Hobmotli* did not slow in the least. While the forward *Tsvortu* units held their ground, retreating *Hobmotli* troops tore into their formations, disrupting them. *Tsvortu* commanders shouted orders, and the Storm demons closed ranks quickly, but the Glass Shadows were upon them before they could become cohesive units again.

The Glass Shadow charge hammered Tyrchon's right wing. The lead Tsvortu legions recoiled from the impact. The physical mass of Glass Shadows moving swiftly battered the Tsvortu front lines. Though Tsvortu spears skewered countless Glass Shadows, the weight of the bodies pulled the weapons down or out of the warriors' hands. Glass Shadows surged into the Tsvortu formations, slicing them up.

"Litviro, roll your Blizzard division forward and bring Fire and Rain over to reinforce the right wing." As she ran off, Tyrchon sprinted forward. He directed himself toward a Malachite Shadow wedge stabbing deep into the Storm division. This also took him head-on into a mass of fleeing Hobmotli.

Restraint bisected the first Devil in Motley that leaped at him, spraying blood back over its comrades. The wolf-warrior brandished his bloody sword, then leveled it at the stunned Hobmotli. "Turn around and fight, you four-armed cowards! They are stone and bone, nothing more! Are you afraid of dirt and sticks, or will you come shatter them with me?"

A few of the Hobmotli jumped away, continuing their flight, but the rest, barely a company, turned and started sprinting back toward the line. More of their fellows emerging from the Tsvortu lines saw them and turned as well, caught up in the ferocity and hysteria of the battle. Hobmotli leaped high into the air, flinging themselves at Malachite Shadows in suicidal attacks. Yet as stupid and useless as those attacks were, the mindlessness of them seemed to infect the Tsvortu and even Tyrchon himself.

He sailed into a gap opening in Storm division and chopped Restraint downward. A Malachite Shadow's arm came clean off, and the sword continued to bite into the construct's thigh. The Glass Shadow began to come apart, with another two Malachite warriors hurling themselves forward into the opening. Tyrchon parried the attack by one, then T*svortu* spears from his bodyguard unit transfixed both of them. The T*svortu* phalanx swept forward, blunting the Glass Shadow drive.

Even with that hole being plugged, Storm division began to fall back. The reinforcements came up to strengthen the line, but they had to deploy to the south as well to prevent Beryl division from curling around and rolling up the flank. Tyrchon withdrew a bit up the hillside and saw what had been a long clean line now being broken by a series of Glass Shadow thrusts. Worse, the Citrine division had completed the drive to the north, freeing the whole left wing to swing to the south.

Without being told to do it, Alkurri had extended the storm to cover the left wing's advance south. The storm seemed to be effective with the other divisions, but as their march took them against the valley's south wall, they naturally followed its curve to the west. Their turn wasn't executed with the precision that would have made it effective, but those divisions would eventually be pointed at his lines, and they would break through.

Damn! Tyrchon watched his force begin to crumble and knew he had to commit *all* his reinforcements, but if he did that, he would only be allowing himself an orderly retreat. *If I commit them now, I won't be flanked, but I have no chance of counterattacking later.*

Then a *Drasacor*, bleeding a glowing greenish yellow

liquid, landed next to him and collapsed at his feet. Tyrchon knelt as the Mist demon clutched at his mail. "Troops in the spur, coming this way. Enemy troops. We have been trapped."

41

"Then you're just going to have to destroy me, Shoth." Len turned and pointed at Fitz. "Kneel in the wall, short it out."

The fitting stool galloped forward and slammed into the wall. It dropped to its knees, letting the metal of its legs ground it. The chain-link pattern flared a deep indigo, and the plastic covering on Fitz's back began to blacken and bubble. The rubber on his neck began to smoke, then the stool sagged sideways. Its limbs began to glow red, but before they began to melt, the blue light sputtered and died.

Sword at the ready, Len dashed forward. He wished he was wearing the magick boots because he wanted to close with Shoth in an instant. With each step he remembered more and more of Shoth. The man encased in crystal became clearer to him. He was being used by Spiriastar and didn't deserve this fate. He deserved better, and though he had already died, his final destruction would be a tragedy.

Shoth looked straight at him, his gray eyes full of terror. Len pulled his right arm back, preparing for a slash that would behead Shoth cleanly, but as he moved into striking range, he faltered. He met Shoth's gaze, then broke it off.

Shoth's left hand flicked forward and a blue spark caught Len over the left hip. Pain shot through the left side of Len's body, followed by absolute numbness. Len crashed down hard. His sword bounced away, and the buckler only stayed with him because his left fist wouldn't open and let it go. Len recognized the sensation as the same as having touched a live wire, and, as he slid to a halt, he felt the tingling pins and needles of sensation returning to his limbs.

Shoth leaned down and shook his head. "I didn't want to, but if I fail her . . . You don't know what she will do." Despite the metallic sound of his voice, the fear came through as easily as the stink of fear sweat rolled off him. "I can't fail her."

Len reached out and grabbed Shoth's ankle with his right hand. "Shoth, don't fear what happens if you fail her. Fear what happens if you *succeed* in her service!"

Shoth hesitated for a moment, then doubled over. Len saw the sorcerer's stomach convulse, then a crystal flow ejected itself from his mouth. Shoth heaved again, and the flow resolved itself into an antling. Shoth straightened up, the hint of a smile beginning to form on his face. Len thought he mouthed the word "Free," and the springtime scent of grasses seemed to confirm that idea.

Then Ghislaine's ax came around and swept Shoth's head from his body.

Len felt Shoth's corpse shudder, then it flopped down next to him. Len's stomach clenched, then the antling that had covered Shoth's leg shifted beneath his grip and pulled itself free. Len opened his hand, then raised it to Ghislaine and let her pull him to his feet. He leaned heavily against her, but she didn't seem to mind and kept him upright.

"Sorry, Len, I know he was your friend."

"And yours as well." Len shook his head. "But that wasn't him. I grabbed him so he'd not see you coming. Thanks for saving my life."

"My pleasure, believe me." She turned and pointed her ax at the rail gun. "What do we do with this thing?"

Nagrendra landed in a crouch at the farside of it. His *Drasacor* touched ground right after him, freed themselves of their harnesses, and became airborne again. The Reptiad sorcerer watched them fly away, then trotted over to the rail gun. Blue light flashed from his hands and played over control surfaces, which Len recognized since they were based, roughly, on the design he'd created for his project. "Seems to be a mix of clairvoyant magick for targeting and conveyance magick for delivering the projectiles."

Len and Ghislaine walked over beside him. Len saw the crest on top of the triggering mechanism and pointed to it. "I'd guess you just drop your thumb on that puppy to shoot." The portion of the control panel that had been designated for the targeting-control system likewise had a crest. "That probably activates your sight."

The Reptiad stepped up to the gun and rested his hand on the targeting crest. Blue light trickled through the crystal gun. "Yes, I see the battlefield, and there is a cross hanging in the middle of the image."

"That's where the gun will shoot."

"Troops are compacted there; I can't get a clean shot

at the Glass Shadows without hitting our own people."
Nagrendra grabbed hold of the triggering lever and
moved it to the right, swinging the gun's muzzle around
to the south. "Besides, Spiriastar is the more important
target, and it looks as if Myat is not doing well."

Len slapped Nagrendra on the shoulder. "Lock and
load, fire at will."

The sorcerer gave him a walleyed stare. "What an
odd incantation, and hardly necessary with the way
the leechspells have been set up here. Touch the
crest, and the work is done for you." Nagrendra made
some minor adjustments with the targeting lever, then
touched the triggercrest with his thumb.

Had Len not known what to look for, he likely would
have missed the elegant simplicity of the rail gun's
operation. At Nagrendra's touch, gold lightning trickled down the targeting lever and blossomed full
through the weapon. The breech snapped open, and
the first of five capsule-shaped projectiles rolled into
it. It closed again, then light pulsed from red through
green and up to violet along the gun's barrel. As the
projectile left the muzzle, a loud boom sounded since
the blue projectile traveled well past the speed of
sound. The moment it had cleared the gun, the second
missile loaded itself and then the third, all five arching
off to the south.

The first three seemed to be headed toward their
target, but the last two didn't make it. The fourth left
the muzzle with a mild *chuff* and blasted away a piece
of the plateau's southern edge. The fifth arced out and
crashed down within two hundred yards of the gun,
then broke into several large pieces that scattered
some of the Glass Shadows and B*harashadi* fighting to
the south.

Nagrendra reeled away, stumbled, and went down hard. Len ran to him and grabbed and immediately felt a chill running through the Reptiad's flesh. "What happened?"

"It draws a lot of energy." Nagrendra's tongue played sluggishly over his lips. "Five was too much. Cold. Must rest."

"At least you got her." Len glanced to the south and still saw light glowing there in the sky. He got up from Nagrendra's side and ran over to the rail gun. He touched the targeting crest and felt a tingle in his left hand. A greenish-neon targeting display magickally appeared in front of him. Len flicked his index finger forward, upping the magnification. He saw Spiriastar in ruby armor, floating on a diamond disc which sported three ornamental crystal ribs curling above her. She didn't look hit or inconvenienced in the least.

"Not good, Nagrendra. She's not down."

Ghislaine helped lever the Reptiad into a sitting position. "I can't shoot again, Len. You'll have to do it."

"Me?"

Nagrendra nodded solemnly. "You have the Dashan's power, even without the boots. It will have to be your shot. Make it good."

Myat's quicksilver disc melted into long fluid tendrils dripping down on the crystals lining the hole, but Spiriastar's magick held her in place. With a flick of Spiriastar's left hand, the Staff of Emeterio flew from Myat's hands and sailed through the sky well above and past Fialchar's head. Myat clutched at the crystal collar, her white fingers a sharp contrast against the red-purple of her face.

The elder sorceress allowed her diamond disc to

turn slowly and solemnly to face Fialchar. "It has been a long time, Fialchar. You have not aged well."

"And you have not aged."

"Ah, the insolence I remember so well. Tell me, did you destroy the Seal in a fit of pique at being excluded from the group that fashioned it, or did you have some other petty motivation for your action?"

Fialchar's head reared back, and corrupt, forced laughter filled the valley. "You must paint it that way in your mind, must you not? You could not allow yourself to admit the truth—that I fostered the debate and maneuvered all sides into the positions where the Seal was created and I was allowed to destroy it. You do realize, don't you, that your enemies provided me with the magicks I needed to do the job. Granted, they just thought I was going to sabotage your effort. Their interests in winning the debate blinded them to the possibilities of what would happen if I used their spells *after* you had completed your work."

Spiriastar's face brightened with a smile—a smile that broadened as Myat gagged when tendrils worked their way down the back of her throat. "So, those who created the Ward Walls, who are viewed as saviors in the Empire, were complicit in the invasion of Chaos."

"A fact they keep hidden from all."

"For now."

Spiriastar's smile tightened down into an angry mask. She whipped her right hand around toward her back, bringing her staff into play. The aft end of her diamond disc became fluid and expanded into a curtain that curled up to protect her back. Three projectiles, one blue and two red, slammed into the curtain. At first it seemed as if they would burst through it, but, instead, they melted into it. The curtain hardened, resolving itself into three columns that arched up over her, all angular, as if they were the tails of giant crystal scorpions there to ward her.

"Your accomplices, Fialchar, are quite determined, and at least one of them is likely now to be dead." She laughed aloud and pointed her staff back toward the north. "The weapon employed against me would suck the energy from any human, leaving a cold husk in his place. My agent could launch five projectiles because I provided him the strength to do so, but no one else could do it, not even this child with her boots."

Fialchar shook his head. "Perhaps I would prove you wrong."

"Give you a chance to do so? I think not." Spiriastar brought her staff around and pointed it at Lord Disaster. "You may have learned much in the past five centuries, but even with your staff, you could not stand against me."

"You would be wrong in making that judgment."

"Perhaps," Spiriastar smiled, "but since you are going to die *now*, there is no way you'll ever find out if that is true or not."

Len's mouth went dry. "Okay, okay, if I have to do this, we need ammo." He glanced over at a pile of projectiles and waved a couple of Black Shadows toward it. "Wrestle one of those things up onto this ramp."

"No." Jhesti leaped from Len's harness onto the rail gun. "You can't shoot her with one of those things. She'll detect it coming, just like she did the ones Nagrendra shot."

"What are you talking about?"

"Len, remember, I don't see things the way you do. All this crystal stuff, it's all linked to her. It's part of her.

She knew when the shots were coming in, and she dealt with them. All the crystal bullets you have here won't hurt her."

Len frowned. "What do I shoot her with, then?"

Jhesti smiled. "Let's just say I've always wanted to be faster than a speeding bullet."

"You?"

"Think about it. I'm plastic, and I'm not from this world. She doesn't have a chance in hell of detecting me." Jhesti rested his fists on his hips and struck a very heroic pose. "And, remember, I'm likely the only smart missile available here."

Len felt a lump rise to his throat. "But, if you hit her, at this speed . . ."

"I'll die?" The little simulacrum of a man shook his head. "I'm plastic, Len. You might have invested a lot of psychic energy into me, but I'm not alive. Or, if I am, I'm making this decision here to put my life on the line. She's gotta go, and I'm the only shot we have. Lock and load me, pal, and make sure I'm dead-on."

Jhesti lay down on the loading ramp and raised his hands above his head. Len dropped his hand onto the aiming lever and maneuvered the crosshairs until they centered themselves on Spiriastar. He saw her raising her staff and pointing it off to the side. The sorceress's lips moved, so he knew she had another victim to play with.

"Ready on the firing line?"

"Ready. Make it good, Len."

"It will be." Len squinted to make sure of his aim again, then jammed his thumb down on the trigger-crest. A wave of cold crashed over him, and his world began to go black. He staggered away from the gun, and the last thing he remembered was stumbling back into Ghislaine's arms.

Spiriastar screamed as Jhesti slammed into and burst through her left shoulder. The impact spun her around and smashed her against the blue pillar. Her left arm whirled off into the air. It blasted into Myat, knocking her from the sky and down onto the pit edge. Spiriastar rebounded from the pillar and fell heavily, but still managed to keep her torso upright with her right arm.

The ruby armor closed around the wound, and the blood that had splashed down over her left flank glistened for a moment before it bled back into the armor. She rose to her right knee, then her staff shrank as the armor absorbed it. In an instant a crystalline arm budded at her ruined shoulder. It grew out swiftly and ended in a razor-taloned hand.

Spiriastar stood slowly, then smiled most grimly. Her voice came hoarse, but no less full of menace for it. "*That* was inconvenient, but I still have more than enough power to deal with you, Fialchar."

"Fialchar!"

Lord Disaster turned to his left as Xoayya, all cut and bleeding, raced back into the pit area. She tossed him the Staff of Emeterio, which he plucked from the air with his skeletal hand. In a second, even before the crystallized half of his body could resume normal proportions, a gout of black energy pulsed from the quartz ball and battered Spiriastar back against the blue pillar. She bounced back from it hard and fell on her face on the diamond disc. Another pulse washed over her, coating her in inky black mud that splashed all over her flying disc.

"Stupid woman! I am F*ialchar*!" The sorcerer brazenly

pumped his staff into the air with his skeletal hand. "I have learned things of which you have only dreamed in your slumbers. First among them, here and now, though a minor thing, is this: I have learned the unmaking of your crystals, and that is more than enough to deal with you."

Xoayya looked on with horror as the mud ate its way through the flying disc and Spiriastar's armor. Blood spurted when the ruby prosthesis dissolved. The tall columns wavered and fell, toppling into the hole. Their loss unbalanced the disc, and Spiriastar clawed at it with her good hand. Her fingers, now stripped of their melted armor, dug into the crystal. Her body sank into it, then through it, and in a glittering diamond rain, Spiriastar fell into the tunnel and vanished from sight.

Xoayya ran to the edge of the pit and peered down into it. "Is she?"

"Dead?" Fialchar flexed his repaired left hand. "Ah, yes, by *now* she is."

"And Myat?"

Lord Disaster looked over at the other woman's body. He gestured at her with the staff, and the crystal collar snapped. "For now, she lives and is mercifully unconscious, but you might want to attend to her wounds."

"What about the others?"

Fialchar shrugged. "Most all our work here is done, and after we finish, we will check on them. If they survive their missions, most likely they will live, too."

42

Tyrchon turned and grabbed one of his bodyguards. "Run to Alkurri. Tell him to hit the Glass Shadows with as much storm as possible, now! Lightning, everything. Hit their Bloodstone and Quartz divisions hard. Send all of our reserves forward and push through Wave division to get at the enemy's center. Go, now, go!"

He stood and double-checked his thinking. With the vast majority of the Glass Shadows hooking south, a drive at the enemy's middle would hammer the weakest part of the line. If the Diamond division did not swing into line because the rain was ruining its communication, only the Bloodstone and Quartz divisions would stand in his way. The fact that the whole left-center had moved north meant a gap had begun to open in the Glass Shadow lines between those wings, which presented him an opportunity to split their force.

Overhead the clouds darkened and spat out lightning. Countless times before Tyrchon had lived in fear of the storm magick practiced by the T*svortu* sorcerers. Bolt after bolt, incandescent and hot, linked sky and ground. Bloodstone Shadows exploded when hit directly. Those nearby stiffened and began to shake so hard their component antlings tore themselves one from another. Looking down from his vantage point, Tyrchon saw Glass Shadows fall beneath the storm assault, but he knew it would be too few to stop the enemy's advance.

Litviro's Blizzard division came charging forward to swell the ranks of Wave division's left flank. They pushed in between Wave and Fog divisions, hitting the gap between the Glass Shadows left-center and right-center. Their assault crumpled the Bloodstone flank and began to drive them south, widening the gap. T*svortu* warriors stabbed deeply and often with their spears, piercing Bloodstone Shadows two or three rows deep in the formation.

Before Blizzard could exploit its advantage, the Amethyst division diverted southwest and slashed at the T*svortu* salient. They didn't hit it very hard—it seemed to Tyrchon as if they just leaned forward to grind down the T*svortu* advance. The press of bodies made any movement all but impossible, and the T*svortu* counterassault slowed. They did not surrender any of the ground they had gained, but they had only pushed ten yards into the enemy formation.

On the right wing, the Storm and Wind divisions began to fall back. Even bringing the Fire and Rain divisions over had no effect, since Beryl's advance forced them to string the flank further out. Tyrchon's army suddenly had a right-angle line, with a hinge between the Wave and Storm divisions. He knew that hinge was the weakest point in his line, and the Malachite Shadows had already eaten into the Storm division. When things started to break down, that was where it would erode most swiftly, and that fact was hidden from no one.

And then, back behind the Glass Shadow lines, he saw the Cinnabar and Hematite divisions execute a smart turn to the northwest that put their backs to the southern spur and pointed them directly at his hinge. With his reinforcements already committed to a floundering attack and reinforcing his right wing, Tyrchon knew the end had come.

A cacophony of shrieks and howls arose at his back. Tyrchon spun and saw a multicolored division of *Hobmotli* with Fryl at its head rushing forward. The little Hob leader had somehow rallied those of his fellows who had run. They had armed themselves with rocks and *Tsvortu* spears, clubs and even a few bones of dead *Bharashadi* warriors. They galloped forward on all sixes like pigmy cavalry.

Tyrchon shouted an order to Storm division and his bodyguards. His personal company moved as quickly as they could to the north, reopening the wound the Malachite Shadows had cut into his line. The *Hobmotli* warriors dashed into it, their war cries rivaling even the thunder in their ferocity. The Hobs hit the Malachite Shadows hard, with those Hobs coming up behind using their fellows' backs to vault them over deeper into the enemy's lines.

This attack, which had more organization to it than the previous assault, eroded the Malachite ranks. The *Hobmotli* warriors in front surged forward to grab and hold and tie down Glass Shadows while those following them smashed and crushed the antlings that made up the warriors. These smashers then moved to the fore, grappling with yet more Glass Shadows, allowing another rank to come in and start smashing. The Hobs sustained injuries, and dead *Hobmotli* bodies littered the line of their advance, but the sheer glee and confidence in their voices as they tore their enemies apart built up in them a momentum that the Glass Shadows could not match.

Tyrchon's own bodyguards had flowed into the gap on the side of Wave division, and, as the *Hobmotli* attack spilled over into the flanks of Quartz division, Wave pushed forward. Litviro sent three of Blizzard's legions to the southeast, directly into the Bloodstone division, while the rest of them fended off Amethyst's attack. What had once been the right-center of Spiriastar's formation now had troops driving into the lines on either side of it. The storm continued to savage it, and as Tyrchon himself stalked forward, sheets of rain driven by cold winds lashed at him.

The wolf-warrior howled madly as he forced his way into the line. His bodyguard cleared a space for him to swing Restraint, and he lit into the Glass Shadows with complete abandon. Knowing the prophecy about swordbearers, he realized there were only two possible outcomes in the battle. One, obviously, was his own death, but the other was victory. He didn't know if victory would be his alone, leaving him the sole survivor on either side. He could see himself, exhausted and cut in a hundred different places, leaning on his sword in one desolate charnel field, but he was determined that would not be the outcome. I *may die exhausted, but if I survive, exhausted though I may be, it will be so that others may survive.*

Restraint blocked one cut high left, then Tyrchon shifted his wrists and slashed down to low right. The blade sliced through a Quartz Shadow, opening it from right shoulder to left hip. It spun away, crashing into another construct, which lost its head a second later to Restraint. The starblade arced low, cutting the legs from beneath more Quartz Shadows. As they went down, Hobmotli finished them, and Tyrchon backed away to check quickly on the advance of the Glass Shadow reinforcements.

As he expected, the crimson and silver divisions had started their march up the hill. They were on a direct line for the hinge. *Even with this headway we've made, we'll still break here.* He looked back to signal Alkurri to hammer the reinforcements, but a series of lightning strikes slammed into their forward ranks. *He's doing what he can, but how long can his people keep the storm going?* Tyrchon's stomach tightened. *No matter how long, it won't be long enough.*

He continued to stare at his enemies for a second, then swiped his hand across his face as rain blurred the world. Tyrchon squinted, then shivered. *Movement, in the spur. The enemy troops are here.*

Troops poured from the southern spur and right on into the rear of the Glass Shadow formation. The initial company rode what looked to Tyrchon to be the most terrifying collection of mounts he'd ever seen, save the lead beast. It was a magnificent stallion of emerald. For a half second Tyrchon took it to be another construct created by Spiriastar, then he recognized it from legend. *That is the Emerald Horse!*

Trumpets sounded, and the riders came at a gallop. Weapons drawn, they crashed into the Hematite rear. Sword and axes, lances and sabers slashed and stabbed, felling whole ranks of Glass Shadows. The riders emerging from the spur after that resolved themselves into cavalry formations organized under Imperial pennants. Two full legions rode north at a full gallop and hooked around to catch the Ruby and Emerald divisions in the flanks. With the storm washing away their communications, the Glass Shadows did not react to these new attacks. Troops intent on carrying out their last orders because they scented no new ones remained ignorant of the fate of their fellows until the fighting came close enough that whatever sense of self-preservation they had could override their orders.

And, by then, the Imperial cavalry slaughtered them.

Tyrchon laughed aloud. "Yes, *enemy* troops to a D*rasacor*, but not to us!"

More Imperial cavalry swept west, cutting into Spiriastar's right wing. The H*obmotli* surged ahead again, tearing into the Malachite Shadows. Litviro's Blizzard division pushed hard against the Amethyst troops, and the D*rasacor* division that had been assigned to the left wing finally took flight, shrieking and raining stones down on the Glass Shadows.

Suddenly a thick green bolt of lightning exploded in the middle of the Glass Shadow formation. A greasy black smoke boiled up from it and rolled out like a malevolent fog. It undulated in waves out over Glass Shadows and, at its touch, they began to dissolve. The forward wave would crest over a rank, then in its trough no Glass Shadows could be seen.

But at the heart of the circle of destruction Tyrchon did see a figure. Tall and gaunt, with a ragged robe that flapped madly in the wet wind, Fialchar swirled his staff around over his head. As if that motion created a huge wind, the fog continued to spread out, eating away at the Glass Shadows.

The fog overwhelmed the Malachite and Quartz

divisions, sending some of the *Hobmotli* in their midst reeling away to vomit. Tyrchon closed his nose against the dark vapor, but caught enough of it to recognize the scent of death. He let the fog move past him, then he trotted forward through a field littered with bones and bodies and glistening puddles that had once been antlings. As he advanced, the storm above the battlefield died.

Tyrchon opened his arms wide. "Is this it, then? You could have destroyed them all with this spell, yet you let so many die here without employing it?"

Gold flames guttered in Fialchar's eye sockets. "What care you? They were Chademons you would have slain without a second thought."

"I care because I care." Tyrchon slowed his advance as the handsome young man on the Emerald Horse came riding over and dismounted. "Locke, is that you?"

"Tyrchon? You were leading the Chaos demons?"

Fialchar laughed with a sound like the gurgling of a throat-cut child. "It was an unholy alliance, Cardew, not unlike the one you and I have had."

Locke looked at Fialchar with disgust on his face. "We never had an alliance. We had a contest you never dared finish because you lost. Why don't you answer Tyrchon's question?"

The lichlord's face darkened. "Spiriastar could have easily blunted this spell. I could not cast it until she was dead, which she is. And I would not have come here and interfered, save that I was compelled to do so."

Tyrchon smiled. "Xoayya and her vision."

"Yes, though about my part in this I think she lied." Lord Disaster nodded toward Locke. "She saw his advent into the battle when she peered into the future. His troops would have been enough to win it."

The wolf-warrior looked over at the younger man. "How is it you're here?"

"Returning from Chaos we ran into the vanguard of the force the Emperor had raised to destroy the Black Shadows if we had failed." Locke's green eyes sparkled with a hint of *Chaosfire*. "We sent Roarke back to Herakopolis with the Fistfire Sceptre, then we took the Imperial troops back here. While I had an agreement with Lord Disaster concerning your safety, I didn't want to leave anything to chance."

"Your lack of trust is really unworthy of you, Cardew."

Tyrchon frowned. "Why does he call you by your father's name?"

"Too many years in Chaos, clearly." Locke shrugged. "I'll explain later."

Fialchar spread his arms wide. "I would note to both of you that my action here destroyed an army that would have severely hurt your troops. Moreover, I have created a gulf between your two forces, so they need not fight each other. Of such a tragedy I do not think you would approve."

"True. Thank you." Locke bowed his head in Fialchar's direction. "Tyrchon, you mentioned Xoayya. She survived?"

"And Nagrendra, too." The wolf-warrior dropped his jaw in a smile. "It's been a rather full fortnight since I last saw you."

"And it is not done yet." Fialchar's spun the staff and surrounded them with a red cylinder. "Now we bring this all truly to an end."

43

The red cylinder flowed away, and Tyrchon found himself standing in Fialchar's sanctum. To his left Ghislaine and Nagrendra flanked Len. He had stripped off his leather armor and cast his weapons aside, though he clutched his buckler to his chest. To the right, past Locke, Princess Myat stood on a dais between her two black guardians. She looked pale and had twin circlets of blood at her throat and collarbone. He'd not seen the sapphire-and-silver armor she wore before, but something about it made him uneasy.

"Where's Xoayya?"

Her voice came from behind him. "Here."

Tyrchon spun and saw her standing there, flanked by her own scarlet guardians and their watchbeasts. He reached out to gather her into his arms, but the way she glanced down restrained him. His insides went cold. "I, ah, I am very happy to see you well." He noticed her clothes had lots of cuts in them, and were stained with blood, but the cuts appeared to have been healed. "You *are* well, are you not?"

"Physically, yes." Her eyes, quite full of *Chaosfire* now, looked up at him. "You are not angry with me for lying?"

"About what?" He jerked a thumb toward Locke. "If I had known Locke was coming, I would have fought differently, and we would have lost. And tricking Fialchar into putting a premature end to the battle, that was genius. If he dared wear a beard again, you'd have tugged a lock or two from it with that one."

Relief flooded through her voice. "Good. I don't want you to hate me."

"How could I?"

"In more ways than you know."

The sharp peal of a staff ringing on stone brought Tyrchon's head around. As he turned to face Fialchar, Xoayya moved from behind him to stand beside him, yet she kept her distance just the same. He found it frustrating, but thrust aside his thoughts as Lord Disaster spoke.

"Through your efforts, a great victory has been won today." The lich smiled most chillingly. "I am inclined to be generous to you."

Locke drew his sword, and one of Myat's guardian beasts snarled and started down the dais steps toward him. The younger man gave the beast a hard stare that stopped it in its tracks, then he reversed his sword and offered the pommel to Fialchar. "I would be pleased to offer you my sword so you can toss yourself on it, or do you not feel *that* generous?"

Fire flared in Fialchar's eyes. "I had hardly thought you so vindictive."

Locke shrugged. "Well, you've ruined the chess set with which we were to play, so I assumed you had nothing more to live for."

"Yes, that." With a casual wave of his hand, Fialchar reverted the chessmen to their original state. The watch-beasts again became rats. Myat shrieked and kicked at one, launching it across the room. "Is that better?"

Locke shook his head. "It depends, I suppose, on your generosity."

"Indeed." Fialchar's staff stood upright, as if rooted in the floor, as he spread his arms wide. "Rewards are in order for all of you. Our visitor first, I think. Len, you wish to be sent home, is that not correct?"

Len's eyes flicked toward Ghislaine, then he nodded slowly. "I guess it is. I . . . I have gotten to know all of you here, and I consider you—well, most of you—friends." He glanced back at a blackened pile of metal that stirred a bit, and Tyrchon recognized it as a badly burned Fitz. "And I've lost friends here. Fitz may recover, but there was Shoth and Jhesti."

Locke looked at Tyrchon. "The Lost Prince was here?"

Tyrchon smiled. "Not exactly."

Suddenly, though the window, flitted a black-and-green creature with big bat's wings. It lit on Len's shoulder, then the wings furled and resolved themselves into humanoid arms. Len plucked it from his shoulder and held the little man in his right hand. "Jhesti? How?"

The little creature shrugged. "I broke up when I hit Spiriastar and was drenched in her blood. You know how everyone else who spends time in Chaos is changed, but she didn't seem to be? We didn't realize it, but she was employing some fairly fierce magicks to keep herself looking normal. All the mutagenic Chaos energy in her had been confined in her blood, and I caught a good dose of it. I managed to pull myself together—seemed like it took forever, but I guess it didn't."

Fialchar cleared his throat. "Prior to leaving her valley I was temporarily able to speed time in that area, to encourage decay and neutralize the place. My work, apparently, had an unexpected side benefit."

Len smiled broadly. "Hey, I guess getting Jhesti back is my reward."

Tyrchon raised a hand. "Don't be so hasty, Len. We consider you a friend as well, but you have friends back in your home the same as we have them in the Empire. You bargained to be returned home, and you should be allowed to go if you want."

"I don't think so." Myat started down the dais steps. She flicked her right hand at Fialchar, and he crumpled to the floor, curled around his stomach, which he clutched in obvious though silent agony. "I believe these boots draw power from you, and your departure from this world will cut me off from that power. You will stay."

Tyrchon dropped a hand to the hilt of Restraint. "Myat, don't do this."

"Do what? Guarantee the safety of the Empire?" She pointed to Fialchar. "I have conquered him, our greatest enemy. None of you can stand against me. With these boots and my power, we need never fear anything ever again."

Len's voice came low and cold. "You said you would send me home again."

"I did let you believe that, and I *may*, sometime, in the future." Myat smiled as she reached the floor and grabbed Fialchar's staff. "If you are good."

"You *promised* I could go home after Spiriastar was conquered."

"I said it would be my *pleasure* to send you home." She laughed throatily. "I believe, in this case, I will delay my gratification."

Len nodded slowly. "I thought so." With Jhesti scrambling up onto his shoulder, Len pointed the buckler at Myat and snapped a little piece of metal down.

The boots on Myat's feet contracted, crushing her feet and ankles. She shrieked in pain, then toppled over. She clawed at the boots and thrashed her feet. Len's hand reversed what he had done before and the boots flew off Myat's feet. A blue spark shot from Nagrendra's hands and grew into a blue blanket. It settled over Myat and ended her struggles by sinking her into a deep sleep.

Len's face had become ashen. "I didn't want to do that, but . . ."

Ghislaine draped an arm around his shoulders. "You were the only brake on her ambition. You did what had to be done."

Fialchar grabbed his staff and struggled to his feet. "Don't any of you have children. They can be very spiteful."

Tyrchon snapped his teeth at Fialchar. "The fledgling seldom falls far from the nest. Perhaps you can atone for her rude behavior by sending Len home."

Fialchar smiled almost graciously. "I would be delighted to do so, but there is a difficulty in doing so." He twirled the staff around in a circle and both Ghislaine and Myat vanished in a red cloud. "Sending them back to Myat's mountain stronghold was nothing, but to send Len home will require a great deal of energy. Energy I do not possess. However, if Len gives me the boots, I can do it, but he has to give them to me of his own free will. If they are not freely given, they will not work."

Len, who had been staring at where Ghislaine had stood, looked at Fialchar gape-jawed. "You think I would be mad enough to give you the boots? No way. Even if it means I spend the rest of my life here, I'd never turn that sort of power over to someone like you. Forget it."

Lord Disaster shrugged. "There is no solution, then."

"Yes, there is." Xoayya stepped into the circle. "Len, give the boots to me. Lord Disaster will teach me the spell needed to send you home, and I will do it."

Len's face brightened. "Xoayya, these will be the best-fitting boots you've ever had, believe me."

"I do, Len." She walked over to the dais steps and removed her own boots. Len scrambled around and gathered up the magick boots and dropped to his knees before her. He worked with the buckler to size them correctly, then eased them onto her feet. Xoayya looked down at them, then let Len help her to her feet. She gave him a kiss on the cheek, then turned to face Fialchar. "Now teach me the spell."

Lord Disaster shook his head. "Why should I?"

The wolf-warrior snarled and drew Restraint. He started to growl that Fialchar would do it because it was the honorable thing to do, but the sheer ridiculousness of that comment stopped him. "You owe it to Len."

"No, his bargain was between him and Myat. My magick caused his friend, Jhesti, to be reconstructed, and Len already said that was enough of a reward for him. I owe Len nothing." Fialchar nodded toward Xoayya. "I think, however, *we* can strike a bargain that will allow me to teach you the spell."

Xoayya's chin came up. "Name it."

"You will become my apprentice."

"Done."

"No!" Tyrchon grabbed Xoayya with his left hand and spun her around. "What do you think you are doing?"

"I'm doing what must be done."

He wanted to shout at her, but he saw the resolve on her face, and the way her lower lip trembled. *She's terrified, but she is facing her terror to do the right thing for Len.* His hand fell from her shoulder, then he glanced over at Len. "Remember this sacrifice, Len. She is trading her life for yours, her happiness so you may know happiness. Don't squander what she is giving you."

"I won't." Len's hands balled into fists, and Tyrchon saw him swallow hard. "It's a new Len Fong that's going back into my life. Things will never be the same."

Fialchar handed Xoayya the Staff of Emeterio. "The staff knows the spell. All you need to do is cast it."

Xoayya had the staff in her right hand and pointed the quartz ball at Len. She closed her eyes, and her lips began to move ever so slightly. A blue-and-silver aura surrounded her, then burned bright in the quartz ball. It leaped out in a coruscating ball of energy that slammed into Len and knocked him backward before it imploded and consumed him.

Lord Disaster plucked the staff from her hand and Xoayya slipped to the floor. A gold cocoon surrounded her and lifted her from the cold stone. It floated her out of the room and down the castle's Grand Corridor. The sorcerer smiled as Xoayya drifted past Nagrendra. "My *apprentice* is tired. She will rest, then her training will begin in earnest."

"If you harm her . . ."

Fialchar turned to Tyrchon. "What will you do? Will you see if I am the foe you cannot defeat with that blade? Xoayya is the mistress of her own destiny, and slaying me will not change that. What you have lost here was never yours to possess, was it, Tyrchon? You know that."

The wolf-warrior nodded once and resheathed his blade. *My fantasies were destined to end. I knew that, and while she did not want to believe it, her vision showed her it was true.* "What I know is this, Fialchar: she may be the mistress of her destiny, but I consider myself a guardian of it. If you harm her, I will see that you will reap the same pain. She is your apprentice and, therefore, your responsibility. Fail in your responsibility to her, and there will be a reckoning."

"I'm certain." The Staff of Emeterio whirled yet again and, after a second of pure agony, Tyrchon found himself with Fialchar, Nagrendra, and Locke back in the middle of the battlefield. "Don't think ill of me as a host, but I would hate to have you overstay your welcome in my home."

Locke turned and petted the neck of the Emerald Horse when it trotted to a halt next to him. "Such a concern for manners, Fialchar. I'd not have thought you capable of it, given your appearance at the Ball last month."

"You took that as unmannerly?" Fialchar sniffed. "Then your reward, Cardew, will redeem me, I am certain. Your intervention here helped preserve my realm, and you are here as part of an Imperial force. Tell your Emperor I have reconsidered my gift to him. I shall give him more time on his throne. More than a year. How much more, I won't say, but more."

Locke sketched a mocking bow. "Given that your realm will be in turmoil over the consolidation of Black Shadow territory for the next year, your generosity is unbelievable."

"Do you value peace so little?"

"This gift is hardly a sacrifice for you."

Lord Disaster nodded. "Your point is taken, and I shall apply it to my next boon." He turned toward Nagrendra. "In the time I have known you, I have not seen you use a staff or any other aid to spellcasting."

The Reptiad nodded. "Becoming dependent on a tool means one is helpless when that tool is taken away."

"Then you shall have to avoid developing dependency." Fialchar held his left hand out and into it flashed a yard-long staff made entirely of a ruby. It ended in a crystal hand that clutched a huge diamond. "This is for you, Nagrendra. An item worthy of you, and of worth to you."

It floated over to Nagrendra, but the Reptiad did not touch it. "Would I be mistaken to assume this was fashioned from Spiriastar's severed left arm?"

"Consider it a tribute to what she once was, back before Chaos allowed her to reach her full potential." Fialchar nodded solemnly. "It will not harm you and might possibly allow you to destroy me, once you unlock its secrets."

Nagrendra reached out and grabbed it. "It is a powerful weapon to be giving an enemy."

"True enough, but without worthy foes, what reason is there for living?" Fialchar's laughter filled the valley. "Just as you live to test yourselves against Chaos, so I live to pit myself against the best the Empire has to offer. In Xoayya I now have one of your greatest champions working with me, and with that staff you have a weapon that will allow you to counter my future threats. A balance has been achieved, and the tipping of the scales shall be an epic worthy of many bard songs."

Fialchar bowed. "I will take my leave of you now."

"Wait." Locke held a hand up. "You haven't rewarded Tyrchon."

A quick look of mock surprise rode over Fialchar's features. "Oh, quite true." The staff came up, and a gold spark struck Tyrchon in the forehead. "There, as we bargained."

Pain shot through Tyrchon's skull, driving him to his knees. He clapped his hands to his head and screwed his eyes shut. He caught the faint scent of rot and a quick pop as Fialchar vanished, but his head felt wrapped in layers of wool. He heard a series of clicks that sparked aches in his head, then his lungs started to burn. He felt himself smothering, so he threw his head back, attempting to stretch his throat and allow air to get into his lungs.

It worked, but a second later he felt something strike him between the shoulder blades. His mail absorbed the force of the blow, and cool air soothed his lungs. He felt a trickle of sweat work from his brow down into his closed eyes, so he swiped a hand across his forehead. He flicked the droplets of sweat away without thought, then he realized what he had done.

He opened his eyes and saw both Locke and Nagrendra staring at him with their mouths open. He raised his hands to his face and felt cold, clammy flesh. His nose had shrunk to almost nothing, and his teeth—he played his tongue along them and discovered they did not include fangs. Tyrchon smiled and realized he actually *could* smile again.

He drew the *vindictxvara* from his belt and held it out to catch his reflection. The pale image superimposed itself over the blackened tracery on the blade, and except for the white halo around his head, the images were identical. Tyrchon reached up and pulled a long lank of his hair around to where he could see it, then he laughed. *Save for the white hair, Fialchar had it all right.*

Tyrchon stood and resheathed the dagger. "When Lord Disaster asked me to work for him in this matter, he promised me my humanity again as a reward. My wolf cloak is once again just that, a cloak."

Locke smiled. "So much for *vindictxvara* forged in your honor."

"True enough." Tyrchon shivered. The aspect of himself that had made it easier to accept Xoayya's rejection of him had been removed, but so had she. *Fialchar must have known.* "Doesn't really matter, though, does it?"

Nagrendra frowned. "What do you mean?"

"Wolf's-head or not, I'm still a Chaos Rider. There will be plenty of time for Chademons to forge new *vindictxvara*." Tyrchon smiled as broadly as his new face would allow. "And I'll be happy to provide them as much inspiration in those endeavors as they can handle."

EPILOGUE

The pain in Len's back and shoulders faded to a dull ache as he opened his eyes and stared up at shelves filled with boxes of shoes. Several boxes had fallen on top of him, and shoes were strewn in the narrow corridor between shelves. Len looked down between his legs to see if he could find Fitz, but the fitting stool was not tangled in his legs.

Good, he stayed behind where he can get well again. A shiver shook Len with that thought. *But none of that could be real, it couldn't.*

Comrade Corbett appeared at the head of the aisle. "Sales Associate Fong, what happened?" The slender man from Corporate appeared behind Corbett and looked quite alarmed. "Explain yourself and"—Corbett wheezed as he stooped and scooped something off the floor—"explain this." Corbett brandished Jhesti as if the doll was a bloody knife.

Len scrambled to his feet. "I, ah, Mr. Corbett, I, ah . . ."

He fell silent as his boss's dark angry eyes bored holes into him.

"Come on, Fong, out with it!" Corbett thrust the doll at him. "What is this?"

"This," said Jhesti in a loud voice, "is me, Jhesti. I'm a little prototype of an action figure that Len here created—on his own time—because he knew what Dancing Joker Shoes really needs is a spokesman that will appeal to kids. Face it, no parents like taking their kids to get shoes, but if the kids want to come here because they like me, Jhesti, then their parents will bring them. And the parents will buy our stuff, too."

The man from Corporate blinked. "That's not a bad idea."

Corbett smiled. "Of course it is, that's why I had Fong work on it, isn't it, Fong?"

"Get real, you fat idea thief . . ."

Len reached out and covered Jhesti's mouth with his hand before taking the doll from Corbett's grasp. "Enough of the ventriloquism act—just wanted to give you a taste of the effect in the ads."

The corporator frowned. "What did you mean by idea thief?"

Corbett's face closed, and Len knew he'd get fired if he said another word. Fear ran through him, but it seemed nothing in comparison to what he had faced while away, wherever that was. *Dream or not, it doesn't matter.*

Len swallowed hard, then lifted his chin. "What I meant was that Mr. Corbett here appropriated the idea of the Bo Gesters from me and some coworkers, in a conversation we had here. He was part of it, to be sure, but we came up with the idea, and, without telling us, he sent it on to Corporate. I don't mind his having done that, though I think the implementation would have been better had you been party to the whole conversation, but I don't like our not having gotten any credit for it."

Corbett's eyes blazed. "That is a blatant lie, Fong. You're fired!"

The man from Corporate laid a hand on Corbett's shoulder. "Let's be honest here, Chester, you've never had an original idea in your life. Your psych profile told us that much at headquarters, which was good because we don't want idea people in retail management. We want good little soldiers who will do what our idea people tell them to do. Part of the reason I'm here is not just to oversee the introduction of Bo Gesters, but to figure out where you got the original idea. Looks like I found it."

Len blinked. "What? You're kidding."

The corporator shook his head. "Not at all. Given your evaluations, Len, and your background, we figured you were probably the guy behind the Gester idea. We were hoping you'd have claimed credit on one of those suggestion slips that came in your pay envelope."

"Suggestion slips?"

Jhesti added. "We only ever get our checks—no suggestion slips, no envelopes."

The guy from Corporate smiled. "You are good, very good. Your lips don't even move."

Len nodded. "It's almost supernatural, isn't it?"

"It is." The corporator nodded. "Since you created this prototype on your own time, we'll need to work out a compensation package for you. We'd like to move you into our merchandising department—it needs new blood and some imagination. You've got a good imagination, don't you?"

"Yes, sir."

"Good. If this Jhesti thing works out, you could be put in charge of the whole division that develops him into a property. Good pay, good perks, and you never have to touch another sweaty foot in your whole life."

Len's mouth hung open. "Wow."

"You in?"

Jhesti answered for him. "We need some time to think about it, but it sounds good. I say we talk about this tomorrow, over lunch. You can get my number from my personnel file. I know you'll be busy dealing with Comrade Corbett here for the rest of the day, so I'll just get out of your hair."

"Please, take the rest of the day off. Mr. Corbett will work the floor for you." The Corporate guy moved out of the way to let Len slip past. "See you tomorrow, Mr. Fong."

Len beamed as he paused in the doorway between the back and the sales floor. "Wow, this is incredible."

"Not bad at all, is it, Len? It was good the way you faced up to Corbett."

"Yeah, dealing with your fears head-on isn't bad." Len smiled and headed out through the store. He glanced back and saw Corbett emerging from the stockroom with an armload of Dixie-trix boots. He laughed and turned to leave, when a hand on his shoulder stopped him.

"Could I ask you a question?"

Len turned and looked up at the woman speaking to him. Her long black hair had been gathered in a thick braid, and she wore a maroon blazer and skirt over a black-silk chemise. Her blue eyes sparkled as she smiled at him. "Ghislaine?"

The woman's dark brows flashed together for a second in a frown, but it lost to her smile in the war to dominate her face. "No, I'm Giselle. I work in the jewelry store next door. I was wondering, I spend a lot of time on my feet, and I'd like some shoes that would stop them from hurting."

Len stared at her for a second, then looked down. "I can find you shoes like that."

"Is something wrong?" She maintained her smile, but concern bled into her voice. "You were smiling, and now you sound so sad."

"It's just you remind . . ." Len forced a smile back on his face. He was about to turn and show her some shoes when he felt Jhesti drawing in a breath so he could speak. Len slapped a finger over Jhesti's mouth and sharpened his eyes. "You remind me of someone I saw in a dream. I must have based her on seeing you in the store next door. What I'd like to know is if you would like to go out with me."

Giselle's smile didn't die, but it contracted. "Ah, you're a shoe salesman holding a doll."

"This *doll* is going to be the focus of a multimillion dollar ad campaign for this chain, and I'm going to be running that show." Len laughed lightly and gave her as confident a smile as he could. "That aside, I think you're going to find I'm one of the most adventurous and inventive people you'll ever get to know. Some people are content to disengage from life, to sit back and let it roll on by. Not me, not anymore. I can't promise everything will be perfect, but I will promise it won't be dull and boring."

Her eyes narrowed, then she pursed her lips and tapped a finger against her chin. "Under ordinary circumstances, I'd probably turn you down, but I like your laugh, and there's something in your eyes. It's something a little wild, a little fiery. It's different."

"Chaotic?" Len offered.

"That works." Giselle nodded solemnly. "Doing anything Saturday night?"

"Nothing I can't get out of for you." Len offered her his hand. "I'm Len Fong."

"Giselle Franklin."

"Pleased to make your acquaintance, Giselle." Len waved her toward one of the store's chairs. "Let me take care of your shoe needs, then let's get out of here. We'll have lunch or something, *anything*, as long as it is well away from here. Life is far too precious a gift to squander in a shoe store."

AFTERWORD

You may have noticed, on the book's title page, the name of William F. Wu listed as the coauthor of this book, but his name is not on the cover or the spine. The reasons for that are varied and kind of confusing, so I'm writing this afterword to explain what's going on.

Back in 1989 I put together a bible for the Chaos world—a world I had developed for Flying Buffalo Inc., back when I was on staff for them. Rick Loomis graciously allowed me to use the world as a setting for novels. The bible, which ran to more than 200 pages, was enough to convince Christopher Schelling of ROC Books to buy two novels based on it. I was to write the first book, and Bill Wu, a good friend, would write the second one. The books were supposed to be between 75,000 and 90,000 words and we both turned them in to ROC in the spring of 1991. Bill actually finished his book before mine, even though it takes place a month after mine starts. We'd exchanged outlines and were

448   Michael A. Stackpole

working from the same bible, so the stories fit together pretty well.

Book contracts contain in them a variety of clauses, and one of them concerns the "window of publication." It specifies the amount of time a publisher has to get the books into print. With the ROC contract they had twenty-four months to get the books into print, which means they would be published by the spring of 1993.

The spring of 1993 came and went with no books. My agent sent a letter to ROC formally asking for the reversion of the rights to the books. What that means is that we'd get the books back and would be able to shop them around elsewhere, keeping the money ROC had paid us for writing them. In the publishing world if an author gets the books in on time and they are accepted, it's up to the publisher to bring them out on time, or the advances remain with the author and they get to shop the book around again to another publisher.

ROC's editors said they really wanted the books and in a meeting in the summer of 1993 they said they'd get them on the schedule by the end of the year. A bit later the list of scheduled books was printed in an industry magazine, and the Chaos books weren't included on the list. I asked ROC what was going on, but they'd had an editorial changeover and asked for more time. I told them that was fine and within six weeks or so, they said they'd like to keep the first book, but they wanted me to expand it by half again so they could make it a lead title and really push it.

Making a book a lead title is a good thing since it means the book will have more copies in the stores and more folks can buy it. (If a store only stocks three copies, you can only sell three copies. If you stock a dozen and only sell eight of them, you're still moving more copies than if three are in the store.) I was willing to expand the book, but since the contract had expired and they wanted more work *and* since the books hadn't been put in the schedule when they said it would, I asked them how much it was worth to have me do the work.

About two weeks later I got the original manuscript returned to me with a note saying ROC was no longer interested. Okay, that sort of stuff happens. My agent turned around and started asking around to see if anyone else was interested in buying the books. As it turned out, Christopher Schelling had moved from ROC to HarperPrism, and he was happy to see the books become available. By October of 1994 we struck a deal to buy the books, provided I would expand the books up to 120,000 words.

Piece of cake. I expanded my novel by adding in a new character with the full intent of rolling that character on into Bill's book. It was decided that I would expand Bill's book as well as my own, so the two of them could be tied together more tightly. I also had the time in my schedule to do the work. In 1996 I expanded A *Hero Born*, and in 1997 sat down to do the same to Bill's book.

I immediately saw that expanding Bill's book would be difficult because of the nature of the story he had written. Grafting another story line into it just wasn't going to work very easily, especially with the characters I wanted to drag in from the first book. I broke his novel down into the various story lines, kept the core character and conflict of it, then wrapped the fabric of a new story around it. Bill and I spoke several times about the changes I wanted to make, and I proceeded with his blessings.

Those of you who have read Bill's wonderfully imaginative prose will recognize his touches here. Without his input on the book, it would have been far more staid and traditional than it is. Working with Bill forced me to expand my horizons, and I learned a lot; and, as a writer, you can do much worse than take lessons from Bill Wu.

> *Michael A. Stackpole*
> Scottsdale, AZ
> *5 November* 1997

ABOUT THE AUTHOR

MICHAEL A. STACKPOLE got his first rejection slip in 1964, at the tender age of six. He got the next one in 1976, and they arrived with more frequency after that. Clearly clueless about the fact that other folks didn't think he could write, he persisted. Shifting his sights temporarily, he moved into the game industry, writing and designing products for companies like Flying Buffalo, Inc., TSR Inc., Mayfair Games, FASA Corp., Interplay Productions, Steve Jackson Games, and West End Games. In 1987—self-deluded into believing rejection could no longer hurt him—he convinced the folks at FASA to let him write novels for them, which they did (the twelfth of which will see print later in 1998).

In the realm of fiction he is best known for his best-selling Star Wars X-wing Rogue Squadron novels. An Enemy Reborn is the fourth novel he has written in a universe of his own devising (or as some folks put it, this is his fourth "real novel"—save for those pundits in the SF industry who consider anything containing magick to be trash.) (And he'd live in terror that said pundits might see this sort of contemptuous remark and think ill of him, but he really doesn't care what they think).

In his spare time he plays indoor soccer (and at this writing has a three-game scoring streak going), rides a bicycle, and has actually cut down on his television watching (yet another sign of the coming apocalypse). He lives in Arizona with Liz Danforth and three Welsh Cardigan Corgis: Ruthless, Ember, and Saint.